THE MADMAN'S

Megan Shepherd was 'born' into the book world, growing up in her parents' independent bookstore in Western North Carolina. She is the author of *The Madman's Daughter* trilogy. When Megan is not writing, she can usually be found horseback riding, daydreaming at coffee shops, or hiking in the beautiful Blue Ridge mountains.

Visit Megan at www.meganshepherd.com.

MEGAN SHEPHERD

The Madman's Daughter

HARPER
Voyager

HarperVoyager
An imprint of HarperCollins*Publishers*
77–85 Fulham Palace Road,
Hammersmith, London W6 8JB

www.harpercollins.co.uk

A Paperback Original 2013
1

A catalogue record for this book
is available from the British Library

ISBN: 978 0 00 750020 8

Set in Meridien by Palimpsest Book Production Limited,
Falkirk, Stirlingshire

Printed and bound in Great Britain by
Clays Ltd, St Ives plc

To Jesse –
I love you, madly.

ONE

The basement hallways in King's College of Medical Research were dark, even in the daytime.

At night they were like a grave.

Rats crawled through corridors that dripped with cold perspiration. The chill in the sunken rooms kept the specimens from rotting and numbed my own flesh, too, through the worn layers of my dress. When I cleaned those rooms, late at night after the medical students had gone home to their warm beds, the sound of my hard-bristle brush echoed in the operating theater, down the twisting halls, into the storage spaces where they kept the things of nightmares. Other people's nightmares, that is. Dead flesh and sharpened scalpels didn't bother me. I was my father's daughter, after all. My nightmares were made of darker things.

My brush paused against the mortar, frozen by a familiar sound from down the hall: the unwelcome *tap-tap-tap* of footsteps that meant Dr Hastings had stayed late. I scrubbed harder, furiously, but blood had a way of seeping into the tiles so not even hours of work could get them clean.

The footsteps came closer until they stopped right behind me.

1

'How's it coming, then, Juliet?' His warm breath brushed the back of my neck.

Keep your eyes down, I told myself, scouring the bloodstained squares of mortar so hard that my own knuckles bled.

'Well, Doctor.' I kept it short, hoping he would leave, but he didn't.

Overhead the electric bulbs snapped and clicked. I glanced at the silver tips of his shoes, so brightly polished that I could see the reflection of his balding scalp and milky eyes watching me. He wasn't the only professor who worked late, or the only one whose gaze lingered too long on my bent-over backside. But the smell of lye and other chemicals on my clothes deterred the others. Dr Hastings seemed to relish it.

He slipped his pale fingers around my wrist. I dropped the brush in surprise. 'Your knuckles are bleeding,' he said, pulling me to my feet.

'It's the cold. It chaps my skin.' I tried to tug my hand back, but he held firm. 'It's nothing.'

His eyes followed the sleeve of my muslin dress to the stained apron and frayed hem, a dress that not even my father's poorest servants would have worn. But that was many years ago, when we lived in the big house on Belgrave Square, where my closet burst with furs and silks and soft lacy things I'd worn only once or twice, since Mother threw out the previous year's fashions like bathwater.

That was before the scandal.

Now, men seldom looked at my clothes for long. When a girl fell from privilege, men were less interested in her ratty skirts than in what lay underneath, and Dr Hastings was no different. His eyes settled on my face. My friend Lucy told me I looked like the lead actress at the Brixton, a Frenchwoman with high cheekbones and skin pale as bone, even paler against the dark, straight hair she wore swept up in a Swiss-style chignon. I kept my own hair in a simple

2

braid, though a few strands always managed to slip out. Dr Hastings reached up to tuck them behind my ear, his fingers rough as parchment against my temple. I cringed inside but fought to keep my face blank. Better to give no reaction so he wouldn't be encouraged. But my shaking hands betrayed me.

Dr Hastings smiled thinly. The tip of his tongue snaked out from between his lips.

Suddenly the sound of groaning hinges made him startle. My heart pounded wildly at this chance to slip away. Mrs Bell, the lead maid, stuck her gray head through the cracked door. Her mouth curved in its perpetual frown as her beady eyes darted between the professor and me. I'd never been so glad to see her wrinkled face.

'Juliet, out with you,' she barked. 'Mary's gone and broken a lamp, and we need another set of hands.'

I stepped away from Dr Hastings, relief rolling off me like a cold sweat. My eyes met Mrs Bell's briefly as I slipped into the hall. I knew that look. She couldn't watch out for me all the time.

One day, she might not be there to intercede.

The moment I was free of those dark hallways, I dashed into the street toward Covent Garden as the moon hovered low over London's skyline. The harsh wind bit at my calves through worn wool stockings as I waited for a carriage to pass. Across the street a figure stood in the lee of the big wooden bandstand's staircase.

'You awful creature,' Lucy said, slipping out of the shadows. She hugged the collar of her fur coat around her long neck. Her cheeks and nose were red beneath a light sheen of French powder. 'I've been waiting an hour.'

'I'm sorry.' I leaned in and pressed my cheek to hers. Her parents would be horrified to know she had snuck out to meet me. They had encouraged our friendship when Father was London's most famous surgeon, but were quick to forbid her to see me after his banishment.

Luckily for me, Lucy loved to disobey.

'They've had me working late all week opening up some old rooms,' I said. 'I'll be cleaning cobwebs out of my hair for days.'

She pretended to pluck something distasteful from my hair and grimaced. We both laughed. 'Honestly, I don't know how you can stand that work, with the rats and beetles and, my God, whatever else lurks down there.' Her blue eyes gleamed mischievously. 'Anyway, come on. The boys are waiting.' She snatched my hand, and we hurried across the courtyard to a redbrick building with a stone staircase. Lucy banged the horse-head knocker twice.

The door swung open, and a young man with thick chestnut hair and a fine suit appeared. He had Lucy's same fair skin and wide-set eyes, so this must be the cousin she'd told me about. I timidly evaluated his tall forehead, the helix of his ears that projected only a hair too far from the skull. Good-looking, I concluded. He studied me wordlessly in return, in my third-hand coat, with worn elbows and frayed satin trim, that must have looked so out of place next to Lucy's finely tailored one. But to his credit, his grin didn't falter for a moment. She must have warned him she was bringing a street urchin and not to say anything rude.

'Let us in, Adam,' Lucy said, pushing past him. 'My toes are freezing to the street.'

I slipped in behind her. Shrugging off her coat, she said, 'Adam, this is the friend I've told you about. Not a penny to her name, can't cook, but God, just look at her.'

My face went red, and I shot Lucy a withering look, but Adam only smiled. 'Lucy's nothing if not blunt,' he said. 'Don't worry, I'm used to it. I've heard far worse

4

come out of her mouth. And she's right, at least about the last part.'

I jerked my head toward him, expecting a leer. But he was being sincere, which only left me feeling more at a loss for words.

'Where are they?' Lucy asked, ignoring us. A bawdy roar spilled from a back room, and Lucy grinned and headed toward the sound. I expected Adam to follow her. But his gaze found me instead. He smiled again.

Startled, I paused a second too long. This was new. No vulgar winks, no glances at my chest. I was supposed to say something pleasant. But instead I drew a breath in, like a secret I had to keep close. I knew how to handle cruelty, not kindness.

'May I take your coat?' he asked. I realized I had my arms wrapped tightly around my chest, though it was pleasantly warm inside the house.

I forced my arms apart and slid the coat off. 'Thank you.' My voice was barely audible.

We followed Lucy down the hall to a sitting room where a group of lanky medical students reclined on leather sofas, sipping glasses of honey-colored liquid. Winter examinations had just ended, and they were clearly deep into their celebration. This was the kind of thing Lucy adored – breaking up a boys' club, drinking gin and playing cards and reveling in their shocked faces. She got away with it under the pretense of visiting her cousin, though this was a far step from the elderly aunt's parlor where Lucy was supposed to be meeting him.

Adam stepped forward to join the crowd, laughing at something someone said. I tried to feel at ease in the unfamiliar crowd, too aware of my shabby dress and chapped hands. *Smile*, Mother would have whispered. *You belonged among these people, once.* But first I needed to gauge how drunk they were, the lay of the room, who was most likely not to laugh at my poor clothes. Analyzing, always analyzing – I couldn't feel safe until I knew every aspect of what I was facing.

Mother had been so confident around other people, always able to talk about the church sermon that morning, about the rising price of coffee. But I'd taken after my father when it came to social situations. Awkward. Shy. More apt to study the crowd like some social experiment than to join in.

Lucy had tucked herself on the sofa between a blond-haired boy and one with a face as red as an apple. A half-empty rum bottle dangled from her graceful fingers. When she saw me hanging back in the doorway, she stood and sauntered over.

'The sooner you find a husband,' she growled playfully, 'the sooner you can stop scrubbing floors. So pick one of them and say something charming.'

I swallowed. My eyes drifted to Adam. 'Lucy, men like these don't marry girls like me.'

'You haven't the faintest idea what men want. They don't want some snobbish porridge-faced brat plucking at needlepoint all day.'

'Yes, but I'm a *maid*.'

'A temporary situation.' She waved it away, as if my last few years of backbreaking work were nothing more than a lark. She jabbed me in the side. 'You come from money. From class. So show a little.'

She held the bottle out to me. I wanted to tell her that sipping rum straight from a bottle wasn't exactly showing class, but I'd only earn myself another jab.

I glanced at Adam. I'd never been good at guessing people's feelings. I had to study their reactions instead. And in this situation, it didn't take much to conclude I wasn't what these men wanted, despite Lucy's insistence.

But maybe I could pretend to be. Hesitantly, I took a sip.

6

The blond boy tugged Lucy to the sofa next to him. 'You must help us end a debate, Miss Radcliffe. Cecil says the human body contains 210 bones, and I say 211.'

Lucy batted her pretty lashes. 'Well, I'm sure *I* don't know.' I sighed and leaned into the doorframe.

The boy took her chin in his hand. 'If you'll be so good as to hold still, I'll count, and we can find our answer.' He touched a finger to her skull. 'One.' I rolled my eyes as the boy dropped his finger lower, to her shoulder bones. 'Two. And three.' His finger ran slowly, seductively, along her clavicle. 'Four.' Then his finger traced even lower, to the thin skin covering her breastbone. 'Five,' he said, so drawn out that I could smell the rum on his breath.

I cleared my throat. The other boys watched, riveted, as the boy's finger drifted lower and lower over Lucy's neckline. Why not just skip the pretense and grab her breast? Lucy was no better, giggling like she was enjoying it. Exasperated, I slapped his pasty hand off her chest.

The whole room went still.

'Wait your turn, darling,' the boy said, and they all laughed. He turned back to Lucy, holding up that ridiculous finger.

'206,' I said.

This got their attention. Lucy took the bottle from my hand and fell back against the leather sofa with an exasperated sigh.

'I beg your pardon?' the boy said.

'206,' I repeated, feeling my cheeks warm. 'There are 206 bones in the body. I would think, as a medical student, you would know that.'

Lucy's head shook at my hopelessness, but her lips cracked in a smile regardless. The blond boy's mouth went slack.

I continued before he could think. 'If you doubt me, tell me how many bones are in the human hand.' The boys took

7

no offense at my remark. On the contrary, they seemed all the more drawn to me for it. Maybe I *was* the kind of girl they wanted, after all.

Lucy's only acknowledgment was an approving tip of the rum bottle in my direction.

'I'll take that wager,' Adam interrupted, leveling his handsome green eyes at me.

Lucy jumped up and wrapped her arm around my shoulders. 'Oh, good! And what's the wager, then? I'll not have Juliet risk her reputation for less than a kiss.'

I immediately turned red, but Adam only grinned. 'My prize, if I am right, shall be a kiss. And if I am wrong—'

'If you are wrong' – I interjected, feeling reckless; I grabbed the rum from Lucy and tipped the bottle back, letting the liquid warmth chase away my insecurity – 'you must call on me wearing a lady's bonnet.'

He walked around the sofa and took the bottle. The confidence in his step told me he didn't intend to lose. He set the bottle on the side table and skimmed his forefinger tantalizingly along the delicate bones in the back of my hand. I parted my lips, curling my toes to keep from jerking my hand away. This wasn't Dr Hastings, I told myself. Adam was hardly shoving his hand down my neckline. It was just an innocent touch.

'Twenty-four,' he said.

I felt a triumphant swell. 'Wrong. Twenty-seven.' Lucy gave my leg a pinch and I remembered to smile. This was supposed to be flirtatious. Fun.

Adam's eyes danced devilishly. 'And how would a girl know such things?'

I straightened. 'Whether I'm right or wrong has nothing to do with gender.' I paused. 'Also, I'm right.'

Adam smirked. 'Girls don't study science.'

My confidence faltered. I knew how many bones there

were in the human hand because I was my father's daughter. When I was a child, Father would give physiology lessons to our servant boy, Montgomery, to spite those who claimed the lower classes were incapable of learning. He considered women naturally deficient, however, so I would hide in the laboratory closet during lessons, and Montgomery would slip me books to study. But I could hardly tell these young men that. Every medical student knew the name Moreau. They would remember the scandal.

Lucy jumped to my defense. 'Juliet knows more than the lot of you. She works in the medical building. She's probably spent more time around cadavers than you lily spirits.'

I gritted my teeth, wishing she hadn't told them. It was one thing to be a maid, another to clean the laboratory after their botched surgeries. But Adam arched an eyebrow, interested.

'Is that so? Well then, I have a different wager for you, miss.' His eyes danced with something more dangerous than a kiss. 'I have a key to the college, and you must know your way around. Let's find one of your skeletons and count for ourselves.'

Glances darted among the other boys like sparks in a fire. They prodded one another, goading each other on in anticipation of the idea of a clandestine trip into the bowels of the medical building.

Lucy gave me an impish shrug. 'Why not?'

I hesitated. I'd spent enough time in those dank halls. There was a darkness there that had worked its way into the hollow spaces between my bones. A darkness that clung to the hallways like my father's shadow, smelling of formaldehyde and his favorite apricot preserves. Tonight was supposed to be about escaping the darkness – if not in the arms of a future husband, at least in a few lighthearted moments.

I shook my head.

But the boys had made up their minds, and there was no convincing them otherwise. 'Are you trying to get out of a kiss?' Adam teased.

I didn't respond. My desire for flirtation had evaporated at the mention of the university basements. But if Lucy didn't balk at the idea of seeing a skeleton, surely I shouldn't. I cleaned the cobwebs from their creaky bones every night. So what was holding me back?

Lucy leaned in and whispered in my ear. 'Adam wants to impress you with how brave he is, you idiot. Swoon when you see the skeleton and fall into his arms. Men love that sort of thing.'

My stomach tightened. God, was this what normal girls did? Feign weakness? I could never imagine Mother, with all her strict morals, doing something so scandalous as slipping into forbidden hallways on a dare. But Father – he wouldn't have hesitated. He would have been the one egging them on.

Dash it. I snatched the rum and poured the last few swallows down my throat. The boys cheered. I ignored the queasy feeling in my stomach – not from the rum, but from the thought of those dark hallways we were soon to enter.

TWO

We bundled into our coats and slipped into the cold night, crossing the Strand toward the university's brick archway. This late only a few lanterns shone in the upper windows. The boys passed a bottle around with hushed laughter at being on school grounds after hours. I wrapped my arm around Lucy's and tried to join the mirth, but the warmth didn't spread below my smile. For the boys, this taste of mild scandal was titillating. They'd never known real scandal or how it could tear a person apart.

Adam led us to the side of the building, through a row of hedges to a small black door I'd used only once or twice. He unlocked it and held it open. Hesitation rooted my feet to the ground, but a gentle tug from Lucy led me inside. The door closed, plunging us into darkness broken only by the moonlight from one high window.

The hallway filled with the eerie silence of unused rooms. My hands itched for a rag and brush as a legitimate reason to be here. Coming on a lark to settle a silly wager, risking my job – it didn't feel right.

Lucy squinted into the darkness, but I kept my eyes on the tile floor. I already knew what lay at the end of the hall.

11

'Well?' Adam asked. 'Which way to the skeletons, Mademoiselle Guillotine?'

I started to head for the small door to the storage chambers, but a light at the opposite end of the corridor caught my eye. The operating theater. Odd; no one should have been there this late. Something about that light chilled my blood – it could only mean trouble.

'We're not alone,' I said, nodding toward the door. The boys followed my gaze and grew quiet. Lucy slid off her glove and found my hand in the dark.

Adam started toward the operating theater, but I grabbed the fabric of his cuff to hold him back. The hallways were filled with the normal smells – chemicals and rotten things. Usually it didn't bother me, but tonight it felt so overpowering that my head started to spin. A wave of weakness hit me and I grabbed his wrist harder.

'Are you all right?' he asked.

I waited a few seconds for the spell to pass. These spells were not uncommon, coming upon me suddenly, usually in the late evening, though I wasn't about to explain their source to him. 'The skeletons are the other way,' I said.

'Someone's in the theater after hours. Whatever they're doing, it *has* to be good. The skeletons can wait.' His voice was charged. This was a game to them, I realized. If they got caught, the dean might give them a stern talking-to. I would lose my livelihood.

He cocked his head. 'You aren't scared, are you?'

I scowled and let go of his cuff. Of course I wasn't scared. We made our way silently down the hall. As we approached the closed door, a sound began to gnaw at my ears. It took me back to my childhood, when I would hide outside the door to Father's laboratory, listening, trying to imagine what was happening within before the servants chased me off.

The sound grew louder, a *scrape-tap, scrape-tap*. Unaccustomed to being in a laboratory, Lucy threw me a puzzled look. But I knew that sound. The scrape of scalpel on stone. A gesture surgeons made to clean the flesh from the blade between cuts.

Adam threw open the door. A half-dozen students huddled around a table in the center of the room, over which a single lamp formed an island of light. They looked up when we entered, and then after a few seconds their faces relaxed with recognition.

'Adam, you cad, get in and close the door,' said one of the students. He threw Lucy and me an annoyed look. 'What are they doing here?'

'They'll be no trouble. Right, ladies?' Adam raised his eyebrow, but I didn't answer. A good part of me contemplated bolting out the door and leaving them to their sick lark. Yet I didn't. As we drifted closer with hesitant steps, I could feel the stiffness in my bones easing, as though releasing some pent-up, slippery curiosity from between my joints.

Why *were* they in the operating theater after dark?

Adam peered over the surgeon's shoulder. Their bodies blocked the table, but the metallic smell of fresh blood reached me, making my head spin. Lucy pressed a handkerchief to her mouth. Memories of my father flooded me. As a surgeon, blood had been his medium like ink to a writer. Our fortune had been built on blood, the acrid odor infused into the very bricks of our house, the clothes that we wore.

To me, blood smelled like home.

I shook away the feeling. *Father left us*, I reminded myself. *Betrayed us*. But I still couldn't help missing him.

'They shouldn't be here,' I murmured. 'This building's closed to students at night.'

But before Lucy could answer, the scrape of the scalpel sounded again, drawing my gaze irresistibly to the table. We stepped forward. The boys paid us little attention, except

Adam, who moved aside to make room. My breath caught. On the table lay a dead rabbit, its fur white as snow and spotted with blood. Its belly had been sliced open, and several organs lay on the table. Lucy gasped and covered her eyes.

My eyes were wide. I felt vaguely sorry for the dead rabbit, but it was a far-off sort of thought, something Mother might have felt. I wasn't naive. Dissection was a necessary part of science. It was how doctors were able to develop medicine and how surgeons saved lives. I'd only ever glimpsed dissections a handful of times – peeking through the keyhole of Father's laboratory or cleaning up after medical students. After work, in my small room at the lodging house, I'd studied the diagrams in my father's old copy of *Longman's Anatomical Reference*, but black-and-white illustrations were a poor substitute for the real thing.

Now my eyes devoured the rabbit's body, trying to match the fleshy bits of organ and bone to the ink diagrams I knew by heart. An urge raced through my veins to touch the striated muscle of the heart, feel the smooth length of intestine.

Lucy clutched her stomach, looking pale. I watched her curiously. I didn't feel the need to turn away like normal ladies should. Mother had drilled into me the standards of proper young ladies, but my impulses didn't always obey. So I had learned to hide them instead.

I looked back at the rabbit. Creeping vines of worry wound around my ankles and up my legs.

'Something's wrong.'

The student performing the surgery glanced up, irritated, before selecting another scalpel and returning to work.

'Sh,' Adam breathed in my ear. My chest tightened as my eyes darted over the rabbit. *There*. The rabbit's rear foot jerked. And *there*. Its chest rose and fell in a quick breath. I clasped Lucy's hand, feeling the blood rushing to the base of my skull.

My brain processed the movements disjointedly, with an odd feeling like I had seen all this before. I gasped. 'It's alive.'

The rabbit's glassy eye blinked. My heart faltered. I turned to Adam, bewildered, and then back to the table, where the boys continued to operate. They ignored me, as they ignored the rabbit's movements. Something white and hot filled my head and I gripped the edge of the table, jolting it. 'It's not dead!'

The surgeon turned to Adam in annoyance. 'You'd better keep them quiet.'

'It isn't supposed to be alive,' Lucy stammered, her face pale. The handkerchief slipped from her hand, falling to the floor slowly, dreamlike. 'Why is it alive?'

'Vivisection.' The word came out of me like a vile thing trying to escape. 'Dissection of living creatures.' I took a step back, wanting nothing to do with it. Dissection was one thing. What they were doing on that table was only cruel.

'It's just a rabbit,' Adam hissed. Lucy began to sway. I couldn't tear my eyes off the operation. Had they even bothered to anesthetize it?

'It's against the law,' I muttered. My pulse matched the thumps of the frightened rabbit's still-beating heart. I looked at the placement of the organs on the table. At the equipment carefully laid out. It was all familiar to me.

Too familiar.

'Vivisection is prohibited by the university,' I said, louder.

'So is having women in the operating theater,' the surgeon said, meeting my eyes. 'But you're here, aren't you?'

'Bunch of Judys,' a dark-haired boy said with a sneer. The others laughed, and he set down a curled paper covered with diagrams. I caught sight of the rough ink outline of a rabbit, splayed apart, incision cuts marked with dotted lines. This, too, was familiar. I snatched the paper. The boy protested but I turned my back on him. My ears roared with a warm crackling. The whole room suddenly felt distant, as though I was watching myself react. I knew this diagram. The tight handwriting. The black, dotted incision lines. From somewhere deep within, I recognized it.

Behind me, the surgeon remarked to another boy in a whisper, 'Intestines of a flesh-toned color. Pulsing slightly, likely from an unfinished digestion. Yes – there, I see the contents moving.'

With shaking fingers I unfolded the paper's dog-eared right corner. Initials were scrawled on the diagram: *H.M.* Blood rushed in my ears, drowning out the sound of the boys and the rabbit and the clicking electric light. H.M. – Henri Moreau.

My father.

Through his old diagram, these boys had resurrected my father's ghost in the very theater where he used to teach. I was flooded with a shivering uneasiness. As a child I'd worshipped my father, and now I hated him for abandoning us. Mother had fervently denied the rumors were true, but I wondered if she just couldn't bear to have married a monster.

Suddenly the rabbit jolted and let out a scream so unnatural that I instinctively made the sign of the cross.

'Good lord,' Adam said, watching with wide eyes. 'Jones, you cad, it's waking up!'

Jones rushed to the table, which was lined with steel blades and needles the length of my forearm. 'I gave it the proper dose,' he stuttered, searching through the glass vials.

The rabbit's screams pierced my skull. I slammed my hands against the table, the paper falling to the side. 'End this,' I cried. 'It's in pain!'

Lucy sobbed. The surgeon didn't move. Frustrated, I grabbed him by the sleeve. 'Do something! Put it out of its misery.'

Still, none of the boys moved. As medical students, they

should have been trained for any situation. But they were frozen. So I acted instead.

On the table beside me was the set of operating instruments. I wrapped my hand around the handle of the ax, normally used for separating the sternum of cadavers. I took a deep breath, focusing on the rabbit's neck. In a movement I knew had to be fast and hard, I brought down the ax.

The rabbit's screaming stopped.

The awful tension in my chest dripped out onto the wet floor. I stared at the ax, distantly, my brain not yet connecting it with the blood on my hands. The ax fell from my grasp, crashing to the floor. Everyone flinched.

Everyone but me.

Lucy grabbed my shoulder. 'We're leaving,' she said, her voice strained. I swallowed. The diagram lay on the table, a cold reminder of my father's hand in all this. I snatched it and whirled on the dark-haired boy.

'Where did you get this?' I demanded.

He only gaped.

I shook him, but the surgeon interrupted. 'Billingsgate. The Blue Boar Inn.' His eyes flashed to the ax on the floor. 'There's a doctor there.'

Lucy's hand tightened in mine. I stared at the ax. Someone bent down to pick it up, hesitantly. Adam. Our eyes met and I saw his horror at what I'd done, and more – disgust. Lucy was wrong. He wouldn't want to marry me. I was cold, strange, and monstrous to those boys, just like my father. No one could love a monster.

'Come on.' She tugged me through the hallways to the street outside. It was cold, but my numb skin barely felt it. A few people passed us, bundled up, too concerned about the weather to notice the blood on our clothes. Lucy leaned against a brick wall and pressed a hand over her chest. 'My God, you cut its head off!'

Blood was on my hands, on the tattered lace of my sleeves, even dotting the diamond ring my mother had left me. I stared at the paper in my fist. *The Blue Boar Inn. The Blue Boar Inn.* I couldn't let myself forget that name.

Lucy braced her hands on my shoulders, shaking me. 'Juliet, say something!'

'They shouldn't have done that,' I said, feeling feverish in the cold night air. The paper was damp from my sweating palms. 'I had . . . I had to stop it.'

I felt her hand squeeze my shoulder tighter. 'Of course you did. Our cook kills a brace of hares for dinner all the time. That's all you did – killed a rabbit that was already going to die.' But her voice was shaking. What I had done was unnatural, and we both knew it.

A cold breeze blew off the Thames, carrying the pungent smell of sweat and Lucy's perfume. I drew a shallow breath. The rumors of so long ago crept through the streets, coming back to life. All I had were slips of memories of my father: the feel of his tweed jacket, the smell of tobacco in his hair when he kissed me good night. I couldn't bring myself to believe my father was the madman they said he was. But I'd been so young when it happened, just ten years old. As I matured, more memories surfaced. Deeper ones, of a cold, sterile room and sounds in the night – recollections that never entirely disappeared, no matter how far I pushed them into the recesses of my mind.

I didn't tell Lucy about the diagram with his initials in the corner. I didn't tell her that he used to keep it neatly in a book in his laboratory, a place I glimpsed only when the servants were cleaning. I didn't tell her that, after all these years trying to accept that he must be dead, a part of me suspected otherwise.

That maybe my father was alive.

THREE

London society was not kind to the daughter of a madman. To the orphan of a madman, even less. My father had been the most celebrated physiologist in England, a fact Mother was quick to mention to anyone who'd listen. My parents used to host elegant parties for his fellow professors. Long after bedtime I would creep downstairs in my nightdress and peek through the drawing room keyhole to take in the sound of their laughter and the smell of rich tobacco. How ironic that those same men were the first to brand him a monster.

After the scandal broke and Father disappeared, Mother and I were shunned by the company we once called friends. Even the church closed its doors to us. We were forced to sell our home and possessions to pay for his debts. We were left penniless for months, relying only on Mother's prayers and a string of grumbling relatives' sense of duty. I was young at the time, so I didn't understand when suddenly we had an apartment again, a small but richly appointed second-story flat near Charing Cross. Mother would take me to piano lessons and have me fitted for gowns and buy herself expensive rouge and satin undergarments. An older gentleman came by, once a week like clockwork, and Mother would send me out for chocolate biscuits in the café downstairs. He wore strong cologne that masked a pungent, stale smell, but Mother never said anything about it. That's how I knew he must be rich – no one ever says the rich stink.

When consumption took my mother, the old gentleman hardly wanted to keep the dead mistress's bony daughter around. He paid for Mother's funeral – though he didn't attend – and let me stay in the apartment for a week. Then he sent over a brusque maid who boxed up and sold Mother's things and handed me a banknote for their value. No doubt he considered himself generous. I was fourteen at the time, and totally on my own.

Fortunately, a former colleague of my father's named Professor von Stein heard of Mother's death and inquired at King's College for suitable employment for a young woman of distinguished background. Once they found out who my father was, though, the best offer I got was to be a part of Mrs Bell's cleaning crew. It paid just enough for a room at a lodging house with twenty other girls my age. Some were orphaned, some had come to the city to support younger brothers and sisters, some just showed up for a week and vanished. We came from different backgrounds. But all of us were alone.

I shared a room with Annie, a fifteen-year-old shopgirl from Dublin who had a habit of going through my belongings whether I was there or not. She once came across the embossed, locked wooden box I kept at the back of our closet shelf. I never told her what was inside, no matter how much she begged.

The night I killed the rabbit, I kept the blood-spattered diagram under my pillow. At work the next day I tucked it into my clothing, like a talisman. It infused my every waking thought with memories of my father. Every remembrance, every gesture, every kind word from him had been eclipsed by the terrible rumors I'd heard in the years since.

I slipped away from my mop to find Mrs Bell scrubbing towels in the laundry room. Her light eyes, narrowed as if she knew I was up to no good, found mine through the billows of steam.

I picked up a bar of soap and chipped at it with my fingernail. What did I expect to find at the inn, anyway? My father, raised from the dead, smoking a cigar in his tweed jacket and waiting to tell me a bedtime story?

'Mrs Bell,' I asked, setting down the mutilated bar of soap. 'Do you know where the Blue Boar Inn is?'

I had to wait until Sunday after church before I could follow Mrs Bell's directions south of Cable Street, avoiding the swill thrown out from lodging houses. As I paused at the corner to find the right street, I became aware of someone watching me. It was a girl around my age, though her face was caked with powder and rouge that made her look older. A striped satin dress limply hung on her thin frame. She stared at me with hollow eyes. I looked away sharply. If it hadn't been for my employment at King's College, that might have been me on the corner, waiting for my next gentleman. I leaned against a brick wall, queasy. Lucy had told me what happened at brothels. That had been my mother's desperate solution, at the expense of the virtues she held so dear. I might not have as many virtues to lose, but I was determined that wouldn't be my future.

The prostitute ambled down the street, coming toward me leisurely, and I hurried in the other direction, until I suddenly came upon a faded blue sign swinging above a thick door, painted with a tusked beast I assumed was once meant to be a boar.

The inn was a wooden three-story building, keeling slightly toward its neighbor. I tugged on the heavy iron latch and entered. It took a moment for my eyes to adjust.

Little sunlight passed through windows coated with smoky residue. I found myself in a dining hall, among sullen patrons murmuring in low voices over their midday meal. The furniture was worn but made of heavy oak that had recently been polished. None of the patrons looked up except a thin man twice my age, face marred with pox scars, who stared at my Sunday dress and the Bible I clutched in my arms. It seemed the Blue Boar did not see many young ladies.

A portly woman came out from the kitchen and raised her eyebrows. She wiped her hands on her apron and looked me over: my face that hinted of aristocracy and clothes that spoke of poverty. 'Come for a room?'

'No . . . I haven't,' I stammered. 'I'm looking for a man. A doctor.' My heart pounded, warning me not to get my hopes up. 'His name is Henri Moreau.'

She peered at me queerly. I must have been the color of ripe tomatoes. 'We aren't in the habit of giving out our patrons' information. You understand.' It was a command, not a question. Was he there, I wondered, in the same building, maybe right above our heads?

'I mean no trouble. I only need to speak with him.'

Her face didn't budge. 'No one by that name here.'

The ground fell out from beneath me. She was mistaken. She had to be. Or else I'd been a fool, thinking some old paper meant my father was here, in London, the city from which he'd been banished.

The set of her mouth softened. She took my elbow and pulled me away from the diners to a staircase that led into the shadows of the upper floors. 'We've no one by that precise name, but there is a doctor.'

My heart leapt. 'Where is he? What does he look like?'

'Calm down, now. You say you don't want trouble, and nor do I.' Her gaze slid to the dining hall, nervously. 'But if

22

it's the doctor you're after, you should know Dr James has been nothing but trouble since he arrived.'

Dr James. Not Dr Moreau. A pseudonym, perhaps? My mind was grasping, trying to form the parts of the equation into a reasonable solution, but there was only one logical conclusion: Dr James was someone else entirely, one of a hundred visiting doctors in London. And yet my curiosity wouldn't be satisfied without proof.

'I'm sorry to hear it. Perhaps if I may speak to him . . .'

'Mind you, the young gentleman is gracious enough. It's that companion of his. Makes the other guests nervous, you understand.'

'Certainly.' I nodded, breathless. No one would describe Father as young. So could the odd companion she spoke of be my father, then?

She turned her attention to my dress, narrowing her eyes, and spoke in a low voice. 'I won't question what a pretty young lady wants with that pair, but I doubt you're a relation. This is a reputable establishment. I don't want no trouble, you hear?'

'Yes, ma'am.' A nervous bloom spread across my cheeks at the realization of what she was implying about a young woman alone with two strange men.

Her chin jerked toward the stairs. 'Second floor. Room on the left.'

I dashed to the second-floor landing, gripping the railing to steady myself. To my left was only one door, tucked into an alcove. A tarnished mirror next to the door reflected my face, wide-eyed and flushed. I looked like a madwoman. I paused. What was I doing chasing a whim? I should have been with the other girls from the lodging house, gossiping about the handsomest boys in church this morning.

But here I was. I slid my Bible into my bag and knocked cautiously.

23

There was no answer. Should I wait? I rapped again, harder. Behind me, low voices and the sounds of clinking glasses floated up from the dining hall.

A wild idea struck me. I tried the knob – locked, of course. It wasn't a sophisticated lock, though, so any skeleton key might do. I rifled through my bag for the key to my wooden box at the lodging house. At last I found the small bronze key and compared it to the door's lock. Too small. I knelt, peering into the keyhole. Inside was a small room with an unmade bed and stacks of steamer trunks. I tried the key again, willing it to reach the tumbler, and I almost had it before it slipped out of my hands.

'Blast,' I muttered, bending to retrieve it. As I stood back up, I brushed the hair out of my eyes, the movement reflected in the mirror. I looked again at my face, studying the hollows under my cheekbones, the shadow around my eyes, wondering if Father would even recognize me now. Suddenly, a second face appeared behind my own – a dark face covered in a thick beard that obscured a man's heavy features. His forehead slanted with an odd deformity, leading to a brow that thrust forward, hooding his eyes. I gasped and tried to turn, but his beastly hands dug into my shoulders. The key fell as he forced a cloth over my mouth. The last things I saw before passing out were his yellow-green eyes glowing in the mirror.

FOUR

I awoke, head throbbing, the taste of chloroform in my throat. I was on the same wooden-framed bed I'd seen through the keyhole. I bolted upright. Scanned the room for my attacker, for a weapon, for an explanation as to why I was there.

I remembered in flashes. The face in the mirror. The cloth against my mouth.

Drugged.

A rush of panic sent my vision blurring and my ears roaring as I ransacked my clothes, relieved to find no signs I'd been harmed. Regardless, I needed something to use as a weapon – a fire poker or a letter opener. But a wave of nausea knocked me back to the pillows. I squeezed my eyes shut until my foggy head began to clear.

I was alone at least. In someone's room – the deformed man's, most likely. From the angle of sunlight pouring into the room, I must have been out for hours. A sick taste rose in my throat as I recalled the feel of his hairy hand against my mouth. My breath came fast, faster, until I thought I might black out. I gritted my teeth, holding in the urge to scream. Panic would get me nowhere.

I opened my eyes, slowly. Testing the door wasn't an option until my head cleared enough for me to stand. But the room was full of clues about my abductor. Crates and trunks were stacked by the door three deep, surrounded by packages wrapped in brown paper. He was traveling, then, and somewhere far away, judging by the cargo. A caged parrot on the dresser eyed me warily while picking at the bars with its beak. I stared at it.

My abductor traveled with a parrot?

A second door, which I assumed led to an adjoining room, was shut. Beside the bed was an open trunk, which I managed to lean toward without too much nausea. It contained rows of glass bottles, partially obscured by packing straw. I brushed the straw aside and took out a bottle: Elk Hill brandy. My father's favorite.

Before I could piece together what it meant, the door to the adjoining room swung open, revealing the beastly face from the mirror.

'You!' I cried. I coiled my fist around the bottle neck, ready to swing. I tried to stand but my feet wouldn't obey, and I grappled for the bedpost for support.

His was not the face of a monster, as I'd first imagined, but it was disfigured nonetheless. A wild black beard covered a protruding jaw below a snub nose and deep-set eyes. He moved with an odd lurch, as though he was unused to his own legs. Despite his disfigurement, he didn't seem so threatening now, partly due to the tray of tea and biscuits he was holding.

Still, my body tensed. He stepped forward with a shuffle, just far enough to set the tray on the foot of the bed. He scurried back and twisted his mouth into what might have been a smile.

The strange act of kindness only made me more uneasy. 'Get away!' I cried. I hurled the bottle at him, but my vision was distorted from the drugs, and it fell uselessly past his shoulder into a crate of clothes. I climbed over the bed, stumbling with vertigo, grabbing at his wrinkled linen shirt and hammering him with my fists. 'Someone, help!'

The man did not speak. He merely cringed and let me pummel him. But the side door jerked open again with a squeal of hinges and another man rushed in, a young man with shirt half-buttoned and suspenders at his sides. He threw his arms around mine to keep me from tearing the beastly man apart.

'Let me go!' I cried. But he was powerfully built, and it didn't take him long to pin my wrists in the shackles of his hands.

'Juliet! Stop this!' he said.

I froze at the gruff sound of my name. The young man let me go and I whirled on him. His face was deeply tanned, odd during the London winter. Loose blond hair fell to his broad shoulders. My lungs seized up.

I knew him. I'd have known him anywhere, despite the years.

'Montgomery,' I gasped. But what was he doing *here*, with my abductor? I'd expected to find my father, if anyone at all. The last person I'd expected to find was my family's former servant.

My knees buckled from shock, but he grabbed my elbows, holding me up. I had thought I was alone in the world. But here he was, the one person who knew me, the only one left who shared my dark secrets. Just seeing him started to untangle the swollen tightness in my chest.

I pulled away from him, not ready for the fragile, preserved knot of my heart to unravel so quickly.

'It's safe. You're not in danger.' He held out a hand as though he was calming a wild horse, his handsome features set with seriousness and concern. The recognition in that

27

expression nearly unbalanced the cadence of my heart. He was two years older than me, the son of our scullery maid. After his mother died when he was very young, my parents kept him on to help with the horses and Father's research. I'd had one of those hopeless crushes on him girls get before they even know what love is, but he had disappeared six years ago, the same time as my father. Wanting nothing more to do with our terrible family secrets, I'd assumed.

Now here he was, flesh and blood and blue eyes and a total mystery.

Montgomery glanced at the hairy-faced man, who shuffled nervously. 'Leave us,' he said, and the man obeyed. A part of me relaxed to see his deformed shape disappear into the other room. But then I realized I was alone with Montgomery, totally unprepared. My hand shot to my coiled braid, which had fallen loose and wild in the commotion. *Blast*. I must have looked like an idiot.

He finished buttoning his shirt and slid the suspenders over his shoulders, throwing me hesitant glances as he tied his blond hair back. He wasn't a thin, silent boy any longer. In six years he'd become a well-built young man with shoulders like a Clydesdale and hands that could swallow my own. Montgomery and I used to spend so much time together as children, though he was a servant and I the master's daughter. I'd never been at a loss for words with him.

Until now.

'I am sorry about the chloroform,' he said at last.

I swallowed. 'Odd way of greeting an old friend, don't you think?'

He paused while buttoning his cuffs. 'You *were* trying to break into our room. Balthazar behaves irrationally sometimes. But he meant you no harm.'

I pulled the pins out of my hair and raked my fingers

through it, hoping for some semblance of sanity. 'Balthazar? That beast has a name?'

'He's my associate. Don't let his appearance frighten you.'

The word *associate* made me hesitate. Montgomery wasn't even twenty yet, barely old enough to be anyone's associate himself.

He sat on a footstool and rested his elbows on his knees, peering at me with that same seriousness he'd had as a boy. It struck me, with a rush of blood to my cheeks, that he had become extremely handsome. I looked away quickly, before he could see my thoughts reflected in my face.

'I didn't expect to find you here,' I said.

Something like a smile played on the corner of his mouth. 'It's a coincidence that you were breaking into my room?'

'No.' My face burned. Words weren't coming out right. My mind still couldn't comprehend that he was actually sitting here, an arm's length away, grown into a handsome young man. I wondered how I looked to him, and if I was much changed from the sullen little girl he used to push around the courtyard in our wheelbarrow in an effort to make her smile.

My bag rested on the dresser next to the parrot's cage. I loosened the string and took out the folded diagram from between the Bible's pages. I handed it to him, but he gave it only a glance, as if he didn't even need to look at it.

'You've seen that before,' I concluded.

'Yes.' His features grew serious again. 'It belongs to me. At least, it did. I acquired it from an old colleague of your father's, but it was stolen two weeks ago with other documents. So you see why Balthazar reacted as he did. He thought you were a thief.' He unfolded the paper and raised an eyebrow. 'The blood spatters are new.'

My face turned red. How could I explain what had happened? I still felt the weight of the ax in my hand, remembered the frightened look on the boys' faces. Like them, Montgomery would think I'd gone mad. He sat here in his well-tailored clothes, a servant at his call, crates of expensive items around him. The scandal obviously hadn't brought *his* life crashing down. He'd changed from a servant to a gentleman, and I'd done exactly the opposite. I must look terribly pathetic to him. And the small scrap of pride I had wouldn't let Montgomery think me lacking.

I stood. 'I should go. This was a mistake.'

'Wait, Juliet.' Montgomery held my arm. For a second, his eyes flashed over my dress, my face. He swallowed. 'Miss Moreau, I should say. I haven't seen you in six years, and now I find you breaking into my room.' A muscle clenched in his jaw. 'You owe me an explanation.'

He'd been our servant, I told myself. I didn't owe him anything. But that was a lie. Montgomery and I were bound together by our past. This was the boy who had secretly taught me biology because my father wouldn't. Who'd told me fairy tales late at night to distract me from the screams coming from the laboratory.

I sank back down, not sure how to act around him. His blue eyes glowed in the hazy light from the window. He moved the tea tray to a side table and poured me a cup, adding two lumps of sugar, then breaking a third in half with a spoon, crushing it, and stirring it in slowly – the peculiar way I used to prepare my tea when I was a little girl. I was so oddly touched that he remembered that I didn't tell him I'd given up sugar in my tea long ago. As I took the cup, his rough fingers grazed mine and I bit my lip. Just the brief touch sent the muscle of my heart clenching with a longing to feel that bond with him again.

My throat felt tight, but I forced out words. 'I found the diagram and recognized it. I thought, maybe, it meant Father was here. Alive.' Spoken, it sounded even more foolish. I braced myself for his laughter.

But he didn't laugh. He didn't even flinch. 'I'm sorry to disappoint you,' he said softly. 'It's only Balthazar and myself.'

I took a sip of the tea, which had grown cold, but its sweetness replaced the chloroform's lingering tang. I wondered what Montgomery thought of me, showing up here, looking for a dead man. Father's death had never been confirmed – just assumed. I think the world wanted him dead, or simply forgotten.

But a girl couldn't just forget her father.

'Do you know what happened to him?' I asked. I wanted to ask if Montgomery believed the rumors, but the words wouldn't come. I was frightened of what his answer might be.

He looked toward the window, foot tapping a little too fast against the table leg. He shifted in his stiff clothes, as though his body wasn't used to them. It struck me that a wealthy medical student wouldn't pick so uncomfortably at his starched cuffs as Montgomery was doing. I wondered how recently he had acquired his fortune.

As if sensing my thoughts, he loosened his shirt's collar. 'The day he disappeared, I ran away too. I was afraid I might be accused as well, because I sometimes helped him in the laboratory. I've heard speculation . . . that he died.'

The teacup shook in my hand. I felt at the point of shattering with warring emotions. I wondered if that was what Father had felt like before he went mad – shattered. The teacup rattled more, and I set it next to the blood-spattered paper. 'What do you even want with this?' I nudged the dotted lines that formed a split-open rabbit. I knew it was abhorrent, but my gaze kept creeping back to the black lines, obsessively tracing the graceful arcs of the body.

'I study medicine. I'm not a servant anymore.' His words were pointed.

'But *this*? Vivisection?' It was hard to talk about these

things with him. The corset I had worn under my Sunday dress suddenly felt too tight. I pressed my hands against my sides. I thought of that rabbit, its twitching paws, its screams. Not even science could justify what those boys had done. And I knew Montgomery, deep in my marrow. He wasn't like them. He had a strong heart. He'd never do something he knew wasn't right.

His foot tapped faster and his gaze drifted around the room until it settled on the parrot. His throat tightened. 'It was among a collection of documents, that's all.'

He'd always been a terrible liar. I studied him from the corner of my eye, wondering. His gaze darted again to the parrot on the dresser, and I stood up and started toward the cage, just wanting to look closer at its iridescent feathers as some sort of distraction from everything that was happening. Montgomery's eyes were too real, too evocative, too familiar. I didn't know what to do with myself around him.

But as soon as I reached for the cage, Montgomery shot up, knocking over the footstool, and beat me to the dresser. His hand closed over a small silver object next to the parrot's cage. I blinked, uncertain, surprised by his actions.

'What is that?' I said quietly.

His fist clamped the object like a vise. His chest and arms were tensed. He'd always been strong. Now he was powerful.

Curiosity made me bolder. My fingers drifted away from the parrot's cage and rested a breath above Montgomery's closed fist. I wanted to touch his hand, feel the brush of his skin against mine, but I couldn't bring myself to do it.

'Montgomery, what is that in your hand?'

His face was broken with things unsaid. 'Miss Moreau . . .' The title sounded too formal on his lips. *Juliet*, I wanted him to call me.

My fingers trembled slightly. 'Please. Tell me.'

Something changed in his face then. He seemed so grown

up, but it was all an act. I knew because I'd played the same role for years. But being with him tore down that facade and left me stripped, vulnerable, just like the look on his face now.

'Don't be angry, Miss Moreau.' His voice was little more than a whisper. He looked away, softly, and opened his fist. The object dropped into my palm.

A pocket watch. I turned it over in my hand. Silver, with a gouge in the glass face and an inscription on the back that had all but worn away. It didn't matter. I knew the words by heart. *Thou shalt honor thy father and thy mother*. Unlike my mother, who'd maintained her devoutness even after becoming a mistress, Father had a scientist's skeptical fascination with religion. The watch had been a gift to him from his father, a bishop of the Anglican Church. Father had little use for the Ten Commandments, but the inscription was one rule he believed in and expected me to uphold.

Father had carried this watch every single day. He'd never have left it behind. Which meant either Montgomery had stolen it, or . . .

Montgomery folded my hands over the watch, and his hands over mine.

'I'm sorry. He made me swear never to tell you he was alive.'

FIVE

The pocket watch, Montgomery explained, had broken. He'd been instructed to have it repaired by a clockmaker in the city and brought to my father along with the rest of the supplies.

But I didn't care about his explanation.

'You lied to me,' I said.

He dipped his head, avoiding my gaze. 'I said I'd heard speculation that he died. That's true enough.'

'He's been alive this whole time and you've known it.' I sank to the bed, closing my eyes. Seeing Father's watch had brought that wall back up, reminding me that I *wasn't* a child anymore. I couldn't afford to let my guard down, not even with Montgomery.

He turned toward the window, twisting the watch chain. 'He thought if the world assumed him dead, they'd leave him alone.'

Father was alive and had never tried to find me – the painful realization of that betrayal ripped open the last tender stitch in my heart. 'But I'm his daughter.'

His only response was to pour me a glass of brandy and one for himself. He, as well, had returned to the act of playing adults. He sank into the desk chair. 'I still work for him, but no longer as a servant. I'm his assistant now. He isn't here, if you're wondering. He refuses to come back to England. We live on a biological station, of sorts. An island.' He swallowed the brandy and considered the empty glass. 'It's very far. He wanted a private place to continue his work undisturbed. I leave every eighteen months or so for supplies.'

I set my glass down, untouched. 'And your associate? Are all his kind like him?'

'The islanders.' Montgomery hunched over his glass. His hair had come loose again, veiling his face. 'They are, yes. You needn't fear him. He's harmless.'

As though he'd heard himself mentioned, Balthazar came in with a fresh pot of tea on a tray. He was a monster of a man, twice my size, with hands like bludgeons. He set the tray down and daintily removed the sugar bowl's tiny lid. Montgomery thanked and dismissed him.

He prepared my tea again with my childhood sugar ritual. The steam from my cup rose like the words of an oracle, forming a haze between us. I took a sip, hoping the tea would soothe my nerves. I tried to remember him as a child. He'd been quiet, especially about what went on in the laboratory. But Mother had been, too, as had the other servants, and all of us. None of us wanted to talk about the puddles of blood on the operating-room floor or the animals that went in and never came out or the noises that woke us in the night. Father said those were the ways of science and I shouldn't question them. Montgomery, at least, had taken good care of the animals before they went in.

I took another sip of tea. 'How did you find my father after so many years?'

'Find him? I never left him. The story about running away . . . it wasn't exactly like that.' He brushed the loose strands of hair behind his ear. 'After his colleagues made their accusations, your father knew he had to flee. He thought Australia might look upon his work more favorably. He took me with him. We found an island off the coast that suited his needs. I didn't want to leave you and your mother, but I hadn't a choice. I was twelve years old.'

'And you've been there this whole time?' The teacup trembled in my palm.

'There is much you don't know,' he said. 'I was just a boy.'

'Well, you aren't a boy anymore,' I snapped, even though I knew that wasn't entirely true. He dressed like a man, but he was too stiff in his clothes, too uncomfortable. He was only pretending to be a gentleman, and making a fairly poor show of it. 'You don't have to keep working for him. You can come back to London – he can't return or they'll arrest him.'

Montgomery bristled, as though the idea of returning to London was like agreeing to be locked in a cage. He didn't want to return, I realized. The city, with all its mechanization and soot and rigid society laws, had lost its hold on him.

But he said nothing. He only jerked his chin at the pocket watch and then at last said, 'It's not that simple. He's been like a father to me.'

'He's no father!' I curled my fingers into the armrests, suddenly angry that my father had left me behind and raised a servant boy instead. 'Haven't you heard? He's a madman.'

His face tightened. 'He's your father, too, Miss Moreau.'

'Would a father abandon his wife and daughter? Mother died and I heard nothing. He left no money. I'm one step away from the streets.' The words poured out before I could stop them. They'd been buried such a long time.

'I'm sorry.' His throat constricted. 'I wish the last few years had been easier for you. If I'd been here, maybe . . .'

Maybe Mother wouldn't have died? Maybe I wouldn't be living in poverty? Maybe . . . what? His eyes dropped to the pit of my elbow, hidden by my sleeve. I pressed my fingers against the sensitive place, protectively.

He nodded toward it, his voice lower. 'You still give yourself the injections?'

I drew back, clutching my arm as though the skin had been stripped back leaving the veins exposed and vulnerable. Montgomery knew things about me even Lucy didn't know. Like my illness. I rubbed my inner elbow, thinking of the glass vials in the back of my closet at the lodging house. The ones in the embossed wooden box Annie kept asking me about. They held a treatment – a pancreatic extract – I injected into my arm once a day. If I kept to a rigid schedule, I rarely showed symptoms. The few times I'd missed a dose, I'd gotten feverish and weak. My eyes would play tricks on me, hallucinate things that weren't there. Sometimes, in the evenings, the weakness would come anyway. Just thinking about it now made a cold sweat break out across my forehead.

Father had diagnosed the condition when I was a baby. A glycogen deficiency so rare it didn't have a name. I would have died if he hadn't discovered the cure. Now, I'd slip into a coma if I ever missed more than a few weeks' treatment.

I hesitated. Speaking of my illness made me feel exposed. It was just one more thing linking me to my mad father. But this – this was new. Montgomery already knew everything about my illness. It was an unfamiliar and comforting thought to know I didn't have to hide from him.

I nodded slightly.

He leaned forward with concern. 'And you haven't had any symptoms?' He reached out to take my wrist, but I jerked away. There was a limit to how much I'd share, even with Montgomery. 'I study medicine,' he said. 'Please. Let me see.'

I thought of the game those medical students had made up as an excuse to touch every bone in Lucy's body. Montgomery had given me anatomy lessons, but not like *that*. He would have been as uncomfortable with that lurid game as I'd been. Cautiously, I laid my white palm in the cradle of his tanned hand. He rolled up my sleeve, then brushed a finger against the sensitive skin of my inner elbow. My breath caught. I was alone in a young man's room, letting him touch me in places he shouldn't even see. But he wasn't just any young man – he was Montgomery. His touch sent my mind whirling. My body was already leaning forward, drawn toward his presence uncontrollably, before my thoughts could catch up.

'Good,' he muttered, and I came back to the present, blushing wildly. His finger still rested against my arm, rubbing absently, burning a hole in my skin. 'Have you had trouble getting enough of the treatment?'

I took a deep breath. 'No. Any chemist will make it if I give them the instructions and the raw supplies. Though they look at me oddly enough.'

He nodded. 'I'm glad. I've worried.' Slowly he released my arm. I rolled the sleeve back down quickly, smoothing the cuff over my wrist.

The silence was heavy.

'When do you depart?' I asked quickly.

'Soon,' he said just as quickly, as though it couldn't be soon enough. He sat back in his chair. 'Day after tomorrow, maybe.'

I swallowed, trying to hide my disappointment. 'Back to the island?'

'Yes. Balthazar has been working to arrange our return voyage. Not many ships want to take our cargo.'

'Cargo? The trunks and things?'

'That's only part of it. The rest is . . . well, the doctor's supplies.'

38

My curiosity was piqued. Surgical tools? Specimens? But I shook the questions out of my head. I wanted my father's truth, not his science.

'Does he ever speak of me?' I asked in a rush. I had to ask before he sailed away, forever.

Montgomery grinned, one second too late. 'Yes. Of course.'

I didn't smile back. I knew that grin, one side pulled back just slightly, jaw set harder than it should have been. Montgomery had given me that grin before, when our house cat had run away. He promised me all cats knew their way out of the city to the farms where mice grew fat as pigeons. But the cat hadn't made it out of the city. Later I found out Father had drowned it for bringing fleas into the house.

That grin meant Montgomery was lying.

I stood so fast the teapot rattled. I pushed my chair back, looking for my bag. I realized I wasn't ready to learn the truth. And Montgomery . . . I hadn't felt such intense and confusing emotions in so many years that I didn't know what to do but run.

'I need to go. I was supposed to work tonight.'

He stood, surprised. 'Stay. It's been so long—'

'It was good to see you,' I said, stumbling toward the door. I'd forgotten the time. Mrs Bell had asked me to help clean the operating theater before a lecture Monday morning. She'd be furious I wasn't there.

Balthazar poked his head out from the other room, giving me a quizzical look. The parrot pecked against the bars of its cage. 'I'm sorry about trying to break in,' I said.

'Miss Moreau, please! Wait.'

I was out of the room before Montgomery could finish. I hurried down the stairs, into the dining hall, where the proprietress was mopping the floors. She looked up, but I didn't stop until I was outside.

*   *   *

The streets were empty. St Paul's church bells tolled as I made my way along Cannon Street. My head was as foggy as the night. Eight, nine, ten tolls. Ten o'clock. *Blast*. Mrs Bell would skin me alive. I picked up my skirts – my Sunday best, which would take too long to change out of – and ran through the back alleys to my boardinghouse. Annie gave me a quizzical look as I threw open the door and grabbed my basket of cleaning supplies, but I couldn't waste time on an explanation.

I ran back out into the night, down the Strand toward King's College. Mrs Bell and Mary would probably still be there, seething that I was late. I tried to ignore the other thoughts clouding my mind: My father was alive but hadn't contacted me. Montgomery was back, and yet he'd soon return to my father, as though our roles as servant and child were reversed.

At last I made it to the entrance of the medical building and dashed up the granite steps, tugging on the front door. Locked. I set down my basket and gathered a few bits of broken stone from the street and tossed them at the high first-floor windows, praying Mary would hear me. Mrs Bell would give me an earful for being late, but it was better than not showing at all. My aim wasn't good, especially since my bare hands were cold and trembling, but a light went on in one of the windows.

'Thank God,' I said, cupping my freezing nose. I picked up my basket of cleaning supplies. I'd help them finish and then scramble home to my warm bed, where I could bury my thoughts in a downy quilt. I'd find a way to get a message to Lucy about my father being alive. She'd know what to do.

The door jerked open. I hurried inside but stopped when I saw the face lit by candlelight.

'Dr Hastings—' I said. He closed the door, plunging us

into darkness lit only by the glowing flame. When he slammed the door behind me, the sound echoed through the empty hallway.

'Juliet. It's quite late.'

'I'm to help Mrs Bell,' I stuttered, holding up my basket. His eyes were on my Sunday dress. No coat, no gloves. I must have looked suspiciously out of place on a cold night. I swallowed. 'I'll just go find them—'

I started down the hall, but he laid a hand on my shoulder. 'They've already left. They finished not ten minutes ago.' His fingers tightened. 'It's only me in the building tonight.'

My stomach clenched. 'Then I suppose I'm not needed. I'm sorry for disturbing you.' I twisted toward the doorway, but he blocked it.

'You're freezing,' he said, clutching my bare hands. 'What a silly girl, without a coat on a night like this. Come to my office. I have a fire going.'

'Thank you. But I should get home.'

His parchmentlike skin grazed my palm, so unlike the strong feel of Montgomery's touch. I tried to slip my hand away, but he didn't let go. I jerked my arm, but his grip only tightened. He smiled. Anger and fear spread throughout my body like an infection.

'Now, now,' he said, with a sickening smirk. 'What sort of mischief have you been up to, out alone late at night in your finest dress?' He licked his lips, his eyes glowing in the candlelight. 'You've been with a man, haven't you? I can smell his cologne. It would be a shame for Mrs Bell to find out. She'd have to dismiss you, of course. King's College has a reputation to uphold.'

The threat raised the hair on my arms. My body started to tremble with a feverish anger that seeped from my bones, tangling in my veins, urging me to lash out at him. My hand tightened on the basket handle as I fought to stay

41

calm. 'It's no business of yours who I've been with. If it was a man, you can be sure he wasn't a balding, dried-out old git.'

He smirked. 'A dried-out old git, am I? You're a pretty one, but you'll have to cool that temper if you want to keep your job. Now come to my office and do as you're told, and there'll be a sixpence in it for you as well.'

A bilious mix of fear and disgust rose in my throat, but my lips felt sewn together. I had to get out of there, quickly. He was twice my weight. If I tried to run, he'd be on me in an instant.

His spindly fingers pried the basket from my hand and set it on the entry table. My thoughts beat in time with my frantic pulse, trying to devise a solution. He reached for my waist, but I stepped backward.

The thin line of his mouth tightened. 'I'm losing patience with these games of yours. I'm going to have you tonight, and you might as well be a good girl and you'll get something out of it.' Wax dripped from the half-forgotten candle in his hand onto the floor. I'd have to clean that hardening wax before this night was out. My fear started to harden, too. My eyes caught the blade of the mortar scraper in the basket, and all sorts of ideas came to mind of what I'd like to do with that sharp point. I might be cleaning up splashes of his blood, too, unless he left me alone.

'You're a lucky girl, Juliet, that I still take an interest in you even after your father's transgressions. Not every man would show such kindness.'

Kindness. A bitter laugh sounded in my head. The last thing Dr Hastings showed was kindness. If he only knew about Montgomery, the man he'd just accused me of having been with. Montgomery would have slammed his fist into Dr Hastings's lump of a nose. My eyes drifted back to the basket. The mortar scraper was within reach. The palm of my hand

42

was hungry to hold its worn handle. To do something . . . I might regret.

Dr Hastings took my silence as consent. He snaked a hand up my arm, his fingers squeezing my flesh like ripe fruit. *Run*, I told myself. But what about the next time? He'd retaliate. He'd come at me harder.

There couldn't be a next time.

'It's a good thing your father's dead,' he said, his fingers curling around my shoulder, suggestively rubbing the place where my worn lace collar met bare skin. 'He wouldn't want to know all the vulgar things I'm going to do to you.'

I started to twist away, but he pushed me against the entryway table. My hip connected with the sharp corner as a bolt of pain shot through me. I winced, and he took the opportunity to pin me against the table with the weight of his own body. His fingers found my throat greedily and ripped the collar of my dress. Buttons rained to the floor.

My cleaning basket was just behind me. His thin lips breathed a disgusting moan against my collarbone. Although he had me trapped, my right hand was free. A tiny voice warned me I'd regret what I was about to do, but my head echoed with a roar. My fingers had already closed over the mortar scraper. A sort of madness took me over, pushing away the fear and terror. Before Dr Hastings realized what was happening, I had the sharp edge of the mortar scraper pressed against the fleshy triangle in the base of his palm where all the flexor tendons met.

His face twisted with anger, but I pushed the blade harder, almost breaking the skin. I didn't want to enjoy this. But I did, so much that my hands shook with the silent promise of the blade in my hand. 'Don't move, or I'll sever every tendon in your hand,' I hissed. 'My father was a surgeon. I know how important motor function is to you, Doctor. I can end your career in about half a centimeter of flesh.'

'I told you I was tired of these games,' he growled. 'Now put the knife down and finish taking off your dress.'

'It isn't a knife. It's a cleaning tool, but I wouldn't expect you to know the difference.' I pressed harder, barely able to restrain myself. 'And I'll use it unless you swear to never touch me again.' I let the blade dip into his skin, just enough to draw a dark line of blood.

'You're as mad as your father!' he cried. He spit a thin stream of saliva that landed on my cheek. 'I'll see you run out of town just like him.'

My hand tightened around the mortar scraper. Anger snapped in my nerves, shooting electric rage though the synapses.

To hell with it.

I thrust the blade into his pale skin until I felt the edge of the flexor tendon attached to his right index finger. A flick of my wrist was all it took – no more pressure than cleaning blood from the mortar. And my God, as wicked and wrong as it was, I enjoyed it.

He howled and crumpled to the floor, clutching his hand. I dropped the mortar scraper, realizing what I had done with a growing horror. I wouldn't need the scraper anymore. My employment was over.

I found the doorknob behind me, turned it, and ran into the cold November night.

SIX

The next morning I sat in Victoria Gardens with a tattered carpetbag and seven shillings, my entire savings. The carpetbag, a parting gift from Mrs Bell at my dismissal, was probably worth more than the contents – a few threadbare dresses, Father's *Longman's Anatomical Reference*, my Bible, and the embossed wooden box containing the syringe and a small supply of medication. Only the diamond ring Mother had left me was valuable. I took off my glove to watch it sparkle. I'd have to sell it. Even that would give me lodgings for only a few weeks. And staying in London was no longer an option.

'Oh, Juliet, I'm so sorry.' Lucy jogged across the lawn and collapsed on the bench, throwing her arms around me. She pulled back and touched a gloved hand to my face. 'Is it true, what they're saying?'

I nodded.

She shook her head. 'I'm sure he deserved even worse,' she said, her voice brimming with anger. 'He's lucky you didn't sever his *other* appendage.'

I gave a weak smile. But not even Lucy's friendship could get me out of this mess, and we both knew it. Dr Hastings had gone straight to the police, wanting to have me arrested. Mrs Bell had shown up at my lodging house an hour before dawn, banging on the door so hard that even Annie woke. She thrust the carpetbag into my hand along with the week's wages and told me to leave town before the police came inquiring.

A man reeking of whiskey passed by our bench, and I hugged the carpetbag closer. My chest felt hollow. How would I even leave? I hadn't money for a train, and surely my reputation would follow me. I'd never find employment as a maid again.

'What will you do?' Lucy asked.

I fiddled with the carpetbag's leather handle. 'It's either the workhouse, or . . .' I didn't need to finish. My mind drifted to the girl outside the Blue Boar Inn, with the hollow eyes and stained silk dress.

Lucy pushed a few coins into my hand. 'I took these from my father's desk. It'll get you as far as Bedford. There must be something you can do. A shopgirl, maybe.'

I counted the coins. Enough for the train, but not room or board. I'd have to spend the night in the station, and from there it was a short – and usually forced – leap to the gutter. Had my mother faced a similar dilemma? She'd done what she did out of desperation, and at least it kept us clothed and fed. My father had left with no note, no parting words, nothing. Was he really the kind of man to simply walk away from his family? Was he really the monster they said he was?

The truth was, I knew next to nothing about him. He was little more than a hazy memory and a slew of scandalous rumors. But he was *alive*. Out there, across oceans. Living. Breathing. For the first time in my life, I could simply ask him if the rumors I'd heard about him were true.

Lucy glanced across the park. Her mother had caught sight

of us and was striding straight through the grass. My stomach tightened. If Mrs Radcliffe didn't approve of me before, she must positively detest me now.

Lucy jumped up, her face suddenly white. She pressed her cheek against mine, hard. 'Write to me, won't you?' She was breathless. 'Let me know where you've gone? I'll try to send money. I'll try to visit, wherever you are.'

Mrs Radcliffe was so close I could see the clench of her jaw, and I pushed Lucy away. 'Go. Now. I'll write. I promise.'

Lucy dashed across the lawn to stop her mother. I grabbed the carpetbag and hurried the other way, dragging its weight along the length of the Thames. Lucy's mother said something biting, but I swallowed hard and didn't look back.

I kept walking, past the bridge and Temple Bar, where the archway used to stand. I crossed Cable Street to the main thoroughfare, to an inn with a swinging sign above the door. I pushed my way in, past the crowded dining room, and climbed to the second floor. I knocked. Then I pounded. The mirror beside the door reflected my wild desperation.

I should have told Lucy she couldn't visit. Where I was going, she couldn't come. It was a bit farther than Bedford.

Montgomery opened the door, clearly surprised. 'Miss Moreau. What are you doing here?'

The carpetbag fell at his feet. My heart was racing.

'I'm coming with you,' I said.

Early the next day, our carriage rumbled south of town to the Isle of Dogs. I pushed aside the gauzy curtain. Outside, the massive hull of a cargo steamer rose toward the sky, dwarfing the fleet of barges that clustered around the dock. Everywhere men swarmed like insects, hawking services or bearing trunks twice their size.

Beside me, Montgomery compared a handful of banknotes

47

against a small ledger, erasing and redoing sums with a frown. I wondered if he thought me a burden.

He looked up, as if sensing my question. The carriage lurched, and the ledger slid from his lap. We both reached for it, our hands grazing. I pulled back.

'It's not too late to change your mind,' he said.

I shook my head and concentrated on the ships outside. I'd made my decision. We had argued all day and night since I had shown up at his door. He'd flatly refused at first. He said the voyage was long, with a rough crew, and the island was no place for a lady. I told him I certainly wasn't a lady, thanks to my father's abandonment, and it was either the island or the streets. Or worse, prison. I didn't tell Montgomery my *other* motive, the one deep within my rib cage that beat in time with my heart: The world knew my father as a villain. I knew him as a thin man in a tweed suit who carried me on his shoulders during the Royal Guard's parades. I needed to know which man my father was – the monster, or the misunderstood genius.

In the end, Montgomery conceded only when I dragged him to the window and pointed out the prostitute my age. He said nothing of how Father would receive me on the island, and I didn't press.

'Is our ship like any of those?' I nodded toward the magnificent four-masted cruisers lined up in port.

Montgomery barely glanced at them before giving a hint of a smile. 'I'm afraid not.'

'It's an older ship?'

'Most likely. The reputable ships turn us away. They don't like Balthazar's appearance. Nor our destination.'

Outside, the relative order of Union Docks gave way to a more run-down part of the wharf. I covered my nose against the smell of rotting fish. Here, the docks were crammed with rusted parts and torn netting. There were no women – even the prostitutes stuck to the better end of the quay.

As we came around the bend, Montgomery pointed to a hulking two-masted brigantine docked alone at the Isle of Dogs. 'There,' he said. 'The *Curitiba*.' I frowned. It looked far too old and neglected to sail more than halfway across the Pacific. A windy storm might blow holes straight through it.

The driver stopped the carriage and we paid him a few coins. He seemed glad to leave us.

'There's Balthazar,' I said, shading my eyes. He sat by the gangway on a steamer trunk that looked more like a child's toy chest next to his size. A rabble of dirty sailors threw him uncertain glances as they dawdled around the rest of the cargo; rough as they looked, even they gave Balthazar a wide berth. A skeletal older man with a grizzly beard stumbled down the gangway in a mildewing black jacket that looked robbed from the dead. He stopped in his tracks at the sight of Balthazar and went the other way.

'Is that our crew?' I asked Montgomery hesitantly.

'Afraid so.'

'They look a shady bunch. Good thing Balthazar could knock them flat if they tried anything.' I watched as Balthazar hoisted the trunk and carried it onto the ship.

'He's not a fighter. But luckily for us, they don't know that.' From the rigid outline of the muscles beneath his shirt, I realized Montgomery probably could have knocked them all flat, too. He was no longer the gentle-natured little boy who caught kitchen mice and placed them outside to save them from the cat's sharp teeth.

He took my carpetbag. 'Come on. Lady or not, I'm going to lock you in your cabin. I don't trust this lot.'

I followed closely. My head spun as we crossed the gangway to the deck. A short walk, but a scary one. The ship's odd

49

swaying made my legs quake. There were a handful of men on deck, though I hesitated to call them sailors. *Pirates* might have been more accurate. Montgomery pulled me out of the way of two men loading a trunk.

'You'll get used to the rocking in a few days,' he said, leading me toward the quarterdeck. My mind whirled at his easy confidence. He carried himself almost as surely as the sailors, though he was far younger than most.

A monstrous barking tore through the air, and I nearly leapt into his arms. A pair of cages stood on the deck, containing three snarling bloodhounds and one matted sheepdog who barely lifted its head, a web of drool dangling from its jowls.

'Quiet,' Montgomery called to the dogs, and then turned to me. 'Stay here. I'll find the captain.' He wove around the cargo toward the rear of the ship.

The dogs had stopped barking at his order. I was surprised to find more cages beyond them. A panther, black fur matted with filth, flattened its ears and hissed from between the bars. And beside it was a small sloth that opened one sleepy eye and shut it again. And others. A monkey. Rabbits. A capybara – an enormous rodent I'd only read about.

I stepped closer, brushing my fingers against the monkey's cage, both incredulous and uneasy at the same time. A movement caught my eye as Balthazar poked his head up from the hold. He hurried toward me.

'Stay away from the cages, miss,' he said in his coarse English. 'It isn't safe.' A tarpaulin had slid off the sloth's cage, and Balthazar replaced it with great care. 'It doesn't like the sun,' he explained, patting the cage gently.

'These are for my father, aren't they?' I asked. My uneasiness grew. 'For his research.'

Balthazar scratched his ear. Folded his mouth tight. Didn't answer.

I told myself there were plenty of legitimate reasons a scientist might want live specimens. It didn't mean, necessarily, that the animals were intended for vivisection. I caught sight of Montgomery coming back toward me, but I couldn't bring myself to ask him. I wasn't sure I was ready to learn what types of boundaries my father might have crossed out there in the dark, silent sea.

'Come meet the captain,' Montgomery called, waving me aft, where the grizzly-bearded man waited for us at the hold. The man swayed slightly. The cloying stench of alcohol hovered around him like yellow London fog.

I climbed around the cages and cargo, my steps uneasy on the swaying deck.

Montgomery took my hand to help me over a coil of line. 'Miss Moreau, this is Captain Claggan. He'll show us to our quarters.'

The captain eyed me closely, either shortsighted or sizing me up. 'Damn wild animals,' the captain muttered. 'Damn lass. Ain't good luck, I say. If you hadn't paid up front . . .' He spit to the side and led us down a steep ladder into a low hallway darker than a coffin. 'Crew's quarters at the rear. My cabin's up top, below the quarterdeck. The hold's below.' He tapped his foot on a trapdoor.

He stopped at a closed door and jiggled the latch, then threw his shoulder against it with a curse. The door swung open into a tiny room with a small bed and desk, so cramped I could feel the heat from Montgomery's body.

'You're all staying in here together, eh?' The captain leered. Blood rose to my cheeks.

'My man and I will sleep above deck, if the weather holds,' Montgomery answered, a hint of red at his cheeks, too. An unwed young man and woman sharing a room together only meant one thing to the sailors.

The captain smirked and left.

51

Montgomery set the bags on the bed. 'We should have free run of the ship, except the crew quarters and the boatswain's hold. Just the same, I'd rather you stay here. It's safer. Passengers have been rumored to disappear under Captain Claggan's watch.' He hesitated, and I wondered if he might try to talk me out of coming one last time. It was so strange to see him like this, almost grown, capable beyond his years. He couldn't have had much of a childhood. So much strength had to hide some sort of vulnerability. But then he brushed past me to the door before I could finish my thought. 'I'll be back once we've left port.'

I closed the door behind him. My stomach was rolling. I let myself fall onto the bed. By the time I awoke, we were already at sea.

SEVEN

Montgomery was right – it took time to grow accustomed to the ship's movement. For the first few days I could barely sit up in bed. Montgomery lashed a lantern to the desk and left a bucket by the bed, though he quickly learned to lash that down, too. Balthazar brought me food from the galley, but I couldn't stomach the rock-hard dried meat and slimy canned vegetables. At last Montgomery brought up a tin of Worthington's biscuits from Father's cargo. It was the only thing besides water I could keep down, and the water turned rancid after two weeks. From then on, it was bitter beer.

After over a month in the dark, cramped cabin, I started going above deck once a day for fresh air and sunlight, but the smell of turpentine and piss usually drove me back even before the sailors started leering. Montgomery came down sometimes, but the ship was shorthanded and the captain kept him and Balthazar busy above deck, never mind that they were paying passengers. Montgomery did the work without complaint. The dogs barked incessantly. I thought I'd gotten used to the ship's rocking, and even believed we'd make it to the island with no incidents – until the storm hit.

That night the waves sent the ship tossing and made

sleep impossible. Every lurch had me clutching the sides of the bed to keep from falling, and my stomach felt flipped upside down. I couldn't imagine what was happening above deck. The animals must be going wild, or else terrified and huddled in the corners of their cages. Not so different from how I felt.

Someone pounded at the door. I stumbled across the dark room to let in Montgomery and Balthazar, who were drenched to the core. I lit a match for the lantern, but the ship lurched and the flame wavered and sputtered before catching. Montgomery bolted the door against water creeping in. He pulled off his shirt, cursing and shivering.

As the weeks passed, I'd spent more time above deck, and it wasn't uncommon for the sailors to go shirtless. But this wasn't some stranger. This was Montgomery. It was hard to keep my eyes from trailing back to steal glances at his bare chest.

He wrung out his shirt and hung it over the back of the wooden chair to dry. 'It's a squall,' he said. 'Captain's ordered all but a handful below. Damn drunkard. We lost a trunk over the side before he thought to batten everything down.'

I sank onto the bed and pulled a blanket around my chemise. It didn't cover my ankles, which I tucked underneath me. Montgomery might be accustomed to showing his bare skin, but I wasn't.

Balthazar sank to the floor and rested his head against the wall. He didn't seem to care that he was drenched. His trousers and white shirt were now just one dull shade of dirty gray.

Montgomery pulled out the desk chair. His skin glowed in the lantern light. The first time I'd seen him in London, I'd noticed how tanned his skin was for a gentleman in winter. He looked considerably less like a gentleman now. Sunburned shoulders. Salt ringing the hem of his trousers.

Hair tangled and loose, and an edge in his handsome blue eyes. No wonder he bristled at the idea of staying in London – he was as wild as the caged animals.

We sat in silence, listening to the storm rage. I recalled an old song Lucy used to sing about a fisherman lost in a squall who returned to his beloved as a ghost. I didn't realize I was humming the tune until Montgomery leaned back and closed his eyes.

'That's nice,' he said.

'It's just an old song.'

'Well, don't stop. Please.'

But I was too embarrassed to continue. Montgomery toyed with the lantern's latch, raising the flame to a blaze and then back to a whisper of light. When we were children, I could tell what he was thinking even without words. Now his thoughts were a puzzle to me.

'Do you still play piano?' he asked at last.

It took me by surprise. 'It's been a few years.'

'We have one on the island. It's probably out of tune. I never had an ear for music like you.'

My cheeks warmed at the thought of him remembering that I played. 'How did you manage to bring a piano to an island?'

'It wasn't easy. I hadn't a clue what I was doing, but I wasn't going to tell the merchants that. I'd chipped three keys and broken a leg by the time we reached the island.' He paused, and I blushed as I realized he was staring at my bare ankles, which had drifted free of the blanket. I tucked them under me.

'The piano's limb, I should say,' he said curtly, clearing his throat. 'I'm sorry. It's been a long time since I've been in the presence of a lady.'

I smiled. There was a time when the word *leg* wasn't mentioned in polite company, even when referring to inanimate objects. My mother had tried to train Montgomery in etiquette. Apparently a few things had stuck.

'You've been gone from London too long,' I said. 'No one gets upset over mention of a leg these days.' My neck felt increasingly warm. 'Besides, you forget that I'm not a lady anymore.'

'Don't be ridiculous, Jul— Miss Moreau.'

'If you haven't noticed, *Mr James*, I'm alone in my night-dress with two men, after being thrown out into the streets.' I lightly ran my fingertips over my dry lips. My nails had grown so jagged and unkempt that Lucy would have called them claws.

'What else does Father have you bring?' I asked.

He laughed, almost a bark. 'Four cases of butterscotches. The full collection of Shakespeare, the same edition as from his library on Belgrave Square; you remember the ones? I had a devil of a time tracking those down. And once he asked for a copper bathing tub. It fell from the crate and sank while we were loading it.'

'What peculiar things.'

'Yes, well, he can be very peculiar.' His jaw clenched. 'I'm sure you recall.'

I drew the blanket tighter around my shoulders. A peculiar disposition didn't make a madman.

Not that alone.

'Montgomery, what do you . . .' I paused. The words were an experiment, and they came out stilted and half formed. 'About the accusations . . .' My throat closed up. I felt his intense gaze but couldn't bring myself to ask. If I'd still been ten years old, I wouldn't have hesitated. But there were years between us now.

'Is it only you and him on the island?' I asked quickly, instead.

'And the islanders,' he said. Balthazar shifted in the corner.

I had almost forgotten he was there. He had a way of settling into the shadows.

'Don't you get lonely?'

'The doctor, he doesn't mind. Sometimes I think even I'm too much company for him. And he certainly can't abide *their* presence.' He glanced at Balthazar, making me wonder who exactly 'they' were. 'It will be different with you there. At times he can get so distracted that he forgets years are passing.' He lowered the light to the barest hint of a flame. 'We're getting close. Another week or two.'

I hesitated. 'Do you think he'll be pleased I've come?'

Montgomery brushed back his hair. 'Of course he will be.' A faint smile tugged at the corner of his mouth, the smile I remembered as meaning he was lying. I pulled the blanket tighter against the sting.

The heel of Montgomery's boot tapped nervously against the floor, as if he knew he was a bad liar. 'I can't say how he'll take the news at first. He can be unpredictable, but in the end he'll be glad you came.' He leaned forward, his blue eyes simmering. His boot tapped faster. '*I'm* glad you came.'

His words set every inch of my skin sizzling, and I nearly dropped the blanket in surprise. I'd always idolized him, but I'd been a little girl. The crush I'd had on him then seemed silly now that I knew how the world worked. Servant boys didn't grow up and marry their masters' daughters. Instead, women fell from privilege and sold themselves on the streets. Men could be cruel, men like Dr Hastings. As much as I believed in Montgomery, the fairy tale was gone.

I sneaked a glance at him. Wondered what his life must have been like, alone on a remote island with only my father and the natives for company. Perhaps he was as hungry as I was to feel that connection we once shared, to get back a little of that fairy tale. I felt myself drifting closer to him as the blanket slipped from my fingers.

The ship jerked suddenly, and I flew backward. My head struck the wall. Montgomery tumbled out of his chair and would have fallen on top of me if he hadn't braced himself against the wall with quick instincts. I clung to his arms as if I were falling, but we weren't going anywhere. My fingers tightened. He was a finger's distance from me. Closer. Close enough to feel the brush of his loose hair on my face, to feel the heat from his sunburned skin. If it hadn't been for the thin fabric of my chemise, we'd have been skin against skin, his hard muscles against my soft limbs. My jagged fingernails curled into the bare skin of his biceps. His lips parted. He drew in a sharp breath. Being so close to a half-naked man – *to Montgomery* – made me breathless.

He winced. I was hurting him, I realized.

I let go. Blood and reason flooded back to my head. I hadn't meant to grab him. Instinct had made me do it. And now he would think . . . what *would* he think?

The ship righted, and Montgomery sat up, his lips still parted. A line of red half-circles marked his arms from my fingernails. His eyes were wide.

'Blasted storm,' he said, a little gruffly. He was breathing as heavily as I was. 'How's your head?'

I touched the back of my skull absently, still dazed from being so close to him. 'Just a bang.'

He pulled his damp shirt back on, hiding my nail marks. A bloom of pink spread over his neck. 'I should probably check on the animals.' He seemed suddenly unable to look me in the eyes. 'Try to sleep if you can.'

He disappeared into the forecastle hatch, leaving me alone with Balthazar. The big man stared into space, then gave a shudder that sent seawater spraying, like a dog. He smelled of wet tweed and turpentine. I doubted I smelled much better.

I realized I knew almost nothing about this man who

hung at Montgomery's heels like a shadow. It was impossible not to be intimidated by his size and looks, despite how gentle he was with the animals.

'You're a native of the island, aren't you?' I asked. He seemed surprised that I addressed him and remained mute through the next lurch of the ship.

'Aye, miss,' he grunted at last.

'So you know my father, the doctor? Henri Moreau?'

Balthazar pulled his legs in to his chest. His eyes darted nervously. 'Thou shalt obey the Creator,' he said.

'Creator? God, you mean?'

'Thou shalt not crawl in the dirt. Thou shalt not roam at night.' He rocked slightly.

I peered at him uneasily. His words had the ring of commandments, but none I'd ever heard. 'What are you talking about, Balthazar?'

'Thou shalt not kill other men,' he said, rocking harder. The ship dipped suddenly and I grabbed the wall for support. Balthazar no longer seemed aware of the storm. He rocked faster, eyes glassy.

'Who told you all this?' I asked. 'My father?' His recitation had the feel of Father's commanding influence all over it.

'Stop saying these things,' I said. 'Please. Calm down.' My thoughts raced. Did the natives see my father as some sort of supreme ruler? Father had scorned religion, so I couldn't imagine he would permit such ridiculous chanting. I wanted to ask Balthazar more, but he leapt to his feet and hurried from the room without another word.

The storm lasted through the night and into the morning. When the *Curitiba* returned to its normal rocking, I stumbled above deck to gasp fresh air and feel warm sunlight. The foremast boom had buckled under the weight of the canvas sail, which now cracked and whipped in the heavy breeze. The dogs sprawled in their cages, quiet for once, under a waterlogged canvas tarpaulin. They didn't lift their heads as I passed. Only their eyes followed me.

Montgomery and Balthazar stood on the quarterdeck, peering into the rigging.

'Is the ship still seaworthy?' I asked.

Montgomery jerked his chin toward the sailors, who fought to tame the sail under the captain's slurred curses. 'We won't sink, but we won't go far if they don't fix the sail. Anyway, we have our own problems.' He looked back into the rigging. On the top spar, a dozen yards above us, was the monkey. 'His cage shattered in the storm.'

'Can't one of the crew climb up to fetch him?'

Montgomery glanced at the foresail. 'They won't bother themselves for an animal.'

I studied the complicated puzzle of rigging, spars, and sails, looking for a solution. But wherever a man might cut off the monkey's passage horizontally, it could always move vertically.

'You'll have to wait for him to come down,' I concluded.

'Not possible. Captain's given me no choice.' His face went serious and he made a gesture to Balthazar, who shuffled to a stack of crates and came back with a rifle. He handed it to Montgomery.

The blood drained from my face. 'Don't you dare shoot it!' I said.

He shook his head a little too forcefully. 'Captain says the monkey's added weight can affect the sails.'

'That's not true. It's basic physics. You know that, Montgomery.'

'Very scientific of you, but it won't make a difference to the captain.' He split the barrel and checked inside. 'Balthazar, go belowdecks for a few minutes.' Balthazar nodded, grinning naively, and shuffled off to the forecastle hatch. Montgomery clicked the barrel back into place. 'You should go as well, Miss Moreau.'

'I shan't. I'll talk some sense into the captain.' I pointed at the rifle. 'And don't even think about using that.'

'Miss Moreau, wait.' His voice begged. 'Juliet!'

I ignored him and crossed the deck. While trying to tame the loose sail, the men had torn a gash down its center, and the captain cursed something furious.

'Captain Claggan, a word, please.'

He whirled on me with bloodshot eyes and breath like a tannery. His nose and cheeks were splotched with broken blood vessels that made him look like the devil himself. 'What do you want?' he bellowed.

I took a step back. The deckhands glanced my way, their faces hardened. I'd find no support there.

'I asked you what the devil you want!'

'The monkey,' I said, getting irritated. 'It weighs too little to do any damage. The laws of physics—'

'Physics! Devil take you, lass! I'll shoot the wretch down myself. And you, too, if you don't mind your own business!'

I wasn't used to being threatened by a bony drunkard, and it didn't sit well with me. Anger stirred deep in my bones. At just sixteen, I had already had a lifetime's experience with men like him. The last one ended up without use of his hand. The river of anger flowed from my capillaries into veins and straight to my heart, lodging there like a hardened bit of glass. Before I knew what I was doing, I'd brought my palm across his face.

The crew went silent. The captain touched his cheek, blinked twice, then stumbled toward me with black rage. Suddenly Montgomery was beside me. He snatched my hand and tucked the rifle under his arm.

61

'Is there a problem, Captain?' he growled. In an instant Montgomery had turned into a hulking animal, powerful and dangerous.

The captain's bloodshot eyes steadied on the rifle. Montgomery casually adjusted it so it pointed at his gut. The captain hesitated, then spit a thin mess of tobacco a few inches from Montgomery's feet. 'Keep your little bobtail below where she belongs.'

I gasped at the insult, but Montgomery squeezed my hand so hard I couldn't think of anything else. 'Our apologies for the disruption,' he said, his blue eyes cold. 'It won't happen again.' He pulled me to the side, where I leaned against the rail, shaking with anger.

'Did you hear what he called me?' I said, face burning.

'He's a liar and a drunk, so what he says is of no consequence to us.' His hand tightened over mine. 'I'm less concerned with your reputation than your safety. Men like him are dangerous. He may be checked by Balthazar's size and by my rifle, but he could do anything to us out here, Juliet, and no one would know.'

His large fingers swallowed my own. He could have let go, for we were quite safe now.

But he did not.

I cleared my throat. His presence had a way of making my anger dissipate, but in return it set loose a swell of other feelings. 'I should thank you, then.' I didn't know exactly what to do with myself. What to say.

He still didn't let go of my hand. He took a step closer, interlacing his fingers in my own. I swallowed the nervous jitters rising in my throat.

'I suppose I've made this voyage very difficult for you,' I said. My voice shook, but the thought of silence was more frightening.

'As I said, I'm glad you came.' His eyes held mine, leaving

little doubt as to his meaning. Montgomery wasn't one for games.

My corset felt even more constricting than usual. I wanted to rip the stays apart and fill my burning lungs with air. His touch was thrilling. His whispered words, *I'm glad you came*, turned my insides molten. Emotions were a puzzle, something to be studied and fitted together carefully. But the edges of this puzzle didn't fit within the lines I knew. I focused on the loose white thread on his cuff rather than on our intertwined hands.

'I've thought of you over the years, Juliet,' he said, his voice low as he brushed a blowing strand of hair out of my face. 'More than I should.'

Juliet, he'd called me. He'd dropped the pretense of using my surname. I studied the waves beyond our hands, trying to work out the equation of my emotions. Since I'd seen him again, in that room at the Blue Boar Inn, there'd been a tightness inside my chest whenever he was around, like string lashed around my heart. I felt it tug at his little gestures that brought me back to our childhood. I felt it at his kindness to Balthazar. At the way circumstances had forced him to grow up too quickly. At the way he made me feel safe, for the first time in years, and yet passionately alive. It was something I could never have felt with Adam or any of those silly boys.

The waves' caps blurred into a dizzying blue mass. I felt myself swaying and gripped the rail. My corset was bound too tightly. Blood wasn't flowing to my brain. I didn't know how to process these feelings. Safety. Warmth. Affection – God, I wasn't a little girl anymore – maybe it was more than just affection.

I pressed my fingers against my eyes and looked back at the waves. A strange sight: a dark mass against the sea. I blinked to clear my head.

A hundred feet away from us a battered dinghy bobbed, half sunk. I squeezed my eyes shut.

'Juliet, are you all right? Did you hear what I said?'

But when I opened my eyes again, I saw that the dinghy was real.

So was the hunched body inside.

EIGHT

'Captain! There's a man adrift,' Montgomery yelled. I dug my fingers into the chipped rail. The dinghy was quickly taking on water, sinking lower and lower.

'Could he be alive?' I gasped.

'Doubtful. Must have been drifting for days. We've been at sea nine weeks and haven't seen another ship.'

The captain shuffled over, cursing loudly, and shoved me aside as he peered over the rail. 'Bloody devil,' he muttered, and signaled to the first mate. 'Turn us alongside her!'

A red-nosed young deckhand helped Montgomery lower some line, hand over hand, so fast that watching made me dizzy. As the ship swung to aft, the sinking dinghy drew closer until it knocked against the hull. The waterlogged body lay curled in the bottom, a hideous display. The tatters of a coat, bleached and salt stained, covered his upper half. Torn trousers ended midcalf over bare feet that were scarcely more than bones. What would we find under the clothes? A bloated corpse? Bleached bones scoured clean by salt and sand? I found myself leaning dangerously far over the rail.

'Larsen, you're lightest,' Montgomery said. The deckhand

swung a leg over the side and disappeared. I waited tensely
with the group of sailors. Even the monkey watched from
high in the rigging. A cloud passed overhead, stealing our
sunlight. A few fat raindrops fell on my face.

Suddenly, a rough hand took my wrist and pulled me
away. Balthazar. He led me to the sheepdog's cage, where
we could watch from a distance, sheltering us from the coming
rain with a canvas cloth.

'Thank you,' I muttered, hugging my arms, though I still
wanted to be watching from up close.

'Montgomery says a lady must be protected.'

I looked at him askance. If Montgomery and Balthazar
thought I'd never seen a gruesome image before, they were
mistaken. I wasn't that kind of lady. I started to say as much,
but Balthazar seemed proud, as if he was protecting a proper
young woman, so I kept my mouth shut.

A murmur spread through the men like spring rain, and
I strained to hear. I caught only one word, but it was enough.
Alive.

I itched to move closer, but knew I should stay with
Balthazar. Another sailor climbed over the side. The line
jerked wildly, held fast by the second mate and his watch
crew. At Montgomery's signal, they pulled. Several feet of
line came up. The sailors hoisted up Larsen along with the
castaway. The unconscious body fell upon the deck, dripping
with seawater. The crew swarmed closer.

Unable to resist, I tore away from Balthazar. He called
after me not to look, but I felt compelled to, dragged forward
by an invisible hand. I slipped quietly among the sailors,
catching glimpses between their swarthy frames.

Montgomery rolled the body carefully to its back. It was
a young man, a little older than me, unconscious and so
battered and beaten by the sea that I couldn't believe he
had survived. His hand clutched a tattered photograph as

though, in his last hours of consciousness, the image was all he'd had left to cling to.

I blinked, paralyzed by the image of that bruised hand holding a photograph. A coldness stole my breath. I had been drawn by morbid curiosity like a vulture to carnage. But this wasn't some lifeless corpse – it was a person, with a heart and a hope. Alive.

I drifted along the outskirts, keeping my distance, almost afraid that if I stepped closer, my curiosity would once again take control of my limbs. I glimpsed a blood-soaked bandage wrapped around his leg. I imagined him alone and desperate in the dinghy, tending to his wound and wondering if he was going to die out there.

Montgomery's lips silently counted the young man's pulse. 'Fetch some water!' he called.

A sailor shifted, giving me a clear look at the castaway's face. I'd never been one to turn away from blood, but my heart twisted at the sight. A crusted and seeping gash ran down one side of his face, just below his eye. Sun blisters covered his cheeks and forehead. His salt stained dark hair tangled like the seaweed that washed up at low tide in Brighton. His eyes were closed.

It struck me he was almost a ghost, straddling the fine line between the living and the dead. I wanted him to live, to see again whatever was so important in that photograph, as if it would make up for my morbid fascination.

The rain came harder now. A sailor pushed past me with a flask. Montgomery held it to the castaway's lips, but he didn't wake, so Montgomery poured the water over his face instead. A slight moan. A cough. And then the castaway jerked awake, blinking, rain streaking down his face. His wild eyes darted back and forth.

'We found you at sea,' Montgomery said. 'Can you speak? What's your name?'

But the castaway shook his head, muttering something I couldn't make out, clutching the photograph so hard it crumpled. He grew more agitated with each breath, kicking and tearing at some invisible demon. The gash on his face reopened, and a line of dark blood rolled down his neck.

'Calm yourself!' Montgomery threw his weight on him. The castaway was no match for his size, but delirium made him fierce, and Montgomery had to struggle to hold him down.

'Sea madness,' Montgomery said. 'Balthazar, get the chloroform.'

The castaway clawed at the deck, nearly grabbing my foot. Montgomery jerked his chin at me. 'Get back, Juliet!' he yelled.

But all I could do was shuffle back a few inches, wondering what was happening in the young man's mind. He seemed to think he was in some other place. But then his eyes found mine and he stopped struggling, like the mad fog had lifted. Like he remembered something – no, recognized something. An odd sensation tickled the back of my neck. *Did* he recognize me? I'd never seen him before in my life. His desperation was familiar – I had only to look in a mirror to recognize that – but he was still a stranger. His lips formed a few voiceless words that drew me closer, fascinated, wanting to hear, wanting to know who he was.

'Juliet, I said stay back! He might be dangerous.'

Montgomery's voice broke the spell and I tore my eyes away. All the sailors were staring at me. I shrugged hesitantly, as curious as they were.

Balthazar stumbled up beside me, clutching a glass bottle and cloth soaked with chloroform. The castaway took one look at Balthazar's hulking form and started straining again. He twisted out of Montgomery's grip and slammed a fist so hard against the deck that the weathered boards splintered.

My lips fell open. That sort of strength came only with powerful delusions. He didn't know what was happening, I realized. A part of him had slipped away out there in the open sea. He let out one hoarse yell before Montgomery thrust the cloth over his mouth and nose and he slumped to the deck.

The captain sank to a knee to rifle through the castaway's pockets. Montgomery frowned as he handed the cloth back to Balthazar and glanced at me, a question in his eyes: What was it about me that had made the castaway go silent?

But I was as much at a loss.

'Might as well pitch him back overboard,' the captain said, turning out only empty pockets. 'You saw him. Mad. Can't have a madman hanging about.'

'If you throw him overboard, that's murder,' Montgomery said tensely. 'And I doubt you'd be saying that if you'd found money in his pockets.'

'Ain't murder if he can't pay.'

'You're not throwing him overboard.' Montgomery's voice was hard.

The captain sat up, eyeing him with something like a challenge. 'You going to take him with you, then, boy?'

Montgomery hesitated, giving Balthazar an uneasy glance before turning back to the captain. 'Look at his buttons – silver. He comes from wealth. Give him a few days to regain consciousness, and I'm sure he'll offer to repay you generously.'

Balthazar wrapped an arm around my shoulders and started to lead me away. My feet went with him as if of their own accord, but I couldn't tear my gaze from the castaway. The gash across his face, the bruises on his bare arms from being tossed about at sea. He seemed so eager to cling to a slip of life. He was a survivor, like me.

NINE

Montgomery attended to the castaway day and night. A rumor circulated that the young man didn't remember his own name, or how he'd been shipwrecked, or if he was the only survivor. The captain lost patience and threatened to throw him overboard again, but Montgomery slipped the captain the last of our coins in exchange for setting up a cot for him in the galley. It was one of several places on the ship I wasn't allowed, but after a few days without seeing Montgomery or hearing more than snatches of gossip about the castaway, I couldn't stay away.

The galley was as dark and damp as the inside of a rotting cellar. The only light came from the cooking fire and a few lit candles. The sailors had laid the young man next to the chimney, where the bricks would keep him warm, but in sleep he looked as cold as death.

Montgomery glanced up when I entered. We both knew I wasn't supposed to be there. Rather than scold me, he handed me a dirty cloth and nodded toward a copper pot on the hearth. 'Boil this. Add a few drops of chlorine to the water. The vial's next to the fire.'

Our hands grazed as I took the cloth. My skin still tingled with the memory of our fingers intertwined.

'I hear you're quite the doctor,' I said, adding a few drops of chlorine to the pot. Steam billowed in the dank space around me.

Montgomery carefully peeled back a bandage on the young man's leg, airing the wound. It oozed with angry white pus. 'Hardly. Your father says I'm useless.' He reached for a bottle of Elk Hill brandy and splashed some onto the scraped flesh. The castaway moaned but didn't wake.

The boiling water tumbled over itself in great bubbles, and I submerged the soiled cloth in the pot with a wooden spoon. 'My father used to call everyone useless, from the scullery maid to the Dean of King's College. You're far from useless.' I stirred the pot slowly, throwing glances at the castaway's face in the candlelight. 'How is he?'

'He'll live.' Montgomery picked up a needle and a length of black thread. 'If we'd found him a day later, maybe hours, he might not have been so lucky. I'd hoped this would have healed, but it got infected. Not a damn clean thing around here.' He pinched the skin around the scrape and punctured it with the needle.

I memorized his gestures as he stitched the wound closed. His movements were like a long-acquired habit, something he did so often, his hands could practically think on their own. When he was younger, he used to build fires in my room's small fireplace with the same certainty of action. For Montgomery, work came as naturally as an afterthought – it was keeping up his strong front that required concentration.

'Has he been awake?' I asked.

'Off and on.'

'Did he tell you what happened to him?'

Montgomery started on the next stitch, tugging the skin

tight. He paused to toss me the old bandage, which I added to the pot. The billowing water turned a murky shade of brown. 'He remembers a little more each day. Yesterday he told me he was a passenger on the *Viola*, bound for Australia, but it took on water from a cracked hull some twenty days ago.'

'Twenty days! Was he the only survivor?'

'He gets confused when I ask questions. But in his sleep, he says as much.' His eyes flashed. 'He's asked about you.'

I nearly knocked over the boiling pot. 'Me? What did he ask?'

'Who you were. Where you were going. What a pretty girl was doing on this kind of ship. It seems you made quite an impression.' There was a flicker of jealousy in Montgomery's voice that made me focus on the pot, studying the rising steam.

'What did you tell him?'

'The truth,' he said. 'You've come to find your estranged father.'

'So you don't think he's dangerous?'

Montgomery tied off the last stitch and bit through the thread. 'No, he isn't dangerous.' He stood, wiping his hands on a rag, and came to the hearth. Steam made sweat bead on his forehead. I was suddenly aware of the intense heat in the small galley, and that we were, with the exception of the sleeping castaway, alone. 'He's the gentleman type. You saw the silver buttons. Probably never had a true day of hard work in his whole life.'

'Still, he survived a shipwreck.'

Montgomery brushed his hair back, studying me with those deep blue eyes. 'What has you so interested in him?'

The tone in Montgomery's voice made me stir the water faster, aware of the red creeping up my neck. Lucy would have said something coy. She believed the way to keep a man interested was to make him jealous, but Montgomery wasn't mine to begin with, and he had no good reason to be jealous of a half-dead castaway, silver buttons or not.

'He had a photograph,' I said into the pot. 'Did you find it?'

Montgomery reached to the shelf behind me, between the larder and block of salt. A trace smell of spiced brandy clung to his hands. He pulled down a scrap of crumpled paper and handed it to me. The photograph, waterlogged and torn beyond recognition.

I could only make out an overcast brown sky, the vague shape of people. I glanced at the castaway. What had it meant to him?

'The helmsman spotted debris in the water this morning,' Montgomery said. 'We're getting close to the island. It's just a matter of days now.' His voice held the relief of reaching home after a long voyage. But there was an undercurrent of worry. 'I don't like the thought of leaving him here, especially without a doctor aboard. That wound will get re-infected without treatment. And if he can't convince the captain he can pay, once we leave there's no telling what will happen. They don't owe him anything.'

The castaway muttered something in his sleep and tossed around in the cot. I brushed my hair back, stealing a glance at the black stitches in his leg. 'You want to take him with us,' I said, reading Montgomery's thoughts.

His jaw tensed indecisively, but he shook his head. 'It crossed my mind, but no. Your father doesn't allow strangers on the island. There's nothing to be done for him.'

'He's been in a shipwreck. Father will take pity on him.'

Montgomery shook his head harder. 'It was a foolish idea. Forget I said anything.' He took the pot off the grate and set it on the cook's table. 'Watch him for a moment, if you would. I have to check on the animals.'

'What if he wakes?'

A corner of his mouth turned up. 'Say hello.'

And he left me with the castaway, the wooden spoon, and my thoughts drifting in and out of the swirling steam.

A few days later I stood on the sun-bleached deck, squinting into the rigging, chewing on a fingernail. I was studying the monkey. It studied me back. Bribing the captain to spare the monkey's life had been easy – apparently he valued a few bottles of Father's brandy over being right. But getting the creature down was now my problem. And with our arrival imminent, I was running low on time.

'Monkey, look!' I held up my father's silver pocket watch. One of the crew had told me monkeys liked reflective objects, but I dangled the watch for the better part of an hour with no results.

Balthazar and Montgomery chuckled behind me.

'Be quiet!' I chided. 'You frighten it, Balthazar. And you too, Montgomery. It remembers you wanted to shoot it.'

'Have you tried a banana?' Montgomery offered.

I scowled. 'I haven't got a banana. And unless you do, clear out!'

Laughing, he went back to tending the caged animals. I folded my arms, puzzled and frustrated. I'd been methodical in my attempts to get the monkey down. First I tried setting a trap, then luring it into a cage with food, and then climbing into the rigging until the boatswain and the whole first watch tried to look up my skirt. Nothing had worked.

I slid the watch into my pocket and watched the monkey swing effortlessly from bowsprit to boom, graceful as a bird. Its skill was astounding. It never missed, never hesitated, never doubted. I was overcome with an urge to try myself, though I knew it was impossible. I'd learned enough from Montgomery's lessons and Father's books to know we weren't built for climbing and swinging, though humans and monkeys had the same basic limb structure. The only major differences were the double-curved spine on a human and the flexible ligaments in a primate's feet. Both easily alterable through surgery. My mind wandered, curious whether science would ever find a way to make us as graceful as animals.

'Don't you wish you could do that?' I called to Montgomery over my shoulder. 'It's like it's flying.'

There was no answer. I turned, but Montgomery had gone below. In his place was the castaway; awake, upright, watching me from across the deck. Surprise drenched me like a splash of cold water.

The sun blisters on his face had faded, though the gash on the side of his face was a constant reminder of the shipwreck. He'd cut the tangles out of his dark hair, and it now fell just below his chin, unfashionable but at least clean. Only a whisper remained of that haunting apparition, and now he was merely flesh and blood and bone and bruises. He looked naturally lean, so his gauntness was even more pronounced, yet there was something undeniably strong about him.

He waved.

I hesitated, and waved back.

TEN

The next afternoon I found a lidded bowl full of live worms and roaches outside my door with a note written in a gentleman's handwriting. It wasn't in Montgomery's hand, and none of the sailors could write, so it took little reasoning to determine who it was from.

Monkeys adore insects, it said.

I went above deck, set the teeming bowl under the rigging, and removed the lid. One roach saw its chance to escape and crawled up the side, but I flicked it back in. I hid behind some crates, settling in to wait, but heard the sound of the ceramic bowl moving within only a minute. The monkey was so engrossed in the bowl that he didn't even notice when I sneaked up behind him and slipped a collar around his neck. I let him finish eating before putting him in his new cage.

Monkey secured, I found the castaway sitting in the corner of the forecastle deck outside the boatswain's hold, his back to me, leaning over an old backgammon board balanced on top of a barrel. He was studying the game's red and black tokens by the fading sunlight. They were set all wrong. He didn't seem aware of the sailors throwing him angry glances for taking up space on the deck.

76

I studied him as carefully as he studied the game. Despite the gash along his face, there was something undeniably attractive about him. Not handsome in a classic way like Montgomery, but more subtle, deeper, as if his true handsomeness lay in the story behind those bruises and that crumpled photograph. Something to be discovered, slowly, if one was clever enough to decipher it.

'They say you're mad,' I said.

His arm jerked as he turned toward my voice. The backgammon game spilled to the floor, red and black tokens rolling across the deck. I fell to my knees to collect them, and he bent to help. He seemed reluctant to meet my eyes. Reserved. His fingers absently drifted to the gash under his eye. A muscle twitched in the side of his jaw. He was scarred from the shipwreck, of course, but there was something in his guarded movements that spoke of more, as though the scars might continue deep below the surface.

'I couldn't remember much at first,' he said, daring a glance at me. This close, I saw that his brown eyes had flecks of gold that caught the fading sun. 'But it's coming back to me.' His hand dropped away from his face. A sailor passed, kicking one of the tokens down the deck and grumbling curses about cadging stowaways.

The castaway added, 'I'm not mad.' For a moment his eyes shifted oddly to the left, as though half his mind was still trapped in that dinghy or had sunk with the ship. He had suffered so greatly, and the sailors seemed keen to make him suffer more.

'Mad enough to come above deck and get in the sailors' way. You aren't making yourself popular with them,' I said, and then lower, 'You should be careful.' I handed him the tokens I'd collected and nodded at the board. 'Would you like to play a round?'

The corner of his mouth twitched again, this time in a

half smile. He straightened the backgammon board and stacked the tokens one by one.

I folded my legs and sat across from him. I tried not to stare at the bruises on his arms and face. His knuckles were scraped raw nearly to the bone, and I remembered that hand clutching the photograph, clutching to life. Hard to believe this was the same person.

'Do you remember what happened?' I asked. 'The shipwreck?'

His eyes slid to me, only a flash, judging whether or not to trust me. He picked up the dice. 'Yes.'

'And your name?' I asked.

'Edward Prince.' He said it slowly, as though he had little information about himself to share and had to ration it carefully.

'I'm Juliet Moreau.'

He nodded slowly. 'Yes, I know.' And I remembered he'd asked Montgomery about me.

It was my turn to stare, wondering what he'd thought of me that first day, when he'd been lost in a whirlpool of delusion. He'd said something that none of us had heard. Now he stared at the tokens, just slices from an old mop or broom handle, with the dice waiting in his hand. The tokens were still set wrong, and I instinctively reached out to re–arrange them before starting our game. It felt good to put something in order.

'How did you survive?' I asked.

My question caught him off guard, and his hand curled around the dice. He gave a cautious shrug. 'The grace of God, I suppose.'

I watched his broken fist working the dice, the twitch of his bruised jaw, the strength in his wiry shoulders. His words came too easily. He'd said what he thought I wanted to hear, not what he was truly thinking.

'I don't believe you,' I said. He tilted his head, surprised. 'Twenty days at sea. No food. No water. No shade. The sole survivor of dozens of passengers. God didn't save you. *You* saved yourself. I'd like to know how.'

He studied my placement of the tokens on the board, memorizing it, learning everything over again from scratch. 'Montgomery's first question was about the family I must have lost,' he said. 'The grief.' He rolled the dice, a little too hard. His reaction told me I should have had more sympathy, like Montgomery.

I blinked, unsure of myself. I hadn't meant to be cold. 'I'm sorry. Your family . . . were they with you on the *Viola*?'

'No,' he said, surprisingly flat. 'I was traveling alone. My father's a general on tour abroad now. The rest of my family is at Chesney Wold – our estate. Probably entertaining dull relatives and glad to be rid of me.'

His tone was so cavalier as he scratched his scar with a jagged nail and studied the board. Something felt a little too forced. There was almost a harsh, layered tone that spoke of pain and anger and made me suspect he wasn't being entirely honest. 'But you said—'

He shrugged. 'I thought it strange you were more interested in the details of my survival than the dozens who died on that ship.' He started to move his tokens, and I should have thought about how heartless I must have seemed, but instead all I could focus on was how badly he was playing backgammon.

He slid a token slowly around the points. 'Montgomery told me you're to be reunited with your father. A doctor of some sort,' he said.

'That's right.'

He picked up the token, running his finger over the rough-hewn wood. 'It's odd, don't you think, for a wealthy doctor to want to live in such a remote place? It makes one wonder.'

I caught the undercurrent in his voice, and it intrigued me. Whatever he was insinuating wasn't good, and it was awfully bold to speak it aloud. Maybe there was more to him than a sea-mad castaway who'd never worked a day in his life.

I picked up the dice. 'What do you mean?'

'What would make a man give everything up to come out here?'

I shook the dice and spilled them out across the deck. 'I could ask you the same thing, Mr Prince. What made you leave England if all your family is there?'

His jaw twitched again. 'You've come to find your father. I've come to get away from mine.' Once more, that subtle layer of anger laced his voice.

'Why? What did he do?' I moved my tokens like an afterthought.

He paused. 'He didn't do anything. I did.' And then he shook the dice and threw them, abruptly, as if he'd said too much. A three and a six. He started moving the token in the wrong direction.

'Captain Claggan isn't exactly pleased I'm here,' he added, and the change in subject caught me by surprise. 'Did you know he came with that first mate of his, last night after Montgomery was asleep, and dragged me to the rail? He was going to throw me over until I told him I had relatives in Australia who would pay dearly for my safe return.'

My hand was frozen in midair. The game suddenly didn't seem to matter anymore. 'Did you tell Montgomery? He won't let the captain get away with that.' I shifted on the rough floorboards. 'Just the same, it's lucky about your relatives.'

He gave me a guarded look, though something like amuse-ment peeked through. 'I don't know anyone in Australia. I just made that up. I sought passage on the first ship I could

80

from London, regardless of its destination. The *Viola* just happened to be it.'

'So what happens when you get to Australia and he finds out there are no wealthy relatives?' Once we were gone, without Balthazar and bribery and guns, Edward Prince would be on his own.

His fingers drummed on the wooden board. The last ray of sun slipped below the horizon, casting half of his bruised face in shadows. 'I don't know.'

A cry from the crow's nest made me drop the token in my hand. The castaway and I exchanged a breathless glance.

'Land ho!' the watchman called.

Night fell quickly that day, obscuring the land the scout had spotted. The sailors sent Edward back to the galley and me to my quarters and told us to stay there. But obedience wasn't one of my virtues. I found Montgomery on the quarterdeck speaking in hushed voices with Balthazar below the glowing mast light. The captain and first mate stood by the gunwale with a lantern held above the sea charts.

I leaned over the rail and studied the black horizon. Moonlight reflected on the waves like scales of some dark dragon. I couldn't tell where the night ended and the sea began. Between them, somewhere, was my father.

Montgomery caught sight of me and rushed over, a spark of energy to his movements. I'd forgotten that this place was his home. He pointed to the horizon. 'It's volcanic. Do you see the plume?'

My mind scanned the horizon for dark shapes, but my eyes found nothing to settle on. Then I discerned a faint line, like a column of smoke, rising to the stars.

'I see it. It looks so far away.'

'A league and a half maybe. There's a sandbar around the

harbor, so we're here for the night. We'll dock in the morning.'

'What about Edward?'

The boyish excitement on Montgomery's face faded. He studied the cold sea. 'What about him?'

The edge in his voice made me hesitate. 'We can't just leave him here. You said yourself—'

'He can't come with us.' He cursed under his breath and leaned on the rail. 'I shouldn't have said anything before. It's impossible.'

'But why? It isn't safe here. There's no doctor, and the only reason the captain hasn't thrown him overboard is because he thinks he can ransom him once they reach Brisbane, which is a lie.'

'You don't understand. It isn't safe on the island either.'

I looked back at the island. The plume of volcanic smoke snaked toward the dark sky like tendrils escaping a gentleman's pipe. My eyes found a single light, halfway up the hill, the only sign of civilization.

'Not safe?'

Montgomery took my shoulder and turned me away from the island. His face softened. 'There's no room, I mean. We've one extra bedroom, which you'll have. He'll have no place to stay, and there are wild animals in the jungle. Besides, your father is a very private man. He'd be furious if I brought a stranger.'

I traced the wood grain on the rail. Would Father consider *me* a stranger? No, of course not. I was his only family, the little girl who used to crawl onto his lap with a dusty volume and beg him to read theories of how birds were once great, lumbering lizards. But then why had he never once sent a letter? Why did I have to learn he was alive from a bloodstained diagram at a late-night vivisection?

'He's *my* father,' I said. 'He'll listen to me. He'll understand it's safer for Edward to stay on the island. It's just until the next ship comes.'

'It crosses his wishes, Juliet.'

I leaned against the rail, studying his worn clothes, his scuffed boots. 'You keep saying you're no longer his servant, but you don't act like it. You can think for yourself, you know.'

Montgomery's jaw tensed, but he didn't argue. I knew I'd hurt him, but I didn't know how to take it back, because it was true. He strode away, bristling. The sudden solitude made the thoughts in my head louder. I wanted to go back to that moment when Montgomery and I stood on the deck, hands interlaced, as he told me he'd thought about me often. But a shift had occurred, slight but significant enough that things weren't exactly the same between us. I leaned on the rail and measured the moonlit distance between me and the island.

The next morning, I was packed before dawn, though maddeningly, because of the tides, we couldn't dock for hours. While I waited, I dressed in new white summer clothes that I'd bought with Lucy's money before we left. The startling clean whiteness hurt my eyes. The rest of my things – my medication, the worn books, even an old hard-bristled brush of Mrs Bell's – I tucked away in the carpetbag. I left out Father's copy of *Longman's Anatomical Reference*, flipping anxiously through the black-and-white drawings. The book of a scientist. A madman, too, perhaps.

Either way, I was about to find out.

When I climbed above deck, I was distracted by a flurry of activity. The mizzen boom was rigged to unload the cargo and cages. A handful of sailors dragged the panther's cage toward a hook bigger than my head. But what stole my attention was the mountainous green island looming off the port side, big as a kingdom, with a column of wispy gray smoke coming from its highest point. After weeks of water as vast as the known world, the island seemed unreal. A soft line of sand touched the sea, edged by a cluster of palms waving in the breeze. The palms gave way to a wild tangle of jungle, packed as tight as stitching with vines and the canopies of trees I couldn't identify. I wondered what lay under that green curtain, waiting for me.

Edward watched the island as well from the forecastle deck, until he caught sight of me. He touched his forehead, an old-fashioned gesture one used when greeting a lady. I'd have to dissuade him of that notion someday.

He came down the steps, wincing slightly from his bruises. 'Montgomery said I may come to the island until the next supply ship passes,' he said. 'I suppose I have you to thank for that.'

Surprised, I stood a little straighter. Montgomery had changed his mind – my jab about acting like a servant must have struck a sensitive nerve. As guilty as I felt, I couldn't help but smile that he'd finally made his own decision. 'Are you going to come, then?'

'If my choices are between spending more time with Captain Claggan or with you, it's an easy decision.' He brushed a dark strand of hair back from his face, not taking his eyes off the ocean. My stomach tightened at the compliment, unexpectedly. I wasn't used to getting compliments from gentlemen. I picked lightly at my dry lips, realizing this meant I'd be spending a lot more time with Edward Prince. Scarred, clever, sea-mad Edward Prince. Who was surprisingly bad at backgammon.

His fingers drummed on the rail. 'Montgomery didn't seem entirely happy about it, though.'

I cleared my throat. 'He's worried what my father will think. He shouldn't; he's not a servant anymore.'

'A servant?' Edward interrupted. His hand fell away from his face.

'Montgomery was our scullery maid's son. He used to work in the stables. Didn't he tell you?'

'I was under the impression that you were traveling together . . . Sharing a cabin . . .' His eyes slid to me, asking a question without asking.

There was no breeze to cool my burning face. 'He's my escort,' I said quickly. 'That's all.' I would have liked to say more to prove otherwise, but the evidence was against me. We *had* spent the night in the same room, more than once. And I couldn't pretend the idea had never crossed my mind.

'Well, I'm not sorry to hear that. I'm glad you're not spoken for.' He paused. 'I like getting to know you, Miss Moreau.'

I kept silent, watching the island, though inside I was a mess of confusion. I wondered if I should acknowledge his comment. He was probably a perfectly nice young man. But I'd seen too much of what men were capable of to trust a stranger. And there was something unsettling about him. He had even said himself that he was running from something he'd done. It must have been serious if he had to flee England. I glanced at him askance, wondering what the wealthy son of a general had to run from.

Edward matched my silence, too reserved to say what else was really on his mind. But then again, so was I.

The *Curitiba* sailed toward a natural inlet that opened like a yawning mouth. From the farthest point, a narrow dock extended toward us, beyond the breakers, longer than any dock I'd ever seen. Waves washed over it, threatening to swallow the whole structure. At the edge, next to a bobbing launch, stood a small party of figures. They began to take shape as the *Curitiba* drifted closer.

There were three men as large as brutes, larger even

than Balthazar. They had the same odd hunch to their shoulders as Balthazar, and their heads seemed set too low on their necks. I wondered what had made all the natives so disfigured. It was as though God had started here before he made man.

One of the hunched men shuffled to the edge of the dock and crouched on his haunches like a beast. As he moved away, I saw another man behind him, this one of regular size, with a straight back and spindly limbs. He wore a white linen suit and shoes so polished the sunlight reflecting off them made me squint. A parasol shaded his face from the sun and my eyes, but my heart would recognize him anywhere.

As I stared, the parasol slid back and the man's eyes met mine.

I gasped.

He was my father, and yet he wasn't. The face was the same, as was his stiff posture, but his once carefully groomed dark hair flew wild and gray like a swarm of wasps about his head. What unnerved me most was the peculiar way he calmly stared back at me, unflinching, as if he'd known I was coming.

As if he'd been waiting for me.

ELEVEN

I ducked behind the bulwarks where I couldn't be seen. Edward dropped beside me. I tried to calm the sudden rush of blood to my head. I don't know what instinct drove me to hide after I'd come so far to find my father. I just had to get away from those watching eyes. I was imagining things, I told myself. He couldn't have known I was coming. A girl in a white dress was an odd sight on any ship, worth a curious look.

Edward frowned. 'Your father, I assume.'

I rubbed my tired eyes and nodded. Paranoia had crept into that part of my brain usually reserved for reason. 'Yes. I suppose I didn't give him much of a greeting.'

He gave me a hand to pull me to my feet, and now I felt silly for my reaction. 'It's natural to be nervous.' Instead of letting go, though, he pulled me closer. 'And I still think it's odd for a gentleman to live out here alone. Be careful, Miss Moreau. I don't want you to be hurt.'

I pulled my hand back defensively, wiping it on my dress. 'I'm capable of taking care of myself.'

Montgomery had given me a similar warning. They might think me helpless, but they had no idea that for a poor girl on her own, the streets of London were filled with far more dangers than a tropical island.

I glanced at Edward. 'And please call me Juliet. I'm not a lady.'

'Drop anchor!' the captain bellowed. I braced myself as the anchor found bottom with a lurch. The launch was so full it could take only one passenger at a time, so Montgomery went first with the rabbits, claiming he needed to oversee the unloading from the dock, though I think he really wanted a chance to warn Father about Edward and me and to spare us Father's unpredictable first reaction.

Father hated surprises. That much I remembered.

My lace collar itched as we watched Montgomery's launch fight against the tide to reach the dock. One of the hulking men lifted the rabbit hutch as easily as a flake of hay. Father helped Montgomery out, giving him a friendly slap on the back. Montgomery was gesturing toward the ship, and Father spun the parasol lazily. Suddenly it stopped. I again had the feeling that, even at such a distance, he could peer deep into my mind.

Then it was my turn to go ashore. Because I was small, they decided I could squeeze in on Balthazar's trip. A sailor with a twitching eye leaned in as he helped me into the launch. 'Good luck,' he said.

Once in the water, it took Balthazar half the time it had taken Montgomery to row ashore. I wiped my sweating palms on my skirt, wishing they would stop shaking. I told myself it was the deficiency. Even with the daily injections, I still sometimes felt weak.

We reached the solid reality of the dock. Father stood there, silent, in his crisp linen suit. I couldn't bring myself to look up from my feet and meet his gaze.

Balthazar clambered out and helped me onto the dock with a meaty hand. Even on firm land, I felt dizzy. Montgomery leaned in as if to whisper something quick and urgent, but sharp footsteps interrupted us.

Father.

He used the folded parasol as a cane, tapping the end slowly and deliberately against the weathered boards. Thick eyebrows hooded his dark, penetrating eyes. A few days' beard clung to his jaw, as it used to when his work so consumed him that he didn't emerge from the laboratory for days. He was gaunt, as though all the excess muscle and fat from his youth had been spent and what remained was only the hardened core.

'Get your paws off my daughter, boy.' He poked the parasol's end at Montgomery's chest. His mouth pursed. 'Your hands are dirty.'

My gut clenched, worried. Montgomery held his hands up, stepping back. But then he grinned. Father laughed. It was a joke, I realized. My stomach unknotted. Father was smiling. Laughing. The tension in the air broke like a dam. My lungs exhaled a lifetime's worth of worry, and I rushed into his arms.

He stiffened briefly but then wrapped an arm around my back. 'Juliet. Daughter.'

I buried my face in his suit and breathed in his scent. Apricot preserves and faint traces of formaldehyde, just as I remembered. The flood of memories almost choked me. Having a father again after so many years left me shaken.

He held me at arm's length, searching my face. Looking for the little girl he had left behind, perhaps. His eyes had that calculating look that had so unnerved his students, but to me it was just his way.

I'd missed it.

'Look at you,' he said. 'You should be looking for a husband, not some wrinkled old man.'

My head spun. I'd imagined meeting him again so many

times that it was hard to believe it was happening. I'd come all this way to find out which man he was – the madman or the misunderstood genius – but already I could see that it wouldn't be so simple. This was a living person, not some theory I'd decided to test. Had I really thought I could just show up and ask if the rumors had been true? I could barely form words to speak at all.

'I had to come,' I stuttered. The dock, the waves, the hulking men – they were all spinning. 'I thought you were dead.'

'Hell hasn't claimed me yet,' he said. He took my chin, tilting my head to both sides. 'You look like your mother, but you must take after me in spirit. Montgomery said you practically held a knife to his throat to come here.'

'She's persistent, for sure,' Montgomery said lightly.

Father pointed the parasol at the jungle wilderness. 'You won't find many of the comforts of London here.'

I almost laughed. Dr Hastings's wandering hands were hardly a comfort. I wondered if I should tell him that my other options had been fleeing London or standing outside the Blue Boar Inn in a stained dress.

But none of that mattered now. 'I don't need comforts,' I said, meaning it.

He nodded, considering this. I bit the inside of my cheek to ground myself. He was alive. I wasn't alone anymore. I twisted my fists in my skirt's soft cotton, not sure how to deal with the tangled feelings pushing around inside me.

Father squeezed my shoulder. 'This isn't a holiday retreat, you understand. We grow our own food. See to our own safety. It's not a place for young ladies.' He pursed his lips. 'But we'll find some use for you.'

I nodded. He was being rational. Still, I tried not to show my disappointment that his thoughts immediately turned to how I could be of use.

The splash of oars sounded behind us. The launch had returned with Edward. Suddenly I was forgotten. Father's eyes narrowed. His knuckles were white on the parasol's delicate handle. He looked at Edward with the intense stare of a surgeon.

Edward climbed out, brushing off his trousers. His gaze held steady on my father, as if he sensed the battle he was about to face. Maybe I hadn't taken Montgomery seriously enough when he'd said Father didn't allow strangers. The way Father looked at Edward wasn't just suspicion – it was an unsettling, intense dislike that made me hesitate.

'Father, this is Edward Prince,' I said. 'He was a castaway. I told him he would be welcome here until a ship can take him home. He's been ill. Montgomery saved his life.'

Father's eyes shifted to Montgomery and back to Edward. 'Can't speak for yourself, eh, boy? Prince, was it?'

Edward stood tall. 'I was a passenger on the *Viola* before the hull breached. I ended up on the *Curitiba* by chance.'

'Chance? Is that so? And why should I let you set foot on my island?'

I threw Montgomery a look. This was beyond mere inhospitality. Isolation had driven Father to paranoia, I realized. Maybe worse. A seed of doubt planted itself deep in my brain.

'I'd be grateful if I could wait here until a ship comes,' Edward said, slowly. 'I'll be no trouble, I assure you.'

Father's eyes glowed like embers. Like a storm, the tension in the air returned, crackling like lightning. 'Well, Mr Prince, I'm afraid you're wrong. You'd be nothing *but* trouble, you see.' And he jabbed the parasol at Edward's chest.

Edward stumbled back, losing his footing, and fell into the churning harbor with a splash that drenched my white dress.

TWELVE

'Edward!' I stumbled forward, but it was too late. I collapsed, wincing as my knees slammed into the hard dock. My fingers curled around the warped boards as I watched him sputter to the surface.

'Take my hand!' I reached as far as I dared, but the distance was too great. Edward slapped at the water uselessly, trying to pull himself up through the unsolid waves. He opened his mouth to shout, but I never heard what he said. He slipped under the surface.

My fingernails dug half-moon trenches into the rotten wood. The dark shape that was Edward hovered just under the glassy surface, like an apparition. I kept thinking I had seen it wrong. It had been an accident. And yet I'd *seen* Father push him.

I pressed my palms against the dock and stumbled to my feet. Father calmly adjusted the rumpled cuffs of his shirt. 'Have you lost your mind?' I shouted. 'He's not well. He'll drown!'

Edward surfaced again, sputtering as he breached the water, only to sink again. Father watched as patiently as if he were waiting for a frog to die in a chloroform-filled jar. A wave of anger rolled up my throat.

Beside him, Montgomery's face was slack and uncertain.

'You can swim,' I said to him. A desperate request, and he looked at me with hesitation. I understood then. He didn't want to cross Father, not even to save Edward. Here, he wasn't the strong, capable man I'd seen on the ship. He was just a boy.

'Please, Montgomery,' I said. He swallowed hard and lurched toward the water. But Father swung the parasol in a swift, graceful arc that blocked his path.

Montgomery's boots skidded on the dock, as if the parasol had been a six-foot iron fence and not just a few bits of wood and lace. His eyes met mine. Everything felt wrong, so wrong. He should have been apprenticing himself to some craftsman back in England, meeting girls after church. Instead he was a slave to a madman's whims.

With a growl, I lunged at the parasol and wrestled the flimsy thing from my father's hand. To my surprise, he surrendered it easily with an amused chuckle that made me shiver. I knelt at the edge of the dock and held it out to Edward. His fingers grazed at the handle, but he was too far away. The last thing I saw before he slipped under was the gold glint of his eyes, fixated on Father.

'To hell with it,' Montgomery muttered. He dived into the water.

For a painfully long moment I was alone with my father. The late-afternoon sun crept over the dock, casting long shadows. I was afraid to look behind me. I'd come so far, only to find that the rumors must be true – only a monster would patiently watch a man drown. What had happened to the father I remembered, the father who sneaked me chocolates when Mother wasn't looking, whose warm tweed coats blanketed me when I fell asleep on the sofa? Were those memories nothing more than fantasies?

I realized I had no idea who the man in the white linen suit was. Fear slipped out of me in little gasps, the only sound except the slap of the waves against the piles. Farther down the dock, the hulking islanders loaded cargo into a horse-drawn wagon. They might as well have been in a different world, though they were only paces from us.

Montgomery surfaced at last with his arm circling Edward's waist, shattering the awful spell. I threw aside the parasol and reached out to help him as he paddled to the dock.

'Hold on to him while I climb up,' Montgomery said. I clutched Edward around the shoulders while Montgomery pulled himself up; then he dragged Edward out of the water and onto the dock. I leaned over Edward, touching him cautiously, afraid the episode would bring back terrible memories of his shipwreck.

'Are you all right?' I asked.

He leaned to the side and coughed, and then his hand found mine. He squeezed the life out of it. 'Juliet . . . you looked even more beautiful when I thought I was dying.'

I stared at his hand holding mine, not sure how to answer. *Thank you?*

Father offered no assistance. 'You should have let him drown,' he observed.

Montgomery only tore at the laces of his dripping boots, trying to get the heavy things off. His knuckles were white. He might have been raised to never question one's master – but *I* hadn't.

I snatched the parasol and thrust it at Father's own chest, not hard enough to push him, just hard enough to show my anger. 'How could you?' I cried. An amused look played on his face.

I raised the parasol to jab him again, but he grabbed it and wrenched it from my hands. The lace tore and the handle splintered. 'Calm down,' he said. The smile was gone, along with his patience.

I heard a watery choking behind me. Edward leaned over the dock, coughing out more seawater. Father grabbed my chin and turned my eyes to meet his. 'He doesn't belong here, Juliet. He isn't one of us.'

I jerked out of his grasp. 'Then maybe I don't belong here either!'

My chest rose and fell quickly with troubled breath. I ached to rip off the corset. The starched lace collar of the white dress scratched at my neck, and I cursed myself for being such a fool that I ever wanted to impress a man I barely knew, father or not.

The sound of wood striking wood made us all turn. A sailor was back in the launch with more trunks. The second launch followed with the caged panther, which hissed and let out a high-pitched, eerie growl.

Father picked up the parasol. He opened it, observed the shredded and soiled white lace, and then folded it back carefully. The three hulking islanders approached in their odd, lumbering gait and secured the launches. Their startlingly fair eyes threw nervous glances at my father, their master. I could barely stand to look at them. Balthazar's deformities were unfortunate, but these brutes were the things of nightmares.

Father turned to Edward. 'Mr Prince, is it?' His lips pursed. 'It seems my daughter has an interest in your welfare. As I have an interest in hers, I suppose you may stay with us.' He pointed the tip of the parasol at the waves. 'Though I would advise you to learn to swim.'

He muttered a command to the islanders and then smoothed his wild gray hair. 'Come, Juliet. Balthazar will stay and see to the unloading.' He extended his hand to me.

I stared at Father's waiting palm. It was surprisingly small, with a pink glow and soft, delicate curves. It was the hand of a gentleman, unused to wielding any tool larger than a surgeon's scalpel.

I hesitated, still unsure of what I'd seen.

His lips twitched in that calculating way of his that made my own feel dry. Then he laughed. 'You thought I'd really hurt the boy.' He clapped his hands together. 'Juliet, you'll have to forgive me. I am aware my sense of humor veers toward the black. I only wanted to put the fear of God in him, to show him who runs this island.' He tilted his head at Edward, whose head was bowed, shoulders slumped as he wiped the seawater off his face. 'You see, it worked.'

I glanced at Montgomery, but he wouldn't meet my eyes. He was suddenly a servant again in front of my father. He finished unlacing his boots and kicked them off. Water seeped out and dripped between the wooden slats of the dock.

Dark clouds began forming overhead. Tension cracked in the air like lightning. Father's hand still waited for mine. His black eyes drew me to him like an anchor to sea. I placed my hand in his, cautiously. His fingers closed around mine with surprising strength.

'Come along, Prince,' he called. 'Or are we going to have to drag you?'

I glanced over my shoulder to see Montgomery help Edward to his feet. Edward took a few shaky steps, waving Montgomery away. Montgomery picked up the rabbit hutch by its crossbeams, and they followed us down the dock.

Father placed my hand in the crook of his elbow, like a gentleman. We walked toward the waiting wagon as casually as a couple strolling down the Strand. If I hadn't known better, I'd have thought we were just a father and daughter enjoying a warm breeze on a sunny day. But my head was swimming. It was all I could do to keep putting one foot in front of the other.

My head throbbed as if my skullcap was fitted too tight. I stumbled as the end of the dock gave way to sand. The beach stretched the length of the cove, fringed with palms just like in a tropical painting, except for the heavy thunderclouds overhead that cast shadows in the dark places between the trees. The wagon waited, hitched to a huge draft horse with golden hair falling in its eyes. The islanders had already loaded two steamer trunks and some bundles into the back.

'After you, my dear,' Father said. He opened the wagon gate. Edward and I climbed in, and Montgomery loaded the hutch behind us. He started to say something, but Father interrupted. 'We haven't all day, Montgomery.'

Montgomery straightened. He brushed his hair out of his face with one hand, and the hutch slipped. I jumped up to catch a corner before it tumbled out of the wagon.

'Careful,' Father said. 'If one of those rabbits gets loose, it'll mean hell for us.'

The muscles in Montgomery's neck flexed. He slammed the gate closed.

I sat back down on a trunk next to Edward. Sand caked his feet and trousers up to his knees. I tried to think of something to say, but words couldn't make up for Father's actions. Edward's face was blank, but his hands were shaking slightly. God, if he'd been suffering from sea madness before, this certainly wouldn't make him any saner.

'Maybe you can go back,' I whispered. 'Captain Claggan might still take you to Australia.'

His eyes slid to mine. 'I don't want to go back.'

A question formed on my lips, but Edward looked away. Folded his arms, tight. I pushed away the voices that wondered if it had anything to do with what he'd said on the ship – that he was glad I wasn't spoken for.

Montgomery climbed into the driver's seat. Father drew

a pistol from his jacket and passed it to him. My throat tightened at the sudden gleam of metal. Montgomery casually tucked it into his belt as though this was their daily routine. But why would they need pistols?

Montgomery took the reins. We moved forward in jerks until the wheels found solid ground and then rumbled over uneven earth and vegetation. I watched the *Curitiba* looming off the coast. I had a sudden urge to jump from the wagon and swim back to it. But I hadn't ever learned to swim. And I hated Captain Claggan and his stinking ship. But at least I knew what to expect from it, which was more than I could say for the island. I dared a glance at my father. I had so many questions, but they had all tumbled in an unsettling direction when he'd pushed Edward.

Presently, we picked up speed as the path became more substantial, and the jungle soon swallowed our last view of the beach. Entering the jungle was like going into a hothouse – the humidity increased even though the canopy blocked out all but dappled late-afternoon sunlight. The broad leaves of unnamed plants formed a tunnel around us, slapping the sides of the jerking wagon and making us duck every few seconds.

'This is a biological outpost,' Father said over his shoulder, as though we were all suddenly old friends. 'Montgomery and I have spent years cataloging every specimen on the island. Extraordinary diversity.' I glanced at Edward, wondering what thoughts must be going through his mind, but he'd retreated somewhere within himself.

The wagon hit a rut and I bounced off the trunk, catching myself before I collided with the hutch of rabbits. I came nose to nose with a dirty white rabbit, which reminded me far too much of another rabbit, worlds away now, in an operating theater in London.

'You're stuck with us for some time, Prince,' Father

continued. 'It's a rare thing indeed when a ship passes our way. A year or more.'

The rabbit twitched its nose ceaselessly. The dimwitted little animal didn't even know it had come all the way from England to end up with a scalpel through its belly. My finger rested on the latch – all I would have to do was squeeze my finger to free the rabbit.

As if he could sense my thoughts, Edward placed his hand over mine and shook his head.

The path grew gradually wider. We rode for an hour, maybe longer. The sun was sinking low behind darkening thunderclouds, throwing shadows among the trees. I was usually a good judge of passing time, but my mind had wound down like a clock. Thunder rumbled overhead. Odd sounds whispered through the branches, though I told myself it must be the trills of unfamiliar insects. At last, Edward pointed ahead.

A stone compound loomed in a clearing. The terracotta-tiled buildings were all arranged within a circular wall gated by two heavy wooden doors. The single bastion of civilization on an untamed island.

'This used to be a Spanish fort,' Father said over his shoulder. 'It was in ruins when I found it. The missionaries slept in it like dogs. And they called themselves civilized.' He snorted.

'Missionaries?' I asked.

'Anglicans, come to proselytize,' he mumbled, but his attention was on the compound. From within came a steady hammering and the smell of woodsmoke. Despite the tremble in my hands, I told myself this was not a place to be feared. Montgomery lived here, and so did my father. There was nothing within those walls that would hurt me. In fact, the danger was outside, in the jungle, where Montgomery had to carry a pistol.

So why was I so nervous?

Ten yards from the compound, Montgomery stopped the horse. A door slammed from within, making me jump, and a boy appeared, running in a strange skipping manner toward us. He took hold of the horse's bridle while Montgomery climbed down and ruffled the boy's hair. I couldn't help but stare. The child's jaw protruded at an odd angle below a nearly nonexistent nose. A dark, fine hair covered his bare arms. A shiver ran over my skin. It was as if my father had stumbled upon some collection of natives whom the theory of evolution – were Mr Darwin to be believed – had skipped by.

Another face peered out from a side door I hadn't noticed. I caught only a glimpse of a bald head and a flash of white shirt. Father climbed down from the wagon as nimbly as an insect and went over to speak to the man.

Montgomery opened the back of the wagon, his sea-soaked boots laced together and slung over one shoulder. The silver butt of the pistol in his belt reflected the dark roiling of the sky. I stumbled as I tried to climb down. Montgomery's hands caught me around the waist and lingered, stealing my breath.

'Are you all right?' he whispered. I glanced at the stark compound walls. Father had already disappeared within, and we were alone with Edward and the child.

'It's the deficiency,' I said. 'After so long on the ship, without proper food . . .'

He didn't look convinced. His hands tightened on my waist. I'd told Edward there was nothing between Montgomery and me, and yet I couldn't deny the way I floated inside when he touched me. It was more than that – I trusted him, and I didn't trust anyone.

'Don't be afraid of the doctor,' Montgomery said. 'He's spent so long on the island that he sometimes forgets the proper way to act. But he'd never hurt you.'

'And Edward?' I asked. Hearing his name, Edward climbed out of the wagon. Montgomery let his hands fall to his sides. My waist still felt the ghost of their touch.

'You're owed an apology, for sure,' he said to Edward. 'He's protective of his work and wasn't expecting a stranger. I am sorry.'

Edward just rubbed his shoulders, as though he was cold. 'You've nothing to apologize for. I'm sure it was only a joke.' But his face said otherwise.

'In any case, you're here now.' Montgomery gave him a brotherly slap on the shoulder, though Edward remained as tightly wound as a spring. 'Come on, we'll get you a good meal and a comfortable bed, and you'll feel better.'

The little boy let out a soft grunt, struggling to tighten one of the harness leathers that had slipped from its buckle. Montgomery pressed his weight against the horse to make it shift and then freed the loose strap and pulled it taut. He smiled. 'You'd have gotten it in another minute. Cymbeline, this is the doctor's daughter, Miss Moreau.'

The boy looked at me shyly through long lashes, producing a sweet smile that revealed a missing front tooth. The humanity behind such a deformed face troubled me deeply. Instead of returning the smile, I turned away guiltily.

With a groan of metal hinges, the great wooden doors to the compound opened. Father stuck his gray head out. 'Well, come on. The rain is coming. Every day like clockwork.' He stuck his head back in.

As if to answer, a crack of thunder shook the sky. The clouds hung like too-ripe fruit, ready to split and burst over the island. Montgomery grabbed the rabbit hutch and braced it on his knee while he shut the gate. The rabbits hopped and sniffed at the new smells of the island.

Plunk. A fat drop of rain fell on my forearm. I looked up, and another one landed on my cheek. All around, the trees quaked and danced under the falling drops. The noise on the broad jungle leaves was like nothing I'd heard before, a thousand tiny wagon wheels on a wood-slat bridge. Another second passed, and the few drops turned into a deluge.

I shrieked. I didn't know rain could fall so hard and fast. Montgomery and Edward ran for the compound. I picked up my skirts and ran behind them, slipping in the quickly forming mud. A second before I crossed the threshold, I startled. Above the entrance, two sets of eyes watched. I blinked away the rain. Two figures were carved in the stone: the Lamb of God and the Lion of Judah. Their eternal eyes, chipped and streaked with lichen, seemed to rumble with the rolls of thunder. I tore away from their spellbinding gaze and hurried through the wooden doors.

THIRTEEN

The interior of the compound was rimmed with a covered portico that gave us shelter from the rain. I hunched into myself like a drenched cat that has been thrown into the gutter. My white dress was covered in mud and sludge and sand. My skin itched for the feel of warm, dry clothing.

Montgomery set down the rabbit hutch and leaned into the heavy wooden doors to ease them closed, sealing out the jungle.

The compound was bigger than it looked from the exterior. Stone walls surrounded a dirt courtyard rapidly filling with mud puddles. A vegetable garden and chicken yard had been built on slightly higher ground. Next to the garden, a pump stood over a sunken pool of water, whose surface trembled in the rain.

A handful of buildings clustered around the courtyard. I wondered which one Father had disappeared into. Next to the wooden gate was the largest edifice, with windows on its two stories shaded by wide-slatted shutters. Wispy smoke rose from a tin chimney. A weathered old barn with wide eaves sat across from the big stone building. The little boy, Cymbeline, reached out from the barn's half door to catch raindrops in his open palm. There were a few smaller buildings, probably no larger than a room each. Directly across from me hunkered a squat building with tin walls, painted blood red. No windows. Something about it lodged a dull pain in my side, as if a fractured rib now pierced my right lung.

'What's that building?'

Montgomery didn't even glance up. 'The laboratory.'

I wiped the rain from my face. That low red building made me uneasy, but the rest of the compound was in good working order. This was clearly someone's home, not the wild den of a madman. The portico had been freshly swept and the garden was well tended, despite the mud puddles. My skirt grazed against the interior wall and came off with a coating of chalky dust from fresh whitewash.

Beside me, Edward leaned against the wall, taking long breaths. He pinched the bridge of his nose, closing his eyes for a moment. Part of me felt oddly protective of him. But he was a survivor. He'd been through worse than this and come through it.

'You'll be all right,' I said.

'It isn't me I'm worried about,' he whispered, giving me a penetrating look. 'I'm not sure you should have come here, Juliet. There's something strange about this island. About your father.'

I folded my arms, not wanting to hear more. I didn't altogether disagree with him, but I wasn't ready to admit that aloud. The rain lightened, and the little boy darted across the courtyard into one of the small apartments. The sound of a hammer started up again.

Montgomery ran a hand through his soaked hair. He was quieter than usual, as if worried I might be disappointed by their simple home.

A slamming door made us both jump.

Father stepped onto the portico from the large building, rubbing his hands. 'I've put the kettle on,' he said, his eyes traveling from my dirty dress to Montgomery's bare feet to Edward's seawater-soaked clothes. He frowned. 'Good Lord. You're all disgusting. Good thing we've no neighbors. The tea can wait. Montgomery, be so good as to show Juliet to her room while I have a bath prepared.'

Father frowned at Edward. 'Prince, I'm afraid there's only the one spare room. Perhaps we can make a place for you in the storage shed. Hitherto, it has been used to store feed for the horses.'

'I'm sure it will do fine,' Edward said, but his knuckles clenched white as bone behind his back.

Father stared at the muddy hem of my skirt. 'I need to look over the shipment while there's still some daylight. That should give you a few hours to make yourself presentable, Juliet, and then we can talk civilly.' He waved Edward toward the main building. 'Come inside, Prince. It will take a few minutes to ready your room, and I've a question or two for you if you're to stay here.'

I threw Edward a nervous look, but his face was calm. For a boy used to a privileged life, he was surprisingly brave. I wondered what he'd told himself to get through those long, desperate days on the dinghy. Then I remembered the photograph, with that tingle of curiosity, and wondered again what he was running from.

'This way,' Montgomery said. I tore my eyes from Edward and followed Montgomery through the portico. The boots hung over his shoulder dripped water onto the stone floor as he led me toward one of the apartments. A few scrawny chickens huddled in the top of the henhouse to stay dry. As we passed the garden, Montgomery darted into the rain to gather a few pea pods. He handed one to me.

The sweet, earthy taste was paradise after weeks of dried

105

meat and tinny canned vegetables. I pointed to the chickens. 'I wouldn't mind one of those for supper.'

'They're only for eggs,' he said. 'We don't eat meat here.'

'That's a bit unusual, isn't it?'

He shrugged. 'Not fish nor flesh. That's the rule.'

'Another of Father's commandments?' I couldn't keep the edge from my voice.

He stopped outside the door of one of the smaller apartments. His handsome face was tense with exhaustion, and I felt a stab of guilt that I'd taken a hard tone. It wasn't Montgomery's fault. He'd saved Edward a second time, even against Father's wishes.

'The doctor's peculiar about his diet,' Montgomery said. 'Doesn't want them to develop a taste for meat.'

'*Them?* The natives, you mean?'

But he'd already turned to the door. It had a strange knob: a smooth, straight cylinder and a hook latch with holes for the fingers. The keyhole had been soldered closed.

'Isn't there a key?' I asked.

'No need. Only the main gate is locked.' He tugged on the latch a few times with his middle finger. 'The interior doors have a safeguard. Only five-fingers can open them.'

'Five-fingers?'

'Sorry. I mean, it's a special mechanism. It keeps wild animals from getting in but lets those of us in the compound come and go as we please.'

'Even into my room?'

He grinned briefly and pushed open the door. 'You haven't anything to fear from *us*, Juliet.'

I followed him inside. The room was large and airy, with a wooden bed and a table and chair. A screen fashioned from a bit of old netting split the room into a bedroom and a dressing area with a dusty mirror. I crossed the room to a barred window that framed the fading sun, muted now behind rain clouds, as it sank below the rolling treetops toward the dark horizon. Far below, I could see the three hulking islanders coming up the road with trunks slung across their backs.

I was alone with Montgomery and the unsettling images of the islanders' twisting limbs. Mother's voice whispered in my ear that drawing attention to the deformities would be impolite, but my curiosity wouldn't be silenced. I turned away from the window.

'What's wrong with the natives?' I whispered.

Montgomery tugged on the window bars, testing them, eyes flickering to the figures on the road. The pistol was gone from his belt but not from my mind. What was out there? Tigers? Wolves? We'd sailed across the Pacific with a panther that Montgomery had treated like a harmless kitten. If a panther didn't frighten him, what outside my window did?

'What do you mean?' he asked.

Wasn't it obvious? 'The deformities. Are they some sort of product of an isolated development?'

'To be sure,' he muttered. Instead of meeting my eyes, he tapped his bare foot against a dusty old trunk in the corner. 'Anyway, take a look at this.'

He was avoiding my questions again. Hiding things.

I knelt by the trunk anyway. He lifted the lid. Inside, folded and pressed, was a stack of ladies' dresses. I ran my hand over the soft fabric. Silk. Tulle. These were expensive pieces, a few years out of fashion, in good condition except for faintly yellowing lace at the cuffs. I sorted through the first few dresses. Below were an assortment of things: undergarments, a shawl, a wide-brimmed hat with a pink ribbon.

'They belonged to your mother,' Montgomery said.

I looked at him in surprise. I touched the dresses again, more gently this time. 'How did you get these?'

He shrugged. 'There was an estate sale when I went to London a few years ago. I thought the doctor might want them.' His foot tapped nervously against the edge of the trunk. I knew Father wasn't the sentimental type. He'd never care about a trunk of old dresses. It must have been Montgomery who wanted these, to remember her and our old life. A string tugged around my heart.

He'd loved my mother like his own.

'Anyway, now you've something clean to wear,' he said, suddenly flummoxed as I pulled out a soft handful of satiny undergarments.

I peered at him, seeing the quiet boy I once knew. Maybe I'd judged him too harshly, before, for obeying my father so strictly. He must have felt so alone out here with only the sea as company. 'I can't wear these dresses in the jungle. They'll be ruined.'

'You haven't much choice. The closest shop is in Brisbane.'

I replaced the dresses carefully and closed the lid. Something about wearing Mother's dresses felt wrong. Unearthing her dresses was like unearthing her long-buried corpse.

I stood, twisting her diamond ring. 'They're fine. It just . . . brings back her ghost.'

He nodded. I wondered what he remembered of his own mother, buried in a common plot somewhere in an overgrown London churchyard. He intertwined his fingers in the mesh dressing screen, pushing it gently in the breeze. I feared I'd said something wrong, stirred up ghosts from the dark places of our pasts. At least I had a father. What did Montgomery have? A story about a Danish sailor who shipped out two weeks before he was born and never returned. Was that why he was so reluctant to tell me the truth? Because no matter how awful the truth was, no matter if I loathed and shunned and hated my father, at least I had one.

'Montgomery.' My voice was a whisper. I stepped closer until only a small space separated us. It was the first time we'd been alone in a long time. His fingers continued to twist restlessly in the mesh strings. My chest swelled with things I wanted to ask – about him, about the island, about my father. I parted my lips to speak, but the words wouldn't form. I intertwined my fingers in the mesh screen next to his. I opened my mouth to ask if the rumors were true.

But I couldn't.

Instead, something else came out. Something unexpected. Something I should have told him six years ago but never had the chance.

'I'm sorry about Crusoe.'

Just saying the name twisted my heart. Montgomery's head jerked as suddenly as if I'd grabbed him by the throat. Crusoe had been our dog – Montgomery's dog, really – raised from a pup at his heels. Crusoe died the day before Father disappeared. The reporters claimed the dog was a victim of my father's criminal experiments. I'd heard all the grisly details of how they found Crusoe's body. Cut up, pieced together, barely alive. The police had killed him out of pity. No one spoke of such things, and so I hadn't either. Until now. Because it was wrong for a boy to lose his dog, and the passing years didn't make it any easier.

Montgomery remained silent for some time, his face flushed. He slowly unwound his fingers from the mesh screen and brushed a loose strand of hair behind his ear. His lips were shaking. I felt my own heart trembling, remembering the dog that I'd loved, too.

Suddenly he brushed his rough thumb against my jaw, catching me by surprise. Heat erupted across my face as I drew in a sharp breath. Was he going to kiss me? My eyelids sank closed. Our bodies were practically touching. It was wrong to be so close to a boy – every moment of Mother's upbringing had taught me that. But I didn't care. We were bound together, he and I.

Someone knocked at the open door. My heartbeat faltered. He pulled away, taking a little piece of my heart with him.

I glanced at the door.

Balthazar. At least it wasn't Father. If he tried to kill Edward for just setting foot on the island, what would he do to Montgomery for almost kissing the master's daughter?

'What is it?' Montgomery barked.

'Bath's ready for you, miss.'

Montgomery took a few steps toward the door. I could still feel the heat of his presence. 'I should go,' he said.

I nodded, aware of the change in the air. The moment had slipped away. I wanted to hold on to that feeling, that closeness with Montgomery. I felt safe with him. Complete. Like the world wasn't such a puzzle anymore.

But he was already gone.

The bathhouse was simple but pleasant. A large wooden tub held a steaming pool that gave off traces of some sweet herb I couldn't identify. I peeled off the summer dress and eased into the bath. It was hot enough to turn my skin red. I scoured every inch of my body with a sea sponge and a bar of lavender soap that seemed out of place on an island full of men. The old me flaked off with bits of mud and sand. The steam eased those tight feelings I'd carried forever, shame and worry and uncertainty. I took a deep breath, shocked at how full my lungs could be without a corset's restriction.

After the bath I put on a dressing gown and returned to my room. The clouds had parted, though the sun was all but gone. I lit the lanterns and slowly untangled my hair with a silver comb I'd found among Mother's things. The bath had worked all the thought out of me. My mind was blank. It was a strange feeling.

I stretched out on the bed. Before I knew it, the lantern flickered, and I felt myself giving in to sleep.

I dreamed of Montgomery's rough hand on my cheek. His palm was warm, familiar, as it ran over my jawbone, over my shoulders, his thumbs brushing across my clavicles in an echo of the game the medical students played counting Lucy's bones. The game didn't seem nearly so silly now that it was Montgomery's touch. But something changed in that witching hour between waking and sleep. My mind conjured a man's body, with strong, alluring hands, but they were cold. It wasn't Montgomery but Edward. That safe, protected feeling I'd had with Montgomery was gone, replaced by a deep chill that sent shivers running down my limbs. In my dream the edges of Edward's body slipped and slid like a ghost, only half bound to this world.

We were back in Father's laboratory on Belgrave Square. There were the familiar rows of cabinets, the specimen jars, everything so meticulously laid out. I was flat on the operating table. Something held me down — not the usual canvas restraints used by doctors, but something heavy and metal, like chains.

Edward stood over me. He rolled his shirt cuffs back slowly, first one, then the other, preparing for surgery. A reference book lay open on the table next to him. I tried to lift my head to see the diagram, but something was holding my head down, too. I tried to jerk free. His gold-flecked eyes slid to me.

'Don't struggle,' he whispered. 'It won't do any good.'

He turned to the table, sorting through instruments that clanked with the familiar ring of steel. I should have been frightened. But, strangely, I felt only an abnormal calm and the suffocating weight of the chains.

'Remain still, Juliet,' he said.

The swinging kerosene lamp above the table lit up the

tool in his hand. A dented old bone saw, rusted and flaking. A butcher's tool, not a surgeon's. I noted this calmly, wondering what a bone saw was doing in my father's old laboratory.

Edward's other hand flickered ghostly, fingers fading in and out, but when he brushed the hair off my face, he felt solid enough. He traced a hand down my cheeks, tilting my head, examining my face. I thought he might speak, but he didn't. Instead he raised the saw.

I felt a jolt, somewhere near my feet where I couldn't see. Then came the awful squeal of metal. He was sawing, I concluded. But a bone saw wouldn't cut through chains. You'd need at least a crosscut-tooth hacksaw for that. It was most perplexing.

The squeal and groan of metal continued. I wanted to cover my ears, but my hands were immobile. Edward came back into view. The bone saw was gone. His hands were covered in blood. I frowned, trying to deduce its source. Had he cut me? I mentally inspected my feet, my legs, my chest, my arms. I didn't feel pain. But I didn't feel anything else, either, except the strangling chains.

His fingers wrapped around something next to my head. He pulled with straining forearms. Sweat poured off his forehead. The rim of something metal came into the edge of my sight. The sharp edge sliced into his fingers, breaking the skin. The blood on his hands was his own, I realized.

The more he peeled back the metal, the more I could move my head. At last I twisted so I could see. He'd cut off a metal bonnet with a copper flower and a ribbon of steel and then peeled it back with his bare hands.

Very peculiar.

Edward moved to my chest. Another squeal of metal. Straining muscles. Blood dripping onto the table. I could breathe at last. Air rushed into my body, waking my senses.

112

I sat up, shaking off the cold detachment, breathing in lungful after lungful of air. I nearly cried when I saw what he'd freed me from. A metal corset, and below that a metal skirt, already peeled back. There'd never been any chains, I realized. What held me down was a metalwork dress. And Edward, with a butcher's saw and bloody hands, had painstakingly undressed me.

Beneath the steel dress I was naked, and I covered myself with my hands, still trembling with the feeling of air and freedom and something else, earthy and corporeal. It was as if I'd woken from a harsh London night into an Italian painting, where the world was lush and warm and passionate.

I swung my legs off the table. Sweat and blood dripped off Edward's brow. His hands were latticed with cuts. He didn't look at my naked body, but instead he inspected my face. He brushed my hair back, studying my features, his eyes dark and unreadable.

Without the restriction of the clothing, I was filled with a constellation of sensations. I was aware of the smell of cologne mixed with his blood, the rough feel of his trouser fabric grazing against my legs, the desire that seeped from the cuts in his hands, staining the floor.

He slid a hand behind my waist, his fingers like ice. My bare skin was flush against his bloodstained clothes. His hand brushed through my hair.

He pressed his lips to mine.

Coldness flooded into me like a splash of springwater on a winter morning. I gasped with the sensation, feeling suddenly painfully *hungry*.

I kissed him back, breathless, wanting so much more.

FOURTEEN

I woke burning with sweat. The dream was still fresh in my mind, so fresh I touched my lips with shaking fingertips. I told myself I'd had the dream because of the almost kiss with Montgomery. It had nothing to do with Edward. And now it was daylight, at least midmorning. Mottled sunlight and the distant sound of waves filtered between the bars on my window.

I'd slept through dinner and all night. I might have slept for days, for all I knew. I wiped my damp palms on the bedcovers. When had I crawled under the sheets? I was wearing a nightdress I didn't recognize, something expensive with lace at the collar. But when I'd fallen asleep, I'd still been wearing my dressing gown.

Someone had undressed me.

I pushed back the sheets as if they were on fire. The memory of the dream flooded back, making me dizzy. Edward's hands on my naked body. The crisscross of cuts on his hands from peeling back the metal dress. Had Edward undressed me? Was that why I'd dreamed of him?

No, surely not. He was a gentleman and so shy he'd barely look at me. But then who? Had one of Father's beastly servants removed my clothes? The thought made the fibers of my stomach shrink.

I threw open Mother's trunk, looking for something plain, and found a simple blue dress. I unlaced the unfamiliar nightdress hurriedly, but a breeze from the window made me pause.

Whispering. The rising and falling cadence of words, carried on the wind, spoken in a language other than human.

I drifted to the window, watching the trees. Beyond the jungle the sea stretched forever. There were no curtains, making me feel suddenly exposed in only the half-unlaced nightdress.

I caught sight of my reflection in the mirror. My arms and face were tan. The meager food and harsh weather on the *Curitiba* had stolen the softness from my face. I slipped the nightdress off my shoulder, turning to see my back in the mirror.

The puckered flesh of a scar I'd carried since I was an infant ran the full length of my spine. When I was a child, Mother dressed me only in high collared shirts to keep it hidden. She said it reminded her of my difficult birth and deformed back. My father's gifted hands had put it right, but not even he could operate without leaving scars.

Mother was long gone, but not her spirit. *Keep it covered*, she seemed to whisper. I hurried out of the nightdress and into a chemise, then pulled the blue dress over my head and pulled the collar high around my neck. I'd have to skip a corset. Mine was filthy, and Mother's were so old-fashioned that I couldn't lace any of them without assistance. Without it I felt strangely light, and I touched my ribs, thinking of the metal dress in my dream.

Someone knocked at the door. I squeezed the strange latch, expecting Father or Montgomery or one of the natives.

But it was Edward.

'Oh.' The one word was all I could manage. Seeing him brought back the dream with a powerful rush. I bunched my hands in the soft fabric of my skirt to remind myself I was dressed. This wasn't a dream. He wasn't some shifting specter. I closed my eyes and leaned in the doorway, dizzy.

'Juliet? Are you well?' Concern crinkled the skin around his eyes. He took my arm and led me to the desk. He poured water from a pitcher into a glass. 'Sit down. Have some water.'

I took the glass with shaking fingers.

'I came to see if you were awake. You've been asleep nearly eighteen hours.'

'My carpetbag. In the corner. Bring it here, please.'

He picked up the ragged thing and set it on the desk without question. I dug through it for the embossed wooden box that held my medication. I opened it and removed one of the glass vials and the syringe. He raised his eyebrows, curious.

'It's a chronic illness,' I said. 'A glycogen deficiency. I have to take a daily injection or . . . I get dizzy.' I left out the part about the coma. Edward had his secrets. I could keep a few of my own.

'I've never heard of that.'

I set the tip of the needle against the vial's opening. 'It's rare.'

He watched, fascinated, as I punctured the vial lid and drew in twenty-five milligrams of the treatment. My hands knew the movement by habit, but I'd never injected myself with someone watching.

I concentrated on the syringe. When it was full, I set it aside and unbuttoned my shirt cuff, rolling it slightly past my inner elbow. Edward shifted closer. I cleared my throat, the dream still too fresh.

I pressed the tip of the needle to my elbow, above the

ghostly blue vein just below the skin. I slid it past the surface, barely flinching, and pierced the vein. My thumb depressed the plunger, and the treatment melted into my blood. I let out a sigh.

Edward watched from the corner of his eye. I withdrew the needle, wiped it carefully, and put it back in the box.

The sunlight flickered over the walls. Clouds were forming.

'You spoke with Father yesterday,' I said. 'What did he say?'

The flecks in Edward's eyes glowed. He didn't answer.

'Did he apologize for nearly drowning you, at least?'

His gaze drifted, cataloging every item in my room. 'He strikes me as the sort who's never apologized for anything.'

'You *are* perceptive.'

'We worked out a bit of an . . . arrangement. I don't think he has any intention of murdering me in my sleep, if that's what you're asking.'

I rolled down my sleeve and fastened the button. The treatment was already making me clearheaded. I peered at Edward, the flesh-and-blood young man in my room, not the dream specter. Whatever he and Father had spoken of, he wasn't going to tell me.

'Well, *I'm* sorry. If I'd known that's how he would react—'

'Don't. It's hardly your fault.'

I ran my fingers around the worn box edge. 'I suppose you're going to tell me your suspicions were right. That only a madman would live out here.'

He leaned closer. 'It's not just him, Juliet. They carry an arsenal just to step outside. What are they so afraid of?'

I drummed my fingers on the box nervously. Remembering how in my dream the light from the swinging kerosene lamp lit his face as his hands traced over my naked skin.

'Did you undress me last night?' I asked bluntly.

He couldn't hide his surprise. He ran his hand over the tangled hair on the back of his neck. '*Undress* you?'

I squeezed the box, feeling foolish, like I had tested a theory too early. 'Never mind,' I said quickly.

'Why would you think . . . ?'

'I woke up in a nightdress I didn't put on.'

For a moment his eyes searched mine, trying to peer into my head. Studying the sound of our silence. His lips parted, asking a question without ever saying a word.

Would you want me to undress you?

He'd hinted at his interest, but how could he expect me to think about such things at a time like this, when I'd just met my father after years apart? And there was Montgomery to consider, and that near kiss, and Edward didn't even begin to know me. If he knew some of the things I had done, the dark things I sometimes thought, he'd change his mind.

'I didn't undress you,' he said, and the silence that came next was heavy between us.

Breath slipped from my lips, pressed by some invisible force. A connection was growing between us, pulsating between us, in time with the beating of my heart. That might not be my last dream about Edward Prince, I realized. And the next one might not be unwelcome.

FIFTEEN

We left my room and found Father and Montgomery in the main building. The entire ground floor was one large, high-ceilinged room with wide shutters angled to let in air but keep out the sun. A dinner table sat behind a seating area with a fireplace and stone mantel. A simple staircase led to a second-floor landing with two shut doors, and another door on the ground floor that might have led to the kitchen.

The furnishings were an eclectic mix of fine but threadbare Rococo-style furniture and a few crudely handmade wooden chairs and tables. In the corner was a piano, its black wood dented and one leg broken, but polished to a high gleam. A sigh slipped from my lips. A breath of elegance whispered here that I hadn't expected to find.

Montgomery looked up from cleaning a rifle on the table. He jumped to his feet, wiping his hands on a rag. Just seeing him made me blush, remembering the near-kiss in my room that had caused me to unwittingly transform him to Edward in my dream.

But maybe I'd been misinterpreting. Maybe Montgomery had just been caught up in the dizzying memories of the past, and it hadn't meant anything more. *I'd* been the one practically throwing myself against him, after all. The ways of men and women were such a puzzle. And I could barely decipher my own feelings, let alone anyone else's.

Father put down his book and looked me over. 'Ah, you're wearing one of Evelyn's dresses. She didn't like it, I seem to recall. Too plain. Come sit and have a cup of tea. You've missed breakfast by a few hours, I'm afraid.'

My feet stumbled into the room on his order. A strange sensation overcame me, as though I were stepping into a memory. Something about the placement of the furniture perhaps. Or the smell of Father's tobacco. Something from long ago that had sunk into that delicate space between the conscious and subconscious.

I rested my fingertips on the back of the sofa, trying to remember. The feel of the worn velvet evoked shadows of a memory. I stared at my fingers. Had I seen that sofa before?

The memory almost surfaced, but one of the island natives entered, frightening it away. Dressed in a loose cotton shirt and old blue military trousers, he carried a tea tray and sandwiches. I tried not to stare. Balthazar and the little boy were abnormally hairy, but this man hadn't a hair on him. Instead, his scalp was covered with lumpy, flesh-colored skin like scales. He was thin, normal height, with nervous eyes, and whereas the others lumbered with their strange legs, he slunk about. He set the tray on the coffee table too abruptly, rattling the cups. He tugged at the cuffs of his shirt, where I saw that the scaly affliction continued to his fingertips.

'Ah, thank you, Puck.' Father smiled.

The man's shifty eyes looked me over, like he'd never seen a woman before. For all I knew, maybe he hadn't. He slunk off toward a back room, and I let out an exhale.

A clock on the mantel ticked loudly. *Tick, tick, tick.* Like the pulsing of my veins. 'Where did you get this sofa, Father?'

He raised an eyebrow. 'I'm surprised you remember. You

were so young.' At my questioning look, he motioned to it. 'It's from the house on Belgrave Square.'

Belgrave Square. Now I remembered. The sofa, the green chair, the writing desk by the window. This had been our furniture. The same sofa I used to nap on as a little girl. A tear in the fabric ran along the seam. I slid a finger over it, as if by magic I could sew it shut. 'Everything was auctioned off years ago. How did you find it?'

'It's Montgomery's doing,' he said, pouring a cup of tea. 'A chair is a chair, if you ask me, but he wanted them. And he has a knack for finding things.' He waved a hand toward the bookshelf by the window. 'He's collected quite a variety of trinkets from our former life. You'll remember some of them, no doubt. But first, sit down. You're making me nervous, hovering about. You too, Prince. We're going to have to find some use for you, you know.'

I glanced at Edward. He settled slowly into one of the worn leather chairs, and I took the sofa. Father poured me a cup of tea. 'How are you feeling? You've been diligent about your injections, I hope.'

'Yes. I feel well. Although . . .' I took a sip of tea, wishing it would soothe my trembling voice. 'I woke in a nightdress that wasn't mine. I wondered if someone else had been in my room.' I spied Montgomery from the corner of my eye. If not Edward, then maybe . . . ?

Father dismissed it with a wave. 'Oh, that was Alice. She found the nightdress in your mother's trunk. Ah, speak of the devil.' His gaze hovered in a space behind my left ear. 'Come meet our guests, Alice.'

A shiver tickled the back of my neck. Had there been another person in the room behind me, and I hadn't noticed? And another woman, on this island full of men? I twisted to look.

A girl, two or three years younger than me, stood in the

shadows at the rear of the room. I started. There wasn't a single twist to her joints or hunch to her back. Her frame was small but perfectly proportioned. I realized that after being surrounded by the natives' lilting gaits and protruding jaws, it was her ordinariness that struck me as odd.

'Don't be shy,' Father said. 'This is my daughter. You've heard Montgomery and me speak of her. Come introduce yourself.'

The girl stepped hesitantly out of the shadows, her chest rising and falling quickly. She was pretty in a natural way, though not entirely without deformity. Her upper lip split and curled to the base of her nose. A harelip. She hid her mouth behind her fingers as she gave me an almost imperceptible nod. She needn't have felt so self-conscious. A harelip might have caused her great distress in England but was a minor blemish compared to the islanders' deformities.

'Pleased to meet you, miss,' she said, so softly I could barely make it out. Her eyes were wide as marbles. Her gaze darted to Montgomery, as if seeking reassurance.

Father waved absently toward Edward. 'And of course you met Mr Prince last night.'

She studied the floorboards with those big eyes and didn't utter a word. I imagined she'd never met a fine young gentleman before. With his loose hair and dirty boots, Montgomery hardly counted as one.

'Now, Alice, won't you see if Balthazar needs help with the animals?'

She ducked her head and slipped across the room. She paused at the door to speak to Montgomery. They exchanged a few words I couldn't hear. Then he laid a hand on her shoulder and smiled.

I quickly looked away, feeling as if I had observed something I shouldn't. I realized that I was new to the island, but Montgomery wasn't. This was his home. He'd likely known Alice for years.

'And you, Montgomery, see if Puck and the others have the cargo stowed. I don't want the rats getting into it like last time.'

Obediently, Montgomery went to the door, where a canvas jacket hung on a peg. A light rain had begun to fall outside. He slipped the jacket on before going outside. It jabbed me like a thorn in the side that he was so quick to do Father's bidding when he wasn't a servant anymore. I stood up and went to the bookshelf to find the trinkets Montgomery had collected.

The top row was filled with books that I vaguely remembered from my childhood. Agrippa, Paracelsus, Albertus Magnus. Shakespeare's full collection, bound in green with gold embossment. *Troilus and Cressida, Edward III, Twelfth Night*. I traced the gold lettering with my fingers, trying to remember the stories Father had read. On the next shelf were more books, a glass bottle, and a tin of pipe tobacco. I unscrewed the lid and inhaled deeply. 'You used to smoke this back in London. Your professor friend brought it to you from the Caribbean.'

'Quite right. Professor von Stein. Now that was a man who knew his way around a bottle of brandy. Brandy and a cigar at the Café du Lac, overlooking London Bridge. It didn't come much better.'

I didn't tell him that Professor von Stein had been the one who'd found me employment at King's College after his banishment. Nor that the professor, like all of Father's previous colleagues, had renounced his friendship and slandered him as a monster to any who would listen.

'If you liked it so much, why trade it for such an uncivilized place?' Edward asked.

I only half listened to them. I wanted to hear Father's

123

answer, but on the second shelf down I found a framed photograph that consumed my attention. A woman holding a baby in a christening gown. I picked up the frame.

'Curious, are you, Prince? Well, it wasn't totally uncivilized. There were some Anglican missionaries who came on the ship with us. It was from them that I heard of the island's existence. Thought they'd make a paradise of it.' He stared into the bottom of his empty cup. 'But they are long gone.'

'And you've never returned to England?'

'Montgomery makes the voyage if there's need. Most of our supplies can be acquired from traders passing to Australia or Fiji, though by and by there comes an errand that requires a longer voyage.'

Their conversation was like rustling leaves in the background. I stared at the picture, transfixed. The woman was my mother. Her young face was so beautiful, so smooth. In her final weeks, she'd looked as worn as Death.

Puck came through the doorway, quiet as a murmur. He whispered something in Father's ear. Father glanced at the ticking clock on the mantel.

'I'll have to miss lunch and supper,' Father announced. 'I started on a new project last night that requires my immediate and prolonged attention.' He stood and kissed me briefly on the temple, like I was still just a child. Like I hadn't traveled so far and risked so much to find him.

I shouldn't have expected him to change. He'd disappear into his laboratory for days, and I'd be lucky to glimpse him at mealtimes. Just like it used to be.

Edward drummed his fingers on the arms of the leather chair, watching. His jaw twitched slightly.

I got the sense he understood my feelings. He'd left England to get away from his own father, after all, though he'd been evasive about the details. He'd done something, something that seemed to have haunted him long before the *Viola* sank. Anyway, he had to know a thing or two about domineering fathers.

But this time, Father didn't instantly disappear into the laboratory. His black eyes glanced at the frame in my hands and then searched my face. 'Let me make this up to you. Tomorrow we'll take a picnic to a point where you can see all the island. I am curious to know what kind of person my daughter's become.'

My lungs expanded, filling with fresh air and childlike happiness. I glanced at Edward, beaming. But he'd gotten up, arms folded tight, his back to me as he looked out the window.

And then Father said the one thing I'd most hoped to hear. 'I'm glad you came, Juliet.'

SIXTEEN

The next day we were to leave in the early morning, before the afternoon heat made travel through the jungle a miserable affair. I waited with anticipation, but Montgomery came at dawn, already sweating and smelling of horse, and told me there'd been a problem. An accident on the far side of the island. Some natives injured – one even killed. The picnic would be delayed a day. That day passed, and then another, and another, and Montgomery stopped bothering to tell me. Father was in charge of the island, so naturally he had duties and responsibilities more pressing than a picnic. But that didn't begin to fill the hollow pit of my disappointment.

I spent those first few days exploring the compound, putting my cleaning skills to use when I could. It was a simple place, a farmstead, and the order and logic behind it was pleasing. Everyone had a job, even the little boy Cymbeline, who picked peas from the garden and fed the chickens. There was nothing of London's chaos and filth and crowds and mechanization. After a few days, I got used to the rhythm of island life. *I could have a future here*, I thought. The idea made my head spin.

Alice stayed mostly in the kitchen, half hidden by

woodsmoke and her own shyness. Edward kept to himself as well, brooding as if the island's desolation made him anxious, though I managed to get one game of backgammon from him.

One morning, as I was brushing my hair with the silver comb, I heard a soft rap at the door.

'Yes?' I asked, turning the knob. Alice stepped back shyly, keeping her scarred face turned away. Her fair hair looked shockingly white in the early daylight, and her eyes locked on the silver comb in my hand.

'The expedition will be leaving shortly, miss. The doctor asked me to see if you were ready.'

'What expedition?'

'Well, the picnic, miss.'

I blinked. I'd pushed the picnic out of my head with all the rest of my father's unfulfilled promises, and it took me a moment to dredge it back into daylight. 'Yes,' I stuttered. 'Yes, I'm ready. Five minutes.'

She didn't take her eyes from the comb. There was something so delicate about her, so vulnerable, and yet mature beyond her years. I'd seen it in the other lodging-house girls, especially the younger ones. I guessed she was an orphan. I knew what that awful loneliness felt like, though for me there'd been a happy ending – a long-lost father. For Alice, I doubted such luck.

I held out the comb. 'Take it, if you like.' Her eyes widened. She didn't move. I reached for her hand and pressed the comb into her palm.

'No, miss, I couldn't.'

'I don't need it.' I motioned to the matching silver brush from the dressing table. 'See? I certainly don't need both.'

A brief smile flickered on her face as she slipped the comb into her apron pocket. But then she covered her scarred mouth and, with a timid nod, slipped back to the kitchen.

She wasn't one of the islanders, that was certain. How had such a young girl come to the island and found herself in my father's employment?

I braided my hair and tried on Mother's floppy sunbonnet in the mirror. The fashion was out of style, yet it made me look glamorous and bold. Someone to be proud of, I hoped. I found the wagon outside in the courtyard, loaded with a wicker basket and blankets from the salon. Edward leaned against the side of the wagon in crisp, clean clothes. He was recovering fast, and the bruises on his face were almost gone. I couldn't help but notice that if it hadn't been for the faint scar down his face, he'd have been almost painfully handsome.

Montgomery hitched the harness to the horse, Duke, struggling with a stiff leather strap.

'Ah, Juliet,' Father said. A bouquet of bright yellow wild-flowers rested next to him on the wagon bed. 'Ready to go?'

The flowers, the food, the effort on my behalf. I nodded, afraid of speaking. Words might make it all go away. Not in a million years would I have expected my pragmatic father to have picked flowers for his daughter.

'What beautiful flowers,' I said at last.

He looked at them blankly. 'Oh yes. Montgomery thought they'd add a touch of elegance you might be homesick for. He arranged for this, the food and all. You know I've little skill for that sort of thing. Where did you find them, Montgomery?'

Edward stood a little straighter, picking a little too hard at a splinter in the wagon gate.

Montgomery strained against the leather cinch. At last the buckle clicked into place. 'North side of the island,' he said gruffly.

I could feel blood rushing to my cheeks. Montgomery had gotten the flowers. Sometime yesterday he'd picked wildflowers like he used to when we'd visit cousins in the country. Mother would put them in a glass jar on the servants' kitchen table, saying the grand dining table was only for proper arrangements.

Edward wiped his brow, eyes lingering on the flowers. And then they slid to Montgomery, who was looking at him with equal hardness. I swallowed. Were they *jealous*? Of each other?

'Are you coming with us?' I asked Edward.

He started to speak, but Father cut in.

'Family only,' Father said. I briefly wondered if he counted Montgomery in that or if Montgomery was coming along merely to drive the wagon. 'I've given Prince a project anyway. Cataloging the pantry supplies. Well-educated boy like you can manage that, can't you, Prince?'

Edward turned away, a little too abruptly. 'Enjoy your flowers,' he muttered to me before sauntering off toward the salon. I took a deep breath. Lucy had never said how complicated boys could be.

Father offered me a hand. 'Let's go before the sun melts us.'

I climbed into the back. Montgomery tied off the last straps and took the reins in the driver's seat. Puck and one of the hunchbacked servants opened the gate for us, and we were off.

The day was beautiful. A blue sky stretched as far as the ocean, which we glimpsed between breaks in the trees. I'd traded a bitter English winter for the lush tropical sun and beautiful calls of faraway birds.

As we rode, Father described the unusual vegetation and wildlife that I'd only read about in books. I listened, though my thoughts kept sliding between Edward and Montgomery. If I'd been in London, and still wealthy, this coming spring would be my Season. Lucy and I would have talked endlessly about the boys – the *men* – at the dances, the galas, the summer picnics in the park.

But after we lost our fortune, I couldn't afford to think about boys. I was just trying to stay off the streets. And now there were two boys my thoughts drifted between. Yet one had been a servant, I reminded myself. And the other . . . well, the other would surely leave the island the first chance he got.

Montgomery stopped the wagon on a windy bluff high above the compound, just below the volcano's smoking rim. I climbed out and made my way to the bluff's edge, where the full expanse of the island stretched below us, meeting the sea in a line of sandy beach. The wind pulled at my skirt, blowing loose my hair, and I closed my eyes, enjoying it.

'Not too close,' Montgomery murmured. My eyes snapped open.

'Over here,' Father called. 'Out of that confounded wind.'

We made our way back to the wagon. Montgomery started unloading the supplies. He stretched out the blankets in a shady spot away from the cliff. *He's not a servant anymore*, I reminded myself, watching him unpack the baskets. Even if he still did the work of one.

'You'll have to forgive our basic fare.' Father uncorked a carafe of water. 'We live simply here out of necessity. I'm afraid we've only cold vegetable stew with bread. And some fruits from the jungle.'

'I don't mind.' I settled onto the blanket. Montgomery casually laid the bouquet of flowers near my feet before filling our china bowls. Father and I tucked into the meal.

'Well, Juliet, what skills have you acquired?' Father asked expectantly.

'Skills?' I briefly met Montgomery's eyes. He knew that the

130

only skills I'd acquired were cleaning mortar and avoiding the gutter. Not exactly what Father hoped for. 'After Mother died, I found employment at the university.'

Father raised an eyebrow. 'A *job*? Shouldn't a relative have taken you in?'

I paused. This wasn't going to be easy. He disapproved of his daughter working, yet he'd been the one who'd put me in that position.

I took a sip of water, trying not to feel irritated. I suppose he hadn't had much of a choice. Maybe he thought that by leaving, he was doing the best for us. He hadn't known Mother would die. Or that the relatives' kindness didn't extend very far.

'It wasn't so bad,' I said. I don't know why exactly, but I didn't want to make him feel guilty. Our relationship was so fragile, like one of the trailing vines bursting with soft white flowers along the garden wall. One harsh word and the flowers might shrivel. 'I learned to clean. To sew a little.'

'To sew? To clean?' He looked unimpressed. 'A professor's daughter shouldn't do that sort of work. What about piano? Needlepoint? All those things your mother taught you.'

I swallowed. 'I might remember a little piano.'

'I see.'

I looked to Montgomery for help. He rested an arm on his knee, tapping a thin twig against his shin. 'Little good needlepoint would do us around here,' he said. 'We're lucky Juliet is so practical. Maybe she could help Alice with the cleaning.'

I gave him a slight, grateful nod, but Father only bristled.

'No daughter of mine is going to scrub anything,' he said. 'I hardly think a future husband wants a girl with calluses on her hands.' He waved toward my chipped nails. My face went white.

'Juliet,' Montgomery said softly. 'What he means is—'

'Thank you, Montgomery, I'll speak for myself. Don't misunderstand my criticism, Juliet,' Father said. 'It's my duty as your father to see you well married. You can't remain on this island forever, and when you leave, you'll need to find a husband. Your mother should have seen you prepared to please a man, but alas, she died too soon. I am merely trying to determine what's to be done with you now.'

What's to be done with me. It was like a barb in my side. I clearly wasn't marriage material, but I was too high-bred to be of use on the island. What did that leave?

'I know something of medicine,' I said in a rush. 'I've studied the books you left behind. I worked at King's College in the operating rooms, and I know anatomy and biology. Perhaps I could help you in your work.'

Even Montgomery's face went white at this. Father gave me a good, hard stare and then laughed. 'A girl interested in science. How *modern* of you. I suggest you find more appropriate interests. Montgomery, we've an old needlepoint set, haven't we?'

'But I can help you—'

'That's admirable, Juliet, but you'd only be in the way. Science is best left to men. Women have too delicate a constitution.'

I fought against my bubbling urge to argue. I wanted to tell him all the things I'd seen. My God, the things I'd done with my own hands. But I wasn't ready to trample on the delicate flowers of my new relationship with my father.

'You're right,' I said, hating myself even as I said it. Father had a way of bending everyone to his will – apparently I was no different. 'Of course.'

Montgomery gave me a questioning look. But he was hardly in a position to judge me.

The sound of horse hooves broke the tension. Balthazar

came along the trail on Duchess, two bandoliers across his chest, his face pinched and eyes darting. A rifle was strapped across the saddle. Puck jogged behind on foot, another rifle in hand. Montgomery leapt up to meet them.

I started to stand, but Father shook his head. 'It's nothing to concern yourself with, I'm sure. Montgomery will attend to it.'

'What if someone's hurt?'

'It's all under control,' Father said, eating a strawberry. 'I know everything that happens on this island. You must trust me.' He tilted his head, studying me like a specimen. His eyes were like black stars, making me forget the rifles and the commotion and Balthazar's worried face.

Almost.

I watched Montgomery run a hand through his hair, his muscles tense, as he said something I couldn't hear. Puck slunk about, whispering low and hushed words that made Montgomery's hand tighten on his pistol.

I looked over the shimmering water, the savage but beautiful island below us. Whatever was happening, this was my home now, at least until the next ship came. I wanted to be a part of it.

'I didn't come here to do needlepoint,' I said firmly. 'You can use my help. Montgomery does the work of ten men. At least let me help you in the laboratory. If not with your experiments, then taking notes. There has to be *some* use for me.'

His black eyes bored into me, studying, thinking, analyzing. I could almost see the clockwork gears clicking into place. He chewed another strawberry slowly.

'Help me with my work, eh?' He absently ran his fingers over his shadow of a beard. His eyes weren't focused on me anymore, but somewhere beyond the ocean. 'Yes, perhaps you could be of use to me after all.'

133

I smiled uneasily. His words were just what I wanted to hear, and yet, between the guns and that peculiar look in his eye, something felt wrong. 'Good,' I said. 'I won't disappoint you.'

Suddenly his eyes snapped back to me with a fiery intensity. 'What do you know of that boy, Prince?'

'Edward?' I sat straighter. 'Not very much at all.'

Father's graceful fingers stroked the wiry hairs on his chin. I remembered the conversation that Edward was so reluctant to talk about, and I wondered what Father could possibly have wanted to say to him after trying to drown him.

'Perhaps we should change that,' Father said.

I couldn't bring myself to ask what exactly he meant. Getting to know Edward couldn't possibly help him with his work – unless it got me out of his way. Or unless he thought the quickest way to fulfill his fatherly duty was to marry me off to Edward Prince.

SEVENTEEN

On the way home I couldn't help but notice Montgomery's tense hold on the reins and Balthazar's wide-eyed scan of the jungle. They were on alert. Something bad had happened, regardless of what Father said. Ever since that native had accidentally been killed, they'd all been uneasy.

Alice fetched me for dinner that evening, saying Father expected proper dining attire. I dug through Mother's trunk until I found a suitable white blouse and lavender skirt. Elegant clothes didn't fit such a savage place, but this wasn't just any island. It was my father's island.

I paused outside the French doors leading to the well-lit salon. Inside Father and Edward talked over a brandy, surprisingly amicable, while Montgomery looked out the windows, arms folded, watching the dark jungle. The dinner table was set with all the finery of a London salon, out of place on the primitive island.

When I entered, all eyes turned to me. Edward straightened. The conversation died between him and Father. Apparently Mother's elegant clothing was something of a sight. Montgomery gave me one long, speechless look and went to the side table to pour himself a brandy.

Edward wore a fine suit borrowed from Father, with a dark-gray vest that would have been at home in any London drawing room. He smiled, though the muscle in his jaw twitched. 'You look beautiful. Like one of the angels Milton wrote about.'

'A fallen one, maybe,' I said.

Montgomery watched us from across the room in his worn riding trousers and loose linen shirt. He'd washed his hands and face but little else. He wasn't a gentleman like Edward. He belonged in the wild.

'Please take a seat,' Father said, pulling out my chair. 'I'm afraid Montgomery and I have grown lax in our manners. Now that we've guests, it's time we remind ourselves that we're not animals.'

Montgomery sat down across from me, fidgeting with the silverware. I wondered if he often thought about that moment when our lips had been so close. If so, he'd said nothing. Could that attraction have been only my imagination?

Alice came in and filled our wine glasses, followed by Balthazar with a soup bowl. She kept her head to the side and wouldn't look at anyone but Montgomery. She positively turned white when she had to serve Edward, with his fine suit and elegant manners.

For a while we ate in silence. I think the sudden sophistication and elegant attire took us all by surprise, and we didn't quite know what to do with ourselves. The clock ticked away the seconds on the mantel. I stole glances at my father, wondering about what he'd meant when he'd said I should get to know Edward better. Wondering what had made Balthazar and Puck interrupt the picnic with so many guns.

'Well, Prince, it seems you are now somewhat familiar with us. We have the disadvantage, however, of knowing next to nothing about you.' Father tapped absently against the base of his wine glass and slid me a look. 'Juliet, in particular, is curious about you.'

I studied the curve of my spoon in detail, and wished Father didn't have to be so obvious about whatever plans he was making for Edward and me.

'You come from a good family, I assume?' Father asked him.

'My father is a general.'

'A high post. Strange you would turn your back on him.'

My soup spoon paused halfway to my mouth. I was intrigued by Edward's story, even without Father pushing me toward him. Edward had given me only glimmers. I had never directly asked him what had made him leave England in such a rush, but then again, he'd never asked me to lay bare my history so he could dissect it, either. It felt like an unspoken agreement. He could have his secrets and I could have mine. Though it didn't make me any less curious.

Edward rubbed the silk napkin between his fingers, clearing his throat. I absently wondered what his hands would feel like against my skin. Strong, yet smooth. Like they had in my dream. The spoon slipped from my fingers into the bowl with an embarrassing clatter.

'We didn't agree on many things,' Edward said.

'Still, one must obey one's father, don't you agree?' Father ran his middle finger along the rim of his wine glass. It hummed with a shrill and unnerving pitch.

'There comes a point when one must make one's own decisions. Live one's own life.'

The hum of the wine glass grew louder and louder. And then, suddenly, he stopped. 'I hope for your sake, Mr Prince, that your father comes to forgive you. I, for one, am glad to have an obedient child,' he said, giving me a tight smile.

He was waiting for me to smile back. *Obediently.* I'd seen

him work his spell on my mother, his colleagues, his students. He had a way of swaying people's emotions like a hypnotist. I so badly wanted to believe that everything was fine on the island. And that pushing Edward off the dock had been a joke, nothing more. But the thing was, I wasn't swayed by my emotions. I was analytical. Logical.

I was like him.

I sat straighter, toying with my napkin. 'Why did you never send any letters?' I asked. 'Or come back to see me?'

The room went silent except for the *tick tick tick* of the mantel clock.

His face shifted almost imperceptibly. He set down his steak knife. 'I wish I could have, of course. But I can never return to England. There's the small matter of a warrant for my arrest.'

'But it's unfounded, isn't it? You're innocent of the things they accused you of.' My voice was harder than it should have been. Not exactly obedient. *'Aren't you?'*

His fingers drummed on the wine glass. 'It seems perhaps my daughter shares your questioning mind after all, Mr Prince.' His voice was tightly controlled. He took a deep breath and leaned back in his chair. 'The last thing the justice system is, is just,' he said. A bitterness stained his eyes, but I realized it wasn't my question that had him angry but the memory of false accusations. 'My academic rivals schemed to slander me so they could steal my work. Unfortunately, they succeeded.'

'But if it's not true—'

'It isn't about truth, Juliet. It's about what people want to believe.' He rubbed his brow. 'You're young. You haven't experienced how unjust the world can be.' He sighed. 'You're upset I didn't bring you with me. You've every right. I thought it was no life for a child, running, hiding out on an island a hundred miles from anything.'

138

He was right in that at least. It wasn't a good life for a child. And yet he'd taken Montgomery.

Father leaned forward. He took my hand across the table. The hypnotist was gone, and he seemed only tired and old and lonely. 'I was wrong, Juliet.' His long fingers consumed my small hands. 'Now, what do you say to putting the past behind us?'

Puck hovered behind him, a dusty champagne bottle in his hands to celebrate our elegant meal. His scaly fingers unwrapped the foil, hesitating to pull the cork until I spoke. Father's eyes crackled with the promise of a life together, of a family again.

Alice handed me a champagne flute. The rim was chipped. Like my soup bowl and my brandy glass and all the beautiful, expensive dishware. Everything had a chip or crack. Nothing here was perfect, but it still worked.

I met Father's gaze and nodded. Behind him, Puck popped the cork.

After supper, a comfortable silence settled over the room. The ticking of the clock seemed not nearly so harsh, and I rather enjoyed the small reminder of civilization.

Father smoked a cigar as he used to do, his gaze settling on the dark night beyond the compound walls. 'Yes,' he reflected, 'it's good to have you here. A father should know his daughter. I'm starting to not even mind you so much, Prince.'

Edward didn't laugh.

Father sent a small cloud of rich, earthy smoke toward the high ceiling. 'Why don't you play us a tune on the piano?' he asked me. 'It's been a long time since we've heard proper music, though Balthazar attempts a melody every now and then.'

Montgomery looked up from the table where he'd been

rubbing a crack in the surface, no doubt thinking of how to fix it. I remembered on the ship he'd said he wanted to hear me play again. My heartstrings tightened.

'Of course.' I stood, hoping I looked more confident than I felt. We all retired to the sitting area. Montgomery leaned against the doorjamb, keeping his distance. The piano bench beckoned, and I sat on it hesitantly, as if afraid it might bite. I hadn't played in years, and I vaguely wondered if I could rescind my agreement until I'd had time to practice.

I played a C-major chord.

'It's out of tune, I'm afraid,' I said.

'For the life of me, I can't tell,' Montgomery said. I shot him a look over my shoulder. He wasn't helping.

I ran my fingers lightly over the keys. They were worn, so unlike the perfectly crafted piano we'd had on Belgrave Square. I'd taken lessons every week from a piano tutor. Mother said I would one day play for suitors, then my husband, and then teach my own children. But after Father left, the piano was the first thing sold.

There was a Chopin piece she used to play. Dissonant, with an odd melody like wind in the night. It was haunting, and it seemed suited to the island. I closed my eyes and laid my fingers on the keys, trying to remember the feel of the music. I played the first chord, adjusting for the stiffness of the keys. Humidity and grime made the strings stick and the wood warp, but it was music nonetheless, and for this piece, somehow it fitted. And then the feeling came back to me, sitting next to my mother on the bench, watching her long fingers on the keys. Like a bird in an unlocked cage, music flew out of me.

I had forgotten what I loved about the piano. The precision of the notes and the mathematical intricacy of the notes and measures. It was like a complicated equation that you work out with your heart instead of pencil and paper. I concentrated on the keys, letting my mind clear. I played and played until the final bar, where I let the chord ring until the last trace of sound faded. My fingers slipped off the keys. Then I opened my eyes.

To my surprise, Alice and Balthazar and Puck stood around the table, halfway through clearing the dishes, with the queerest expressions on their faces. Tears glistened in Balthazar's eyes. I realized they might never have heard proper music before.

Father stood and brought his hands together, slowly, and then the others took up the clapping as well. The room suddenly felt warmer. I'd finally done something to please him.

They all rushed me – Edward and Alice and the servants. They had so many questions. What was the piece, and where had I learned it? Would I play more? Would I teach Alice? I was used to being overlooked as just another maid. Their attention was overwhelming.

I caught Montgomery's eye. He smiled at me like we shared some secret. And then I remembered why that piece out of all of them had come back to me. It had been his favorite. I'd found him at the bench one day, when we were children. His wax and polish brush were forgotten on the floor. I sat beside him and put his hands over mine so he could feel the movements of my fingers pressing the keys. I started to play a Vivaldi, but he shook his head. *Not this one*, he'd said. He'd wanted to play the one that sounded wrong.

The Chopin.

Montgomery looked away. He busied himself with a splinter in the doorframe.

'Lovely. Simply lovely.' Father gave a tight-lipped smile. Next to him, Balthazar brushed aside a tear. I suddenly felt crowded, as though they were pressing in. The rush of emotions was too much, drowning me. I slouched on the piano bench, desperate for a breath of air.

'Are you well?' Father asked. Suddenly the smile was gone, replaced by a physician's cold determination. He felt my forehead.

'I'm just a little dizzy.'

But I might as well have been a cold body on the dissection table. He felt my wrist for my pulse, then pushed up my sleeve. The syringe's pinprick flashed, red against the pale skin of my inner elbow. Redder than it should have been. Swollen.

'What's this?' he barked.

'Just a small infection. From the ship.'

'Have you been taking your treatment?' His lips pursed. 'You haven't missed a day, have you?'

I pressed my other hand to my forehead. Suddenly every sound in the room was magnified. Alice clearing the table. Edward's quick breaths. The scaly man whispering to Balthazar.

'I'm fine!' I cried. I wrenched my arm back. 'I'm fine. I just need some rest.'

Father glanced at the clock above the mantel. 'Midnight. I've kept you up.'

'It's all right, I'm just tired,' I said. I tried to stand, but my legs were weak.

'Someone help her to her room,' Father said.

Edward and Montgomery were suddenly both by my side, each taking an arm.

My face burned as I looked between them. Two boys, two sets of hands on my wrists. One rough and calloused, the other strong yet smooth. My emotions knotted tighter, threatening to cut off my circulation.

'You take her, Prince,' Father said. There was an odd tone to his voice that made me think of how he wanted me to get to know Edward better. Edward seemed pleased enough to escort me, but Montgomery squeezed my wrist harder. Not wanting to let Edward have me.

'Father, won't you take me?' I asked, trying to keep things peaceful. 'Like old times.'

Father grunted but helped me stand. I leaned on his arm, overpowered by the chemical smell coming off his jacket. Had he been in the laboratory before supper? I hadn't noticed the smell earlier. I looked closer. Three thick black hairs glistened on his collar. I realized I hadn't seen the panther or the monkey or any of the animals since arriving.

What had he done with them?

Father escorted me into the courtyard, where the night air cooled my cheeks. The chickens were gone, roosting in some cool, dark corner. The footfalls of our shoes echoed through the portico, the only sound of humanity among the trilling, whispering jungle sounds.

Maybe I should have felt out of place so distant from the noisy streets of London. But there was a serenity here, as though I had crossed the threshold into a place both familiar and novel. This gray-haired man wasn't a stranger. He was my father.

He stopped outside my door and patted my hand – the one with Mother's ring – as if the scandal had never happened. *And it hadn't*, I reminded myself. It had just been rumors.

'I hope you don't regret coming,' he said. 'I don't know what you thought you would find, but I realize an old Spanish fort and an old wrinkled man are probably a disappointment.'

'I'm not disappointed.' I laid my hand on top of his, squeezing before turning to my room and the odd door latch.

'Oh, and Juliet,' he said. I turned back. Half of his face was thrown in deep shadow, while the whites of his teeth gleamed in the distant lights from the salon. 'I'll be working in the laboratory late tonight. I've a good start on the new specimens. Don't be alarmed if you're awoken. The animals – they scream, you know. An unfortunate effect of vivisection. It keeps the whole household up.'

For a breath, the world seemed to freeze. And then the clouds rolled again, the wind howled again. I realized that he had charmed me, just like he charmed everyone. I'd thought I was so clever. I thought I could see past his manipulations. But I'd heard only what I wanted to.

He'd never said the accusations were untrue. Just unfair.

EIGHTEEN

The noises started sometime in the night, during the hour when the moon was at its highest. Not screams, exactly. More like moans. Howls. Sounds I couldn't put a name to. I lay in bed, wide awake, staring at the odd shapes the moonlight threw against the whitewashed walls. I couldn't tell what type of creature he was working on in that blood-red, windowless laboratory. I'd heard the panther make all types of howls and cries on the ship, but nothing like what came from that building.

Whatever it was, it was large.

Tears pooled in the hollows of my eyes. I wiped them away angrily. All I could think was that I'd gotten what I wanted – answers. Why should I be surprised? Hadn't I suspected the rumors were true, somewhere deep in the creases of my mind? And what about all the other strange things happening – the islander dying, Balthazar showing up at the picnic with rifles? Father had lied to me about everything.

The angrier I got, the more thorny memories began to surface, like drowned bodies rising to the water's edge. I remembered his voice calling to Crusoe, *Here, boy, there's a good dog*, and the laboratory door locking shut with a quick, dull click. I remember how the servants' eyes were bloodshot and sunken on the mornings after he'd operated. The screaming kept them awake, too. But none of us ever spoke of it. Least of all Montgomery.

Thinking of Montgomery made my hands twist at the sheets. He'd spent almost half his life on the island. He must have known of my father's guilt. Why hadn't he told me? And then I remembered how he'd tried to talk me out of coming. He'd warned me without putting it into so many words. But I'd insisted. I'd said I'd have to sell myself on the streets if he didn't take me with him.

But was this any better? This terrible, anguished truth?

A painful bellow tore through the night. I kicked the sheets off, sweat pouring down my neck. Was it the sheepdog? I didn't know any creature that could make such an ungodly sound. As the screams dragged on, haunting my every breath, my mind started to wander to darker and darker places. Wondering what would cause an animal to scream like that. Imagining the beast spread out, shackled down, dotted lines traced on its skin in black ink. And why? What purpose did Father have for such wanton cruelty? He was beyond dissecting for knowledge's sake. He already knew every corpuscle, every bend of nerve. No, he wasn't studying. He had to be working on something new. Something different.

My mind searched for an answer among the moonlight splashes on the walls. Whatever experiment he was working on, it had begun in his laboratory on Belgrave Square when I was a child. Over the years he withdrew inside himself more, working later and later hours. Even when he was with us, his eyes would stray to the door, as if half his mind was always tethered to that laboratory. Whatever it was – his new discovery – it had consumed him enough to abandon everything else in his life. It was more important than his reputation, his wife, even his daughter.

It was this idea that drew me out of bed. After years of wondering what science he'd unlocked in that damp basement, a science that he loved even more than he loved me, I had a chance to *see it*. My feet swung into a pair of house shoes as though they had a mind of their own. The need to know pulled me like a puppet, commanding me to dress quickly, to open the door, to find out what my father was working on that had brought him to the edge of madness.

A single lantern hung in the courtyard, swinging softly in the breeze. It threw the light at odd angles, making shadows lengthen and then disappear. A faint glow came from beneath the laboratory door.

I waited until the lantern light dimmed, then darted around the portico, past the servants' bunkhouse and the barn to the laboratory, where I pressed my back to the tin wall. The thrill of finally learning Father's secrets took little bites out of me, making me feel savage. The screaming had stopped, but my head pounded, clouding my senses. A low, mournful sob began from within, then grew into an ear-splitting wail. I dug my palms against my ears.

This was madness. This curiosity inside me was unnatural. It had pushed me further from my mother, further from reason and rules and logic. But there were times I still couldn't resist it.

I rested my forehead against the wall and closed my eyes. It wasn't just my curiosity, or my fascination with anatomy, or how I could unhesitatingly chop a rabbit's head off with an ax when a roomful of boys couldn't. Those things were all symptoms of the same sickness – a kind of madness inherited from my father. It was a dangerous pull in my gut drawing me toward the dark possibilities of science, toward the thin line between life

147

and death, toward the animal impulses hidden behind a corset and a smile.

Turn back, I heard Mother whispering. *It's wrong, what he's doing.* But she was no longer here to scold me. I was free from her and society and the watching eyes of the church. I could do whatever I wanted. But what *did* I want? To follow that slithering curiosity to Father's laboratory door, or to listen to Mother's ghost and go back to bed where I could close my ears to the screaming?

One last wail came from the laboratory. Air slipped from my lungs. A tuft of snow-white fur blew slowly across the stone portico. I picked it up and rubbed it between my fingers. Next to me the dark entrance to the barn gaped like a chasm. I peered inside cautiously.

Out of the darkness came a white shape, hopping to the edge of the barn, just inches from my toes. One of the rabbits. Somehow, it had escaped its cage.

Father didn't eat rabbits. They were intended, rather, for the sharpened blade of a scalpel. To pursue science. But the difference was that my father wasn't accused of practicing *science*. He'd been accused of *butchery*. He'd already crossed that forbidden line long ago. And I couldn't lie down on my feather mattress and just listen to it. To understand my own curiosity, I needed to understand his.

I returned to the laboratory. The tin door had the same latching doorknob as the rest of the buildings. I squeezed it slowly with bated breath. I felt the latch catch and release. It opened in my hand, silent as the night, but I dared not enter.

The sharp smells of rubbing alcohol and formaldehyde slipped from the cracked doorway. In an instant, I was a little girl again, sneaking into her father's laboratory. The memory was so strong, I almost shut the door and ran back to my room.

But a whisper came from the dark.

I held my breath to keep the smells at bay. Peeking through the cracked door, my eyes adjusted slowly. At the end of the room, a shadowy figure stood over a wooden operating table surrounded by a lantern and candles on a high shelf. The candlelight reflected in dozens of dark glass jars lining the walls, like the glowing prayer candles in a dark cathedral. Only these jars didn't hold votives, but things I could only imagine.

Specimens. Experiments. Nightmares.

And the figure at the front, the unholy priest, was my father. His back was to me, but I knew the tight set of his shoulders and shape of his head. Whatever was on the table was half covered by a sheet, and all I could make out was the shape of thin limbs, the scarlet spill of blood on the sheet, a pile of towels at Father's feet, the silver gleam from the surgical instruments. The sound of fluid slowly dripping reminded me of the ticking clock in the dining room. Father said something in his low voice. I imagined more of his haunting commandments, some kind of terrible prayer, but it was only mental notes to himself. He lowered the blade to the table. The scalpel pressed against firm flesh, which gave, the muscle opening like butter.

The thing on the table jerked to life with a painful squeal. Its cry was a blade to my heart. Thick leather manacles bound its limbs to the corners, but it writhed wildly under the sheet. My sweaty palm slipped on the door latch. I wiped it on my skirt. As terrified as I was, my eyes were riveted to that table.

Father seemed unfazed by the thing's torment. The manacles strained and rattled, but they held. Father kept cutting, a slice here, another there, as graceful as an orchestra conductor. He hummed a few notes of a melody. *The Chopin piece*, I realized with a sickening lurch. I caught only glimpses as his hands flew over the creature. A flap of skin, pale and still dripping with subcutaneous fat, pulled back on its shin. A white bit of bone flashing in the candlelight. Father covered it with a towel to stanch the blood, but the towel soaked quickly. He peeled it off carefully and dropped it into the growing pile at his feet. So much blood. It made me tipsy. For a moment my thoughts slipped out of my control, into a primal hunger. *What was he doing?* This wasn't just vivisection. It was much more than that.

He was *creating* something.

He stepped away, clearing my line of vision. I got a look at the leg under the sheet, and my throat tightened. Instead of toes, there hung a stump wrapped in a bloody bandage. *No, no, this is wrong.* It was my own voice now, not Mother's. It didn't matter what he had discovered, what higher purpose he thought he was following. He'd crossed the line into a place you couldn't come back from.

The thing's skin looked pale, sickly. He must have shaved the creature, because its leg looked almost human except for the twisting hinge of the knee. I swallowed – I'd seen that same awkward twist before, in Balthazar and the other islanders' lurching limbs.

It couldn't be a coincidence. An inkling of what he was doing in that laboratory ruffled my thoughts. He was operating on the islanders . . . but why?

Father came back with a wooden clamp that he set over the ankle, holding it still. The toneless humming faded as he pressed his fingers delicately along either side of the knee. With a grunt, he threw his weight against the leg and cracked the knee socket, buckling it against the brace.

I cried out. I couldn't help myself. But the creature's wail matched my own and drowned my voice. Its cry rattled the glass cabinets. A candle fell from the shelf and crashed onto Father's hand. He cursed and jerked his hand back, knocking the sheet off the creature.

I looked away, but it was too late – I'd already seen the animal body stretched out unnaturally, limbs splayed like a human's. Impossible to tell what creature it was or had once been.

My stomach threatened to bring up supper. I blinked back angry, frightened tears. Frightened for the beast, and frightened for myself – for inheriting my father's sick curiosity. I should have run back to my room and forgotten all of it. It wasn't the blood or the flesh that made me sick, but what he was doing. Evil. He was what they said he was. A madman. A demon.

A monster.

Through the crack in the door came his voice.

'Blasted devil. Boy, come hold it down!'

He was speaking to someone. I pressed my eye against the door crack. The thing on the table had worked free of one manacle and was rattling the table in an effort to get loose. A second figure appeared from some dark corner, looking ghostly through the screen of my tears. As he approached the candlelight, I recognized the blond hair falling into his eyes, the handsome tanned face. He threw his weight on the thing on the table, pinning it down, and jabbed a needle into its arm. My heart shot to my throat.

Montgomery. He was more than just aware of Father's experiments – he was *assisting* him. I squeezed my eyes shut.

Not Montgomery.

My knee slid and knocked into the tin laboratory door. It shook with a loud metallic tremble that made my breath catch. I dared a glance into the laboratory to see Father turn, peering keenly at the crack in the door.

'Who's there?' he barked. And then, 'Find out, Montgomery. Use the dogs if you must.'

I slammed the door shut. My limbs screamed to get away. *Run.*

151

But where to? The gate was locked. I was trapped.

I dashed into the warm darkness of the barn, hiding, fleeing, pacing. I glanced at the roof. It was thatch, so there was a chance I could climb through. The wilderness beyond was uncertain, but that was better than the certainty of what was happening in the laboratory. I grabbed a pitchfork and, balanced on top of a sawhorse, thrust it through the roof, dodging falling straw and sticks, until a shaft of moonlight poured through the hole. I hoisted myself up onto the wide rafter beams, kicking my feet, and pulled myself through the thatch into the warm night air.

It didn't matter what was out there as long as it was away from the truth.

Heavy footsteps sounded in the courtyard. Montgomery. He'd soon find out I was gone and hunt me down with the bloodhounds. He'd drag me back to Father's nightmare in minutes.

I climbed down into the barn again, kicked off the hutch latch, and pulled out two kicking rabbits. They squirmed in my hands. I climbed back onto the sawhorse and pushed them through the thatch hole, then went back for the rest before pulling myself after them. The rabbits wouldn't stop the dogs, but they might slow them down.

I dropped to the ground. Pain shot through my shins. Then I was tearing blindly through the jungle.

NINETEEN

I didn't stop running until the first rays of daylight broke through the canopy. The dogs' barking, distant as ghosts, might only have been my imagination. Closer, the sound of water led me to a stream. I collapsed on the bank to fill my dry throat with cool water.

That frantic night before, under moonlight echoing with the sound of screams, fleeing had seemed imperative. But in daylight I doubted my decision. My arms were covered with red scratches. I knew my face must look the same. The house shoes were little more than shreds. I peeled them off, wincing, and tossed them into the stream. They'd be useless to me now. I eased my bruised feet into the water. I buried my face in my hands, losing myself in the rushing sound of the stream.

A hand touched my shoulder.

I jerked up, ready to scream, but just as fast another hand was covering my mouth.

'Shh. It's me.'

Panic made me twist away, tearing Mother's dress against the river stones. 'Edward!'

Sweat ran down his face from running. I could only stare

as if he were a ghost. He'd followed me. My dream came back, the blood on his hands, that cold kiss.

'What are you doing here?' I asked between breaths.

'I saw you from my window tearing through the jungle like a demon was after you.' He splashed water over his face and neck and wiped it off with his cuff. 'I came after you. It's not safe out here, Juliet—'

'Did you see? Inside the laboratory?'

He paused. Took in my bruised feet, my torn dress. 'No, but I heard the screams. I can guess what he was doing in there. I told you there was no good reason for a doctor to live in such a remote place. But you shouldn't have run. It's dangerous. I couldn't bear for you to get hurt . . .'

My heart wrenched a little that he'd risked his own safety to come after me. And then I remembered why I had run. How my curiosity had pulled me to that laboratory like a hungry animal to a fresh kill. I shuddered, disgusted with myself.

'I had to get away.' I rubbed the life back into my aching feet, pushing hard until I felt sparks of pain. 'I saw something I wish I hadn't.' I looked him in the eye, wondering if he was strong enough to deal with the truth. He'd survived twenty days at sea. He'd had the courage to run away from a wealthy life – not an easy feat. Something in me wanted to test his strength, to see just how much he could take.

He lowered his voice. 'What did you see?'

I closed my eyes and replayed the scene from the laboratory. The twisted limbs, just like Balthazar and the rest of the islanders. All the caged animals. My head had suspected the connection, even though my heart didn't want to believe it: Father might be creating things – *creatures* – out of vivisected animals.

I shook my head. 'It doesn't matter. I can't go back there.

I thought there might be other people on the island. The missionaries, maybe . . .'

'It's dangerous out here. People are dying.'

I frowned. 'That islander who was killed? Father said it was an accident.'

'It was no accident. No one accidentally has his heart clawed out of his chest.'

My spine went rigid, forcing me to my feet. I paced without even meaning to. I'd suspected Father hadn't told me the truth, but not like this. 'What do you mean?'

'They found the body near the beach. Three claw marks to the chest. Not the first one, either. They're still finding some of the bodies. Puck told me some terrible stories.'

I glanced at the dark jungle. It wasn't the dogs Edward was worried about, but a dangerous wild animal. I remembered the bandoliers around Balthazar's chest. Father eating a strawberry slowly, telling me it was nothing to worry about.

I shook my head. 'Montgomery would have said something. He wouldn't have let me come if it was dangerous.'

'Montgomery's been away six months. He didn't know,' Edward continued. 'Neither he nor your father knows what's killing people. That's why I came after you. We have to go back before it finds us.'

'No! I can't face him. Don't you understand? I don't want to ever see him again.'

'It's better than getting clawed to death!' He took a deep breath. 'You need to go back. Whatever you saw in that laboratory, pretend you didn't. Just long enough until we can think of a way off the island.'

'You don't understand,' I said bitterly. 'They lied to me – Father, Montgomery. Ever since I was a little girl, I've heard rumors . . . there was a scandal . . .' I shook my head. Tears were threatening to spill, and I hated myself for the vulnerability. Years of my life had hinged on this one question: What type of man was my father?

And now I knew.

But Edward didn't. He thought I'd simply come to reunite with an estranged father. I leaned forward, cupping my face. 'You don't understand.'

He paused. The tic in his jaw started. 'I know about the scandal,' he said.

My head jerked up. 'How?'

He studied me as if anticipating my reaction. 'When I was in London—'

Something growled in the trees, silencing him. I lost my footing and nearly slipped into the creek. It was an ungodly noise, not human or animal.

Edward flexed his still-bruised knuckles, his words forgotten. 'We have to go back. Can you run?' He glanced at my bare feet.

'I'll manage.'

We tore through the jungle. The ground sloped downhill and we stumbled over vines, over thorns, through dense foliage that clawed at our limbs and tangled our feet. I tripped on a twisted root and slammed into the ground, my knee finding a sharp rock, my hands sinking into the moist layers of rotting leaves. I wiped the stains of the island on my dress as Edward pulled me to my feet.

'Sh,' he said. 'Listen.'

We stood together, my head so close to his chest that I could hear the thump of his heart. There were always sounds in the jungle. Insects. Birds. Creaks and cracking, like whispers. As if someone was always following, watching from the ever-present screen of leaves.

'I thought I heard . . .' His whisper trailed off. For a moment it was just us and our heartbeats in the wilderness.

And then the thing snarled again, sudden and shrill. I could feel its rabid excitement.

Whatever it was, it had caught our trail.

We darted in and out of the foliage, making our way along the narrow spaces between trees, following the slope downhill. As if the island were guiding us. To where, I didn't know.

I glanced back fleetingly, wondering what it was – a wild animal or something worse. But the jungle was too dense. It could have been a stone's throw away and I wouldn't have seen it.

My feet screamed for relief. We came to another stream, and Edward dashed across some rocks, but I paused for a second to catch my breath with my aching feet in the cool water. My heart thudded in my ears. When I looked up, Edward had disappeared amid the undergrowth.

Behind me the thing screamed.

'Edward!' I called. But the rush of the stream drowned my words. I struggled out of the water, slipping on the mud. My fingers clawed at the soft bank. The twisting thorns along the side tangled in my hair, grabbing at my dress, carving their mark into my arms. The island had its claim on me. I tore at the thorns with my bare hands, feeling stings of pain but not caring. The island wasn't going to make me its prisoner.

A vine of thorns snapped back and struck me across the face. I stumbled back into the water, gasping for breath.

If the island wasn't going to let me through to Edward, I'd find another way. I moved with the stream, fast as I could, following its winding bed. The water would wash away my scent, I realized. There'd be nothing for any animals to follow.

Except Edward's trail.

I tried to tell myself he'd be fine. He was stronger than he looked. He was a survivor.

I stopped to catch my breath. For what felt like hours I stood, listening, hearing nothing. Whatever had been pursuing us, I'd lost it. I sank into the water, letting it soak me through, and mixed my tears with the stream water of the island.

Later, I followed the twists and turns of the stream until my feet were numb. I found a gnarled stick to use as a crutch for my left foot, which bled from a gash on the toe. My thoughts grew more frantic with each hobbling step forward. I listened for the dogs, to find my way back to the compound. It would mean facing Father, swallowing back my disgust and disappointment and fear, but at least I'd be alive. Why hadn't he told me the truth about the deaths?

What else might he be lying about?

One way or another my whole life had led to this moment, to *him*, and now I had nothing. I couldn't return to London. I couldn't even be sure about Montgomery anymore.

It was useless anyway. I was hopelessly lost and hadn't heard the dogs for hours.

The stream turned, and a rotting footbridge with a handrail blocked my progress.

I stopped, surprised. A bridge meant people. This one clearly hadn't been used in years, but it was far enough from the compound and old enough that it couldn't be my father's doing. I glanced through the woods, wondering who had built it and if they were still alive – and if they were dangerous. All I could hear was the trickle of water and wind in the trees.

I climbed out of the stream. The ground here was softer, and I followed it cautiously until I broke out of the jungle into a grassy clearing.

A cabin sat decaying in the middle of the clearing.

I stopped.

My feet didn't dare go any closer, though I knew there

might be something useful inside. I tried to remember what Father had said about the island's previous inhabitants. The Spanish who had built the fort. The Anglican missionaries who came later. Father said they'd all gone – what exactly had happened to them, he'd neglected to say.

I circled the cabin cautiously. The soft blades of grass felt like down feathers on my bruised and bloody feet. A support beam had collapsed and the roof sagged on one end. The tin roofing was rusted and eaten away in places. No one could live here now, but the previous occupants might have left an old pair of shoes. Maybe a knife. I'd settle for a strong board with a rusty nail – anything I could use as a weapon.

I hobbled toward the cabin. The wooden steps had long ago rotted and collapsed. I set my stick aside and pulled myself onto the bowed porch. The soles of my feet left bloody prints on the rough old boards, which protested under my weight as I crossed to the doorway. The door hung open a few inches. I only had to push it a little farther.

The hinges groaned, sending gooseflesh over my skin. I peered inside. The interior was as dilapidated as the outside. It was sparsely furnished – a low table, a wooden bed frame. No sign of inhabitants. I stepped inside but felt a tug at my skirt. With a shriek I ripped it away, but it had only caught on a nail in the doorframe. A snag of dingy fur was also caught on the nail.

My throat tightened. Just because the cabin had been abandoned by people didn't mean some wild animal hadn't taken up occupancy.

A wild animal . . . maybe one that was killing the islanders by clawing their chests. I glanced around the clearing, looking for signs I was being watched. Not a blade of grass rustled. I slipped in anyway and closed the door behind me, breathless. There was a crude wooden latch attached to the door that I fumbled to twist closed.

Sunlight poured in from rusted-out patches in the roof, throwing puddles of light on the room. Dust danced in the hazy air.

My breath began to calm. I was alone, I told myself. I cleaned the cabin's one dirty window with the edge of my sleeve. Outside there was nothing but empty porch and my walking stick leaning against a post.

On the table was a nub of tallow candle and a grimy green bottle filled with dust and the petrified husks of flying insects. I spied a cupboard in the corner and twisted open the latch. The door came off in my hand, and a heavy, rusted wrench spilled out at my feet, just missing my toes. I jumped back, my heart in my throat. Several more tools tumbled out with a dull crash of metal. I stooped to look. A claw-headed hammer. A railroad spike. A rusted pair of shears. My hand closed over the shears. Though the blades were dull, they could be used as a weapon. I slipped it into my pocket.

I turned to the bed and sucked in a quick breath. The remnants of a straw mattress and old quilt were matted with thick yellow fur. Something had made a den out of the bed – some animal. Images jumped to mind of a savage beast with claws big enough to slice a man open.

I fumbled with my skirt pocket and pulled out the shears. With my other hand I touched the quilt, hesitantly. The fur felt gritty and rough against my fingers. A creature lived here.

And it might return.

A desperate need to flee pulled at my gut. When I turned, I caught sight of something startlingly white on the mantel above the caved-in fireplace. I stepped closer to see what it was.

On the mantel was a small glass bottle, broken at the top, filled halfway with water. In the bottle was a single fresh white flower.

No animal could do that. Someone had been here. A human.

A chill seized me.

This wasn't the den of some wild animal – it was the filthy home of some person. I hurled myself at the door. But the wooden latch wouldn't turn.

A creak sounded from the porch. I pulled back my hand as though the latch were on fire. My body went still as stone. I closed my eyes.

I waited.

I licked some moisture back into my quivering lips.

Another creak. And another, slow as the shallow breaths I took. Someone was walking on the bowed wooden boards on the other side of the door.

My eyes flew open. I dared not take a step and make my presence known. From my position I could see out of the window's corner. The shadow of a tall figure stretched across the porch.

The latch rattled.

I shrank into myself, feeling a silent scream coming from every pore in my skin. There was no other way out of the cabin. The window was on the same side as the door, and the chimney had fallen in. I looked up into the dappled sunlight blinding my eyes. The roof would never take my weight.

The latch rattled again.

I fought against consuming fear. Panic would get me nowhere. I needed my head. He'd be bigger than me, no doubt, so I couldn't overpower him. The shears were an extension of my hand, deadly and ready to strike. I needed to catch him by surprise as soon as the door opened. Strike something essential but soft, easy to damage with the shears. His abdomen. No – his eyes. I could get away easier from a blind attacker.

The latch rattled again, harder this time. Sweat rolled down the sides of my face. Somewhere beneath the fear, there was a thrill. I could almost taste it, like chimney ash. In the next minute, I might blind a man with my own hands. It made me feel savage and powerful.

Outside, somewhere in the jungle, one of the bloodhounds howled. A small ripple of hope.

Suddenly the door went still. The dog howled again, and then several more joined it. They had picked up a scent. I tried to peer out the window but saw nothing. The shears were slick in my sweating palm.

Then, as sudden as they had come, the footsteps left.

I waited ten seconds. Twenty. I lost count. Still, the door-knob did not move. I forced my legs to walk to the window. The porch outside was totally empty.

Had the dogs frightened him off? Or was he just around the corner, waiting for me? I stood still as long as I could before the dust dancing in the air began to choke me like poison. I pounded at the latch with the shears until I could twist it. Slowly, I inched open the door. Sweat rolled off my face and soaked my blouse. I took a step onto the porch.

There was no one there. He'd gone. But he'd left behind wet footprints on the sagging wooden porch, interspersed with my own bloody prints. I crouched down to study the print closest to the door. It dwarfed my own. He'd been barefoot, which was strange. Stranger still was the number of toes.

One, two, three.

TWENTY

I jerked up from the porch floor, searching the jungle. An eerie feeling of watching eyes crept over me. The island was full of life, and yet I saw none of it. The living things here had a way of creeping silently, like ghosts, keeping to the shadows, whispering. The spaces between the leaves could hold all kinds of dangers.

I snatched the walking stick and jumped off the porch, wincing as my tender bare soles connected with the ground. I hurried to the edge of the clearing. Sweat poured down my neck, pooling in the space between my breasts. Ahead, the grass bent from someone recently having passed through. An insect trilled behind me. The jungle watched my every move.

I turned and cut across the clearing, following the direction of the dogs' barking. Tall blades of grass slashed at my skirt. Through breaks in the trees I could see the volcano plume, but there should have been a second column of smoke from the compound's chimney. Either the fire wasn't going or I was too far away. I decided to circle the island until I found a road. The terrain flattened gradually as I neared the coast, but I hit a patch of dense brambles. My walking stick became a machete. At least beating back the vines gave me a distraction from not knowing which way to go. And not knowing if Edward was all right.

He might be wandering the island, lost like me. *I know about the scandal*, he'd said. But if that was so, why hadn't he said anything earlier? Why had he agreed to come if he knew my father was a madman?

I beat back another bramble with my walking stick. Edward Prince was as difficult to figure out as the twists and turns in the jungle labyrinth. Every direction looked the same. Big, woolly vines clung to the trunks of many-armed trees. Brambles tangled like a wild horse's mane.

A cry sounded in the distance, and a bolt of fear propelled me forward into a run. The three-toed creature was still out there – man or beast or murderer, I didn't know. Maybe watching, even now. Waiting for nightfall. Following my steps like a phantom. The faster I ran, the greater the fear swelled. I wiped slick sweat off my forehead but more took its place. I started sprinting, faster and faster, until I crashed into a copse of leafy stalks. When I fought my way through, I found myself next to a small, winding stream.

I sank on the bank. The thump of my pulse was deafening. A bird warbled, and then another. But no phantom pursuer crashed through the jungle behind me. My breath slowed.

I splashed water on my burning face and lay back on the moss and leaves, letting my lungs fill with air. Nothing about the island was predictable. It was as alive as a person, full of whims and lies and contradictions. I didn't know what to trust. Each snap sounded like a pursuer. Every half-trampled path led to nothing. How could I even trust my own instincts? They had led me to the island to test some theory – some desperate hope – that the world had been wrong about my father.

My instincts had been wrong.

My vision was blurry and my head pounded – I'd missed my injection that morning. I wiped my face and noticed a streak of red on my arm. Blood bubbled from the thorn scratches. I touched my forehead, my cheeks, my neck. Blood stuck to my skin like tar. I'd become prey to the island but, as in my dream, I felt no pain. Only a fascination with the webs of slashes and bloody marks on my body. I was sliding, slipping away from humanity.

Had my father slid the same way?

Something fast and damp darted across my hand. I sat up with a shriek. Across the stream, something flashed again, then closer, moving incredibly fast. It was about the size of a rat but of an odd fleshy color. The longer I sat still, the more creatures appeared, slinking around on the other side of the stream. I bent forward slowly to take a drink, cupping the water in my hands, and looked up to find one standing on its hind legs on a rock, head cocked. I gasped. Not afraid, just bewildered. I'd never seen anything like it. It was a little smaller than a rat, furless, with a face like a snapping turtle. The thing squawked and disappeared back into the foliage. For a few moments, not a single leaf rustled.

Biologists discovered new species all the time, but these rats seemed unnatural somehow. My thoughts were so consumed that I hardly noticed that the water had turned a dark tint like rust. The little creatures congregated on the other stream bank, leaping and chattering.

'What are you so excited about?' I muttered, wading over to them. The creatures scattered, revealing a mauled chunk of flesh and fur – one of the rabbits I'd set free. I jolted in surprise. It was ripped apart but uneaten. Blood still trickled into the stream.

A recent kill.

Something much bigger than the rat things was responsible. Maybe something with three claws, big enough to kill the islanders. I scurried to the opposite bank, tunneling into a thicket of bamboo to hide. The ratlike creatures vanished. The jungle filled with the trickling sound of water and the ever-present calls of birds. Slowly, I made out two voices.

Arguing.

The voices had a strange, rough lilt, like Balthazar's. *Thou shalt not crawl in the dirt*, I remembered him saying. *Thou shalt not kill other men.* The voices of islanders, which meant they were likely loyal to my father and could take me to the compound. But something held me back. There was no proof the murderer was a wild animal. It wouldn't be hard for a man to disguise knife wounds to look like claw marks.

I crept closer, silently.

'He says, Caesar,' one of them said.

'Shalt not eat flesh. Shalt not eat flesh. Nonsense,' another answered.

My chest pressed to the rotting leaves. Between the twisted roots, I made out two figures with their backs to me. Islanders for sure. They shuffled as they argued, making quick, awkward movements. The underbrush hid their bottom halves, so I couldn't see if they were barefoot or count the number of toes.

Through the screen of leaves I could tell one of the men was about Balthazar's size, perhaps even larger, with matted black hair and a canvas jacket like Montgomery's. The other was smaller, with a dingy white shirt. His straw-colored hair was gathered messily at the nape of his neck. These men were even more malformed than the servants at the compound. I reached into my pocket for the shears, just in case.

'Shalt not eat flesh,' the large one grunted, motioning to something in the other's hand. I saw a flash of white – the rabbit's head. A drop of sweat rolled down my face. Montgomery had said they didn't eat meat, but ripping a rabbit in half didn't sound like the actions of a vegetarian. 'Shalt not kill,' he added.

These men were not my allies, that was clear. But it was too risky to creep back to the stream. All it took was one snap of a branch to give me away.

The blond one growled and waved the rabbit head around. 'Nonsense! Nonsense!' He walked more gracefully than the other. His nimble, quick movements reminded me of the panther on the *Curitiba*, pacing, pacing, tensed to spring at any moment. The bigger man lumbered as if he wasn't used to his own feet. They continued arguing.

As terrified as I was, I couldn't take my eyes off them. One of Darwin's books talked about a link between animals and humans, even suggested we came from some primordial animal-like form. These men could be holdovers, evidence of Darwin's theories. Yet I couldn't forget the same odd twist of limb on Father's operating table. So were they creatures from Darwin's theories – or my father's laboratory? The idea hit me with a stab of pain between the eyes. If my crazy idea was right, if Father was *creating* creatures out of the caged animals . . . No. Such things weren't possible.

I felt a sharp prick on my leg and held in a gasp. An ant must have gotten under my skirt. Well, I'd just have to let it bite me. But then something larger moved – a lump the size of my fist, crawling up my leg, making the fabric roll like a wave. Something smooth, like a fleshy hand, brushed against the bare skin of my thigh.

I nearly jumped out of my skin. I shook the skirt frantically until one of the little rat beasts fell out. It scurried away and disappeared under a rotting log. My hands were still shaking. Then I remembered the men and hugged the ground again. Ahead, the smaller man had turned and keenly watched my thicket.

My stomach leapt to my throat. I didn't know if he'd seen

me. In any case, I could clearly see their faces now, and they were horrible to look at. The dark-haired man had Balthazar's same bearlike protruding jaw, though more slovenly, with a tooth the size of my thumb sticking out of his bottom lip.

The blond man's face was equally strange, yet I couldn't look away. His skin was covered in fine yellow hair with faint brown markings. His piercing eyes were set deep below a heavy brow. His nose was wide but flat, giving him a powerful, leonine look. Pointed incisors gleamed as he wrinkled his nose to sniff the air.

My breath caught. So this was what Montgomery had been so afraid of. The guns, the worried glances into the jungle. He and Father were frightened of these creatures.

The blond man looked directly toward my hiding spot. His companion snorted and began to speak, but the small one silenced him with a paw on his arm. He stared at me like a hunter, nose flaring, eyes narrowed. And then he grabbed the black-haired man's jacket and pulled him sharply away into the trees. In a second, all trace of them had vanished.

It was some time before I could think clearly again. Dusk had fallen and the forest was shrouded with haze. The men might have looped back and could be stalking me even now. If they were there, watching, waiting, there wasn't anything I could do about it but keep moving. Shakily, I made my way to the stream. Finding a safe place to spend the night seemed impossible.

As I followed the stream deeper into the island, I heard the sound of falling water. A clearing opened ahead. Moonlight reflected on a waterfall tumbling into a deep pool. After I'd spent so long in the dark tunnel of the trees, the moonlight shone with a silver tint that made everything dreamlike. There was something odd about the waterfall, something extra luminous, as though it glowed from within.

A rocky bank hugged the falls, and I carefully climbed it, feet slipping on the slick rocks. The roar of the water was deafening. I made it to an outcropping, balancing unsteadily on the pitched rock.

There was a gap behind the falls, just wide enough for a person to slip through. I peered inside. The red glow of flames met me.

'Is that fire?' I muttered. But two hands thrust from behind the waterfall, grabbed my shoulders, and pulled me through the screen of water.

TWENTY-ONE

Sputtering, I fought my attacker, but the rush of water blinded me. Then the water was gone, and I was in a shallow cave lit by a small fire.

'Edward!' I said. A gash ran up the side of his shirt and blood stained the knees of his trousers, but, even weary and spent, I threw my arms around him, not thinking, just needing to feel that he was real.

'I was afraid it had gotten you,' I said.

'I'm faster than that.'

My fingers curled around his dirty shirt, pulling at the fabric. I wished I could express how relieved I was to feel his arms around me.

His fingers found my waist, inching me closer, and for a moment I didn't think about impropriety. The rules of society couldn't reach us here beyond the falls. I pulled back to ask if he was all right, but the breathless desire written on his face stole my words. Before I could put together a coherent thought, he kissed me.

His lips were cold like in my dream. I was stunned, barely able to think as his hands pulled tighter on my waist. And then as quick as he'd kissed me, I pushed away and stumbled to the other side of the cave.

I'd felt a shiver from the touch of his lips that I hadn't expected. A surprisingly welcome one.

'Juliet—' he said, half filled with apology, half with lingering desire. 'I'm sorry. I thought—'

'Don't say anything else,' I said. The rushing water was deafening. 'Just forget it happened.'

He paced, somewhat frantically, as though he wanted to come closer but knew he shouldn't. 'I don't want to forget.'

'Edward, please . . .' I slumped against the cold stone, eyes closed. Water had seeped into the inner layers of my clothes, giving me a rash of gooseflesh.

He stopped pacing. 'It's Montgomery, isn't it? You like him.' The fire sent sparks dancing in his gold-flecked eyes as he waited for me to deny it, but I didn't. I didn't know how I felt about any of this. I needed time to think, to analyze . . .

'You said he used to be your servant,' Edward interrupted my thoughts. 'That there was nothing between you.'

'There isn't. Not yet. God, I don't know.'

Edward raised his voice above the roaring water. 'He was in the laboratory, wasn't he? Helping create those aberrations. He's as bad as your father, Juliet! How can you love him?'

'I never said I loved him!'

My pulse quickened with all the boiling arguments forming in my head, but then I paused. Something Edward had said didn't sit right. 'How do you know what they were doing in the laboratory? You said you didn't see.'

A wave of guilt washed over his face and I knew, in that look, he'd been lying. Embers from the fire littered the ground, disturbed by my struggling. He knelt to rebuild it, avoiding my gaze.

171

I watched him sweep the embers together, jerking his hands back to keep from being burned. 'How long have you known?' I asked, trying to keep my voice calm.

He stood slowly, brushing his hands against his trousers. Firelight danced in his eyes. For a moment, we just looked at each other. He was gauging my reaction. Trying to decide how much to tell me.

'Since the *Curitiba*,' he said. 'Since the first time Montgomery said the name Moreau.' He flexed his scarred knuckles nervously, starting to pace again. 'My uncle was acquainted with one of the detectives at Scotland Yard who worked on that case. The King's College Butchery, they called it. They kept it quiet, but they suspected your father was trying to stitch together animals to create something human – more or less. It used to give me nightmares as a boy. And when I saw Balthazar and the other islanders, I knew.' His eyes flashed. He was not just the naive young man everyone had first taken him for – but I'd known there was more to him. 'Scotland Yard's theory was right.'

'Balthazar's my friend,' I shot. 'He's no creation of surgery.'

'Your *friend*? He's a monster!'

I brushed the spray and tears and sweat off my face. Edward didn't know Balthazar like I did. Balthazar might be malformed, but he wasn't a monster.

'He's not,' I said. 'Cymbeline – he's just a little boy. That scaly man . . .'

'Puck,' Edward said.

'Puck.' I kicked at a glowing coal. Like the name of the sprite in *A Midsummer Night's Dream*. A fitting name, since his existence was as unbelievable as any fairy tale. 'They're not all monsters.'

'You're making excuses for your father,' Edward said, his voice rising. We were shouting, but no longer because of the waterfall. 'Trying to justify his work.'

172

'You knew the truth and didn't tell me!' I hugged my arms around my chest, turning toward the falls, letting the rush of water drown my thoughts. Edward was wrong – I wasn't defending my father. I was defending the part of me that knew what my father did was evil but was terribly proud that he'd accomplished it. My father's blood flowed in my veins, too. Didn't he understand that?

It stung. A stranger knew the truth I'd searched for my whole life. 'You should have told me.'

'Why do you think I came here?' he yelled. 'I could have stayed on the *Curitiba*. Did you think I was so afraid of that idiot captain? I came because you didn't know what you were getting into! You were walking into a danger with your eyes closed, not wanting to see the evidence so clearly in front of you.'

I paced, hugging my arms tighter. He'd been right, I realized. I had known all along, in those deep recesses of my brain. It had been my heart – my weak, human heart – that had betrayed me, not my head.

Edward hadn't lied to me. I'd lied to myself.

I ran a shaky hand over my face, feeling like the world had flipped upside down. 'You should have stayed on the *Curitiba*, then. There's nothing for you here.'

'I came here for you, Juliet!' He was so close to the falls that water danced on his shoulders like fine rain. He wiped the spray from his eyes. 'I came because I couldn't stop thinking about you. I still can't.'

For a moment, the water roared around us. He'd come here, knowing my father was a madman, for *me*. My heart thumped so loudly, I thought the whole jungle must hear it. I touched my lips, wet from the waterfall's spray, still cold from his kiss. Still *wanting*. But this was wrong. My heart belonged to Montgomery, not Edward. But Montgomery had been helping my father do his terrible work. So much had happened that I was unable to decipher my own feelings.

I sat down at the edge of the cave, closing my eyes, sealing out the rush of emotion.

Edward paced a bit more and then sighed. He eased himself down beside me, wincing.

'You're hurt,' I said at last. Hoping to change the subject.

'I tripped after we got separated. I might have cracked a rib.'

I picked up a thin twig from the cave floor, twirling it in my fingers. Trying not to think about how Montgomery was helping my father while Edward, who'd come to protect me, had just kissed me.

After a minute Edward pulled a steak knife out of his pocket.

'Where did you get that knife?' I asked.

'While you were chatting over dinner, I was stealing the silverware.' He started to whittle at the pointed end of a stick. Trying to make a spear. God, were we that desperate? His grip was too tight. He didn't know what he was doing any more than I did. He'd probably only read about spears in *Robinson Crusoe*.

The twig stopped in my fingers. 'How did you know you'd need one?'

'Your father tried to kill me five minutes after I arrived. That was a pretty good indication.'

I rolled the twig between my fingers, scraping the thin bark with my thumbnail. At last I threw the stick into the fire.

'I came across two of the islanders in the jungle,' I said. 'They weren't like Balthazar or those big ones on the dock. They were wild. They killed one of the rabbits – ripped it in half. I don't know what they'd have done if they'd known I was there.' I shivered at the memory of the spotted one's piercing eyes. He'd looked directly into the bamboo grove. Had he really not seen me?

174

The knife paused in Edward's hand. 'That's strange. Montgomery said no one eats meat on the island.'

I'd had the same thought. I studied Edward, impressed that he wasn't scared out of his wits. Firelight danced across his strong features. His face belonged half cast in shadows, with warm light on the planes of his nose and forehead. He would have looked out of place in the bare electric lights that were becoming so popular in England. I wondered if we would ever again see London. In the small world of the cave behind the waterfall, it felt like we were the last two people on earth.

'So what do we do?' I asked. 'We can't stay out here forever. It'll be a year before another ship comes.'

'Other ships must pass nearby on the way to Australia or Fiji. Montgomery said there's a Polynesian shipping lane not far off the coast.'

'So we take our chances with a raft and hope a ship finds us?' I pulled my arms in tight, shivering. 'We'll drift off course. Or go down in a storm. Or die of thirst. You should know better than anyone.'

He sat back, staring into the fire. The tic in his jaw pulsed, just once. He'd spoken so little of what happened when the *Viola* sank. He didn't have to. It was written in the sun blisters that still marred his face. 'What choice do we have? Your father's gone mad out here. What's to say he won't find a use for us after all? Strapped to his operating table, perhaps.'

'He wouldn't do that. He's my *father*.' I didn't want to hear it. Didn't want to speculate how far Father had gone over that line.

Edward placed a finger on my cheek to turn my face back toward him. 'You know how I feel about you. You don't have to say anything in return – it doesn't matter. I came here to protect you and that's what I intend to do. Tomorrow we'll find our way back to the compound. We'll act like everything is fine – we just got lost in the jungle while exploring. And

175

then we'll find a way to get off this island.' He brushed my hair behind one ear. 'I won't let anything hurt you.'

I studied the tender new scar that ran just below his eye. His bruises had faded, but that didn't mean they weren't still there, under his skin, beaten into his bones.

'What was the photograph?' I asked before I could stop myself.

Surprise registered on his face for a second. And then the fold between his eyes deepened. 'What photograph?'

'You had a photograph. It was too water-damaged to make out. I haven't seen it since the ship.'

He gave a slight shrug, brow furrowed, as though thinking back to the time in the dinghy unsettled him. 'I don't remember any photograph.'

We stayed like that for some time, listening to the water in our own private world behind the falls. I didn't believe for a minute he'd forgotten the photograph, but the secret was his own, and so were his reasons for lying. The night got cooler, and my soaking dress made my skin turn white. I self-consciously stripped to my chemise to let the dress dry next to the fire. I was too aware of my bare ankles, my bare arms. Edward's eyes shone bright in the dying firelight, not like a gentleman anymore. But he didn't try to kiss me again.

The closeness of the cave pressed in, as hard as the memory of his kiss. I knew Edward wouldn't hurt me. And yet I didn't exactly feel at ease with him.

I lay down next to the fire, aware of every stone and crack in the ground. Edward lay down behind me, a respectful two feet away, but close enough that I could feel the heat from his body. I fell asleep to the sound of the roaring water and a thousand questions tumbling in my head.

I awoke halfway through the night to find the embers barely smoldering. Edward and I had found our way together in our sleep, my head against his chest, his hands wrapped fiercely around my waist, our legs scandalously intertwined. It wasn't safety I felt with him, no, more like a deep connection I didn't even understand. I had a vague memory, more like a dream, of him wrapping his arms around me, breathing in the scent of my hair, muttering against my cheek. I could have stopped him. But I kept my eyes closed instead, and held him closer.

In the morning Edward was gone. The coals were cold in the light filtering through the screen of water. The cave looked different in daytime, without shadows clinging to the dark corners. It was only a damp outcropping, bare except for clumping moss near the puddles and more spiders than I cared to notice.

The knife, which Edward had left by the fire while we slept, was gone too.

I peered through the gap in the falls. A young man's naked form bathed in the shallows of the pool. I jerked back with a gasp, embarrassed to see Edward undressed. I'd never seen a man naked before. The memory of his body against mine all night and the brief, unreturned kiss made me feel suddenly very warm.

I splashed water on my face from a puddle. Went to check on my dress. Washed the cuts on my arms. No matter how I tried to busy myself, I couldn't stop throwing glances at the waterfall.

'Oh, dash it.' I tiptoed back to the gap. My heart thumped in my ears.

He had his back to me. He waded up to his chest and ducked underwater, whooping as he came up, holding his hurt rib lightly. I'd never seen him so carefree. And I'd certainly never seen him so . . . exposed. He didn't have Montgomery's impressive physique, but there was something undeniably strong in his wiry arms. Arms that had held me last night.

I fanned a little air onto my face.

He scrubbed his head and climbed out of the pool. My fingers twirled the soft ribbon of my chemise's neckline, knowing I should stop watching. He might turn around at any minute. The thought gave me goosebumps.

He pulled his trousers and shirt down from a tree branch, taking care with his ribs, and dressed quickly. He started toward the waterfall and I hurried back to the makeshift fireplace to wait for him. I slipped my dress back on and closed my eyes, stilling my heart, imagining what Mother would say if she saw me now. I'd never held hands with a boy. I'd certainly never watched one bathing.

A centipede crept over my toe and I jumped. I realized Edward still hadn't returned. I went back to the gap in the falls, but the pool was empty, and there was no sign of Edward.

'Edward?' I called tentatively. No response. I scrambled down the side of the falls and into the jungle. My foot landed on a rotten yellow fruit. No sign of him.

'Edward, are you there?' I called again. A glint in the fallen leaves caught my eye and I hurried over. Half buried in the leaves was his silver steak knife. Fresh blood stained the blade.

I kicked at the leaves until I found footprints in the soft silt around the pool. Bare prints mixed with the deep tread of Edward's boots. They went every which way. Trying to follow them in the growing heat made me dizzy, dizzier still because I'd missed my injection for two days.

'Edward?' I called one more time. Only a bird shrieked in response.

TWENTY-TWO

I picked a direction and ran as fast as my bruised feet would take me. The shears were heavy in my pocket, but I was glad to have them. And the knife. All I could think of was that rabbit, ripped in half, when supposedly no one ate meat.

Someone had developed a taste for it, it seemed. And was now clawing apart anything with a pulse. I had to find the compound before whatever was lurking out there found me.

My foot slipped on another of the yellow fruits, and I stopped long enough to fill my pockets. I'd seen a bowl full of them in the compound, so they must be safe. It could be hours before I found anything to eat again. I planned to find a stream and follow it to the beach. If I circled the whole island and couldn't find the wagon road, I'd climb to the volcano's rim, or as close as I could get, and look for the compound from above.

A bird called overhead with a sharp, unnatural pitch. I caught glimpses of the ratlike creatures from the corners of my eyes. Had my father created them, too? Was the island filled not only with his lurching islanders but also with all manner of aberrations?

Presently I came across a pile of river stones marking some

kind of trail. I followed the narrow path until I found another pile of stones, where I stopped to rest. The yellow fruits had oozed and stained the inside of my pocket, but they were still edible. I ate a half dozen and dropped the slimy pits on the ground. A trill started up somewhere – an insect, or a bird. I squeezed the knife harder. Then I realized that anyone who saw the pile of pits would know I'd passed this way.

I threw them into the jungle to hide my trail. Satisfied, I wiped my sticky hands on my skirt. As I turned to go, one of the pits sailed back through the air in a graceful arc and landed at my feet.

I clutched the knife and spun around. Something was out there.

'Who's there?' I yelled. My palms were sweaty. I bit back my fear. *Aim for the eyes.*

A catlike snarl emerged behind me and I whirled. 'Come out! Show yourself!' I yelled.

A deep growl came from the brush. The leaves trembled. A figure slunk toward me, keeping to the mottled light, his hunched posture and spots making him nearly undetectable.

It was the blond islander. The one who'd killed the rabbit.

'You,' I breathed, brandishing the knife. Fear mixed with fascination. This walking, breathing creature had been created on my father's operating table. Somehow, my father had accomplished the impossible: turned animal into man – almost.

'Stay back,' I warned.

'"Come out." "Stay back." Make up your mind, girl.' His words came with a distinct hiss. I should have been afraid. I should have been *terrified*. But his mere existence – knowing what he really was – was so spellbinding that there wasn't room for fear.

'Don't come any closer,' I said, raising the knife. He emerged from the leaves but hunkered near the clearing's edge. His white shirt was roughly patched with scraps of linen. The sleeves were rolled to the elbow, revealing forearms covered with thick blond hair. For the first time I could see below his waist, where a tail flicked and swayed. A muscle in my back twitched involuntarily. *A tail.*

I studied the way he moved, so silent, so graceful. The perfect balance of animal and human. My gut tightened as I remembered standing on the *Curitiba*, watching the monkey. That was something I'd once longed for: a way for humans to share the talents of animals.

I was like my father in too many ways.

The creature came closer, recapturing my attention. 'If you try to hurt me, I'll slit your throat,' I threatened.

'Hurt you?' His lips curled into a snarl. 'There are better ways to hurt a lost girl than throwing fruit.'

'Who are you?' I snapped.

'Jaguar,' he pronounced.

'Jaguar? Didn't my father name you, like the others?'

'Jaguar,' he said again.

'Did he make you? Did he turn you into this? Answer me!'

'Lost girls must be careful. The jungle is dangerous, they say.'

A drip of sweat rolled down the back of my neck. He was trying to frighten me. But if he truly meant to attack, surely he would have done so already.

I kept a firm grip on the knife but lowered it. 'Why are you following me?' I asked.

He cocked his head. 'You were following *me*. You were in the bamboo. Watching.'

So he had seen. He could have attacked then, but he hadn't. I narrowed my eyes, wondering why. He curled his lips in response. He was smart, I realized. Smarter than most humans.

'Where is Edward?' I asked.

'The castaway.'

Surprise nearly made me drop the knife. *How did he know?*

My discomposure made him smile all the more. 'Montgomery told me about the castaway,' he said. 'Montgomery says watch the girl. Doesn't say watch the castaway.'

'When did you speak with Montgomery?'

'Questions. Questions. Come with me, now.'

His paw curled, beckoning. The tip of his tail twitched. I felt myself drawn toward his hypnotic yellow eyes. But I caught myself.

'I'm not going anywhere with you,' I said, squeezing the knife. 'This is madness.'

'It isn't safe without me.'

'It isn't safe *with* you!' I stepped back, a branch snapping under my foot. 'I'd sooner take my chances alone.'

'You don't know what hunts you.' His nose twitched. 'I do.'

His words were unsettling. On the whole of the island, I couldn't imagine any beast or man more terrifying than him. And yet, if he hadn't clawed those islanders to death – which I wasn't sure he *hadn't* – something else had.

'What's hunting me?' I asked cautiously.

'The monster,' he said, lips curled diabolically. I didn't know if he was as mad as my father or just toying with me. It was ludicrous, anyway. Talking to a walking experiment. Yet he hadn't tried to hurt me, which was more than I could say for some humans.

'I want to go to the compound,' I said.

He cocked his head. 'The Blood House.'

A tense breath escaped me. *Blood House.* There could be only one place he meant. The red laboratory.

'Come with me, now. No questions. No questions.'

I gave a shaky nod and waved him forward with the knife.

He moved through the undergrowth so silently that he hardly left a path for me to follow. My skirt caught every thorn. I made as much noise as ten of him. I studied the way he stepped, dissecting his movements. Ball of the foot first, then rolling back to the heel, which only grazed the ground. His body moved side to side, swaying almost imperceptibly but giving him better balance. I mimicked his steps and soon I was almost as quiet as him.

He wore no shoes. I'd counted his toes again and again, but always the same. Five. It hadn't been him stalking me at the cabin, but something else.

The monster.

Not once did he look back. At times his specter melted into the jungle like a shadow. I stumbled to keep up with him. My head ached. The heat was relentless. I lost my balance and held on to a tree branch to steady myself. The missed treatments were taking their toll. I could hear the roar of dizziness before I felt it, and then my vision disintegrated into black spots.

The coarse brush of his fur against my bare arm made me jump. I clutched the knife, though I was too weak to raise the blade. 'Stay back,' I said. My voice was barely audible above the blood rushing in my ears. 'I just need a moment to rest.'

But he came closer. I could smell his musty scent, like wool and unwashed man.

'You are unwell.' The warm moisture of his breath misted my neck.

'I'm only dizzy. It will pass.' My fingers squeezed the tender flesh inside my elbow.

The thick pads of his fingers grazed my forearm, turning my elbow gently. The knife in my weak hand flopped uselessly. I closed my eyes.

He ran a finger down the inside of my arm. There was

something familiar yet perverse about his touch. A creature like him shouldn't exist, and yet here we were, in the solitude of the trees.

He sniffed my arm. Something wet and warm nicked at the pinprick.

I jerked my eyes open.

He'd licked me.

'Let me go!' I pulled away.

'The doctor's medicine,' he said.

'Yes.' I clutched my inner elbow. My mouth hung open, searching for words. 'Just keep going.'

He's an animal, I reminded myself. *Dangerous.*

'As you wish.' He nodded.

I kept more distance between us as he led me deeper into a valley. There were only more trees, more vines, as far as I could see. We entered a copse of fernlike trees taller than my head. As his figure faded in and out of the wispy green fronds, I drifted farther back and farther still, until he was just a shadow far ahead.

Then I turned. I didn't know if he'd been taking me to the compound or not. I didn't know if he was the murderer or not.

I didn't intend to find out.

Using his calculated, silent steps, I vanished into the jungle.

TWENTY-THREE

I walked for hours. The jungle rose around me like a fortress of tree and stone. Through the canopy breaks I glimpsed the volcano's ever-present plume of smoke drifting up, up, into the sky.

After a while, I detected the smell of a campfire. It wove into my hair and clothes, pulling me forward until I heard a faint hammering noise. The trees opened ahead into a clearing. I pushed aside the high grass and found myself on the edge of a village.

I immediately covered my nose. The smell of smoke only thinly covered an overpowering stench of rotting food and dirty animals. A few sloppy thatched huts sat at the village's edge, with dirt paths running between them. Big, ugly rats dug through piles of decaying food. One hissed as I passed.

I peeked inside a hut's doorway and glimpsed a few signs of life: a wooden branch shaped into a plow, a tattered cloth pooled in a corner, shriveled onions drying in the rafters.

The pounding began again, making me jump. It wasn't hammering, I realized, but drumming. As I moved closer, I heard chatter and grunts. One droning voice rose above the rest.

I wasn't sure if I should hide or show myself. I didn't trust the islanders, but at least these lived some semblance of normal life in a village, not like Jaguar. I slunk along the next path until I could glimpse the village center. Dozens of islanders clustered, feet kicking clouds of dirt, hands swaying in the air. Most were dressed like Jaguar, in ragged blue canvas, though some women wore faded cloths wrapped around them. They all moved with stilted steps and hunched shoulders.

Seeing so many – a whole village – made it seem inconceivable that my father had actually *made* them. I couldn't deny they were unnatural. But to fabricate something as complex as a man who spoke and danced and dressed in trousers . . . it was impossible.

The crowd parted slightly. In their midst stood a tall man with a powerful set of elk antlers growing out of his tawny-colored hair. My mouth fell open. The odd tusk or horn on the other creatures looked malformed, but this being's antlers looked perfectly suited to him as he held his head and arms high, blood-red robes dragging in the dirt. He was the chanter. His voice droned like beetles. At his side was a boy no higher than my waist. It was Cymbeline, though the wilderness had robbed him of his sweetness. His eyes locked on to me and he pointed.

They all turned. Their faces were things of nightmares. One of them, I thought, might even be a murderer.

Run, my body urged, but it was too late. They had already swarmed me, dirty hands reaching for my hair and pulling at my clothes. They dragged me into their midst. The antlered man raised his staff, silencing their wild chatter.

'Her hand,' he commanded.

Beside me was a slanting-eyed, bald woman with oddly translucent skin that seemed to reflect sunlight. She splayed my hand with four smooth, strong fingers. I tried to jerk away, repulsed.

186

'A five-finger woman,' he said.

The woman hissed, revealing a snake's forked tongue. A python, I thought. That's where I'd seen that skin before. The boar-faced man beside her was also missing one digit on each finger, as were the two dingy boys who pulled at my skirt. Everyone was, except the tall man in the robes whose five fingers were long and stiff and covered in a thick, coarse hair.

'A five-finger woman!' he bellowed, and the crowd pressed closer. Their sour breaths turned my stomach. My illness grappled at me, making me weak, knotting my insides.

'Who are you?' I asked the robed man.

'He is Caesar,' the python-woman hissed, petting my sleeve with strong fingers.

The crowd repeated the word, rolling it like thunder.

Caesar. Caesar. Caesar.

The antlered man brought down his staff. The sharp points of his antlers gleamed in the sunlight. 'I am Caesar,' he said. 'Minister of the island.'

A beast posing as a religious man. It was as absurd as the commandments that Balthazar had chanted on the ship. Montgomery had refused to tell me what they meant, and now I understood why. I'd have thought him mad.

'Where have you come from, five-finger?' he asked.

There was something too human about his dark-brown eyes. 'England,' I said.

The crowd parroted the word, but it sounded foreign on their tongues.

'Across the sea,' Caesar explained. The crowd murmured and nodded, but still seemed vaguely confused.

'You come with the other one.' Caesar nodded to the boar-faced man. 'Bring the five-finger man.'

I strained to see above the bobbing heads as he disappeared into the crowd. The python-woman eagerly petted the smooth skin of my arms, her fingers tickling my skin. Another woman slid forward, reaching for my ring, but the python-woman snapped at her. She grinned at me as though she and I were both in a higher class than the others.

The crowd started yapping as the boar-faced man returned. He shoved a scraped and dirty body at my feet.

'Edward!' I dropped to my knees. He sat up, a hand to his head where a small cut bled. 'Are you all right?'

He nodded, throwing a wary look at the boar-faced man. He wiped the dried blood off his forehead with his shirt cuff. 'As well as can be.' He spit a bloody line of saliva into the dirt. 'They grabbed me by the falls. Your father's behind this. They think he's some kind of god.'

The crowd grew more agitated. They circled us, leaning in, watching our every move. Cymbeline and the two other boys dropped to all fours, crawling closer, but Caesar pointed his staff at them.

'Thou shalt not crawl in the dirt!'

The boys shrank back and stumbled to their feet.

I pushed myself up, but Edward pulled me closer, just for a second. 'Whatever happens, stay close.'

Before I could ask him what he meant, a shadow was cast over his face. The crowd suddenly grew quiet. I spun to find the face of a different kind of beast peering at us, a fresh white parasol balanced on his shoulder.

TWENTY-FOUR

Father smiled. 'Ah, there you are. You've given us a devil of a time trying to find you.'

Edward and I scrambled to our feet. Through a break in the crowd I caught a glimpse of Montgomery standing next to the wagon with a rifle resting on his hip, avoiding my gaze. I was in part relieved to see him. He'd take us back to the compound's strong walls and away from the lurking danger in the jungle. But I couldn't get the image out of my head of the beast strapped to the table, Father humming while the candle wax slowly dripped, and Montgomery *assisting*. I felt betrayed, as though the boy I'd idolized was nothing more than a fantasy.

'I see you've already met our neighbors,' Father said. 'Let me introduce you properly.'

Father was acting like nothing was amiss. I glanced at Edward. We'd said we would play along until we had a chance to escape the island, but this was excruciating. Father had abandoned me. Lied to me. Ruined my life. It was all I could do not to claw his face. I almost would rather have faced the murderer than go back with him.

189

The beasts stared at him with wide eyes and quivering lips. He was king here. And Montgomery hovered on the outskirts like a reluctant prince.

My knees buckled suddenly. The snakes of my illness were coming fast, coiling up my legs. Edward grabbed my elbow but I waved him away, swaying slightly. I needed an injection. I needed to get away from my father's all-consuming presence that stole the oxygen from the air.

I leaned on my knees, drawing in quick breaths. Trembling. Trying to quell the rage at this man I had once called family. I felt Edward's hand on my shoulder, heard a few reassuring words in my ear, but I couldn't make them out. All I could picture was the beast strapped to the table, writhing in pain. Its torturer's blood flowed in my own veins, a cruel inheritance. I pressed my fingers against my eyes to keep from crying. But a single sob escaped.

Then Edward's hand was gone.

I saw it happen from the corner of my eye, just a quick movement. The crowd gasped. There was a crack like a twig snapping. And then a flash of blood.

It happened so fast.

Father stumbled back, clutching his face, the parasol falling to the ground. Blood trickled between the white slats of his fingers. Edward's arm was still balled in a fist. He'd punched Father in the mouth. I gaped.

What happened to pretending everything was fine?

Edward flexed his hand. 'He made you cry,' he explained.

Montgomery rushed through the crowd as the islanders erupted in a frenzy of excitement at the smell of the blood. Caesar raised his staff, the red robes sweeping out like a curtain. Even *his* nose flared at the smell.

Montgomery tackled Edward. They scuffled, kicking up clouds of dust. The python-woman threw herself in front of Father protectively. Several others followed her lead. At last

Montgomery wrestled Edward to his knees and pinned his arms behind his back.

My skull pounded as if I were drunk. Montgomery was slave to my father's will. Helping him with his terrible work, defending him, even at Edward's expense. Montgomery wasn't cruel, I knew that to my core. Father might have dragged him here as a child, raised him to do terrible things, but Montgomery wasn't a monster. He shouldn't act as Father's puppet.

'Don't listen to him!' I yelled, pounding my fist against Montgomery's shoulder. The surprise made him hesitate. I dug my fingers into his hand, trying to pry his fingers off Edward. 'Let him go!'

'Stop this!' Father's voice was like the thunderous voice of God. Specks of blood spattered as he spoke.

A rough hand closed over my mouth. Lumpy scales grazed my lips – Puck. I recoiled in disgust, tasting the sweat on his palm. He wrapped his other arm around my chest and pulled me off Montgomery with the strength of two men.

My chest heaved. Tension still crackled in the air. The islanders fawned over Father, but he waved them away, rubbing at his split bottom lip. I stared at Montgomery. *Don't listen to him*, my every thought urged. *You know this is wrong.*

Montgomery only looked away.

'Really, this is no way to act.' Father drew out his handkerchief and spit into it. Red blood flashed against the crisp white linen. 'We must set a good example for them. You most of all, Juliet.'

'I know what you're doing in that laboratory,' I said. 'You're a monster.'

Father stared, his black eyes deep and unreadable. He tucked the handkerchief back into his vest pocket. 'Release them. They won't run again. They've no place to go.'

A low growl came from deep in Puck's throat, but he released me. Montgomery slowly let go of Edward's arms.

191

Father picked up the parasol, now broken and stained. 'So you've found me out, have you? You saw what was on that table and you've seen my islanders. Of course you've reached the only logical conclusion. You're smart, after all. Smarter than you should be.' His black eyes shone. 'It's a shame you weren't a boy.'

'You've crossed the line,' I said. 'This is God's work, not ours.'

'You sound like your mother,' he said. It wasn't a compliment. He walked among the beasts, picking clumps of dirt from their hair, straightening their ragged clothes, as a father might tend to a child. A shaggy man with striped hair falling in his eyes stood straighter as Father approached. Father placed a friendly hand on his shoulder. 'Juliet, dear, these animals have been given a great gift, made man by careful and studied science. They're exceptional, don't you see? Capable of human thought and action, but without mankind's corruption.'

Anger seeped backward up my spine.

'You've been listening to this silly boy. He's not one of us – I told you that from the beginning. Come back to the compound. You need an injection, and food and water. I shall explain my work to you. It's only the shock of it that has you so tightly wound. Once you understand the science behind it, you'll see things my way.'

My growing anger was overshadowed by an encroaching weakness in my legs. I could feel my illness's cold grip on me tighten. I doubled over, bracing myself on my knees. As my legs faltered, Montgomery's arms were suddenly around me, picking me up effortlessly. His heart beat wildly through his shirt.

'Get her back at once,' I heard Father say, though my senses were fading. 'And you, Prince. When we return, you and I will need to re-examine the nature of our *arrangement*.'

If the arrangement had anything to do with Father's plan

to marry me off to Edward, I couldn't imagine Father was still pleased with his choice for son-in-law.

The village spun as Montgomery carried me through the crowd. The python-woman pushed forward, grazing her fleshy fingers delicately against my cheek. Montgomery ordered her away. I grabbed at his biceps, feeling vertigo. His heart beat faster.

'I tried to warn you.' His voice was a fierce whisper.

I heard the big draft horse grunt, and then the rusty hinges of the wagon's back gate. Suddenly Montgomery's arms were gone, replaced by stiff wooden boards. Something was beside me in the wagon bed, something long and wrapped in cloth. The stench of congealed blood choked my throat. I twisted away from the smell, too weak to sit up.

'You insisted on coming here,' Montgomery whispered harshly. I couldn't tell if he was mad at me or mad at himself. 'I should have refused. I'd hoped . . . Blast, it doesn't matter.'

Then he was gone and the wagon was moving. Each jostle felt like the tossing waves at sea. A sudden bump rolled me into the wrapped fabric. My hand fell into a sticky substance.

I looked down at my hand. Congealed blood clotted between my fingers. I'd rolled over onto a canvas shroud wrapped around what had to be a body. Blood soaked through the fabric in three red streaks across its chest. Another victim.

The monster, Jaguar had said.

The wagon bumped again, and the canvas fell away from the face. It was an islander woman, or had been. The jaw had been ripped away, leaving only long jagged incisors poised in a permanent scream. Gashes streaked her cheeks and forehead, already covered with a voracious swarm of flies. A scream hurled up my throat, but I never heard it. I'd slipped into a welcoming darkness.

TWENTY-FIVE

I awoke in my bed at the compound. My memories were hazy, sunken into the moss-laden swamps of my mind, where I was content to leave them. I remembered only hints. Peeling skin on the dead woman's face. Bloodstains on the canvas tarpaulin. Flies buzzing like thunderclouds. There was a lingering stench of blood in my mouth and the smell of lavender in the air.

A soft humming filled the corners of the room like sunlight. I imagined for a moment that I was back home on Belgrave Square, with Mother humming while she made me tea. But it was a poor fantasy. London had never been so stiflingly humid.

I opened my eyes. The humming was nothing more than an insect's steady drone, but the lavender was real. Alice stood over a steaming copper pot on the dresser, her back to me, rolling the flower between her palms to release the fragrance. Tiny purple blooms tumbled into the pot, filling the room with their calming scent. Montgomery leaned beside her, painting a clear gummy substance onto the mirror with a thick brush. Half the glass was shattered into fine cracks like a spider's web. When had it broken?

Alice brought her fingers to her face, breathing in the soft, earthy scent. She held her cupped hands to Montgomery. He inhaled deeply, giving her an easy smile I hadn't seen since we were children – and even then only rarely. My heart wrenched a little. They were in my room, but I felt like the intruder.

'Alice,' I said. Her name caught in my rusty throat. She and Montgomery turned in surprise. Her hand instinctively flew to cover her harelip. I cleared my throat. Seeing them so playful should have cheered me, but it only twisted something inside me.

Montgomery crossed his arms at the foot of the bed, the lightness gone from his face. 'You're awake. Are you feeling well?'

'There was a body. Someone died.'

His hands clutched the footboard. 'A woman from the village.'

'Another *accident*?'

He didn't reply.

I caught my reflection in the mirror. The gossamer cracks split my face into a hundred little pieces. 'What happened to the mirror?'

He gave it a glance, showing a thousand frowns. 'Don't you remember? You threw your silver brush. It shattered.'

I sat up, studying the fractured wall of eyes. 'Why would I do that?'

'You were aiming for me.'

My reflection smirked. 'I must have been more clear-headed than I thought.'

Alice's wide eyes focused on the towel she dried her hands with. Montgomery's lips fell open and I thought he might say more, but then he shook his head. 'I'll tell the doctor you're awake.'

My reflection caught in the mirror, just a glimmer of a

passing expression. Some part of me was sorry to see him leave. I still cared about him, and that made me angriest of all. Angry because he knew that what he was doing was wrong, yet he was still loyal to my father. It surely hadn't been the mirror I wanted to shatter, but Father's spell on him.

Alice dipped the towel into the copper pot. She dabbed my brow, gently. 'He's a good man, miss. He means well.' Her eyes were alight.

I knew that look.

She was in love with him.

The trickle of water ran down my face and tickled my ears. It made sense, I supposed. He was the only young man without a hoof or claw on the island. And he was handsome. Oh, was he handsome. I felt my face getting warm and blamed it on the steam from the copper pot.

'Your getting lost gave the doctor quite a scare,' Alice said softly, dabbing at my neck. She was a gentle, pretty thing. Had I been ignoring something obvious? An odd feeling crept over me, that maybe her feelings toward Montgomery might be returned. I suddenly felt like an idiot. I'd thought he felt something for me. He'd practically told me as much; he'd almost kissed me . . . Had I been exaggerating his affection in my mind, when it was really someone else who had his heart?

'His creatures gave *me* a scare,' I muttered, my thoughts elsewhere. The lavender mingled with my breath, infusing my body. It was meant to calm me, but I found it choking. 'Did you know about them?'

Alice ran the towel down the sides of my neck, over the bridge of my nose, the curve of my chin. 'Yes, miss. We all know.'

'It's madness. Humans made from animals.'

'It's the way of the island.'

'Aren't you scared?'

The towel paused on my neckline. Her lip twitched. 'Most things scare me, miss.'

She began cleaning under my fingernails with a metal file. The caked dirt didn't bother me, but she went after it with a vengeance.

'He thinks he's God,' I said. She didn't stop scrubbing. The file pressed at the sensitive skin under my nails, making them tingle. 'But he's insane.'

Her hand jerked, and the file dug into my skin. Blood appeared in the hollow under the nail. I can't say why, but I started laughing. The more the blood flowed, the more I laughed, until I felt like a madwoman. Alice squeezed the towel around it, her eyes wide.

'You should rest, miss. You still aren't well.'

The laughter died on my lips. I pulled my hand back, licked away the blood the towel didn't get. It tasted rich, like iron. 'Where are the others? Where's my father?'

'The salon, miss.'

I sat up, throwing a dressing gown over my chemise, and hurried across the courtyard barefoot.

I interrupted a sullen tea in the salon. A few dried-out plain cakes rested untouched on the coffee table. The tea looked cold. Montgomery stood when I entered, but Father waved him back down. I glanced at Edward. No visible broken bones. At least Father hadn't drowned him for that punch in the jaw.

'Are you feeling—?' Montgomery said, but I cut him off.

'To hell with how I'm feeling.' I folded my arms, staring at Father. 'I want an explanation.'

To my satisfaction, Father closed his book. Apparently profanity had a way of making men listen. The clock ticked, slowly. Father nodded toward the leather armchair. I sank into it, gripping the armrests. Montgomery stood again but

197

hung back near the bookshelves. Close enough to listen, far enough to distance himself.

'You think me a monster,' Father began. 'Or a madman. Though I assure you, the research Montgomery and I conduct here is quite the contrary. We are pioneering the science of manipulating living forms.'

'Butchery, you mean,' I said. My gaze flickered to Montgomery, challenging him.

Father didn't flinch. 'I can't control how a handful of ignorant boors label it.'

'And the creature on your operating table?' I snapped. 'What label would it use?'

'It doesn't think in those concepts, Juliet. It was merely a panther, used to hunting. Instead of craving flesh, it will now gather fruit and live in a society with others of its kind. I gave it intelligence. Reason.'

'Impossible. No surgery can do that.'

'My technique is not limited to the physical form. The brain, as well, can benefit from the surgical process. It's a simple matter of mapping the mind, learning what to tweak, to stimulate, to cut out. It requires special instruments and infinite patience, of course.' Father took a sip of tea.

I briefly wondered where cruelty resided in the brain. Whether you could cut it out with a scalpel. I glanced behind me, where Montgomery pretended to read a book. Had he ever tried to stop my father? Was he a prisoner here, or a willing participant?

As if he could read my thoughts, he slammed the book shut and shoved it onto a shelf. His sleeve tore on a loose nail. He pounded his balled fist on the nail as if his anger alone could hammer it down.

'I don't believe you,' I said.

Father smiled thinly. 'The proof is right here. Balthazar, won't you come here for a moment?'

Balthazar shuffled into the room, his hands enveloping the teakettle. Father motioned to a chair. Balthazar sat down, blinking nervously. Across the room, Montgomery's attention focused on us. A flicker passed over his face, a memory maybe, and he smacked the shelf so hard the books rattled. Edward glanced up at the noise, but Montgomery turned and left through the door.

Coward, I thought, *leaving Balthazar to face my father alone.*

'Now, take Balthazar.' Father's voice pulled me back. 'One of my finer creations, even able to pass among the streets of London, though admittedly somewhat unusual with the odd slanting forehead and profusion of body hair. He speaks. He thinks. He's capable of compassion. Why, he even carried a garden slug outside this morning so the chickens wouldn't eat it. Didn't you?'

Balthazar nodded.

'Tell me, Juliet, would you call this man an abomination?'

Balthazar grinned. He thought he was pleasing us. He had no notion that Father was talking about his own horrible origin. I remembered that Balthazar was the one who'd taken care of the little sloth on the *Curitiba*. He'd cried softly when I'd played Chopin on the piano.

'No,' I said gently. Then my resolve hardened. 'But I can't call him a man, either.'

'Nevertheless, a man he is,' Father argued. 'A man carved and wrought from animal flesh. Don't act so horrified, Juliet. It is merely surgery. You are no doubt familiar with some of the more common practices. Setting broken bones, amputations, stitching ruptured skin back together?'

'I am,' I answered cautiously.

'No one questions the hand of a doctor performing such procedures. No one calls it butchery – it is science, and no different from what transpires behind the door of my own laboratory. For it is surgery I perform. Grafting of skin, setting of bones. A more complex scale, mind you. There is a most fascinating procedure, you know, I have only recently perfected, wherein I separate the sternum . . .'

His explanations continued. Examples, details, complications of his work. They made my throat go dry and my mind whirl. He had really done it.

My father had played God and won.

I had so many questions, but the rush of them caught in my throat. How long did the grafting take to set? Why did he choose the human form? What did a heart split open and sewn back together look like? I shocked myself with my hunger to know.

Edward was strangely quiet, shocked by the horror of it, as I should have been. But as much as I knew I should be repulsed, my curiosity burned so brightly it made my humanity flicker and dim.

Father continued. 'Balthazar, for example. He is part dog and part bear.' He traced an imaginary line along the bridge of Balthazar's nose. 'You can see the canine influence in his jaw placement, but examine these ears. Ursine.'

Montgomery's figure filled the doorway, and my heartbeat sped. He knelt by the bookshelf with a hammer in hand. *Thwack. Thwack.* Each strike of his hammer against that loose nail made me cringe.

Thwack. Edward leaned forward, somehow able to ignore the hammering. 'But what about scars?' Edward asked. 'What about broken bones? Your creations don't show any signs of surgery.'

'A happy accident of my banishment. The island's isolation means there is almost no disease here. A body can heal in a matter of days if there is no risk of infection. Quite remarkable. I daresay many of my attempts in London failed solely from the polluted city air.' He drew in a lungful to prove his point.

Thwack. The nail drove deeper, as if Montgomery was driving it into my very heart. How hard was it to fix a loose nail? He hit it again and again, determined to set that bookshelf straight. Determined to do something right, after so much wrong.

I pressed the heel of my hand to the aching space between my ribs.

'But what about the pain?' I whispered. Balthazar's grin faded. From the corner of my eye, I saw the hammer pause in Montgomery's hand.

Father scoffed and took another sip of tea. 'Pain is merely a signal to the brain. Like the urge to sneeze. Uncomfortable, but tolerable.'

I swallowed down something hard and bitter. 'You use anesthesia, right?'

'Can't. It interferes with the vivisection. Causes the body to reject new material. Anyway, animals are used to pain. It's a formative part of their lives. Birth of offspring, fighting over prey, competing for a mate. In fact, pain can be an effective tool. When I am finished with them, they are abnormally docile creatures, through no intention of my own. The pain drives the fight out of them, you see.'

Montgomery slammed the hammer against the nail one final time, hard enough to crack the wood. A shiver raced up my spine, punctuating the horror of what Father was saying. He tortured these beasts with as little regard for their well-being as if they were straw dummies. I narrowed my eyes, wondering if Father would feel any differently if it was a human instead of an animal on his table.

I wasn't sure he would.

Montgomery thrust the hammer into his back pocket. I caught sight of Alice in the doorway. She must have been there long enough to hear at least a little, because her face was white. Montgomery took her hand and led her away.

'What is your intention in all this, Doctor?' Edward asked, with a surprisingly steady voice.

Father folded his hands. 'I am in pursuit of the ideal living form. Just like all of us, wouldn't you say? The same reason we choose mates and procreate. We want to create something better than ourselves. Perfection. To me, perfection is a being with the reason of man but the natural innocence of children – or animals. I have come so close to achieving it. You have no idea how close. I thought, once . . .' His black eyes gleamed at Edward. 'Well, it failed in the end, as they all have failed. It wasn't always humans I tried to create. I started with smaller things. Rats. Birds. Just tweaking their shape, minor alterations. But I wasn't satisfied. I kept creating, kept carving flesh. I've yet to attain perfection.' He sighed deeply, then waved a hand in Balthazar's general direction. 'Montgomery tends to them – these failures. Teaches them English, basic skills, trains the more intelligent ones to work for us here in the compound. Administers their treatments.'

'Treatments?' I asked.

Father held his cup for Balthazar to pour more tea. A drip spilled onto his linen pants, and he waved Balthazar away, annoyed. 'Yes, treatments,' he said absently, dabbing at the drip with a napkin. 'We give them a serum to keep the tissue from rejecting its new form. Without it they revert to their original state. It's another fail-safe, you see. If anything goes wrong, we stop their treatments, and they return to being cows and sheep and whatever other harmless animals they came from.'

'But they're amalgamations,' I said. 'You stitch together different animals.'

He shrugged. 'Then I suppose they would regress into strange-looking cows and sheep perhaps, but harmless nonetheless.' He took a sip, and then thrust the cup angrily into Balthazar's hands. 'The tea's gone cold.'

Balthazar stared at the sloshing tea, uncertain what was to be done with it. I folded my hands around his, taking the cup gently.

'I'll take care of the tea,' I said, biting my words. I hurled the cup into the fireplace, where it shattered in a thousand white pieces that littered the floor like snowfall.

Edward leapt up in surprise, but Father didn't flinch.

Balthazar trembled. I laid my hand on the unnatural hump of his shoulder. 'Don't listen to him, Balthazar,' I said. 'You're not the monster here.' I gave Father a cold glare and stormed into the courtyard.

TWENTY-SIX

I stopped to steady myself on the water pump. In the garden Cymbeline calmly dropped peas into a wicker basket, just another normal day. All traces of the snarling little creature from the village were gone. He sang a strange song, though the tune seemed familiar. The melody slowly took shape until I could hum it, the words gradually returning. 'Winter's Tale.' A lullaby Mother used to sing to me. Sung now on the lips of this poor animal carved into a little boy by a madman.

I dashed into the barn. I needed a place to hide from the world. Chaff filtered through the air like dancing sunlight. I collapsed on a bale of fresh straw, pain gripping me somewhere deep. I buried my hands in my hair. The shame. The rumors. The whispers. Just like I was still ten years old. Only now I knew.

My father was a monster. And a genius.

Mother's voice whispered, telling me everything he was doing was against God, against nature. And yet a small but sharp part of me, like a piece of broken glass lodged in my heart, was almost *proud* of him. I knew that was wrong. But he was part of who I was – how could I *not* feel that way?

Footsteps came from the tack room. I crawled to my knees, peering into the next stall.

Montgomery paused, leaning on a pitchfork, and brushed a loose strand of blond hair behind his ear. Duke nuzzled his shoulder from his stall. Montgomery pushed the horse away affectionately. I fought back anger. Of all people, of course it had to be him. The boy I'd idolized, who now betrayed me with a scalpel and a set of manacles.

'You're good with animals,' I said coldly. 'Or should I say *creatures*?' All the anger from the past few days flooded my brain, made me lash out at Montgomery when it was really Father who was to blame.

He wiped his hands on his trousers, not acknowledging my sting, and picked up the pitchfork to gather a load.

'You enjoy all this, don't you?' I pulled myself up, straw raining from my dress. 'Having these aberrations wait on you hand and foot.' I knew I was being cruel. He didn't deserve it, and yet I wanted him to feel the same angry bite of broken glass that I did.

He dug the pitchfork into a pile of straw. 'Seems to me *I'm* the one mucking out the stall.'

I glowered. 'You're right. Mucking out the stalls. Proper work for a servant. That's what you are, isn't it? Still doing whatever he commands.' I leaned against the wooden stall gate, entwining my fingers in the steel bars. 'Even if it is the devil's work.'

'That isn't fair.' He dumped the straw and went back for another load, his shoulders tense. 'I hadn't a choice.'

'You could have stayed with Mother and me.'

'You don't understand.' The pitchfork scraped the stone floor so hard it squealed. 'I was a boy. I'd already taken part in his work. I was already guilty of his same crimes before I even knew what we were doing.' He dumped the load and shoved the pitchfork against the wall. 'I didn't have a choice.'

For a moment, he rested his hand on the pitchfork, breath ragged. Strands of his hair escaped the ponytail and fell over his eyes, making him look wild, untamed. He'd changed so much from that quiet little boy. He'd had to, growing up with monsters as playmates.

He turned to go.

'Wait!'

He paused, a hand on the barn's half door. I put my hand next to his, keeping the door closed. I remembered the feel of his body. The heat of his skin. Montgomery wasn't my enemy. He wasn't to blame.

Father was cruel – I didn't want to be, too.

'I'm sorry. They aren't your crimes,' I said. His jaw flexed. He started to push the half door open, but I jerked it closed again. 'They aren't. You were a child. He manipulated you, like he manipulated all of us.' I stepped closer. 'We have a choice now. We can stop him.'

Montgomery's jaw tightened. His voice was a gruff whisper. 'Even if we could, what then?'

'We'll leave. You and I and Edward.' My voice broke, thinking of the scene earlier over the lavender bowl. 'And Alice.'

But he shook his head. 'I can't leave them. Without treatment they'll regress.'

'Maybe they should. They're animals. What he's done is unnatural.'

'What *I've* done, you mean. I'm just as guilty.' His words echoed in the barn and set my heart pounding. 'They're not animals anymore. You haven't seen what they can become. You haven't met Ajax.'

'Ajax?'

'He was one of them. The doctor did something to his brain, something we haven't been able to replicate. He became smart. And civil. He was like a brother to me. He's different – he *was* different.'

'What happened?'

'Ajax stopped his own treatment. The others crave humanity. But Ajax knew what he was. He *wanted* to regress.'

'And has he?'

'Not yet. He lives alone. Won't be a part of their village. Won't live here. He waits until all traces of his humanity are gone.' He paused. 'The doctor doesn't know. He ordered me to shoot him, but I couldn't.'

I stared at Montgomery, realizing that he must never have had a true friend since coming to the island. Father was no companion. And Balthazar and the others, well, their company was more like a dogs'. Then I remembered the cabin in the woods, the yellow hair on the mattress, and the single flower in the vase on the dusty mantel.

'Jaguar,' I muttered. 'He calls himself Jaguar now.'

Montgomery's shoulders tensed. 'How do you know that?'

'I met him in the woods.'

'You *what*?' There was fear in his eyes.

'He told me you'd sent him to find me. Didn't you?' A trickle of worry crept at the base of my neck.

'I haven't spoken to him since returning from London.'

'But he knew about Edward. And he knew about me.'

Montgomery leaned his weight against the door. He put a hand to his brow in thought. 'He must be eavesdropping on the compound. It's the only way.' He grabbed my shoulder. 'And he didn't hurt you? Do you swear? He's not some docile farm animal, Juliet. He's dangerous.'

I shook my head, my heart pounding harder. I remembered the feel of Jaguar's rough tongue on my skin. Fearful sweat began to drip down my face. Had I been in the company of the murderer? I hadn't trusted him, which was why I'd slipped away. It might have saved my life.

'He didn't hurt me,' I stuttered. 'But he killed a rabbit.'

Montgomery's hand gripped mine protectively. He squeezed so hard it hurt. 'Killed a rabbit? Are you sure?'

'I saw him arguing with another man about it.' I swallowed, wanting to find some logical explanation. 'They can't be perfect always, can they? They must break commandments sometimes.'

'Not that one. Not to kill. We didn't think they knew how to kill.' An idea seemed to strike him. The blood drained from his face. I remembered the stinking corpse in the back of the wagon. All the other *accidents*. He pulled a pistol off the gun rack in the back of the barn. Checking the chamber, he started for the half door, but I held it closed.

'What's going on?' I demanded.

'You were right. That woman in the wagon wasn't an accident. There've been more bodies. Many. All with three slashes across the chest. We thought it must be an escaped animal. A bobcat got loose once . . . It didn't occur to us that one of them might be responsible.' He grabbed my shoulders. The butt of the pistol lay between his hand and my clothes, a harsh reminder of what was out there. 'Whatever you do, don't go back into the jungle.'

TWENTY-SEVEN

The next morning, in the salon, I peered between the long shutter slats at the courtyard outside. Father and Montgomery argued furiously, tramping up dirt, sweat staining their shirts. They'd been arguing like this for hours. It must have been serious for Montgomery to be so defensive. The pistol butt gleamed in his waistband. I made out only two words: *Rabbit. Ajax.*

I didn't need to hear more.

Edward sat in a chair reading, his attention on the musty pages rather than the argument in the courtyard. I sank into the green sofa opposite him.

'There's a murderous beast on the island. How can you just sit and read?'

He flipped a page. Then another. 'I can't. It's impossible to concentrate.'

'You could have fooled me.' I raised an eyebrow, but my sarcasm was lost on him. I leaned forward to read the title. *The Tempest.* 'I've read that one. Shall I tell you the ending and save you the bother?'

He closed the book on his finger to mark the place he'd stopped. 'I'm not reading it for pleasure.' He cocked his head toward the courtyard. 'I'm trying to find something that might help us escape. The book's about castaways on an island. They get off eventually.'

I rolled my eyes. 'With the aid of magic.'

He dipped his head, going back to the book. 'We'll have to be a little more creative.'

A door slammed outside and I peered through the shutters. Father and Montgomery were gone. Only the chickens pecked in the courtyard. The familiar trickle of worry returned.

'The doctor came in here earlier furious over something,' Edward said, his voice lower.

'It's about that dead rabbit I found. They think one of the islanders killed it. The one who calls himself Jaguar. And so that must make him the murderer.'

'But you think he didn't kill the rabbit?'

I frowned. 'No, I'm sure he did. I saw him waving the bloody head around. It's just . . . never mind.' A dull pain throbbed at the base of my skull. I rubbed the stiff muscles there. My hands still felt the weight of the ax I'd brought down over the rabbit's neck in the operating theater. I couldn't exactly condemn Jaguar for separating a rabbit from its head when I'd done the same.

'Have you at least found anything useful?' I said, nodding at the book.

Edward set the book on a pile of warped leather volumes. 'Not unless you have a magic wand. We need a vessel. That's easy enough – the launch at the dock. We can steal enough food from the garden and the kitchen. There are a few waterskins – not ideal, but enough to survive, I think. The only problem is—'

His words died as Alice entered the room. Her eyes grew wide. She knew she was interrupting something. She quickly flitted around, picking up a dirty towel on a peg by the door, the napkins from breakfast, the rag Puck had used to clean up the spilled tea last night. Her long blond hair floated behind her like that of some ephemeral being. She slipped from the room as silently as she had entered, leaving behind the faint scent of lavender.

'The only problem,' Edward whispered, once she was gone, 'is navigation.'

'Montgomery knows the way,' I said. 'You said he told you there's a shipping lane not far.'

A shadow passed over Edward's face and I knew, in that look, that he didn't want to take Montgomery with us. 'You were awfully quick to forgive him after what you saw in the laboratory,' he said.

'He didn't have a choice,' I said defensively. 'He was just a boy when he came here. You'd have done the same thing in his place.'

'No. I wouldn't have. I'd never choose to hurt anyone.' His voice didn't hold a trace of doubt. He tilted his head, his face suddenly tender. Goosebumps rippled over my arms at the memory of the night behind the waterfall. 'We'll leave this island. You and I. Go wherever you want. You'll forget about him . . .' He swallowed, unable to finish.

I sat straighter. The whalebone corset dug into my ribs, stifling my breath. What could I say? The night behind the waterfall with Edward had been disconcertingly intense, yet there'd been a distance between us since coming back. Nothing I could put my finger on, exactly. More like our connection existed out there, in the wild. It dulled among the books and fine china and lace curtains.

I pulled a worn throw pillow into my lap. I couldn't tell him what he wanted to hear. Montgomery meant too much to me, despite everything. 'We're taking Montgomery and everyone else who has a human heart beating in their chest,' I said, and left it at that.

He didn't press. 'And your father?'

'He can stay here and rot with the rest of the animals.'

Edward and I whispered about escape whenever we could steal a moment alone. As the days passed, those times became scarcer. More islanders went missing. Edward was needed with the search party while I was left alone to think about the murders.

About Jaguar.

One afternoon after the men returned and we'd finished eating a sullen midday meal, I found Mother's crystal earring among the trinkets in the salon and held it to the light of the window, where it sent a spray of dancing rainbows over the walls. That was my mother – color and light and delicate as glass. She would have been repulsed by Father's creations. Not drawn to them.

Balthazar passed on the portico outside, stealing my attention. Puck followed him, and then the rest of the servants, one by one, in their blue canvas shirts and pants. I pressed my face to the window. They gathered under a thatched sunscreen outside the bunkhouse. I put the earring back and pushed open the salon doors.

The islanders formed a loose line, chattering and shuffling their twisted feet. They looked at me curiously as I squeezed to the front between two hoglike men whose bristly hair made me cringe.

Montgomery stood on the other side of a worktable that held his medical bag and a half dozen cloudy glass bottles. He'd smoothed back his hair and put on a fresh shirt. He might have looked like a gentleman if it hadn't been for the open button at his chest and the casual way he stood, as though he'd spent more of his life climbing trees and racing wild horses than walking.

'Come forward,' he said to one of the hog-men. The creature

shuffled to the table, holding out his fat arm like a piece of meat. Montgomery filled a syringe with the cloudy liquid and tapped the man's vein before inserting the needle. The man must have been twice my size, but he cringed like a little girl.

'You're all done,' Montgomery said, drawing out the needle. 'Next.'

I wandered to the other side of the table, watching over Montgomery's shoulder. Another islander slipped to the front of the line. The python-woman from the village. She grinned at me, flashing the tips of thin fangs. Montgomery gave her an injection and checked her name off a roster. She waved as she left. Four fingers.

I picked up one of the vials, studying the cloudy liquid. 'What are you giving them?' I asked.

'Something to restore the tissue's balance.' He waved a gangly-limbed man forward. 'Come,' he ordered. The man shuffled to the table and extended his arm, covering his eyes while Montgomery found a vein.

The next, a man with a folded nose like a goat, approached with his sleeve already carefully rolled up.

I watched Montgomery administer the treatments. The islanders all walked away proudly rubbing their arms, like a child after his first trip to the physician. My hand drifted to the skin on the inside of my own elbow. I drew my thumb in a circle around the red mark from this morning's injection, studying the vial in my other hand. The slight tint, the cloudiness of the compound – it looked remarkably similar to the treatment Father had designed for me. I sneaked a glance at the sheep-woman next to me, at her too-human eyes and the casual way she scratched an insect bite on her neck. I wondered how similar their treatment's chemical makeup was to my own injections.

Montgomery watched me from the corner of his eye while he gave the next injection.

213

'What's in it?' I asked.

'Mostly rabbit blood with hormones added.'

'How often do they need it?'

'Three times a week for the villagers. Once a day for Balthazar and the more advanced ones. Ajax used to need it twice daily.' He finished with Cymbeline, who squeezed his eyes shut during the entire injection.

'There now. That's very good,' Montgomery said.

Cymbeline gave him a smile and took off like a wildcat. Montgomery cleaned the needle and repacked his medical bag, then reached for the vial in my hand, but I held it back.

He shook his head. 'I know what you're thinking. And it's nonsense.'

'What am I thinking?' I asked, clutching the vial. It was a pale yellow color, like the pancreatic extracts I took, but thicker. He snatched it out of my hand.

'You're wondering if your treatment is similar.'

'Is it?'

My bluntness caught him off guard. He clicked his bag shut. 'No. It's nothing at all the same.'

'No one's ever heard of my treatment. The chemists look at me like I'm mad.'

'Your father designed it specifically for you. He tried to produce it for the public, but the medical board shut him down.' He picked up the bag and leaned closer. A strand of hair worked its way loose and fell into his eyes. Nothing about him could be tamed for long.

'Your mind is racing,' he said softly, his voice caressing my worries. 'You're looking for problems where there are none. I've known you from the time you could barely walk. I'd know if there was something . . . unnatural.' His gaze shifted to something behind me in the courtyard. His jaw tensed.

Father strode toward us from the main building. I knew that anger on his face. But it was Montgomery he was after, not me. Still furious that Montgomery had lied about Ajax being alive.

My hand twisted into a fist. I leaned in to Montgomery and whispered before Father could hear. 'Come to my room tonight. I need you to see something.' I slipped around the worktable just as my father stormed up with all the cold rage of a coiled snake.

Night had settled when Montgomery finally came to my room. The air hung with the promise of rain. He'd spent all afternoon beyond the compound walls, digging graves for the deceased. Shadows stretched over his face, handsome still after such grim work.

He stopped in the doorway. His blue eyes glowed in the soft light, lashing my heart like a string. But warning was written in them, too.

'Why am I here, Juliet?' he asked. We both knew there would be trouble if he was caught alone in my room, especially while Father was in a rage.

'Just come in for a moment,' I said. My nervous hands drifted to my blouse's mother-of-pearl buttons.

His lips were sunburned. He glanced around to make sure no one watched from the courtyard. But there were always eyes, somewhere.

He shook his head, reluctant to cross Father. I grabbed a fistful of his shirt, hard buttons and crisp linen, and pulled him gently inside. His eyes still held warning, but there was something else there now. Desire. Seeing it stilled the breath in my lungs. I closed the door behind him.

The oil lamp cast a warm glow over the whitewashed walls. In the semidarkness, his presence blazed even more.

'You've been digging graves,' I said.

A spot of sandy dirt clung to his right ear, missed in his bath. 'Eight dead so far. That we know of.'

'Did Jaguar really kill them?'

'I don't know. Maybe. A year ago I'd have said you were crazy. But things are different now.' He stepped closer. His hair was still damp from the bath. Lye soap mixed with the smell of coming rain. 'Don't worry. You're safe here.'

He thought I wanted reassurance that whatever killed them wouldn't kill me. But no one could make that promise. 'That's not why I asked you here. I need you to look at something.'

He brushed his hair behind one ear, just missing the patch of sand. An urge overcame me to wipe it off with my thumb. But my hand would have shaken, knowing what I was about to ask him to do. I tangled my hands in the folds of my skirt instead.

'What is it?' he asked.

I took his hand and led him into the corner, where we couldn't be seen from the window. His tired feet dragged, but his eyes were alert.

'I want to know why my medication is so similar to theirs.'

He let out a pent-up breath. 'Is that what has you worried? I told you, it isn't the same.'

'Close enough to make me need more proof.'

He touched my shoulder tenderly, like he'd done to Alice. 'It's impossible. You look too much like your mother to have been created in a laboratory.'

I tried to read the unspoken words in the lines of his face. His concern was deep and genuine and honest. He didn't believe I was anything like the creatures. But he could be wrong.

'It's more than that,' I said. 'I feel odd sometimes. Like there's something not entirely right about me, as if I've inherited some of Father's madness. Only now I wonder if it's something more . . .'

His thumb rubbed small circles against my shoulder.

'Everyone feels like that at some point or another. A little mad. Besides, your mother would know if you came from her own womb. She wouldn't have lied to you about that.'

Thunder rumbled outside. The sky was on the verge of spilling open. I twisted a lock of hair, unused to having it long and loose. His fingers tightened, pulling me almost imperceptibly closer. He was right about Mother. She may have believed in denial, but her strict morals wouldn't have let her lie outright.

'And you're forgetting,' Montgomery continued. 'That was sixteen years ago. He's only recently been able to make anything close to the human form. And you've seen them. They look abnormal.' His eyes glowed. 'You look . . . perfect.'

'But there are anomalies,' I said, trying hard not to confuse the reason we were alone in my bedroom. My hands drifted to the back of my blouse that hid the puckered scar. 'Like Jaguar. You said Father did something to his brain that he hasn't been able to replicate. Couldn't the same thing have happened to me? A fluke?'

Montgomery touched a calloused hand to my cheek. Outside, lightning cracked. The smell of coming rain swelled. 'This is nonsense, Juliet. You'd at least have scars. But you're beautiful.'

His thumb brushed my burning skin. The tops of my breasts rose and fell quickly beneath my blouse's tight bodice.

'That's just it.' I swallowed, trying to keep my reason. 'I do have scars.'

The wind blew in the first drops of rain, and I pulled him deeper into the corner away from the window. 'You know his work better than anyone,' I said, breathless. My fingers drifted to the fabric covering the base of my spine. 'I have a scar on my back from surgery. He says I was born with a spinal deformity. I can't help but think . . .'

217

He shook his head, almost laughing at my worry. 'This is ridiculous.'

'Just look!' I said. Too loudly. We both glanced at the door. I dropped my voice to a whisper. '*Please*. Tell me if it looks like the procedure he uses on them.'

I started to untie the ribbons at the back of my skirt, but he grabbed my hand with an iron grip. 'Don't,' he said. 'I shouldn't even be here.'

'We aren't in London anymore. Who's going to gossip?' I hissed. 'The birds?'

'If your father finds out—'

I shook off his hand and pulled the ribbon loose. I stepped out of my skirt and began unbuttoning my blouse. 'I'll only lower my chemise's collar in the back.'

He started to object, but voices came from the other side of the wall and I pulled him closer, resting a finger over my lips. We waited until the voices passed. I finished the last button and removed my blouse, setting it over the chair. My fingers trembled. I told myself it was a medical examination, not some secret tryst. But I'd never taken my clothes off in front of a man before. And Montgomery wasn't just some nameless doctor in a cold examining room.

'Can you help me with the corset laces?' I asked, turning around. I gripped the back of the chair to keep steady.

'Juliet—'

'Please. I need to know.'

He tugged at the laces with the ungraceful hands of a man. At last they loosened. I dragged the chemise's wide collar down over one shoulder. I kept my arms folded, holding the corset against my chest.

'Just look,' I whispered, feeling exposed. His hand brushed the hair off my back, sending shivers along either side of the scar. I hugged the corset tighter. Bit my lip. Worries drove me mad. *Mother lied. I am some creature, a cat, or a wolf, or . . .*

He withdrew his hands. I pulled up my chemise, feeling the warmth rise to my cheeks. He loosely retied the laces of my corset. I smoothed a hand over the whalebone ribbing, waiting.

'Well?' I asked.

'You're crazy,' he answered. His face broke with the traces of a smile. 'It's just as he said. A spinal deformity fixed by surgery.'

My eyelids sank with relief. 'Are you sure?'

'Beyond doubt.' He wet his parched lips. 'I know you, Juliet. You're no monster.'

I studied him closely. The sand still clung to his ear, and I reached up on impulse and brushed it off. His heartbeat sped at my touch. I wanted to believe him. But even if he was right, I knew that one didn't have to be a creation to be a monster. My own family history proved that.

For a few moments he stood a breath away. His fingers found my wrist and traced along the edge of my arm. He cleared his throat and looked ready to say something, but then he shook his head.

'Good night, Juliet.' He left slowly, as if he had to pry himself away before he did something improper. A growing part of me wished he'd stayed.

TWENTY-EIGHT

Father and Montgomery left at dawn the next day. The set-in clouds threatened a storm, but Father was convinced the murderer was Ajax and must be hunted down and brought to justice, despite the weather.

The clouds broke and heavy rain stretched into the afternoon, driving the rest of us indoors. Edward kept to his room with complaints of a headache, a throwback to his time in the dinghy. I spent the day helping Alice hang laundry to dry under the portico's covered eaves. She was quiet, but that suited me.

We heard the horses stamping outside in late afternoon. Alice brushed the hair out of her face with the back of her hand. 'They've returned.'

Puck opened the gate. Steam rose off the horses' bodies. The riders looked like dark, unearthly creatures, covered in mud and black duster coats. They dismounted and crossed through the beating rain to the laboratory. Montgomery glanced at me from under the hood of his duster, a flash of blue eyes and wet hair and unanswered questions.

Alice and I silently returned to the laundry, though we were both on edge. We were halfway through with the laundry when the laboratory door slammed open. I dropped the basket of wooden clothespins. Heavy footsteps echoed over the stone flags as I bent to pick them up. Two muddy boots stopped next to the last clothespin.

My father.

I had nothing to say to him. He was an old man with weathered skin and graying hair and dark impulses he couldn't contain. Not a father.

'You should leave that work to the servants,' he said, raising his voice over the rain. Alice kept her head down as she wrung out a sheet. 'Play the piano if you've nothing to do. Something proper for a young lady. Where's that blasted Prince? Can't he take you for a walk? Show you the view or some such nonsense?'

'Stop trying to push us together,' I hissed, wishing Alice weren't overhearing. 'Edward can make his own decisions, as can I.'

Father raised an eyebrow. 'Is that so? I'm not so sure.' A bolt of lightning lit the sky as he continued to his apartment above the salon. I rested the basket on the side of the laundry bin, biting back words. He was a fool if he still thought he could tell me what to do.

After we finished the laundry, I went to the salon, curious whether Edward was up and feeling better. But it was empty save Puck, laying out dinnerware. The piano had been freshly polished, but I crossed to the bookshelves instead. I admired the beautiful green binding of the Shakespeare collection, each book stamped on the spine with gold emblems. There was a gap where one volume was missing, though I didn't recall which title had been there. I couldn't imagine one of the beasts reading Shakespeare.

I ran my hand along the uneven shelf and thought of Montgomery, hammering it together years ago when he'd still been a boy. Father demanded perfection, but he'd still

221

kept these shelves, crooked as they were. For as much as he ordered Montgomery about, I suspected he loved him in his own warped way. He'd always wanted a son. Lord knew he never cared about his daughter.

I pulled out the brandy stopper and sloshed a healthy dose into a cut-crystal glass. I drank the spicy-sweet liquid in several gulps. My throat burned. Puck stared at me, the silverware forgotten.

'What? Want to try some?' I asked, tipping the bottle toward him. He scowled as he hurried to finish laying out the place settings.

I took the bottle to the window, studying the falling rain outside. The warm smell of supper began to fill the room, drawing in Montgomery and Father, both scrubbed clean but looking grim.

Father tore the bottle from my hands. 'This isn't for a lady,' he snapped.

'Good. Then it's perfect for me.'

Father replaced the stopper and returned the bottle to the bookshelf. 'You're determined to ruin yourself, I see. You think you're an adult and I haven't control over you anymore. That is where you're wrong.'

I bristled as spikes of anger twisted into my gut. He hadn't seen me since I was ten years old. Hadn't left me money or a home, just a crippling scandal. He didn't get to dictate what was right and wrong. He didn't get to tell me who I should marry.

Montgomery saw the look in my eyes and shook his head slowly, warning me. But I couldn't go along with the charade like he could. 'You think I care what you think,' I told Father. 'And that is where *you're* wrong.'

I turned before he could respond. My hands were shaking and I didn't want him to see. Montgomery stood by the door, and suddenly my heartstrings tightened, needing a kind look from him, some reassurance. But Alice touched his arm and whispered something in his ear, and his attention was only on her. I turned my thoughts to the silverware, straightening the already straight knives, trying not to feel stung.

Edward filled the doorway, rubbing his temples. I went to him, in no small part to show Montgomery I had someone else to pay attention to as well. But when I saw the shadows under Edward's eyes, Montgomery really did drift from my mind.

'How's your head?' I asked softly.

'Do I look that awful?' Edward said.

I smiled. The scar down his face was now only a whisper of pain, reminding me of the first time I'd seen him, sunburned and beaten by waves and straddling the line between the living and the dead. I hadn't thought him handsome at the time, and yet the way he wore the bruises had intrigued me. Not complaining, not vain, but like they were an inescapable part of him.

'Like Death's waiting around the corner,' I said.

'That sounds about right.' He folded his arms. One of the cuffs had a frayed white thread that stirred a memory. They were the same clothes Montgomery had been wearing when I broke into his room at the Blue Boar Inn. Montgomery had no use for a gentleman's suit now – he wore loose clothes on the island, clothes you could hunt and ride in.

I touched the thread, and as if seeing the line of my thoughts, Edward pulled it loose. Perhaps he didn't want my mind turning to Montgomery, but it was too late, because Montgomery was coming over.

'Any luck finding Ajax?' Edward asked.

'No. Balthazar's still out with the hounds. I've had enough of that awful rain.'

Father stared out the window. 'The island is in a perpetual

deluge this time of year. Trade winds off the Pacific, you know. Easy for a man to hide in weather like this if he knows the jungle.'

Easier still for an animal, I thought.

Cymbeline entered, straining under the weight of a steaming platter. Alice rushed to show him patiently how to cut and serve.

Montgomery ruffled the boy's hair. 'Smells wonderful,' he said to Alice. 'You're as good a teacher as you are a cook.'

Her cheeks turned a deep shade of peach. A pang of jealousy struck me deep inside, and I flopped into my chair. The others joined me at the table. Didn't Montgomery remember last night, during the storm, running his fingers down the bare skin of my back? *I* did. I could barely think about anything else.

Edward sat across from me, deep in his own thoughts. His hands still bore the scratches from our escape. I wondered if his ribs still hurt him. I absently touched my own, remembering the feel of his hands holding me there, that night behind the waterfall. As if he knew what I was thinking, he looked up and gave me the flicker of a smile. His dark eyes were intense.

I bet *he* remembered.

'Those clothes suit you well,' I said.

'Montgomery was kind enough to lend them to me.'

'I hardly had use for them,' Montgomery added with a slight grin. At least he and Edward were back to being civil. 'Besides, Edward's the gentleman, not me.'

'That's certainly an understatement,' Father said. Outside, a crash of thunder shook the windows. His bitterness killed what little contentment we had. I sat back, appetite gone in a flash. I threw my napkin on the table. Ever since Father had found out that Jaguar was alive and Montgomery had lied to him about it, he'd treated Montgomery like a dog.

But all Montgomery was guilty of was sparing a creature's life.

'When, exactly, were you going to tell us about the murders?' I asked Father, my voice tight. 'Or did you plan to keep calling them *accidents* and having Montgomery bury the evidence?'

Father speared a dumpling and didn't blink at my accusation. 'This is my island, Juliet. Not yours. If you'd stayed inside the compound walls as I instructed, there wouldn't *be* any murders.'

I nearly choked on my food. 'How is this my fault?'

'You set loose the rabbits,' Father said. His voice was cold. 'The islanders didn't even know what killing was before Ajax killed a rabbit. We've found three more rabbits with their heads torn off.'

I turned to Montgomery, who confirmed it with a nod.

I leaned on the table, anger making me as tense as the storm outside. 'Be careful with your accusations, Father. The murders started before I even arrived.'

He dismissed my comment with a scowl. 'I had everything under control before you came. Now you've riled them up. Trying to turn them against me, but it won't work. I'm God to them.'

'God to a pack of bloodthirsty animals.'

Alice's face went white. Montgomery's hand found hers in a reassuring squeeze. I was talking about her friends, I realized. And Montgomery's.

'They weren't *animals*,' Father said. Coiled rage was a tremor beneath his calm voice. 'Not until they tasted blood. They were human!' He slammed his brandy against the table, sending sticky liquid sloshing onto the tablecloth. 'But they won't be for long.'

'What do you mean?' Edward asked. There was an uncertain edge to his voice like a sharp piano note.

Father turned on him, eyes flashing. 'I mean Ajax should be six feet under right now. It's dangerous to let the smart ones live, don't you think, Mr Prince?'

Edward's hands coiled on the table, pulling up folds in the tablecloth. The tension between them was palpable. I had missed something, I realized. Something in their talk that first night. Some threat Father must have made. What had Edward called it? *An arrangement.* Maybe the arrangement hadn't been about me, after all.

'Very dangerous, I should think,' Edward said, his voice holding something back.

'The doctor means that he's ordered me to stop their treatments,' Montgomery interrupted. I whipped my head to face him. 'He intends to let them regress.'

A deep current of fear ran beneath my skin at the idea of beastly, mindless creatures roaming the island. 'You can't do that,' I said. 'If you take away their humanity—'

'Then they'll cease to be dangerous,' Father said.

'They'll be wild. Nothing to check their violence.'

'Don't be so dramatic,' he snapped. 'I told you, most of them are pigs. Dairy cows. Sheep.'

'Not all of them.'

'Don't you think I've considered that? There are safeguards. They all have domesticated components to keep them docile. What's more, what little spirit they might have once had was driven out of them by the procedure. Pain is an incredibly useful tool.' His fingers worked the table, and I imagined he was absently tracing the shape of a body, cutting into it. 'This regression is necessary, Juliet. A fail-safe. When they regress, they lose their dexterity. Everything here – the guns, the cabinets, even the door latches – has been carefully designed to work only for five-fingers.'

'Five-fingers?' Edward asked. He flexed his hand, looking at the web of cuts across his knuckles.

Father held up his open hand. 'Humans. And some of the more advanced creatures, like the house staff.'

'Jaguar has five fingers, too,' I warned.

'Which is precisely why we're hunting him down.' He turned his attention to Montgomery. 'Because *you* let him live.'

'I'm not to blame for this,' Montgomery said. I could see the stormy rage building in him. 'He shouldn't have been created in the first place. None of them should have been!'

I couldn't imagine he'd ever crossed my father so directly. The force of his outburst made me both elated he'd stood up for himself and terrified at what Father would do.

Father grew dangerously quiet. The clock on the mantel across the room ticked away painfully slow seconds. Montgomery's face went white, but he didn't take back his words.

'"Should never have been created,"' Father repeated with a chilling calmness. 'And what of your own part in it? You consider yourself innocent?'

Montgomery stared at the rain outside. His chest rose and fell quickly. 'No. But no one bears the blame more than you.'

'Bah! What do you know? You're hardly a gentleman. You said so yourself. Perhaps you should start acting like the servant you are and keep your useless opinions to yourself. And keep your dirty hands off my daughter!'

I nearly spit out my water. Montgomery's jaw tightened.

I pulled at my collar, needing air. Edward stared at me from across the table, face so slack I might as well have slapped him. Guilt seized me. I'd told him I cared about Montgomery, so he shouldn't have been surprised. But there'd been that night behind the waterfall. I couldn't pretend that had meant nothing.

'I don't know what you're talking about,' Montgomery said, trying to pass it off casually. But his voice shook. He didn't look up from the table.

Father smirked. 'Don't show your lack of intelligence by insulting mine.' He poured himself another glass of brandy. His temper had cooled into self-righteousness. 'Juliet, don't tell me you didn't know. Montgomery's been in love with you since the day you found him again. Long before that, come to think of it. He's been in love with the mere idea of you for years.' He took a sip. 'It's pathetic.'

'Stop this,' I said. My voice was barely audible above the rage boiling in my veins.

But Father was enjoying torturing him. 'We all know it's true. I merely want to inform him that you're too good for him. Prince is a damn fool, but I'd rather pair you with him. At least he's of proper breeding.'

I couldn't bring myself to look at either of them. I just wanted the torture to end.

'What do you say, Prince?' Father said jovially. 'You wouldn't mind a match with my daughter, would you? After all, it's a small island. Limited selection, you understand, unless you prefer the four-legged variety.'

My mouth nearly fell open. My face was burning, but I was too angry to be embarrassed.

Edward slammed his fist on the table. 'I say you're cruel and a madman, Doctor.' He pushed his chair back so hard it grated on the wood floor. 'The sooner this world is rid of you, the better it will be.' He threw his napkin on the table and left the room.

I stared at a chip in my supper plate, stunned. The ticking clock echoed in the hollow cage of my heart.

At last, Montgomery stood. 'I agree with Edward. And I'll add that you're a goddamned bastard.' He stormed out of the room into the rain.

I stood, too, but Father grabbed my wrist.

'He's a servant, Juliet. You'd do well to remember that. Prince would be the better match.'

'Why do you care?' I yelled. 'Why not just leave us be?'

'It's still my duty to see you married. And your duty to do as I say.'

'You've never liked Edward.'

'He's of use to me in this case.'

Father didn't care about people, only how he could use them. And matching me with Edward would mean fulfilling his fatherly duty so he could send me back to London with a husband and never think of me again.

I wrenched my hand from his. I had nothing to say to him.

TWENTY-NINE

Later that evening, I paced the long portico outside my apartment. Rain poured off the roof and into the courtyard. Beneath the door to Edward's outbuilding a shadow passed, back and forth, back and forth, making the light shift and slide. I pictured Edward pacing on the other side, as trapped as I was. Father didn't like Edward, knew hardly anything about him, but was ready to pawn me off on him to get rid of me. It stung that I meant so little.

I leaned against a post, listening to the storm. A light shone from the barn, where Montgomery must be attending to the horses, wishing the mess over dinner could be cleaned as easily as brushing down a horse. Above all the embarrassment and the anger, I was proud of him for standing up to my father.

I made my way around the portico, stealing glances at the barn's cracked half door, wanting just a glimpse of him. The horses stamped and whinnied within. I hadn't intended on going inside, but as if by their own accord, my fingers softly pushed the door open. Inside, rain slowly leaked into murky puddles in the straw. The whites of the horses' eyes flashed in the lantern light.

Montgomery groomed Duke with quick, tense strokes.

I let the door ease closed behind me, but the hinges groaned. Montgomery's eyes slid to mine. They were dark. Cold. Warning me away. He brushed harder, sending dust dancing in the air.

'He didn't mean it,' I said. I hugged my arms close. 'He would have said anything to wound you.'

The brush kicked up more dust, almost obscuring his face. The rhythmic sound of hard strokes against the horse's hair was hypnotic. Montgomery's jaw was set hard, the cords in his muscles strained.

'I know,' he said.

He finished brushing the horse's hindquarters and back legs, then used a metal pick to pull the knots from Duke's tail. When he finished, he threw the pick into a tin bucket. The metallic ring echoed in the small space, giving me shivers.

He rubbed down his hands with an old rag and stood in the stall opening. His presence warmed the room more than the lantern.

'But he wasn't wrong,' he said. Desire flickered in his eyes like firelight.

My heartbeat stumbled. *He's been in love with you for years*, Father had said. I'd thought Montgomery's affection lay with Alice, but could I have been wrong? If so, how could he love someone whose father had been so cruel? What if I misunderstood him still? What if—

He stepped closer, lowering his head. His face was inches from mine. Then he pulled me to him, digging his hands into my arms. His lips found mine. I jerked back, just for a breath, shocked by his passion. It was totally improper. But as he grabbed my chin and kissed me again, harder this time, I forgot about decorum. Suddenly I couldn't be close enough to him. I clutched the collar of his shirt so hard the fabric ripped.

His lips found the pulsing vein on my neck. I could hardly think. It was familiar and new, all at once. This was the little boy who'd taken care of me when Father was consumed with work. The little boy I'd idolized since I could barely walk.

He pushed my back against the stall door, kissing me. Edward had tried to kiss me, but I'd been so shocked I'd barely had time to explore how it felt. Lucy had told me stories of shady corners and sweaty palms. But this was passionate. Wild. Something I'd never known.

'Have you kissed a girl before?' I whispered.

He ran a thumb over my cheek. His eyes lingered on my lips. 'Yes,' he said. I thought of Alice, her pretty blond hair, the split lip that made her so vulnerable. But it wasn't her name he said. 'A woman at the docks in Brisbane. She didn't mean anything. I was lonely. It wasn't love.'

A prostitute, he meant. So he'd done much more than kiss her. Suddenly I didn't know what to do, as though I were still just a child and he a grown man. 'Just once?'

'Twice.' His fingers twisted in the hair at the back of my neck. The pupils of his eyes were wide and black, like an animal's. 'Does it matter?'

I bit my lip. I felt dizzy as a spinning top. In my old life I never would have risked my reputation. Never would have stepped outside the line.

But that life was behind me.

'No,' I said. I stood on my toes, pressing my lips to his.

The sound of barking dogs made me jump. I'd lost track of time, swept up in the storm of Montgomery's passion. He had pulled me into a dark corner of Duke's stall, murmuring my name as his lips grazed my throat, my shoulder, my temples.

I fought to my senses and put a hand on his chest. 'Do you hear the dogs? Balthazar's returned.'

He paused, listening, but his grip tightened on my waist. His hair hung loose over the sides of his face, hiding all but his fierce eyes.

A voice called from the courtyard. It was Father's. I gasped.

'Montgomery! You worthless fool, are you in here?'

Montgomery's fingers curled into the folds of my dress, protectively. My lips fell open but he placed a finger against them. I pressed farther into the barn wall, wishing I could disappear into it.

Montgomery pulled his hair back. He stepped out of the stall, blocking me from Father's view. 'Duke stumbled on the ride today. I thought he might have a sprain.' I detected an edge to his voice. After all, their earlier argument wasn't the sort of spat that would blow over easily.

'Get him saddled,' Father snapped. 'And Duchess as well. Ajax has killed again. That striped fellow, Lear. The beasts are rattled. It's time to put an end to this, storm or not.'

I kept a hand pressed to my mouth, afraid to make the slightest sound. Father couldn't find me here. I wouldn't put it past him to kill Montgomery.

Montgomery met my eyes briefly before closing the stall gate behind him. I heard the sound of his footsteps on the stone floor.

'Balthazar is gathering the men,' Father said. 'Prince will come with us. He may be a fool, but at least he can hold a gun.'

'And Juliet?'

'She'll stay with Alice. This was a fortress once. Nothing can get through these walls.'

I heard the sound of jangling bridles in the tack room. And then Father's voice, lower.

'And don't think I've forgotten your insolence tonight. The minute Ajax is dead, you and I will have words.'

I heard the creak of the door's hinges as Father left. A moment later, Montgomery unlatched the stall gate.

'He's gone to the salon. Quick, hurry to your room.'

'Be careful,' I said.

He pressed his lips to my forehead tenderly, flooding me with warmth. 'Be safe, Juliet.'

I slipped out of the barn, dodging every shadow for fear of the dark, and dashed back to my apartment. I pulled off my skirt and blouse and slipped into my nightdress. The last light faded over the sea as an overwhelming feeling of darkness grew in my heart. Whatever lay in that jungle, Montgomery and Edward were going to face it.

Alice knocked at my door. She looked terrified. 'Miss? Have you heard?'

'Yes.' I wanted to crumple in the corner with my face in my hands. It would be so easy to give in to the fear. But fear was written on Alice's face too. I took her hand, forcing back my own terror. 'Don't worry, Alice. We'll be safe.'

'They've all gone. We're alone.'

'I know.' I squeezed her hand, trying not to let my own worry show. 'I know.'

THIRTY

Formalities disappeared in the face of fear. It didn't matter that Alice was a servant and I the master's daughter. We climbed into my bed, huddling together like sisters frightened by a howling storm outside. Alice's eyes were wide and haunted. Maybe she was worried for Montgomery's safety. Or for the islanders'. Or for our own. Either way, there'd be no sleep for us that night.

I remembered that Montgomery had mentioned a needlepoint kit in my mother's trunk. I got up and dug it out and untangled the colored threads. We needed something to keep our hands busy.

'What's this, miss?'

I found a few tarnished needles. 'You've never seen needlepoint?'

She shook her head.

'How I envy you.' I unfolded a worn pattern of a blue bunny rabbit. She knew the basics of sewing, so she picked it up quickly, though her hands trembled with each lightning-crack outside. I plucked at my own pattern – a milk goat – though my thoughts rustled in the wind like the leaves outside. My lips still tasted Montgomery's salty kisses. I could barely think of the murders or our escape or even feel a pang of guilt that I'd rebuffed Edward's advance but kissed Montgomery so willingly.

I pricked my finger with the needle. My distracted stitches had made the goat look more like a horned devil. Alice's needlepoint had drifted off course, too, as her eyes were fixed on the dark window.

'Pay attention,' I said, hiding my own botched stitching under my skirt. 'You have to concentrate.' She looked at her work blankly. Her big eyes crinkled with worry. 'It's all right for a first try,' I added.

'I'm sure it isn't nearly as fine as yours, miss.'

I tucked mine farther under my skirt. 'Why were you never taught needlepoint? Every girl I know has calluses thick as pennies on her fingers.'

'I've no use for something so fine. Just the basics of sewing. Patches and hems.'

'Did your mother teach you to sew?'

Her face darkened. She turned her head, hiding the harelip. 'No, miss. I never knew my mother.'

Her voice was barely audible. She suddenly concentrated raptly on the stitches. It wasn't normal, a young girl alone on a godforsaken island, under the care of a madman. 'Then who brought you to the island?'

'No one. I've lived here as long as I can remember.'

'But you must have parents. How did they come to be here?'

'They came with the doctor.' Her voice dissolved to a whisper. Lightning cracked outside. The needle trembled as she pushed it through the fabric. I was beginning to understand. Her parents had been the Anglican missionaries who came over on the same ship as my father. Meaning she was the sole survivor of whatever tragedy had destroyed them.

No wonder she didn't want to talk about it.

'So who taught you to sew?' I asked, trying to keep my voice light. It wasn't successful. The wind howled outside. Something fell against the roof – a branch maybe. We both jumped.

'Montgomery did, miss.'

The blood rushed to my cheeks at the thought of him. I cocked my head. 'I'd hardly expect him to know his way around mending clothes.'

'Oh, he's quite knowledgeable about everything,' she gushed. Her face lit up, the danger outside forgotten. I'd found a topic to take her mind off the murders, at least. I just wished it wasn't so close to my own pounding heart. 'He does all the carpentry and metalwork, and he treats us when we're ill – he's an extraordinary physician – and he even taught me to cook. Cooking and sewing are woman's work, but Montgomery isn't too proud. Not when there's work to be done.'

The burning color in her cheeks made me uneasy. She was thirteen, maybe fourteen. The age when most girls can't think of anything but first kisses and true love. She was infatuated with Montgomery. I could hardly blame her. But it felt wrong to just sit and listen to her gush about him, knowing he'd just had his lips all over me.

'Yes, he's very talented,' I said.

'And you'll never hear him complain. Even the villagers' – her voice dropped – 'even *they* do as he says. They obey the doctor out of fear, if I may be so bold to say. But they listen to Montgomery because he's kind to them.'

'Indeed.' I pulled too hard at a pink stitch and ripped the thread. A curse slipped out as I reached for another skein.

'In fact, Montgomery told Balthazar he'd like to teach him to read. Can you imagine, miss? Balthazar with a book in his hands? And Montgomery will do it. He always keeps his promises.'

'Does he?' I asked, focusing on threading my needle. The trees outside trembled and shook. Something scraped against the side of the building. I glanced at the window, but outside was only darkness and leaves shimmering in the moonlight. I wished she would talk about something else. Anything else. The feel of Montgomery's hands lingered on my waist, so powerful that I thought it must be obvious with one look at my face. And yet she didn't seem to suspect a thing.

'Oh yes. He promised to take me to London one day. I know he will. He's told me all about it – the tall buildings and the people and the flower markets.' Her eyes were big and dreamlike.

The needle slipped from my fingers. I patted the duvet until I felt the stiff metal against my thumb. Why would he make such a promise? A man and an unwed girl couldn't travel alone without rumors. *I* certainly knew that. It was one thing for him and me to travel together – I didn't have anything to lose, not even a reputation. But Alice did.

So did he have some affection for her? Had he even considered *marrying* her? The thought made me blanch. But it was logical. Before I came, she was the only girl on the island. He certainly wasn't the type to care about her harelip. And she was a sweet girl. The kind a man married. Not like me, a girl who'd just as soon scratch a man as cook for him.

Could I just be a passing fancy to him then? Something new, like the prostitute in Brisbane?

A loud thump at the window made me gasp. I'd been deep in my head. Alice trembled in fright, her needlework forgotten. Even Montgomery was forgotten.

'A coconut fell,' I said quickly. 'The wind blows them down. I hear them occasionally.' I hoped she was too distracted to remember there were no palm trees anywhere near the compound.

She tore her eyes from the window to see if I was serious.

I swallowed the fear creeping up my throat. There was no telling what was on the other side of those iron bars. Jaguar, perhaps. A pack of islanders starting to regress. If only the window had a screen or shutters to seal off that awful darkness.

Another thump sounded. We both jumped. And then a long scraping sound, as if something were running a knife against the side of the building. Alice's small hand found mine and squeezed. My mind raced. I needed to devise an explanation to keep the fear from blooming in our hearts.

'The wind,' I muttered. It was a poor answer, and it didn't soothe either of us. Her breath came in quick little gasps. Something tapped against the iron bars. *Tap. Tap. Tap.* As if the darkness were knocking.

Alice's mouth fell open. I clapped my hand over it to keep her from screaming. She struggled but I wrapped an arm around her, holding her tight, like Montgomery did to calm the rabbits.

'Quickly. Get on the floor,' I whispered.

We tumbled off the bed, hiding behind the mattress, where anything outside couldn't see.

'What's out there?' she asked, squeezing my arm as though she was afraid I would leave her. No explanation came to my lips. It wasn't the *wind*, that was for sure.

'Stay low. You'll be fine.' I crawled across the floor to the dressing table. I pulled the rusty shears out of a drawer and hid them in the folds of my nightdress. Seeing them would only frighten her more.

My heart thumped painfully. Slowly, I pulled myself up and approached the window with careful steps. The wind whistled outside, a thousand malignant whispers.

The shears felt small but powerful in my hand. Heavy clouds blocked all traces of moonlight. Whatever was outside, it could be standing three feet away, or with its face inches from the bars, and I wouldn't know.

Lightning flashed. Fear shot up my throat, making me gasp. I had a quick glimpse of the valley. Shaking leaves. The stormy ocean beyond. No face, not unless I hadn't seen right. The island played tricks on my eyes.

I stepped closer to the window. My face almost pressed against the bars. I held the shears to my chest, ready to strike.

Lightning flashed again. There was nothing out there but the island, erratic and tumultuous. Yet I felt watched.

'Hello?' I called. My voice was hoarse. 'Is someone there?'

'Miss, don't!'

I turned toward the bed. The tip of Alice's head peeked above the mattress, her eyes wide and glassy.

'Get down!' I breathed. Her head disappeared faster than a blink. I tightened my grip on the shears. Maybe the traces of Father's madness in me had its uses – if it made me able to chop a rabbit's head off and maim Dr Hastings, it made me able to fight whatever was lurking outside.

I turned back to the window and forced myself to do what I feared most. Grabbed the iron bars.

'Hello?' I called again.

Only the howling wind answered. What lurked out there, watching?

I heard the scraping sound again, just outside the window. Inches away. My body went rigid. Something inside me screamed to run, but I gritted my teeth, ready to thrust the shears into those watching eyes. *Hungry* to do it.

Alice was forgotten. It was only me and the monster and the rolling thunder. *Tap tap tap*. Coming from so close. The thrill made my blood flow backward. I was ready. I squeezed the bars, knuckles white. In the pit of my stomach I knew that not even iron bars would keep us safe from the thing outside.

The wind howled, blowing cracks and wrinkles in the dark clouds. Faint moonlight broke through and glistened off three long, black claws on the other side of the bars.

Stretching close enough, almost, to graze my fingertips.

THIRTY-ONE

A jolt of fear nailed my feet to the floor. The claws found the stone windowsill, grazing gently, scraping at the rusty bars. Then three slow, sinister taps. *Tap, tap, tap.* Asking for entrance.

My heart crashed and throbbed, trying to break free of my ribs, pulled toward that monster in the night like rivers to the sea. I was hopelessly bound to the thing outside.

I leaned even closer, my trembling fingers a hair away from the glistening claws. I felt a deep, pulsing need to know the nature of the beast still hidden in shadows.

Alice screamed. The spell broke. I blinked, looking at the claws that were even now reaching for me. I slammed the shears into the longest one. It split down the ridge, shattering at the point. I dug the shears harder until I wrenched the broken claw off. The beast howled. The claws were pulled back into the darkness, save for one that fell to the floor.

'Miss, get away from the window!'

I crawled over the bed, fast as I could, and collapsed beside her. The wind whistled, calling me back. I fought the urge and pulled Alice into my arms instead. 'It's gone,' I said.

'It'll return!'

'It can't get through the bars.' My chest heaved. I wanted to tell her we were safe, but the lie wouldn't form. 'Get back on the bed, Alice. Finish your needlepoint.'

'I can't! Not with the monster out there!'

I cocked my head. Something about the way she said it: *the* monster. Not *a* monster. As if she had a certain one in mind. Jaguar had said the same thing. I gave her a sidelong look, wondering if she knew something more than she let on. 'Try.'

She could tell I was serious. We climbed back onto the bed and I picked up my milk goat and stabbed it with the needle. The men should return soon. They had rifles. Horses. We just had to wait it out.

I kept stitching, stiffly, until she picked her needle up, too.

'You called it *the* monster,' I said slowly.

Her hands shook. She didn't look up.

'Did you mean Jaguar? The one they called Ajax?'

She bit her bottom lip. Her needlepoint had apparently become endlessly fascinating.

'What aren't you telling me, Alice?' The edge to my voice slapped her. The harshness of it startled even me – I sounded so much like Father.

'Not Ajax, miss,' she said softly. 'Ajax was friends with Montgomery. They could have been brothers the way they went on. He used to tell me stories. I'd never be afraid of Ajax.'

My needlepoint fell into my lap, forgotten. If she wasn't afraid of Ajax, then why was her voice shaking?

'Jaguar isn't the one killing the islanders, is he?'

Her lips pressed together. It was enough of an answer.

I grabbed her wrist. 'Then what is?' She shrank back. I hadn't meant to scare her. I wanted to protect her, but I couldn't do that without the truth.

'I can't say, miss!'

'Why not?'

'It's listening! It's always listening. It'll kill me if I tell.' Her eyes welled with tears. She was so young – a child, really. A kind person might have patted her hand and told her everything was all right. I dug my nails into her palm instead.

'What do you mean? What's listening?'

'The monster!'

Something scrambled on the roof. Something big. Fast. Tiles crashed to the ground outside.

My breath froze. Alice cried out. I pulled her close, a finger against her lips. We both looked upward. It was right above our heads. The walls had to be twenty feet high. What kind of creature could scale a sheer wall? Another tile fell. Then came a thump in the courtyard. My head jerked toward the sound.

It was inside the compound.

I closed my eyes. My heart hammered wildly. The men were gone. The guns were across the compound in the barn. We hadn't even any proper locks on the doors. All we had was my wits.

'Alice, I want you to crawl under the bed.' I knew, somehow, that hiding from it was useless. But at least she would feel safer.

Her eyes were riveted on the door. 'They can't open the latches unless they have five fingers,' she said. 'The doctor said so.'

There was conviction in her voice. She believed in him blindly, just like his beasts did.

I scowled. 'He said they couldn't get past the walls, either, and that was a lie.' I bit my tongue before I said more. I'd only scare her. He was deluded into thinking himself a god, so adored by his creations that they'd never turn against him.

But animals were animals. And there was only one way of dealing with a bloodthirsty wild animal: kill it before it killed you.

I picked up the shears in one hand and the lantern in the other. 'Stay here,' I said.

'Miss, don't go out there!'

But I already had the door cracked open. 'Montgomery keeps ammunition and rifles in the barn. I'm going to try to make it there.'

Outside, rain poured off the roof into puddles. A lantern hung by the salon door, dimly lighting the court-yard. The tomato plants looked like skeletons in the shadows. A set of slippery tracks staggered across the mud, too muddled to count the number of toes. Leading to where, I couldn't tell.

'Keep the door closed,' I said. 'And stay under the bed.'

'Wait for the doctor and Montgomery, miss, please!'

But I didn't trust Father's promises like she did. The monster didn't obey my father's rules. It had made it into the compound. It had killed wantonly. It would find us.

'I'll be back soon. I promise.' I slipped out.

The compound was quiet, except for the rain and the wind. I moved silently, as I'd seen Jaguar do. *Toe-heel. Toe-heel.* I expected every shadow to jump to life. I could feel eyes watching from some dark place. I tried to tell myself I might be mistaken. In the haze of fear, every noise sounded louder. It might have only been a bird on the roof, or one of the ratlike creatures.

But the tracks didn't belong to a rodent, and no bird could knock tiles off the roof. I held up the lantern, my throat feeling exposed and vulnerable in the light. If it was out there, watching, I was an easy target.

I studied the tracks from under the eaves of the portico. They seemed to go everywhere and nowhere. It was impossible to single out a footprint in the mud and darkness. All I could tell was that they were large.

Very large.

A cry came from the jungle and I leapt. An owl. But it was startling enough to make me dart the rest of the way to the barn, panicked, the lantern light flickering wildly, until I threw open the barn door and closed it behind me, sealing myself inside.

Total darkness. The wind had extinguished the lantern's flame.

I could hear only the rasp of my breath and the steady drip of the leaky barn roof. Smell only the earthy, damp hay. My eyes fought for a glimmer of light to lock on to. Nothing but blackness.

I felt my way to the wall behind me, pressing my back into the wood. Holding tight to the shears. I told myself not to panic. There was no reason the monster would have gone into the barn. The laboratory was more likely, where it could smell the caged animals, or the kitchen with its mix of odd scents.

Get the rifles, I told myself. I'd been in the barn enough to know where the tack room and gun rack were, even in the darkness. I'd never fired a rifle, but I understood the interlocking parts, the burst of gunpowder. Odds were Montgomery kept them loaded. I would aim and pull the trigger. Even if I missed, it might scare the monster away.

But my feet wouldn't take me to the tack room. The wall against my back was safe. Standing still was safe. I had an overwhelming premonition that if I moved, I'd be dead.

I would count to five. Five breaths to return to reason.

One.

I gritted my teeth. Listened to the sound of my own breath.

Two.

Beneath the familiar smell of hay, I detected a pungent odor. And yet it, too, seemed familiar. I'd smelled that lingering scent before, recently even, though I couldn't place it.

Three.

A rustle in the darkness. My breath quickened. I told myself the barn must be full of mice. But I knew better. My hand tightened on the shears. The tracks hadn't led to the barn, I was sure of it. Wasn't I? I'd been so frightened that I'd barely been able to process what I'd seen. But there was that smell, stronger now, as if its source were closer. With a gasp, I recognized it.

Damp fur.

Four.

I squeezed my eyes shut. Something crept closer. I heard it in the sigh of the rafters. The shifting straw on the ground. It was too late for guns, I realized. There was something in the barn with me. Something big. Its presence melted into the darkness as if it belonged there. Fear clutched the soft parts of my throat. I told myself there was a logical way to go about this. The chest would be the largest target in the dark. Thrust the shears low, below the rib cage, where they would do the most damage. Duck low to avoid claws and teeth.

Something brushed my hand, something hard but gentle, shocking me so much that I dropped the shears. They clattered into the darkness.

Five.

I leapt for the tack room. I hadn't a choice. It was instinct now, not logic. I felt a rush of air behind me, like something running. The hairs on the back of my neck tingled. I couldn't hear anything but the pounding of my own heart. I found the doorway and stumbled inside, feeling blindly along the walls for the smooth metal row of gun barrels. My hand found only wood. Empty holsters.

They'd taken all the guns.

My hip collided with the corner of the worktable and I winced. I could hear my fear deep in my throat, a panicked whine like a dog's. I ran my hand over the table, looking for a knife, a hoof pick, anything. My hand settled on a box of matches. I fumbled to strike one against the rough side, and with a spark it burst to life.

I held it high, fingers shaking, eyes searching wildly in the dim light for my pursuer.

Nothing.

I was alone, with only the smell of the match's burning sulfur and the lingering scent of wet fur.

THIRTY-TWO

I told Alice, when I returned to the room, that I had found the beast and it was nothing more than an unusually large rat. Eventually she managed to fall asleep, but my eyes wouldn't close for a minute. We both lay on my bed, the monster's broken claw hidden in the curve of my palm. I put my arm around her, brushing her hair gently like my mother had done for me when I'd been frightened.

Hounds bayed in the distance. The men were returning.

I sat up, easing Alice's head off my lap, and tiptoed to the door. I'd lit every lantern I could find to chase away the darkness. I squeezed the broken claw to reassure myself the terror of the night hadn't been my imagination.

Outside, the front gate groaned open. I peeked into the courtyard. The men came in, muddy, exhausted, not even noticing the blazing lanterns. For a moment I felt a bit exposed in only a nightdress, with the storm raging and men returning, but I had bigger concerns. I glanced back to make sure Alice hadn't woken, and slipped outside the door.

Balthazar brought in Duke with the wagon, the back gate hanging open. One cadaver, swathed in muddy white. Which meant they hadn't found Jaguar, only another victim.

Montgomery and Father struggled to unload the body, but Edward saw me. His gaze was as unreadable as the night stars.

He crossed the courtyard, shielding his eyes from the bright light coming from my doorway. A streak of mud ran down the side of his face, alongside the scar.

'Why are you awake?' he asked. 'Why are the lanterns lit?'

I clutched the claw to give me strength. 'Something happened while you were gone.'

He could tell by the falter in my voice that it was serious. He pulled me into the room, where we had some privacy. He glanced fleetingly at Alice asleep on the bed.

'Your face is white.'

I fingered the claw's broken ridge. Remembering the sounds at the window, the tiles sliding off the roof. The certainty that I wasn't alone in the barn. 'Something tried to attack us. At the window . . .' Something broke inside me, and words didn't come out. Fear did, instead, in a rush. I squeezed the claw.

'Shh, you're safe now.' Edward pulled me to him, barely glancing at the claw. I supposed he'd seen enough of the carnage it had wrought. He ran a hand over my hair like he'd done behind the waterfall when I'd pretended to be asleep. It was a soothing gesture that had the opposite effect. Being so close to him agitated me, as if the dream might become real and I'd find myself with him instead of Montgomery. It wasn't as though the thought had never crossed my mind. Father wanted us matched. Edward clearly felt affection for me. Yet I *couldn't* be with Edward. He was running from something. He had secrets that he hid so well, I sometimes forgot they were there. I wasn't sure he'd let me peel back the layers, even if I wanted to.

'I shouldn't have left you alone,' he said. 'I knew it was

dangerous. I thought it might be safer for me to be out there' – his fingers tangled the ends of my hair – 'hunting whatever demons your father created.'

His whispering lips grazed my ear. It was like an unexpected bolt of electricity. I pulled back, but he didn't let go, lips parted to tell me something. His arms around me no longer felt safe at all. They felt dangerous, as if he might try to kiss me at any moment. I pressed my thumb against the claw's point, the bite of pain keeping me grounded. I knew he cared about me. But so did Montgomery. Oh, Montgomery . . . Being around Edward only confused me.

'We'll leave this island before it comes back,' he said, his voice low so as to not wake Alice.

'The monster, you mean.'

His hands dropped to my waist. Temptation whispered in my ear, ruffling the lace on my collar, drawing me closer. 'Whatever you want to call it.'

The door creaked. Montgomery stood on the doorway, frozen for a beat. I pulled away from Edward, face on fire. Edward toyed with the loose button on his shirt as if nothing had happened.

But something *had* happened, and I wasn't sure how to interpret it.

'I was looking for Alice,' Montgomery said, his eyes shifting between me and Edward almost imperceptibly.

I brushed a strand of hair behind my ear and nodded toward the bed. 'She's here.'

He came in, relieved. 'She wasn't in her room. I was worried . . .'

He checks on her first, I thought. *Not me*. But I shook the jealous thoughts out of my head. I was drawing inaccurate conclusions. When he'd come in and seen me with Edward, he might have come to a similar conclusion. But he'd have been wrong. Surely.

'Something got into the compound. One of the beasts, or else . . .'

'Or else what?' Montgomery asked.

'I don't know. What else might be on the island?' I asked, my eyes flashing, and set the claw on the dressing table.

Alice muttered something in her sleep and turned over. Montgomery's hand hesitated an inch above the claw.

'We can't stay here,' Edward said, voice rising. He picked up the claw and thrust it into the obscurity of his pocket. 'We need to get off this island.'

'Sh!' I hissed. Alice jerked awake, disoriented, crying out.

My first thought was to tell her it had been a bad dream. But Montgomery was already by her side, smoothing a hand over her beautiful fair hair. 'We're back,' he said. 'You're safe.'

Because I kept her safe, I thought. Father obviously wasn't taking care of the island residents, so someone had to.

But she kept shrieking, breathing so quickly I thought she might faint. At last Montgomery scooped her in his arms and carried her out. He passed someone in the courtyard, coming quickly, carrying a lantern.

Father burst into the room. 'What's happened? The barn door is off its hinges and there are a dozen broken tiles.'

I stood up. 'One of your monsters came in over the roof.' Venom laced my words.

'That's preposterous,' he said. 'They can't climb the wall. You're mistaken.'

'The mistake was to create them!'

He struck my jaw. Pain shot up the side of my face. I stumbled back, stunned. Maybe I shouldn't have been surprised. But somewhere deep inside, I still thought there might be hope for him and me.

Now I understood that there would never be.

Edward stepped in, fast, and twisted the stiff lapel of Father's jacket. 'Don't ever strike her.'

Father pulled away, seething. 'Punch me again, Prince, and you'll wish you'd never set foot on this island.'

'Stop it. Just stop it.' I stretched my jaw, testing. Nothing broken, just bruised. I understood now. He didn't care what happened to any of us. He'd gone mad with delusions. But as little as he cared for us, he might still listen to reason. 'Whatever you did to make them docile . . . it failed. They're animals. They won't obey you forever. There's only one choice, and that's to abandon your work. Leave this place.'

Father smoothed his cravat, which had gotten ruffled in his tussle with Edward. His eyes were black as the churning sea. 'As soon as the weather breaks, we're going to the village. You'll see for yourselves that I have everything under control.'

I touched the bruised edge of my jaw, knowing further discussion was useless.

He was beyond reason.

THIRTY-THREE

The storm raged for several days. By the time we were able to leave for the village, the jungle was so humid it felt as though the wagon was rolling underwater. We had to stop every quarter mile to clear the road of downed trees.

I could smell the village long before we arrived. The stench hung like a pestilence. Not just the smell of animals, but a rotten miasma that made me cover my mouth and nose. The beasts were overdue for their treatments, and Montgomery said the change would happen quickly. Father kept insisting they would be peaceful and domesticated in temperament now that the serum was dissipating from their systems.

Pigs, sheep, dairy cows, he'd said.

The road was practically a lake as we neared the village. Duke stopped, unwilling to go farther. Montgomery had to climb out and drag him by the harness.

The village was filthy. Huts had been torn down or clawed. Smoke billowed from piles of burning refuse. I exchanged an uncertain glance with Edward. This didn't look like the work of dairy cows.

We passed a creature wallowing in the mud, belly distended as though it was drunk. Its back legs were so bent,

I doubted it could walk. It watched the wagon pass with a vacant stare. Father motioned to it as we passed. 'Is this the beast that scaled a twenty-foot wall, Juliet?'

I folded my arms. He was delusional. Nothing I could say would change that.

The wagon jerked to a halt. We were in the village center, though I hardly recognized it. Gone was the praying crowd, the man with the sweeping red robe, the beasts clamoring for a glimpse of their venerable creator.

'No one to greet us,' Montgomery observed.

Father dismissed it with a wave. 'That's to be expected. They're like livestock now, I told you. Either wallowing like pigs or rooting out grain somewhere.'

I glimpsed a few eyes watching us from sunken doorways. I hugged my arms, feeling a chill despite the heat.

Edward pointed to one of the few huts still standing. Cymbeline peered at us from within, apparently unchanged except for a hardened, distrustful turn to his mouth. I waved. He hissed, baring inch-long fangs he'd never had before. I hugged my arms tighter.

Father climbed down and dusted off his hands. He extended his arms, smiling, like a savior returning to his adoring masses.

'Come out!' he called. 'Let me see your beautiful faces.'

No one came. I detected a flicker of uncertainty in his face, but it was gone as fast as the buzzing flies. 'You there!' He pointed a long finger at a figure in a doorway. 'Don't be shy. Come on.'

The figure slunk forward on all fours, moving rhythmically. Its limbs popped in the sockets as it moved. It circled us slowly and then stood upright on two feet and slunk closer.

The python-woman. Her face was horribly stretched, and she no longer wore clothing. She approached my father with the grace of a snake.

He smiled, oblivious to her horrible appearance. 'Where is Caesar, my dear?'

'Caesar,' she repeated. She slunk along the side of the wagon. My stomach clenched. Montgomery swore I wasn't like the beasts, but I couldn't help but fear I'd end up like her if I stopped taking my treatment.

She gave a few hissing chuckles. 'Caesar says no more.'

More creatures emerged, creeping toward us slowly. Bodies stretched unnaturally, moving on four legs. Montgomery calmly placed a hand on his rifle.

'Where is he?' Father commanded. The smile was gone. 'Bring him out!'

Python-woman laughed again. Her forked tongue darted in a thin-lipped mouth. 'Bring him out, bring him out, he says.'

Creatures started to swarm like flies, blocking the road behind us. At last we heard a faint wheezing. The creatures bobbed up and down like a restless herd. A giant figure passed through the crowd, taunted as it came forward. I covered my mouth. It was Caesar, antlers broken off, only splintered nubs left. One shoulder twisted at an unnatural angle. Black stains covered the skin around his eyes and mouth.

'We should leave,' I said. But no one responded.

Father took one look at Caesar and moved his hand to his pistol. 'You weren't supposed to stop *his* treatment,' he growled at Montgomery.

'I didn't,' Montgomery said. 'This isn't regression. The others did this to him.'

Father rested a foot on the worn stone stand. 'Recite the commandments, Caesar,' he ordered. 'They seem to have forgotten!'

But Caesar bobbed his head, as if rubbing his antlers on a phantom tree. 'Speak!' Father ordered again, and the python-woman hissed.

'Caesar says no more,' she repeated.

Father grabbed Caesar's jaw and forced his mouth open. There was a gurgle of saliva and clinking teeth, and Father's mutterings to himself. His back went rigid, and then his hand fell away, releasing Caesar. The elk-man dropped his chin to his chest.

Father came over in long, reluctant steps, running a shaky hand over his whiskers. 'They've cut out his tongue,' he said.

I drew back in revulsion. 'My God.'

Father gave me a sharp look. 'We can do just as well without him.' I didn't know if he meant Caesar or God himself.

Father turned back to the crowd. 'Listen! I shall speak the commandments myself, you wicked creatures! You call yourselves human, yet you live in filth. You crawl upon the ground like four-legged things. How soon you have forgotten the commandments!' The shuffling and murmuring in the crowd quieted. The creatures cocked their heads as if remembering a long forgotten song.

'Thou shalt not drink spirits! Thou shalt not eat flesh of living creatures! Thou shalt not roam at night!' Father paused. I knew what came next but I waited, as breathless as the creatures. 'Thou shalt not kill other men!' He stamped his foot. 'This is the word of your god!'

Silence pervaded. The creatures stared with dull, watery eyes. *No*, I wanted to shout. *They aren't the word of any god. They're the words of a madman.*

'Yes!' A husky voice broke the silence. 'Yes, the word of our god!' Low murmurs ran through the crowd. We all strained to find the voice. A hulking creature pushed his way toward us. His gait was lilting. It was the bearlike creature I'd seen in the jungle with Jaguar. His hands were crippled into twisted claws he kept tucked against his chest.

257

He stopped in front of Father. The islanders huddled closer like cattle. 'The word of our god!' the bear-man shouted.

I glanced at Edward. His arms were folded, muscles tight as wire.

'We shall not drink spirits!' the bear-man cried again, dancing on his monstrous legs. 'We shall not eat flesh! The words of our god!'

The beast-people began to stir again, as uncertain as I was. Python-woman slunk up to me, her slanted eyes blinking. She licked her mouth with an unnaturally large tongue. I sucked in a breath.

'Very good, Antigonus,' Father said to the bear-man. His lips twisted in a self-satisfied smirk. 'Now, my fellow, tell me who did this horrible thing to Caesar.'

Antigonus took a few stilted steps toward Father, beckoning with a clawed hand. His other hand was still clutched at his waist. Just as he leaned his bear snout close enough to whisper, a knife blade glinted in his hand. It jerked toward Father's throat.

A shot rang out.

Montgomery had scrambled for his rifle, but Edward had fired first. The creatures panicked, climbing over one another to get away. Antigonus's body fell at my father's feet, spilling blood on his leather shoes. Father's eyes were wide. One of his precious creatures had turned on him.

Montgomery rushed to the body. Dust clouded around them. But I couldn't take my eyes off Edward. He had killed. Defending my father, no less. The pistol fell from his hands. He looked as stunned as I felt.

'Edward—' I said, but I couldn't finish. He was a killer now, too.

His face was blank, wide-eyed. He ran a hand over his head, shaken, staring at the fallen body as though it was going to stand up and haunt him. His eyes held the same look as when we had found him in the dinghy, torn between life and death and sea madness.

He turned and disappeared into the jungle, as though he could run from what he'd done.

We rode back in miserable silence. There was no sign of Edward, no matter how much I'd yelled for him. Montgomery assured me that a man who could survive twenty days in a battered dinghy could make it back to the compound. But at sea the only thing hunting Edward had been the inescapable sun and his own haunted memories, and here there was a monster loose.

Someone shouted ahead. Through the leaves, the compound's walls appeared. Balthazar came running, big chest huffing, eyes rimmed in red. I recalled the first time I'd seen him, when I thought he was hideous. Now, after the horrible faces of the python-woman and Antigonus and the others, he looked as human as any of us. I hoped Montgomery would never stop giving him the treatments. I couldn't stand to see Balthazar regress.

'What is it?' Montgomery asked. His hand tightened on the rifle.

'Come quickly,' Balthazar said, out of breath. His lower lip trembled. 'Hurry.'

Montgomery handed the reins to Father and jumped from the wagon. He took off at a jog with Balthazar. Ahead, I saw the wooden gate was broken. The boards had been splintered by a terrible force.

Father brought up the wagon quickly. No one waited to take it. Puck, Alice, the other servants – they weren't there. Something clenched in my stomach. A primal need to get inside. To find out what had happened.

Father thrust the reins at me. 'Stay here. Hold Duke.'

'But what happened?' I asked. He ignored me. I twisted

my fingers in Duke's mane, watching the men disappear through the broken gate. Why was no one saying anything? Why didn't someone come for the horse?

There were tracks in the mud outside the gate. Slipping, gliding tracks like the monster had made before. But the gate was reinforced with iron bars. The monster couldn't bend iron, could it?

A man yelled. I recognized Montgomery's voice.

'Stay here and be damned,' I muttered, and led Duke and the wagon to a tree. I looped the reins around a branch and hoped he wouldn't try to bolt.

I bunched my skirt in one hand as I climbed through the broken gate. My breath caught. The courtyard was a wreck. The tomato plants had been trampled, the lanterns broken, the chicken house shattered.

Voices came from the kitchen. I stepped toward them slowly.

'The devil take you!' Montgomery yelled from around the corner. 'The devil take you all!' The anguish in his voice made me stop in my tracks. He was usually so controlled, even when he was seething with fury.

I pressed my cheek against the stone wall. They were right around the corner. I only had to look. But somehow, I was afraid that looking would change everything.

'The devil take you!' Montgomery yelled again.

Curiosity took control, compelling me to look at whatever had Montgomery so enraged.

Montgomery and Father were outside the kitchen door with Balthazar and Puck. Montgomery paced back and forth wildly, hulking shoulders straining like a beast's. A trembling hand covered his mouth.

'Calm down,' Father said. His hand was shaking, too. 'You'll drive yourself mad.'

A flash of white on the kitchen floor caught my eye. I

blinked, not sure I was seeing correctly. Alice's white skirt peeked out from the doorway, flat on the ground, with two pale bare feet streaked in mud. A line of dark blood dripped from her big toe into a puddle. The feet didn't move. As certain as I'd ever been of anything, I knew those feet would never move again.

Alice was dead.

THIRTY-FOUR

Montgomery slammed his fist into the kitchen door. The wood splintered too easily, and he growled, unsatisfied. He swung his other fist at the solid stone wall.

I rushed forward. 'Stop it!'

But it connected with a sickening crack. Blood flowed from his shredded knuckles. I locked my hands around his wrist.

'Stop it!' I said. 'It won't change anything.'

'Let go!' His loose hair was caked in sweat and grit. The muscles in his arm flexed like steel clockwork below his skin. It took all my strength to hold his fist back from pounding into the wall again.

'He's going to hurt himself,' Father said. 'I'll prepare a shot of morphine.'

Montgomery reeled toward him. 'I don't want your drugs. I don't want anything from you!'

Father ran a shaking hand over his chin's thin white hairs. For a moment I thought he might apologize or, at the least, offer some condolence. But then his black eyes iced over. 'That suits me. You were worthless anyway.'

Montgomery's arm jerked back. In another second his fist

would have slammed into my father's face, but I threw my arms around him.

'Come on,' I whispered. I touched his hot cheek, his tense shoulders, trying to calm him. Alice's cold flesh lay by our feet on the kitchen floor. Her blood soaked into the mortar. It could have been me. It could have been any of us. The thought nauseated me. 'You need air. You need to clear your head.'

He strained against my arm, pacing like a wild animal, but I was able to gradually pull him away from her body, through the broken gate, and away from the compound.

I found a grassy place against the vine-covered outside wall where we could see the sparkling ocean. I sat down, but it took him some time to calm. I tore a strip of cloth from the hem of my skirt.

'Let me bandage your hand. You're getting blood everywhere.'

His blue eyes met mine. The wild animal was still there, still restless. But there was pain, too. He sat down next to me and tied his hair back. I gently wiped away the blood from his busted knuckles. His jaw had a hard edge. He was so handsome it made my pulse race.

'I'm sorry,' I said, winding the strip of linen around his hand.

He didn't answer.

I pictured Alice's white feet in the mud, glad I hadn't seen her cold, dead face. 'I know she loved you,' I said before I could stop myself. 'And I know I came between you. If I'd never come, maybe she'd still be alive.'

His deep eyes could carry every burden in the world. I tied off the bandage, tucking in the frayed edge. It was already damp with sweat and blood. 'It's not your fault,' he said.

'Did you love her?' She was dead, not even buried, but

I couldn't keep my frantic thoughts to myself. My voice rose in a hysterical pitch. 'If I hadn't come, would you have married her?'

His eyebrows were a line of worry. 'What are you talking about?'

'You always wanted to save people. She was an orphan. The only missionary left. How could you not have fallen in love with her?'

'Blast and damn.' His head fell back against the wall, crushing the vine's little white flowers. 'I wasn't in love with Alice. God, Juliet, I thought you knew. She wasn't one of the missionaries.' He paused, not meeting my eyes. 'She was a creation.'

My breath caught. I pushed my hair back with shaking hands. Alice? The sweet girl who carried the comb of my silver brush set, one of *them*? I felt my head shaking forcefully. 'That's impossible. She was human.'

'She looked human,' Montgomery said. Sweat beaded on his forehead. His wounded hand tensed. 'But she was created two years ago from a sheep and three rabbits.'

'Rabbits?' I put my fingers to my lips, as if I could feel the word. As if that might make it more believable.

Her harelip. *They are all flawed,* Father had said. I tried to piece it together, to make sense of the puzzle. Alice had dodged my questions about her past. God, I'd been such a fool. When I called Balthazar and the others animals, I'd been calling her the same.

'I thought you said it couldn't be done.' I swallowed back my rising fear. 'You said he couldn't make them look completely human.'

The blood drained from Montgomery's face. He took a deep breath. 'He can't.'

It came to me then. A whisper of an idea.

'You made her,' I said. Not a question. An accusation.

264

He rubbed a hand over tired eyes. The wound had reopened, and blood seeped through the bandage.

'How could you?' I whispered, lips trembling. 'Just like Father . . .' Blood rushed in my ears. I tried to stand, but he grabbed my hips and pulled me back to the grass.

'What's done is done! If I'm to go to hell, so be it. But I'm not like him.' The force of his anger was a slap in the face. It wasn't me he was angry at, but himself. He let me go and stood up, grabbing the iron bars outside my window. Like he deserved a prison.

'It was a mistake,' he said. 'I knew that from the beginning. Your father and I had an argument. One of his creatures died on the operating table. I tried to warn him. I saw the errors in his work. But he'll never admit to mistakes. He told me he was the doctor and I was a servant, and it would always be that way.' His knuckles tightened on the bars. 'I wanted to prove him wrong.'

The breeze off the ocean blew a strand of hair into his face. He hadn't said it in so many words, but I understood. By creating Alice, he had bested my father at his own work. With no formal training, as only a teenage boy.

And they called my father a genius.

I looked at him askance. I had underestimated him. We all had. As much as I cared about him, I always thought of him as the handsome, brooding assistant. Edward was the clever, educated one. Montgomery was a workhorse, strong and faithful.

But if he could make Alice, what else was he capable of?

'It was wrong.' He turned away from the window, plucking a flower from the vine and tucking it behind my ear, as thought it could protect me. 'And now she's dead, and so are we if we don't find Ajax.'

'Ajax?' I asked. 'Don't you think it was the monster who killed her?'

He frowned. 'What monster?'

I paused. Didn't he know? Alice had been terrified of something very real, and it wasn't Ajax. Montgomery had been gone for months. Long enough, I supposed, for Father to create some terrible new creature without his knowledge.

The trees rustled in front of us. The sound of footsteps came from the jungle.

I slowly stood. Montgomery stepped in front of me protectively.

The footsteps grew louder.

Something was coming.

THIRTY-FIVE

Montgomery pulled a blade out of his boot. The footsteps were running now. Whatever it was, it tore through the jungle. I clawed at his arm. We had to get back inside the compound.

But Montgomery wouldn't come. His eyes were the steely color of ice. He wanted to be there when the monster returned. He wanted to ram the knife into its murderous flesh.

The leaves trembled just beyond the line of trees. The muscles in his arm tensed, ready to strike.

A figure came out of the woods, tearing at the leaves. I grabbed the blade from Montgomery. I had recognized Edward a second before Montgomery did, and that might have saved his life.

'Devil in hell,' Montgomery cursed. 'You gave us a fright, Prince.'

Patches of blood streaked Edward's shirt. Scratches formed lines over his face. He braced himself on his knees to catch his breath.

'Are you all right?' I asked, just as breathless. 'Is something chasing you?' The jungle was silent, but silence could hide danger.

'I don't know.' He wiped his face with the back of his hand. 'I heard noises. I ran. It might have been only my imagination.' His sleeve was torn. A gash ran down one arm. Blood seeped through his shirt where his shoulder met his neck. He touched the blood, wincing. 'Damn thorns are big as my thumb.' He looked between me and Montgomery. 'What are you doing outside the walls?'

He hadn't been here. He didn't know about Alice.

Montgomery slid the knife back into his boot. 'I have work to do.' His voice was dead again. He wanted it to have been the monster, I realized, to exact his revenge. 'I have a casket to make,' he muttered over his shoulder.

Edward's face went slack. A question formed on his lips.

'For Alice,' I said hesitantly.

Edward collapsed against the wall, wiping a hand over his white face. 'How? When?'

'While we were in the village. Something broke into the compound. It tore down the gate.'

'There are iron reinforcements.'

'Even so.' I took a deep breath. 'Come inside. I'll dress those cuts.' Between him and Montgomery, at least I was getting some use out of my medical knowledge.

We climbed through the splintered gate and passed the area outside the kitchen. They had moved Alice's body, but the tiles were stained red. Edward was silent.

Most of the medical supplies were in the laboratory, but I knew there was a small kit in the servants' bunkhouse. The quarters were spartan, simple, just as I'd imagined. Two beds for Balthazar and Puck and a floor pallet for Cymbeline, though he'd disappeared back to the village when the treatments stopped. The sheets were crisp and white. A woven ring hung above one of the beds, rich in red-and-gold threads, as if it was meant to capture nightmares before they could enter the sleeper's mind.

I pulled open the desk drawers until I found a length of cloth and a pair of scissors.

'Sit down,' I said. 'Take off your shirt.'

He pulled out the stool and obliged. His skin was pale except for his tanned arms and a sunburned ring around his neck. In addition to the cuts on his arm and neck, a dark-blue bruise covered his ribs.

'Thorns did this?' I said.

'Everything here's dangerous. Even the damn plants.'

I poured iodine onto a clean rag. *I should bandage Montgomery's knuckles, too*, I thought briefly. But he'd never sit still long enough. I dabbed the iodine on Edward's cuts. The sting didn't seem to affect him, but when my fingertips grazed his skin, his stomach muscles contracted sharply.

'You're too good for him,' he said.

I dabbed the rag carefully around his cuts. I didn't need to ask who he meant. 'He's a good man,' I said. 'He's smarter than he looks.' I tried to keep my fingers from shaking. *So smart he made Alice*, I thought, but I kept that to myself.

'A good man wouldn't have brought you here.'

I turned away to measure lengths of cloth. It wasn't a discussion I was willing to have. To be honest, I wasn't sure I could win.

'Your father wants us matched,' he stated. As if I needed reminding.

'Don't,' I said. 'Don't talk about that.'

'We have to talk about it! We've all been dancing around it . . .'

'Fine, then.' I balled the cloth in my fist. 'Why don't we talk about why you killed Antigonus, then? I must have missed when you and my father became so close that you decided it was all right to kill to defend him.'

The tic in his jaw pulsed slightly. For a moment his face seemed undecided as he tilted it slightly toward the door.

269

He brushed at his chin as if he could sweep away the tic. 'I wasn't thinking. I saw the blade in Antigonus's hand, and it was just instinct. It wasn't your father I was trying to defend, Juliet. I swore to protect you. To be honest, your father could be sliced through the chest tomorrow, and I wouldn't blink.' He paused. 'I'm sorry. That was heartless.'

I shook my head. I didn't like what the island was doing to us, making Edward a killer and me so unhinged. I tried to tell myself it didn't matter that Edward had killed one of them so easily. It wasn't in cold blood. It was defense.

'It doesn't matter,' I said. 'We need to focus on leaving.' I wrapped the cloth around the gash on his shoulder, glad that at least I could fix one thing. But what was one bandage going to do against the madness out there? I had an overwhelming feeling that the island wanted to sink its thorns into us, to bind us to this place.

'Even if we left,' I said, fighting to keep an even tone, 'even with water and food, how could a ship possibly find us? One tiny dinghy might as well be a piece of driftwood!'

I jerked my head toward the sea, angry at myself for being weak. I should have been stronger. Edward wrapped an arm around my back. I buried my face in the soft bandage on his shoulder.

'We're going to die, aren't we?' I asked bitterly.

He held me so tight I could hardly breathe. But I wanted tighter still. 'Not here. I swear it.'

That evening, the chime of bells mixed with jungle birdsongs. I found the wagon in the courtyard with all the men gathered. The gate had been hastily repaired with scrap wood from the barn. Boards from the same source formed a simple wooden box the length of a small person.

'Let's be done with it then,' Father said. He took a lantern. Balthazar and Puck slid the coffin into the wagon bed.

I pulled a shawl around my blouse. 'Where are you taking her?' I asked.

Montgomery paused with his hand on Duke's harness. The rifle was slung over his chest. A pistol glinted at his side. 'We've got to burn the body,' he said. He swung into the driver's seat.

My stomach turned. 'But you dug graves for the others.'

'That was before. They'll dig her up now. The regression gives them a better sense of smell.'

Balthazar held his hand out to help me into the wagon. I shook my head, remembering the buzzing flies and bloody canvas wrap. I'd rather walk than ride with another dead body.

At a click from Montgomery, Duke heaved at the wagon. We followed its deep tracks into the jungle. Father's small lantern was our one light in the darkness. I matched my steps to Edward's. A rifle hung over his shoulder, too. One of the new ones from London. I raised my eyebrows.

He jerked his head toward my father. 'Apparently killing a man makes me trustworthy enough to get one of the good rifles.'

We walked for some time. The only sounds came from the jungle and the squeak of Duke's harness. I heard the sea before I saw it. The dirt path turned to sand under our feet, and then suddenly we were there, bathed in moonlight, beside the churning tide. Montgomery stopped the wagon. Balthazar and Puck took out armfuls of wood and started down the dock.

Father nodded toward the dark horizon. 'We'll burn her at sea.'

The breeze carried the distant sound of the firewood tumbling against wood. I swallowed. He was going to burn her in the launch. I threw a look to Edward – the launch was the only way off the island.

'Montgomery, get the casket,' Father said.

Montgomery slid the casket halfway out, and Edward took the other end. Father and I followed the wooden box down the beach. Sand gave way to boards that echoed our footsteps. Montgomery climbed onto the launch and settled the box on top of the wood piled in the bottom. His palm rested for a moment on the flat face of the casket before he climbed back onto the dock.

At Father's nod, Puck scattered straw over the launch. Father raised the oilcan, but Balthazar shuffled forward first with something square and black clutched in his hands. A nervous whine came from deep in his throat.

'What do you want?' Father barked.

Balthazar held up a thin, worn volume. A gold cross imprinted on the cover reflected the moonlight. Father made no move to take the Bible.

'Where did you get that vile thing?' Father asked.

'Left behind by the missionaries,' Montgomery said softly. 'He's become fond of the prayers.'

Father shook his head. 'Sorry, my fellow. I wouldn't say a prayer over the body of my own sinful mother.'

Balthazar whined again, lower. Father uncorked the oilcan, but Montgomery grabbed his wrist. 'Stop.' He jerked his chin toward Balthazar. 'Let him say a goddamn prayer for her.'

'Prayer. Christianity.' Father snorted. 'Fairy tales.' He poured the thick, pungent liquid over the casket.

The muscles in Montgomery's throat contracted. He had given life to Alice. Taught her to speak, to read, to sew. He cared about her as a girl, not some scientific experiment.

He cares about all of them.

The realization was a strange one. It was illogical to be so attached to walking experiments, and yet I was beginning to understand it. Before Crusoe died, Montgomery had treated the dog more like a friend than a ratcatcher. The other servants teased him for caring so much about an animal. But they weren't just animals to Montgomery. They had hearts and brains. Maybe even souls.

'"To everything there is a season,"' Edward quoted, breaking the silence. My father bristled at the verse but let it stand. '"And a time to every purpose under heaven: A time to be born, and a time to die."'

Montgomery nodded, a silent thanks.

Father lit a straw and threw it onto the launch. It took flame immediately. The flickers of orange and red ate away at Alice's coffin. The boards cracked and splintered. I watched as long as I could. The smell was unmistakable. I covered my mouth with the shawl.

Montgomery untied the launch. He threw the rope onto the pyre and gave the vessel a shove with his boot to send it out to sea. The waves reflected the flames, making the whole ocean burn.

'So we all shall end,' Father reflected, then tucked his hands into his pockets and started down the length of the dock.

'We shouldn't stay out here longer than we have to,' Edward said, but I shook my head.

'Give us a moment.'

Edward glanced at Montgomery, who stood at the end of the dock watching the smoldering pyre. He left us alone, but I could feel reluctance pulling at him like the tide.

Montgomery kicked the empty can of oil into the water, where it floated for a moment before drowning. Flames highlighted the angles of his face.

'If you're going to judge me for creating her,' he said, 'don't bother. I already know I'll go to hell for it.'

I watched the dying fire. I took a deep breath. 'It isn't your fault she died.'

With a crack, Alice's pyre splintered. The sea bubbled up from beneath, swallowing the flames, pulling the remains of her body to the deep.

Montgomery spun and strode back to the wagon, putting distance between him and Alice's sinking body. I ran after him, but he was already back with the others. My footsteps echoed in the hollow space below the dock. I stopped. If he'd wanted me to catch him, he'd have let me.

Our nerves were as battered as the wagon's old struts and axle on the ride back. No one spoke. I don't know what terrified us more – passing through the jungle at night, or what might be waiting for us at home.

THIRTY-SIX

For days afterward, Father wouldn't speak of what had happened – not Antigonus's betrayal, nor the savage murders that had claimed Alice as the most recent victim. He plunged himself into his work instead, spending all day and night in the laboratory and emerging only for meals or to go on secretive errands into the jungle with Puck. The rest of us lived every moment on alert.

One evening Montgomery, Edward, and I stayed in the salon after an awkward supper during which Father refused to entertain even the slightest suggestion of danger. Montgomery paced by the windows like a caged animal, eyes fixed on the darkness outside. I sat on the piano bench, touching the long black keys one at a time, slowly, listening to the sharp resonance spilling out across the room.

'We'll have to build a raft,' Edward said. 'Between the monster and the beasts, we'll be lucky to last another week.'

I struck a C-sharp. 'That'll take too much time. Father will figure out what we're doing.'

Montgomery paused, folding his arms. His gaze was still focused out the window. 'There's another launch,' he said curtly.

My finger slipped off the key, crashing into the C and D with a discordant echo.

Edward leapt up. 'Where? Why didn't you tell us sooner?' he asked.

'It's not exactly tethered to the dock, waiting for our escape.' He rubbed his forehead. 'It's in the village.'

I took my foot off the sustaining pedal, cutting off the notes. 'We can't go back there. You saw the beasts. And they're getting worse every day.'

Montgomery ran a hand over his hair. 'I didn't say it would be simple. The boat belongs to Caesar. He used it for baptisms.'

'Next you'll be saying those animals take communion,' Edward said.

Montgomery narrowed his eyes. He'd grown up with the islanders, I wanted to remind Edward. Not with governesses and siblings and servants like a general's son would have. 'You think they're not good enough for religion, Prince?'

I pressed the pedal again, feeling the hammer board tighten and release, wishing everything could be as simple as the workings of a piano.

Edward cracked his knuckles, one at a time. The air was getting tense. 'I don't recall the Bible preaching clawing people's hearts out.'

Montgomery's hands curled to fists at his sides. 'You can't blame them for wanting revenge. Do you have any idea of the pain they've suffered at human hands?'

'I don't,' Edward said. 'But I'd wager *you* do.'

I pounded my fist against the lower keys. The room shook with the wild combination of deep notes. 'Stop it! You can box each other to bruises back in London, if you like. But let's get the launch first and get off this island.' I slammed the key cover down. 'Agreed?'

They stared at each other, taut as piano strings. At last

Edward turned away, his eyes meeting mine. I got a chill, thinking of the three of us back in London. Not every problem would be solved by leaving the island.

'Where's the boat, then?' Edward asked.

'There's a church,' Montgomery said. 'It's a stone building in the main square with a wooden cross above the door. The rowboat is in a shed behind it. They might have smashed it for firewood for all we know.'

'We don't have any other options,' I said.

'We should wait until the doctor leaves,' Montgomery said. 'The next time he takes Puck on another fool's errand.'

'How do we know the beasts won't try to kill us?' I asked.

Montgomery folded his arms again, staring out the window. 'Let's hope they feel more loyalty to me than they do to the doctor.'

I couldn't sleep that night. My dreams kept replaying the feel of my kiss with Montgomery. His arms around me in the barn, pulling me closer, his hand running down my hair. The dreams slipped to Edward holding me behind the waterfall, and I awoke, restless. It was very early, though already hot. I sat up and my foot accidentally kicked the wooden box where I kept my medication. I'd run out the day before but I hadn't told anyone. If I didn't take it today, I'd start to feel symptoms.

I pushed the still-locked box farther under the bed. No matter how Montgomery tried to convince me my treatment was different from the islanders', I needed to find out for myself.

I went to the salon just after dawn. The mantel clock sliced little ticks through the thick early-morning silence. Troubling dreams. Father insane. Murderer loose. Alice dead.

Montgomery came in, as surprised to see me as I was to see him.

'I couldn't sleep,' I said. 'The heat.' I left out the dreams.

If he could tell I was nervous, he said nothing. 'I can't say that I mind a little time with you before the world rises.' My stomach pressed against my spine, the air suddenly gone. He took my wrist, lightly. He kissed the soft, sensitive flesh, and then ran his finger up my arm. *This is what people talk about*, I thought, *when they say they could die of pleasure*. I would have gladly died, if it meant he'd press his lips to my skin again. But he stole away his touch and didn't return it.

My eyes snapped open.

'You didn't take your treatment this morning,' he muttered.

I swallowed, surprised, still longing for his touch again. 'How do you know that?'

'Because you're out of medicine. I've kept track of the number of days in your supply.' He pressed his palm to my forehead. 'And you're burning up.'

Maybe the heat I felt wasn't just at the thought of him and Edward, then. I twisted my head away. 'It doesn't matter. I'll drown at sea or be clawed to death before I get sick.'

But he shook his head, his eyes locked to mine. 'You're doing this on purpose. You want to see what will happen if you don't take your treatment. You think you'll become like *them*.'

A bead of sweat rolled down my temple. 'It's an experiment,' I said. 'You have to appreciate that, as a man of science.'

'I told you. You aren't one of them.'

'Then my experiment will prove it.'

His body tensed, the muscles in his biceps straining. He was so close all he'd have had to do was duck his head to kiss me. 'You'll go into a coma and die if you stop taking the injections long enough.'

'Then we'll know for sure,' I said.

278

He sighed. Those fathomless blue eyes swallowed me, making me helpless. 'Juliet . . .'

My cheeks burned. All I could think of was his lips on my pulsing veins. I blinked, trying to regain my reason. He'd be easier to argue with if he weren't so attractive.

'If you kiss me right now, I'll slap you,' I said. But my threat was barely a murmur. The heat from his body made my skin sizzle.

He grinned. 'I'll make you a deal. You told me and Edward to wait until London to work out our differences. You must do the same. Once we're in London, with proper medical care, then you can play your experiment if you insist.'

The clock on the mantel ticked away each long second. He was right, of course. Whatever the experiment proved, it did me little good if we were still stuck on the island.

I folded my arms. 'You know, I suspect you and Edward would be friends if it weren't for this place.'

His eyes were on fire. 'It's not the island keeping us from being friends.'

My pounding heart stole the words to reply to that.

He took my hand, kissing the knuckles gently, sending trails of fire along the length of my arm. 'I've made you another batch of treatment. It's in the lab.'

'But Father . . .'

'He left before dawn. He won't be back for hours.'

Even without my father's overwhelming presence, the laboratory still gave me chills. I could hear the caged animals in the back pacing, their breathing heavy. It was my first time inside, and I could still feel the memories of that unholy operation. There was the wooden table where the thing had been thrashing, now cold and wiped clean of sin. There was the hardened wax on the floor from Father's candles, now extinguished.

279

Montgomery lit a lantern in the windowless room. Dozens of glass specimen jars reflected the flame. I eyed them as we passed. Animal hearts. Fetuses. An organ I couldn't identify. I peered closer. The fleshy shape in the water suddenly moved. It swam into the glass, shaking violently.

'What in God's name is that?' I asked. The thing's toothless mouth gaped like that of a dying fish.

Montgomery led me past Father's desk, with its neat stacks of papers smelling of india ink and traces of chemicals. The tin walls made the room an oven, but it was so dark and still that it should have been underground, somewhere cold, somewhere forgotten.

Montgomery unlocked one of the cabinets lining the back wall. 'You don't want to know.'

He took out his medical bag and a wooden box. He set them on the desk and then nodded toward the operating table. 'Sit. It'll just take a moment.'

He took out a gleaming glass syringe and a large vial. I came to the table hesitantly. A tray of spotless steel surgical tools lay on top. The leather manacles were attached to chains as thick as my wrist soldered to the table.

Montgomery held the vial to the light. Cloudy. A yellow tint. 'It's a slightly different compound,' he said. 'We don't have unaltered cows for the pancreatic extract. I had to make do. But I think this will work. Tell me if you feel unusual.'

'Yes, Doctor,' I said, trying to sound playful. But the sharp edges of the laboratory swallowed the sound. I hugged my arms. It was cold in the room, or else it was my fever. Either way, I had gooseflesh.

Montgomery prepared the syringe and came to the table. 'Do you want to or shall I?'

My whole body was shaking. Chances were I'd miss a vein and stab myself in the arm. I briefly wondered what he'd used to replace the cow pancreas.

You don't want to know, I told myself.

'You do it,' I said.

'Give me your arm.'

I held it out. My fingers quaked like the lantern's flame. Montgomery set down the needle and took my hand in his. He rubbed them together, letting the friction warm me. The warmth spread to my blood, carrying his heat to my heart, to my limbs, to my every pulsing vein.

'You'll feel better soon,' he said. His voice was soft as a caress. Alice had been right. He was an exceptional doctor, if only for the way he calmed his patients. The specimen jars, the manacles, the sound of the pacing caged animals – they all faded into the background.

He picked up the syringe. My stomach knotted.

'Are you ready?'

I nodded. The cold metal tip pressed against the thin skin inside my elbow. I held my breath. He slid the needle under the skin and my breath caught. My eyes closed. The light was dim, but he found a vein immediately. And then a painful pressure filled my arm as he injected the liquid. I'd done it every day. The routine was familiar. But this was not – this feeling of slow, throbbing pain mixed with the thrilling pleasure of his proximity.

My lips parted. The new compound shot through me, making me light-headed. I gripped the edge of the table so hard the surgical instruments rattled. My eyes settled on a strand of hair falling over his jawline.

'Do you feel unusual at all?'

My throat tightened. I felt *something*, but it didn't have to do with the new compound. It had to do with the light reflecting off his face. With his hand that held my wrist, checking my pulse.

'You have dirt on your collar,' I said. My voice was hoarse.

One side of his mouth tugged back in a handsome grin. 'That's normal.'

I brushed the dirt off with my thumb and forefinger. His head turned to my hand, instinctively, his lips grazing the inside of my wrist. I gasped with the sensation. How could such a simple touch electrify every inch of my body?

He pressed his lips into my palm, my knuckles, each of my fingertips, drowning me with a thousand waves of pleasure. He murmured my name. The sound of it on his lips, so aching, choked me with passion.

I grabbed his collar, pulling our lips together. Not knowing if it was wrong or right or today or tomorrow. He hardly needed persuading. He kissed me back so hard the operating table shook beneath us. The surgical tray fell and tools crashed to the floor. I hardly noticed. He picked me up around the waist and sat me farther back on the table, leaning in, his chest rising and falling like a stormy tide. My trembling fingers brushed against a manacle, accidentally knocking it off. It tumbled down with a rattle of chains.

'Juliet,' he muttered. His hand tangled in my hair, and his lips were inches away but he wouldn't kiss me, torturing me with the space between us. 'You shouldn't have anything to do with me. I'm guilty of so many crimes.'

My fingernails dug into his shoulders. I rested my forehead in the crook of his neck. Breathed in the scent of him. There was so much I wanted to say. He thought he was guilty, when he didn't even know what guilt was. He had made mistakes, but he could never be cruel. Not like my father.

Not like me.

'I don't deserve you,' he whispered.

'Leave that for me to decide.' My lips brushed his jawline, tasting him, drowning in him.

The laboratory door rattled. I jerked at the unexpected

sound. The hinges groaned, and mottled sunlight poured in as the door swung open.

Montgomery's hold tightened on my waist. I could have gotten off the table, could have acted like we there for the injection, but it wouldn't have made a difference. Father had already seen enough.

He came in and closed the door behind him.

THIRTY-SEVEN

Father approached slowly, his footsteps echoing in the silent room. Suddenly the laboratory looked menacing again. It was all sharpened metal and glass and ink diagrams of horrible things. Montgomery's fingers twisted in the folds of my skirt.

'I can't say I'm surprised,' Father said. His black eyes gleamed like the glass specimen jars. 'Just like a dog. You tell it not to do something, and that's just what it does.'

I curled my fingers around the edge of the table, angry enough to rip it in two.

'I warned you, Montgomery,' Father said coldly.

Montgomery didn't answer. His fist tightened in my skirt.

'He's not yours to command,' I snapped. Montgomery shot me a wary glance, but I ignored him. 'You've treated him no better than a slave.'

'I treated him like a son.'

'You used him. He was just a boy when you dragged him here.'

Father's eyes were burning coals. He paced along the wall of cabinets, peering at me like one of the specimens. 'Stay out of this, Juliet. It doesn't have anything to do with you.'

'I started the kiss.'

'You're a female. You can't control yourself.'

'The hell I can't.' I pushed off the table, swinging my fist. He dodged it easily and boxed his hand against my ear. Montgomery moved like a flash, throwing my father against the wall of cabinets. A pane shattered and glass rained to the floor. I screamed and covered my head. Somewhere in the chaos, Father pulled a pistol from his jacket. He aimed the barrel at Montgomery's chest. Montgomery started forward anyway.

He was going to take a bullet for me.

'Stop!' I yelled.

He froze. His breath came as quickly as my own. Father dabbed his mouth with the back of his shirt cuff. It came away spotted with blood. He waved the pistol at Montgomery. 'Over there,' he said, his voice creepily calm. 'Against the wall.'

Slowly, Montgomery stepped back. Once he was far enough away not to lunge, Father grabbed my wrist and dragged me to the operating table. 'You've proven my point,' he said. 'Do you know how they control a hysterical woman in the sanatoriums?'

'Let me go!' I yelled. I slammed my shoulder against him, but he was solid for such a thin man, and I was still weak from my fever.

He dug the pistol's barrel into the back of my head. 'They lock her down before she can harm herself.' His free hand worked the buckle of the closest manacle. He threaded my wrist through and tightened the buckle, so hard the metal bit into my skin. Something clicked into place. A lock.

'I'll be back to deal with you,' he told me. I lunged for him, but the manacle kept me chained to the table.

'Don't leave her here alone,' Montgomery entreated. 'The beasts got in once. If they come again, she won't be able to escape.'

Father grabbed Montgomery's collar and dug the gun against his temple. 'I told you,' he said, only a tremor of anger in his voice as he dragged Montgomery across the cold floor. 'They're harmless.'

Mad. He was mad.

'Let him go!' I yelled. I tore at the manacle, but it held strong.

They vanished into the rectangle of morning sunlight.

If he was mad enough to think the beasts harmless, he was mad enough to take Montgomery outside and shoot him. I twisted my wrist. Clawed at the manacle. It didn't give. I studied the manacle and found a small black opening on the side for a key.

I might be able to pick the lock. If I just had . . . yes, the surgical tools. I fell to the floor and reached as far as my shackled wrist would let me. Scalpels, forceps, needles – they littered the floor out of reach. I slid out my toe as far as I could, but I was still inches away.

'Blast!' I yelled. I jerked on the manacle. The chain clattered – the sound of my imprisonment.

I crawled to the desk. My fingertips just grazed the brass drawer handle. I cursed and tugged on the chain. It was twisted. I scrambled to my feet and spun around, twisting the chain the other direction. A straightened chain might give me only an extra half an inch, but that was all I needed.

I reached again for the drawer, and my middle finger barely wrapped around the handle. I pulled it open, hoping for a letter opener or a pen. My stomach sank. Files – dozens of them, meticulously labeled, packed tightly. The laboratory was filled with countless sharp objects, but all I could reach was a cabinet filled with useless paper.

I slammed my fist on the files. Montgomery might already

have a bullet in his skull. Maybe Father would kill me, too. Then again, maybe not. There were worse things on the island than dying.

The sweat on my hand smeared the ink on one of the files. I wiped my hand on my skirt and looked at the word.

Balthazar.

I slid out the file. Inside were pages of notes in tight, controlled handwriting. Sketches. Medical diagrams. Notes on behavior, appetite, origin of the bear and dog he'd been made from. Careful recordings of the exact procedure Father had done five years ago.

I read it quickly. *Five-fingered*, it said. *Passable appearance. Still unable to replicate Ajax's procedure. Suitable for household service.*

I threw the file on the floor and dug through the rest.

Cymbeline.

Othello.

Iago.

Ophelia.

All names from Shakespeare's plays, I realized. That's how he'd named his creations. There must have been a hundred files, each with careful notes and measurements, as though the islanders were only experiments on paper and not breathing, thinking, killing creatures.

My finger paused on a familiar name.

Juliet.

For a moment time slipped away into some dark void. My lips formed that one word, my name – *Juliet, Juliet, Juliet* – over and over, repeating until it all made sense. But it never did. How could it? My hand pulled out the file, but it was like someone else's hand laying the file on the cold ground, opening it, rifling through the few meager pages annotated with my father's distinctive handwriting.

And then time seemed to fracture again and I was back in my own body, all too aware of how my sweaty fingertips caught on the paper, the grit on the ground digging into my legs, as my eyes focused and refocused on the handwriting.

The pages had a date – July 1879, one month after I was born. The notes were briefer and more disjointed than Balthazar's and the others'. The paper wasn't even the same – these pages looked ripped from an old journal. They must have come from a time before Father had developed a system for cataloging his creations. There were only a few scribbled lines describing the surgery he'd performed when I was an infant. The file told me painfully little, didn't prove anything – until I reached a handful of words in Latin I didn't recognize. Except for one.

Cervidae.

Deer.

That was all I needed to see. Feeling melted out of my fingers and I let the pages flutter to the ground. I touched my face, my hair, but sensation was gone – it was like touching flesh that wasn't mine. And maybe it wasn't. Maybe it belonged to some animal, a deer. This body – my eyelashes, my toes, the curve of my waist – was a lie. Such a convincing lie that I'd even fooled myself.

I slumped against the operating table, eyes closed, hugging my arms in tight. Trying to see within me, to *feel* if it was true. At some point the lantern must have gone out, because when I opened my eyes, I was alone in darkness. Hours or minutes might have passed – it didn't matter.

The laboratory's metal door creaked open, and I shielded my eyes from the bright sunlight. The pages of my file lay scattered at my feet. My eyes adjusted slowly to the light. Father came in, his arms folded behind his back like a gentleman. His face was as calm as the afternoon sea. Feeling flooded back into my numb body. My fists balled, slowly.

Anger bubbled in my blood, almost giving me the strength to rip the manacle from the table.

'Where is he?' I asked.

'Montgomery should never have been a concern of yours. His kind are beneath you. His mother was a whore whom Evelyn let scour our pots in her Christian charity.'

'He's smarter than you,' I said, seething. 'He bested you at your own work.'

He lifted a hand to strike me, but his eyes caught on the paper littering the floor. He slid the file closer with his boot. 'And what's this?'

'I found the files,' I said. My words sounded so far away. 'I *know*.'

'Know what exactly?'

I jerked my chin at the open file drawer. 'Know that I'm one of them. An animal you've twisted and taught to speak like some sideshow attraction.' The chain rattled as I inched toward him, as close as I could, wishing I could strike. 'And thank God for it. I'd rather be an animal than have your cursed blood flowing in my veins.'

His eyebrows rose. He picked up the folder and straightened the papers carefully on the desk. 'You have quite an imagination.'

'Don't lie to me.' I jerked the chain. 'There's a file with my name on it, just like the others.'

He flipped through the pages leisurely. 'And what precisely did you find here? Diagrams of rabbits? Notes on how I turned a sheep into a girl and named her Juliet? Funny, I don't see any of that.'

My fingers itched to claw the smirk off his face. 'You named me after a character in one of your books, like them. You stick a needle in my vein, like them. It's written right there.' I pointed a tense finger at the first page.

He followed my finger and tapped the word. *Cervidae*. 'You're mistaken,' he said. 'I don't give you the same treatment as them. I give *them* the same treatment as *you*.' He closed the file. 'You were the first.'

THIRTY-EIGHT

Black rain filled my vision, making me light-headed.

Father continued, 'It's not precisely identical to theirs, but it's the same basic compound.' His fingers stretched and itched as though they missed the familiar clutch of a scalpel. 'You see, when you were born – yes, *born* – your spine was deformed. The doctors said you would die within days. But your mother wouldn't believe it. She begged me to fix you. Whatever it took.'

He leaned against the desk, his eyes wide as they delved into some long-ago memory. 'And I did fix you. It's all right here, in plain print, in your file. But the surgery was unconventional. By the time I was finished, you were missing several essential organs.' He brushed a hand over his chin. 'The medical department always kept a few live specimens on hand for the zoology classes. There was a newborn deer – well, it served its purpose.'

My fingers prodded my rib cage, the taut line of my diaphragm, feeling for something unusual to verify his wild claim. But even if it was true, how would I know? My body was no different than it had always been.

'They said you would die, so I had nothing to lose. I did

291

what any father would have done. Luckily, I was also England's best surgeon.'

I dug my fingers into the soft place in my back just above my kidneys, feeling the lower edge of my ribs. 'You can't substitute a person's organs with a deer's. That's impossible.'

'So is vivisecting a dog and a bear to make a man. At least that's what they tell me. Perhaps they should ask Balthazar.' His eyes gleamed as though I were some fresh specimen on his operating table. 'The injections are to keep your body from rejecting the foreign organ tissue. If you stop taking the serum, your organs will fail. You won't regress like they do. You'll die.'

'You're mad,' I said. My eyes flickered to the glass cases, where a shadow slunk over the rows of jars.

'Don't you see?' he continued. 'They exist *because* of you. If you hadn't almost died, if I hadn't taken the risk of substituting animal flesh to save your life, I'd never have known it was possible. I'd still be in London teaching ignorant medical students how to dissect street dogs.'

I pressed my eyes closed. Even so, I could feel the shadow moving closer.

'I'd never have sliced open that first dog if it weren't for you. I'd never have come to this island. Never rivaled God in his power to create. You've made everything possible, Juliet. You're responsible for all of it.'

I wet my shaking lips, feeling faint. All those years of worry, all those sleepless nights, wondering if my father had unlocked some dark science that made him a monster. And it all came down to *me*. *I* was to blame for all the rumors, the scandal, even Montgomery's years spent as a slave on a madman's island.

It was my fault.

The wind blew the door half closed, dimming the light.

'So you see, you do share my blood. We're more alike than you think.'

I balled my fists, practically feeling his poisoned blood coursing through me like a disease. That was the source of my dark inclinations. *Him.* I could never escape what flowed in my veins, not even if he was dead.

The sound of a boot crunching broken glass came from beside the cabinets where the pane had shattered earlier. The shadow approached. Father turned, but not fast enough.

Edward jammed a needle into his neck. Father clawed at his arms, but Edward held him with an incredible strength for a man his size. At last Father went limp. Edward let him slump to the floor, unconscious.

I fell back against the table. A held breath slipped out between my lips. Edward fumbled in Father's pockets for the key ring.

'I feared he'd hear you coming,' I said breathlessly.

Edward found the small key and unlocked the manacle. 'So did I.'

He took my hand and we raced for the door. I stepped around Father's prostrate body. Maybe I was his flesh and blood. Maybe I was as cold as he. But I wasn't totally without feeling.

I hated him.

We dashed out of the laboratory. My head spun with everything I'd learned, and it was all I could do to stumble behind Edward toward the wooden gate.

'Wait, he took Montgomery,' I said breathlessly. 'He had a pistol. I'm afraid he might have—'

'Montgomery's alive. The doctor has him caged outside the walls.'

Relief spread through me. Alive! We could still escape.

Edward sorted through Father's key ring and then shook his head, frustrated.

'He must keep the gate key elsewhere. We can't go through the barn thatch. They sealed the roof.'

'We don't need a key.' I darted into the barn and dug through the toolbox in the tack room. My hand fell on a smooth, heavy crowbar. Edward and I both had to strain to wrench the boards from the gate. At last a thick plank came free, and we climbed through into the thick grass below the carved Lamb of God and Lion of Judah.

'This way,' Edward said. We hurried along the north wall, where the jungle grew thickest. The early sun beat down on our necks before we plunged into a dark tunnel of trees that seemed to close in on us the farther we went, until we were climbing over vines and branches, pulling ourselves forward. The vegetation pressing in started to make me panic. I imagined the vines holding me there, ensnared, waiting for Father to wake and find us with the dogs. Father, or the monster.

I pushed away a slick leaf, and my fingers grazed something metal. A bar.

'Over here,' I called.

We spilled out into a clearing tangled with overgrown vines. A circle of rusted cages, each big enough to hold a bear or tiger, rose from the jungle floor like a new, terrible kind of thicket.

I caught a glimpse of movement in the farthest cage. Someone standing up.

Montgomery.

I rushed over, threading my fingers through the rusted bars. A deep bruise covered his jaw. 'You're alive,' I said.

He wrapped his powerful hands around the bars. 'He thought to punish me. He puts the islanders here when they disobey. Locks them here for days without food or water or shade. He told me . . . blast, it doesn't matter anymore.' He didn't have to finish his thought. I understood the tender pain in his eyes. Montgomery had believed he was like a son to my father, but in the end we were all animals to him.

Edward searched the rusted cage until he found the lock and tried each key. My heart faltered with each failed try. I paced, chewing on a fingernail.

'How did you know these cages were here?' I asked.

Edward tried another key, uselessly. 'I came across them when I was trying to find my way back after I shot that . . .' His voice seemed to slip from his lips as he remembered killing the beast. The next key turned with a groan, banishing the terrible memories. The cage door swung open on rusted hinges.

Montgomery climbed out, slapping Edward on the shoulder, and gave me a look like he wanted to do all sorts of scandalous things to me. My body longed to touch him, but I told myself there wasn't time for that.

'This way,' he said.

We trekked through the jungle, slowing as the sun rose. Sweat soon poured down our backs. Montgomery led us away from the wagon road, in case anyone was looking for us. He never once hesitated. The island was as familiar to him as our childhood home was to me.

He stopped at the edge of a bamboo grove, staring ahead. I squinted, but all I saw were leaves.

'What is it?' I asked.

'The village. Twenty yards ahead.'

'I don't hear anything.'

'Neither do I. That's why I'm worried.' He nodded at the crowbar in Edward's hand. 'If you have to use that, don't hesitate. They won't.'

Edward's face was a mystery. The sea-mad castaway who couldn't remember how to set up a backgammon board had faded with each day as that rugged part of him took over, the part that would survive at all costs. The island had turned him into a killer. If he was forced to kill again, I feared his soul would fracture.

'You should stay here, Juliet,' Montgomery said.

'Like hell.'

Montgomery sighed. 'Then stay near. Don't make any quick movements.'

We crept through the bamboo toward the village. The tops of huts slowly appeared through the trees, sagging and torn down. There was no hammering, no praying, no sound of people. The wind blew the smell of burnt wood into our faces.

Montgomery went first. He crept along the side of a wooden fence, his body on alert. I peered down the dusty streets. Empty.

'Where are they all?' I asked.

Montgomery didn't answer, but I could tell from the tense set of his shoulders that he didn't know either.

The farther we went, the bolder we became. The few footprints in the muddy pathways were old and dried out. Montgomery stuck his head inside one of the huts. Empty.

'They've all left,' he concluded.

'And gone where?' Edward asked.

Montgomery shrugged. 'It's a big island.' But his eyes weren't so certain. The islanders had lost their humanity now. They could be anywhere: in the trees, in the grass, watching us like the animals they'd always been. He pointed at a stone building behind the main square. 'There's the church. Let's get the boat.'

We hurried across the square. The village was a ghost town, though days before it had been teeming with half-crazed creatures who stank and growled and crawled on all fours. Where was the python-woman? Cymbeline? Caesar?

Montgomery ducked his head into every hut. After each one, his expression grew more troubled. But he said nothing.

The wooden cross had been torn from the front of the church. Montgomery brushed his fingers over the hollow spot where it had once stood and then led us around the side to a rough stone patio in the back. He froze. When Edward and I caught up to him, I understood why.

The shed was gone. Burned. If there was ever a boat, it was now nothing but ash.

'Oh no,' I said. 'Not this. Not now.' My feet sank into the soft earth outside the church's open door. Without a boat, we'd have to wait for the next cargo ship – in a year or more. We'd never survive that long. Just as I stumbled forward, my mind whirling, a spindly set of fingers appeared from within the church and closed over my arm.

I screamed. With brutish force the hand jerked me inside the church, where muted splashes of colored light lit the walls from the few unbroken stained-glass windowpanes. The sudden rush of blues and reds and yellows made me forget where I was until Edward hurried in behind me, crowbar raised like a bludgeon. Montgomery was just behind him.

'Don't!' he cried. 'It's Caesar.'

My erratic heartbeat calmed. This hulking beast, now barrel-chested and hunched at the shoulders, with broken stumps on his skull, was a far cry from the regal antlered minister we had seen before. I barely recognized him. His horse lips gaped at the end of an elongated face. Even if he'd still had his tongue, I don't think he could have spoken. He was too far regressed.

He let me go and crossed the floor on four shaky legs, his back feet bent and hardened like hooves. The church echoed with the sounds of his feet skittering across the ground. Montgomery crouched next to him, unafraid.

'Where has everyone gone?' he asked gently.

Caesar bobbed his head mechanically, the stumps of his former antlers scraping against the stone wall. His eyes were glassy.

'We need the boat,' Montgomery said. 'Did they burn it?'

Caesar's head snapped around, his eyes drifting to the burned shed outside. Then he started bobbing again, faster and faster, getting agitated. He jumped up, pawing around the room. His hardened, curled fingers rested on the lip of a bowl, which he flipped onto the ground. It shattered, spilling dirty water and shards of pottery all over the floor.

With his hoof, Caesar nudged a curved shard across the wet ground, next to a piece of singed wood. He moved the wood closer, then looked at Montgomery.

'What's he doing?' I asked.

Montgomery jumped up. 'He's telling us where the boat is.'

By the time we made it to the coast, the midday sun had given us all a thick sheen of sweat. Montgomery led us to the murky edge of a mangrove forest. Thin, spindly trees grew from the swampy tidal waters like giant skeletons. The ground was spongy under my feet. Something clicked. I paused. Another click.

'It's the trees,' Montgomery said. 'They filter salt from the water. Makes the roots contract and expand.'

I hugged my arms. The clicking sound echoed through the ghostly trees, as though they were telling a story.

'He used to keep the rowboat tied here sometimes. The mangroves protect it from storms. He must have moved it when the regression began.' Montgomery waded into the water, navigating through the tight trees. Mud sucked his boots down. The water was soon up to his waist, and then he disappeared through the watery tangle of trees.

Edward and I stood alone on the shore, an uneasy silence between us. Ever since he'd killed Antigonus, a shadow had settled over Edward. He'd drugged my father so easily. It was the island, slowly corrupting his heart, as it was corrupting everything. We had to leave before it turned us into things we weren't.

Get off this island, I told myself. *Then sort out the messes of our lives.*

The water rippled in graceful arcs that spread across the tidal inlet and lapped at our feet. After a few minutes Montgomery returned, pulling a blue-and-white-painted boat through the water. It looked too cheerful for a bleak, savage island. He beached it in the soft silt. 'Climb in. We'll row to the dock and tie it there. It's too heavy to carry overland.'

Edward helped hold the boat. I bunched my skirt and climbed in, trying to steady myself. My foot slipped, and warm seawater flooded my boot. Edward climbed in with considerably more grace. Montgomery tugged us free of the shore and pulled the boat through the tunnel of trees until the water was at his waist, then his chest, and finally his shoulders. We broke from the trees.

Oh, the open sea. Freedom felt so close. I wanted to tell Montgomery to just keep going, farther out to sea, to never turn back to the island.

Edward was watching me keenly. 'We won't last a day without shade and water,' he said, dashing my hopes.

Montgomery hoisted himself into the boat, water pouring off his massive shoulders. He wiped his face and picked up an oar. The other one he tossed to Edward.

'Hug the coast,' he said, pointing ahead. 'The beach is on the other side of the mangroves.'

The tide tried to drag the boat away from the island, but Edward and Montgomery kept it steady. From outside, the forest of mangroves looked dense and impenetrable. Every few breaths, I heard the roots clicking, reminding us they were living parts of the island.

'We should leave tonight,' Montgomery said. His face was hard, making it impossible to tell what he was feeling. 'Edward, pack as much food as you can in the rucksacks and fill the waterskins. Juliet, go through your mother's things. We'll need parasols. Shawls. Anything to keep off the sun. And take everything you think is valuable. We might have to buy our passage back to London.'

'Assuming we find a ship,' Edward said.

Montgomery studied the sky. 'The full moon was last night. The Polynesian traders might still be out. Their course takes them five miles from the island. The tide will bring us just south of their shipping lane. We'll have to row a few degrees north to cross their course.'

I was starting to feel faint. My insides clenched, threatening to bring up bile from my empty stomach. I couldn't shake the feeling that something would go wrong.

Montgomery rested a hand over mine. 'Don't worry,' he said. 'I know the way. We'll find a ship.'

The mangroves clicked louder. A shadow passed overhead, giving me a sudden shiver. The wind made the water shimmer as if something swam just below the surface.

We rounded a bend and saw the long dock stretching out ahead. I let out a tight breath. Soon the whole beach was in sight.

Tonight, I promised myself. It felt as unreal as a dream. My mind wouldn't let me dare to believe it, but my heart pumped wildly.

Edward's oar hit something hard in the water. He jerked it, but it was stuck. I frowned. We were too far out to graze anything along the ocean bottom. 'It's caught on something.'

'Maybe a coral reef,' I said. 'Or a shipwreck.' I glanced at Montgomery, but his attention wasn't on the oar. He was scanning the beach, body tensed, eyes narrowed like a hunter's.

'What do you see?' I asked, feeling creeping tendrils of fear crawl up my back.

He shook his head, just a quick jerk. 'Nothing.'

But he didn't tear his eyes away. I sat straighter, gripping the sides of the rowboat. Suddenly we felt as small as a bobbing toy in the endless ocean.

Edward leaned over the side, fingers disappearing into the water as he felt for whatever had caught the oar. The boat rocked, suddenly unbalanced by his movements. I clutched the sides harder, as panic made my toes curl.

Montgomery tilted his head, his eyes still riveted on the shore. 'Stop, Edward. Get your hand out of the water. Now.'

Edward started to pull back, but something quick and hard rammed the boat from underneath.

I yelped. The sudden jolt pitched me into the bottom of the boat, scraping my wrists against the rough boards.

Montgomery had braced himself to keep from falling. 'Edward, get your blasted arm out of the water!' he growled.

'I can't!' Edward was shoulder deep in the water, causing the boat to pitch at a dangerous angle. His gold-flecked eyes were focused on me, unreadable. 'Something's got me.'

'What is it?' I said, not daring to lean and pitch the boat farther.

Edward clenched his jaw to keep the panic at bay. 'A hand.'

THIRTY-NINE

I was falling. It happened in an instant. I saw Edward going overboard, dragged into the deep by whatever malevolent hand held him. The sudden movement made the boat rock violently. Water stung my eyes, my ears, flooded into my mouth. I tried to scream, but there was no air.

The boat had flipped. I was underwater.

I couldn't swim. It was the strangest sensation, like panic in slow motion. I kicked and waved my hands, but the water was just that – water. Nothing to grab on to. My flailing limbs brushed against slippery moving objects. Whether I touched Edward or Montgomery or something else, I didn't know. Something slid by me, a person or an animal, with an easy undulation, like a jellyfish, only the size of a man. Scaly tentacles – fingers almost – tangled between my kicking legs. My scream was silent in the water, an eruption of bubbles in the deep.

At last my fingers latched onto something solid. Wooden. I pulled myself up, sputtering as I surfaced.

The world had grown dark and damp. I took a few hysterical breaths before realizing I was underneath the upside-down rowboat, with just enough room for my head.

I clutched the bench seat above me, filling my lungs with air. I stopped kicking, but the churning in the water didn't stop. Dark shapes moved in the water's deep, violently, maliciously.

One shape rose, coming up fast, and then its head broke the surface.

Edward.

I let out a shaking breath. 'Here,' I said. 'Hold on to the bench.' His chest was rising and falling fast. Blood from a gash on his forehead mixed with the seawater pouring down his face. 'What happened?' I asked breathlessly. 'Where's Montgomery?'

'I don't know.' He panted for air.

'What tipped us over?'

'Creatures,' he coughed. 'Creatures in the water. A different kind of beast.'

'Water beasts. Oh God, Montgomery . . .' My voice echoed eerily with mounting panic. 'Did you see him? What happened to him? He must be here, in the water . . .'

Edward pinched the salt water out of his eyes. 'He can swim. I'm sure he's safe.'

Another undulating tentacle slid around my ankle, coiling like a snake. I kicked furiously, fighting the urge to scream. 'You don't know that! He could be hurt. He could be dead!' The darkness beneath the boat was terrible. Only muted sunlight filtered through the water, throwing dancing lines of light on us, barely enough to see the blood trickling down Edward's face.

'Don't just hang there, Edward. Do something!'

'What do you want me to do?' he snapped, matching my tone. 'I can't swim. I don't know where he is.'

'He could have drowned!'

'If I let go, I'll drown too! Is that what you want? For me

to drown trying to find him?' Salt water and blood mixed as he spat the words at me.

'He saved your life, Edward. Don't you dare insinuate—'

'Don't pretend this has anything to do with me! It's never had anything to do with me. If it was me lost in the water, you'd never ask Montgomery to risk his life to find me.' But before I could sputter a response, he ducked under the boat's rim, into the bright world outside the cavern of the upside-down boat.

I was alone. Water swirled between the folds of my dress, my legs dangling helplessly like bait worms into the deep, cold part of the ocean. Montgomery might be down there, a watery corpse, just below my toes. Edward had every right to feel hurt, but hadn't I also a right to care about Montgomery? He'd been with me forever, tucked into the hollows of my heart, lodged like a precious secret they'd have to cut out of me. And now he might be dead.

The worries churned inside me, trying to take shape, trying to find a voice. I squeezed my eyes, wanting to scream. To release the terrible knot of emotions that preyed on my soul.

I loved him.

The words came to me like a crashing wave, and I almost lost my grip. The sharp pain in my side loosened, turned into a low, constant throbbing instead. I'd fallen in love with Montgomery. Edward had read it in the worry in my face, and it had added yet another scar to his collection.

The water around my toes grew colder. I squeezed my eyes closed and ducked under the edge of the boat. I was underwater only the space of a breath, but it was long enough to make my lungs burn. And then my head broke the surface into the dazzling sunlight. I gasped for air. Edward guided my hands to the wooden rim of the boat. The world was shockingly bright. Seawater stung my eyes. I looked everywhere, trying to take in everything at once. The mangroves, the beach, the sea.

'He's a good swimmer,' Edward said, a grudging softness in his voice. 'He must have made it to shore. I'm sorry – for yelling.'

I had to blink to make sure I'd heard him correctly. The blood still trickled from the cut on his forehead, finding the path of his scar and following it to the sea. It would attract sharks, I realized. And anything else drawn to the smell of blood. 'That's all right,' I muttered.

'I'm going to try to flip it,' he said. He shoved the edge underwater, and the other side popped up with a rush of water that brought me to my senses. I helped him flip the boat until it slammed against the waves right side up.

Edward heaved himself into the boat, balancing carefully, and helped me in after. The feel of his cold hands made my insides tighten with guilt. All I could think about was another man, yet he was still helping me. Water poured down my face, out of my clothes, but the guilt didn't drain away.

We paddled to the dock with our hands. Progress was painstakingly slow and full of worries that at any moment something might grab our exposed fingers. Each second that passed was another second Montgomery might be clawed, slashed, stabbed – assuming he hadn't drowned. I tore at the water until at last the bow collided with the dock. Edward tied the lead rope to one of the piles, and we climbed out. I spun in a circle on the dock, scanning the water, the beach, the tangled line of trees.

'There.' Something dark in the sand caught my eye. I raced down the dock, ignoring the burning in my lungs and the ache in my muscles. My dress clung to my legs, slowing me down. Edward's footsteps echoed behind me. My feet sank into the deep sand, and I froze when I saw I was treading on fresh footprints.

Edward wiped the water and blood from his face, breathing hard. 'What is it?'

The sand in front of us was rough and disturbed. Footprints led from the shore into the jungle. About every five feet was a dark spot. Blood.

I pressed my hand into one of the footprints.

Still wet.

Which made it easy to count the unusual number of toes, the abnormally large size of prints that could only belong to beasts. The sun beat down, burning our salty skin.

'Look, there's a smaller set of prints,' Edward said.

I found the ones he was looking at. Smaller boot prints, the size of a man's. I realized the drips of blood were heavier around these tracks.

Panic rose again. 'He's bleeding.'

'That means he's alive,' Edward said. 'And he's walking. They weren't dragging him, at least.'

A strange cry came from the ocean behind us – a seal's guttural bark, only more high-pitched. But the sea looked so calm. I shivered.

'The footprints end at the jungle,' Edward said. 'I don't think we can track him any farther.'

'We can't,' I said. 'But my father can.'

We ran and ran along the rutted wagon road, the jungle a blur, feet aching.

The front gate was open. They'd been waiting for us.

We slowed to a walk. My body was spent. My dress clung to my skin – hot, salt-stained, damp with sweat. Edward's face burned with sun and exhaustion. The road from the beach to the compound had been achingly long. With each pounding step, my panic had transformed to anger.

The beasts had taken Montgomery. Father owed it to us to help get him back.

In the garden, we found Balthazar kneeling to replant the few delicate tomato seedlings he'd been able to salvage. My heart twisted coldly at the sight. Life couldn't just *continue*. Alice's ashes still floated on the wind. Montgomery was God knew where, dead maybe. The monster was out there, lurking, waiting.

'Don't bother, Balthazar,' I muttered. 'There'll be no one left to eat them once the monster finishes with us all.'

'That's not true,' Edward said.

'Yes it is!' The chickens scattered at my yell. 'You know it is. And it's Father's fault.' I grabbed Balthazar's shirt. My fingers left streaks of dirt on his collar. 'Where is he?'

His lips fumbled. 'The laboratory, miss.'

I felt Edward's hand on my shoulder. I let Balthazar go, and he slunk away like a wounded dog. Good. He was right to fear anyone with Moreau blood – we were all a little mad.

I stumbled to my feet, wiping the dirt off my palms. I'd thought the island was driving Edward mad, but maybe it wasn't *his* mind the island had polluted, but rather my own.

Edward's hand tightened. 'Juliet, think carefully. He locked Montgomery in a cage. Why would he help us go after someone he hates?'

'He doesn't hate him,' I said, stumbling away. 'He loves him like a son.'

The latch to the laboratory door was just like the others – deceptively simple, a symbol of Father's arrogance. I slid my fingers into the special holes and squeezed, bristling at his vanity. No locks – he thought himself indestructible.

He was a fool.

I wrenched the door open and found him sitting inside at his desk, peering into the monkey's cage, scribbling notes on a tablet. A set of roughly made children's blocks – Montgomery's handiwork, no doubt – was stacked on the table. Father didn't look up as I approached.

My footsteps echoed along the wall of cabinets. The broken glass had been swept away. The new batch of my serum sat tidily in its box on a polished worktable. No trace remained of our earlier fight save the one empty pane from the glass cabinets. He kept writing, pausing to watch the monkey fiddle with a toy block, then jotted down a few more notes in his tight, meticulous handwriting. I had expected an argument. I'd even expected to be slapped again. But I hadn't expected to be quietly ignored.

'Father,' I said.

'I'm trying something new,' he muttered, not looking at me. 'A new technique. It doesn't involve surgery, but alteration of a different kind. It changes the constitution on a cellular level, without ever having to use a scalpel. If it works, the ramifications could be tremendous.'

I stepped deeper into the room, my shadow casting over the tablet. 'After everything that's happened, you're still focused on your work. Aren't you going to tell me what a horrid, disobedient child I am?' I picked up one of the blocks, inspecting the carefully carved letters on all sides. 'Or do I have to play with blocks like the monkey for you to pay me attention?'

He made another notation on his tablet. 'Unlike the monkey, you no longer show any promise. So I'm content to throw you out with the rest of my failures.'

I slammed the block against the table, toppling the stack. The crash sent my pulse racing, making me hungry for more destruction. I leaned on the table, my hair falling like a fortune-teller's veil over my face.

'Your *failures* are going to find you and kill you. That's what you get for throwing them out.'

He stacked the blocks back into an orderly pile. His refusal to grow angry only made my own rage seethe. 'I've given them a precious gift. Do you really think they would turn on their creator?'

'You gave them pain. They're animals and that's what they've always been, no matter how you've twisted their limbs and minds. They'll get their revenge.'

The monkey tapped the block against the bars of his cage. Father turned back to his note-taking.

'Yet you insist on deluding yourself,' I continued. 'You think yourself safe because . . . why? A few door latches?'

He slammed down his tablet. The monkey screeched and hid in the corner of its cage. But I didn't flinch. I smiled. This was what I wanted.

A fight.

Faster than I could react, Father grabbed my wrist and splayed my hand on the table. My first instinct was to pull away, but I realized he wasn't planning on striking me.

'The human hand,' he said in that steady voice he used for lectures, 'is what most separates us from the animals, did you know that?'

His voice was calm, and yet I detected a ripple beneath it, like the water beasts swimming below the ocean's surface. A chill tiptoed up my spine, one vertebra at a time. He traced his fountain pen, slowly, along the length of each of my fingers, leaving thick black lines. 'The four lateral fingers are extensions of an animal's primary phalanges. We hardly need Mr Darwin to tell us that – it's evident when comparing the musculature of any mammal, human or otherwise.'

He tapped my thumb with the sharp tip of his pen. 'But the opposable thumb – ah, there's the secret. The distal phalanx is attached to the wrist by a mobile metacarpus, giving the thumb unique properties. The ability to clutch objects – weapons, tools. To climb. To build. Why, even to hold a fountain pen.'

The precise black lines he drew along my skin radiated

from the wrist to each knuckle, an anatomical diagram written on my hand. Fingers were so important to a surgeon. It was little wonder that Father was obsessed with the hand, the fingers – even going so far as to base his own safety on cleverly designed latches instead of locks.

'Without the thumb, most animals are simply mindless beasts, unable to advance mentally due to their limited physiology. Which is why they'll never get into the compound. We are perfectly safe as long as the opposable thumb eludes them. And the next stage of evolution shouldn't happen for, oh, a hundred thousand years.'

His words sounded so logical. It might have been easy to believe him if I didn't know he was utterly mad. He'd assumed the beasts couldn't get in over the roof or break through the gate, yet they'd done both. Montgomery had warned me – Father would never admit to his mistakes.

My splayed hand began to shake. I curled my fingers inward, no longer wanting to be part of his lecture. His arrogance was going to kill him. Maybe all of us.

'They took Montgomery,' I said like a slap, wanting him to feel as much pain as the rest of us.

His dark eyes snapped to mine. He let go of my wrist. 'What?'

'They dragged him into the jungle. He was bleeding.'

He set down the fountain pen, fingers trembling slightly. He looked around at the blocks, the monkey, as if seeing it all for the first time. A flicker of humanity showed in the look on his face, the way he wiped a hand over his whiskers. He stood. 'Which ones?'

'Creatures in the water.'

'*Damn!*' The force made me jump. I took a step back, sensing his madness roiling like a storm. He grabbed his canvas jacket from a hook on the wall and removed a revolver from a cabinet. 'This is *your* fault,' he snapped, struggling into the jacket. 'You bewitched him! Everything was fine before you came. I never wanted a girl. Montgomery was lowborn, but at least he was male; at least he could reason, not like some hysterical female. I'd just as soon you'd died with your consumptive mother and left me in peace!'

I blinked. My mind was strangely calm, strangely clear, and yet my body was shaking. 'How did you know Mother died of consumption? The obituary only said a prolonged illness.'

Father's eyes narrowed. He spun the revolver's cylinder into place, snapping the bullets into their chambers. 'I know because Montgomery was there on a supply trip six months before she died. He sent Balthazar back with a letter telling me to come. Those quack doctors couldn't save her, and he knew I could.'

A slow anger uncoiled inside me, weaving between my ribs, plucking my tendons like piano strings. 'But you didn't come.'

'Of course not. I had work here.'

'But you could have. You could have saved her.'

He waved his hand. 'Didn't you hear me, girl? I had work to do. Typical flawed reasoning of a woman, to place mortal needs above timeless research.' He straightened his jacket. 'I'm going to the village. He's either there or torn into pieces on the jungle floor.' He left the laboratory, leaving me alone.

He's mad, I told myself. *He isn't well.* And yet I didn't feel any pity. He could have saved my mother but he didn't. My fingers curled into fists. I looked at the monkey clutching the block, and knew I was about to do something terrible.

Maybe I was a little mad, too.

FORTY

My chest was thumping, but not with fear. With a dark thrill that snaked up my skin, pouring into my nose and mouth like smoke. Consuming me. Controlling me.

I wove my fingers between the bars of the monkey's cage. Father said he wasn't going to operate on this one. He had a new technique – cellular replacement. He intended to change the monkey from the inside out. But you couldn't destroy the animal spirit. The monkey would always be an animal.

Would always be in pain.

My thumb slipped to the cage's latch, a modified version of the door latches Father had designed. The monkey had five fingers, but too small to operate the special mechanism. Anger swelled inside me, building and growing until I thought I would split. My fingernails clicked on the cool metal. The monkey cocked its head.

I threw open the cage.

The monkey exploded out, shoving the cage door with a squeal of hinges that made my pulse race. It dashed over the table, sending the blocks and Father's tablet crashing onto the floor, and out the laboratory door before the papers had even settled.

I gasped. My body felt so alive, demanding more.

I tore open the parrot's cage next. The bird cocked its head. I threw blocks at the bars, scaring it into taking flight. Then I set free the capybara and the sloth, shaking the cages to make the sloth hurry.

'Get out!' I yelled. It was as though the bits and pieces of animal flesh inside my body had taken hold of me. 'Get out of here!' I chased the sloth outside, where it latched onto a post and climbed to the roof. I turned back to open more cages, but my hand paused.

They were all empty. I'd set all the animals free. But my hunger for destruction hadn't subsided. If anything, it had grown, wanting to free more animals, to do anything to ensure my father would never work again.

I paced the wall of glass cabinets slowly, shaking, savoring my secret thoughts. The glass was so delicate, I could smash through it, let it all rain to the ground. My heart leapt with the thought, hungry for destruction. Sunlight reflected off the glass canisters. The living specimen – the jellyfish-like monster with its gaping mouth – lunged for me inside its glass cage.

I smiled grimly. Before I could stop myself, I threw open the glass cabinet and grabbed the jar with both hands, struggling to unscrew the lid. The squirming thing snapped at me ravenously. I hugged the jar to my chest and tipped the contents onto the floor. The glutinous liquid splashed against my feet as it puddled in the center of the room. The thing caught in the jar's neck and I shook it loose. It fell to the floor with a squish.

I ground the heel of my boot into the fleshy center of the flopping thing. Something crunched. I dug deeper until I cut the unholy thing in half.

Madness overcame me like a whirlwind. I threw the jar to the ground with all my strength, letting it shatter into hundreds of sharp pieces. I pulled out another jar, this one with a graying heart floating in blood-tinted liquid. The liquid poured out like a torrent, puddling on the floor, the heart coming last, like a heavy and dead afterthought. The smell of the chemical preservative made me light-headed. My lungs burned for air, but I smashed the empty jar to the floor anyway. Dozens more jars of all sizes shone in the light of the lantern, each containing gray, twisted bits of organ. Nearly a decade's worth of work.

My hands were slick with the viscous fluid. It soaked through my dress. Remnants of animal tissue tangled in the lace hem. I unscrewed the next jar, my fingers leaving wet streaks on the glass. Inside, the aged tissue came off in gossamer sheets like a spider's web. It was almost beautiful. I recognized what half the jars contained – spleen, large intestine, brain. But then there were ones I didn't know. Those both disturbed and fascinated me the most.

The floor pooled with fetid organs and slick preservatives as I emptied jar after jar. I drew the back of my hand across my forehead, leaving a slimy trail. The chemicals choked my pores. I smiled, reaching for the next preserved organ. Ready to smash its glass case to the ground.

'Juliet, stop!'

Edward appeared at the door, rushing toward me. He grabbed the jar before I could drop it. My liquid-covered hands left dark stains on his shirt as he tried to wrench the jar away.

'Let go!' I yelled. My vision was black with rage. 'I have to destroy it!'

'Juliet, calm down! Stop! It's done.'

The jar slipped from my hands, shattering on the ground. One final act of destruction.

Edward didn't flinch at the crash. 'It's done now,' he said, breathing hard.

I swallowed, suddenly aware of the slime on my face, the bits of graying organ clinging to my skin. I'd laid waste the laboratory in a whirlwind of insanity. A trembling panic clutched the back of my brain.

'He could have saved my mother,' I said. 'He thought his work was more important.'

Edward brushed his knuckles against my cheek, wiping away grit and slime, his eyes deep and strong. 'You don't have to explain,' he said.

I swallowed, searching his eyes. Of course I didn't. Edward was scarred, too. Whatever he had done, whatever he was running from, we weren't so different. Edward didn't care that I was a little mad, that I could slip and slide away from reason. Just as I didn't care what he had done that made him flee England. We both had ghosts in our pasts that let us understand each other on a deep level – a level Montgomery never could. Montgomery might be capable of wicked things, but *he* wasn't wicked, not at the core. No matter how much Father had twisted him, he would always be that hardworking, kindhearted boy who couldn't tell a believable lie if his life depended on it. Edward and I were cut from different cloth. Maybe we weren't wicked, but there was something stained, something torn, in the fabric of our beings.

Something warm and wet seeped into my boots – fluid from the specimen jars. Edward's hand tenderly took my own. There was something not right about a boy who could survive twenty days at sea and didn't blink when a half-mad girl covered herself in broken glass and rotting organs.

He's pretending to fit in, just like I pretend. And he was good at it – better than me.

I curled my hands into his shirt. 'What happened to you?' I whispered breathlessly. 'What are you running from?'

For a moment his gold-flecked eyes flickered, and he knew

I wasn't referring to his overbearing father. I meant what he truly ran from – the source of his deep-seated scars. He shook his head, almost violently. 'It doesn't matter. We'll go back to London and none of it will matter. It'll just be you and me. Juliet . . .'

I knew what he wanted to say. He loved me. He loved the half-mad, filthy girl standing in a pool of formaldehyde. But he would come back to his senses once we were in London. He'd hide his scars, as he was so good at doing, and find a girl like Lucy – sweet, rich, sane. And that's how it should be. Besides, I'd already made my choice. Montgomery.

But then why did I still think about the cave behind the waterfall? Why did my thoughts slip from Montgomery's face to Edward's late at night, in the instant before sleep overcame me?

'Montgomery,' I said, though my throat caught. I suppose I hoped that saying his name would evoke his spirit and help ease this heart-clenching tension. 'Montgomery's coming back, too.'

Edward's jaw twitched. His fingers found my waist, pulling me closer until our bodies were touching. The preservatives seeped into his clothes, binding us together. But he didn't let go. His pupils were dilated, black as night. 'I want to tell you something . . .'

I shook my head forcefully. I didn't want him to say he loved me. Because I had recognized a little of myself in him. Too much. And it terrified me.

I put my finger over his lips. 'Father's taken the dogs to the village. He'll find Montgomery. We'll go back to London and we'll never speak of this place again.'

In my room, I peeled off my stained dress and shoved it between the iron bars of my small window. The island could have back the mud and the salt and the sweat. I washed the burning chemicals off my face and hands and pulled on the old muslin dress I'd worn when I arrived on the island. I didn't want Mother's fancy things. I wanted to feel like myself again.

A chill crept up my back as I bent to lace my boots. That odd sensation of being watched. I whirled to the window, but there was nothing. A familiar smell hung faintly in the air, though – wet dog.

'Who's there?' I said.

The tip of a boot peeked out from the cracked door.

'I see you,' I said. 'Come out.'

Balthazar shuffled forward, peering through the crack. Eyes still human, not regressed like the others.

I threw my hands to the buttons at my chest, doing them up quickly. 'What are you doing here?' I snapped. Had he watched me undress? He retreated as though I'd struck him, and I felt a wave of remorse. Balthazar wasn't a leering beast. He was innocent as a child.

I eased open the door. He was holding the wooden box from the laboratory that contained my new batch of serum. 'I'm sorry. I'm not cross,' I said.

He shyly handed me the box. 'I wanted to bring you this.'

I took it, feeling guilty. 'Thank you.'

His big hands, empty now, plucked nervously at his pockets. 'I also wanted to ask you . . . wanted to ask . . .'

I jerked my head toward the room. 'Come inside.' I tried to listen, but my head raced with what needed to be done. I set the box on my dressing table. We still had to fill the jars and waterskins. Find something to use for shade. A weapon would be handy, a pistol or a knife. I dug through the trunks, looking for the shears. Where had I left them?

I glanced at Balthazar, who shifted his weight back and forth. 'Yes? Ask me what?'

'Take me with you,' he said. 'Take me to Lon-don.'

My hands closed over something hard and sharp between two dresses. The shears. But just as quickly, my fingers went slack. 'What do you mean?' I asked.

'Montgomery says you're leaving the island. You and the other . . . five-fingers.' His lip trembled. 'I've got five fingers,' he said, holding up his hand. 'I've crossed the sea. I've been to London. I can pretend. Like actors in a play, Montgomery says. And I will help you. You'll need a servant.' His mouth broke into that odd panting smile that meant he was nervous.

I leaned on the dresser, closing my eyes. He'd clearly spent some time composing this request. It was true that he could pass for human – a mutilated, deformed man whom people shrank from in the streets. But that wasn't why I hesitated.

The reason was because I was terrified of taking Balthazar – or any of Father's creations – off the island. Father's brilliant and horrible discoveries had to stay lost on that small bit of land in the South Pacific, exiled with him, never to leave.

Balthazar was still smiling. He was so hopeful it broke my heart. I stared at my reflection in the fractured mirror, knowing I hadn't the strength to tell him the truth.

'Promise you'll tell no one?' I asked. I hated myself for lying. Destroying Father's laboratory had been simple, but a single lie to this dog-faced beast made my stomach heave. He nodded enthusiastically. I swallowed, trying to keep the bile down. 'You won't be able to tell anyone about this place. It will have to be a secret.'

He nodded again vigorously. 'Like actors in a play.' His hands clamped together.

I looked at a spot just over his left ear. It made the lie easier. 'Then you may come.'

His face broke into a genuine smile. He scratched at his nose, trying to hide his excitement. My heart tore, just a little, right along the ventricular septum.

I shoved the shears into my pocket. 'But we aren't going

318

anywhere if Father doesn't find Montgomery.' I cocked my head, wondering if Balthazar had any sense that his master had been taken. I placed my hand on his hulking shoulder, wondering how to explain. 'Some of the islanders took him. I don't know where. I want you to be strong, no matter what happens. Not to worry. Can you do that?'

He scratched the back of his neck. 'I'm not worried. I know where Montgomery is.'

My body went rigid. 'You do? Where?'

'He's with Ajax. I heard the birds talking about it.'

I stared at him, speechless. The birds *talking*? All those whispers I'd heard in the jungle hadn't been my imagination after all. But that wasn't what disturbed me most. 'Ajax? *Jaguar?* Are you sure?'

'Oh yes, miss, sure.'

I sank to the bed. Balthazar was so calm about it. Didn't he know . . . ? 'Ajax is dangerous,' I said carefully. 'He's no longer himself. He's a beast now. He's regressed – do you know what that means?'

Balthazar frowned. He thought Jaguar was still the man who used to tell bedtime stories to Alice.

Something else he'd said came back to me. 'Father went to the village to look for Montgomery.'

Balthazar shook his head. 'He won't find Montgomery there. Ajax is almost always—'

'In his cabin,' I finished. Father was headed in the wrong direction. By the time he came back, Jaguar might have killed Montgomery, if he hadn't already.

I had to return to the cabin.

FORTY-ONE

I hurried to the barn, fear making my footsteps light as a sigh. Jaguar's cunning eyes haunted my thoughts. Father believed the monster and Jaguar were one and the same, but I knew better. That didn't mean he wasn't still dangerous, though. He was clever as a man, with nothing to hold his predator instincts in check. As far as what the monster was, I could only form half-thought-out theories. A beast that had regressed on its own. Something that had escaped from Father's laboratory. Something worse than I could dream.

Father had taken Duchess, the more nimble of the horses. Duke snorted and pawed the straw when I came in. I touched his velvety muzzle, seeing the fear in his white-rimmed eyes.

'We'll find him,' I said, laying my hand on the white stripe across his nose. I picked up the saddle, staggering under its weight. It still smelled faintly of oil from the last time Montgomery had cleaned it.

'You shouldn't go,' a voice said behind me. I nearly dropped the saddle. Edward stood in the doorway, breathing hard, looking disheveled. 'It isn't safe.'

I propped the saddle on my knee, trying to hoist it onto

Duke's back. I grunted with the effort. 'Father's gone to the village, but Montgomery's not there. Jaguar has him.'

'It's dangerous! Jaguar's regressed. They all have. And the monster—'

'I've seen the monster,' I said. The memory of the claws curling around the bars in my bedroom window made my blood race. I thought of the darkened barn, the smell of the monster, the weight of its presence so close. 'It could have killed me and it didn't.'

'What makes you think it wasn't toying with you? It doesn't have reason, Juliet. It's an animal.'

I straightened the saddle. 'Hand me that girth strap,' I said.

He didn't move. I pushed past him and ripped it down from the wall, then buckled it to one side and ran it under Duke's belly. I looped the buckle and tugged as hard as I could, but the girth wouldn't cinch.

'Blast!' I muttered.

Edward's hand fell over mine. I swallowed, wishing he'd just stay away and make this easier on both of us.

'Don't go.' The softness in his voice wrenched something deep inside me.

'I have to. I'm sorry. Montgomery . . .'

'There's something I have to tell you.' His hand worked the buckle straps like it was me he wanted to be holding, and the saddle leathers were a poor substitute.

He needed to let me go. Because only then could I let *him* go.

'Don't say it,' I said, almost a plea. 'I love Montgomery.'

But deep inside, my God, I *wanted* him to say it. To kiss me feverishly and end this terrible pull between us.

His lips parted. My mouth fell open, struggling for breath. I'd been drawn to him since I first saw him, I realized. So desolate, so damaged. He was close enough that I could smell the salt on his clothes. Desire smoldered in his eyes and stole my breath, and I felt myself drifting closer.

Duke stamped his hoof, letting out a shrill whinny, and the moment was gone.

Edward let out a ragged breath. I fell back, startled by what I'd been about to do. My fingers fumbled to tighten the buckle.

'Then let me come with you,' he said.

I shook my head and pulled myself onto the horse, arranging the folds of my dress hurriedly around the saddle. 'There's only one horse.' But the truth was, if I stayed a moment longer in his presence, I wouldn't trust myself not to fall into his scarred arms.

Under the jungle canopy it was already growing dark. The wagon road was easy to follow, but the leaves blended together in the dusky light, hiding the side paths that would take me to the cabin.

I only knew the general direction: close to the beach, near the winding stream. I hoped Duke would know the way to the cabin better than I. I found what looked like an opening and turned him toward it, but he stopped. I dug my boots into his sides, but he didn't budge.

'Come on, you old block,' I muttered.

A snarl tore through the trees. Duke's muscles tightened between my legs, just a second of warning before he bucked and bolted down the path. I grabbed a fistful of mane, just trying to stay on as leaves and branches slapped against my face.

I gasped as he suddenly lurched off the trail onto a narrow path. I leaned in closer, almost hugging his neck. Thin branches tore at my hair. I kept my eyes squinted to focus. A single low branch could throw me from his back.

The trail turned sharply into a valley. Each bounce nearly sent me flying. I gripped Duke's sides with my ankles, tugging on the reins. But it was useless. He slowed only when we reached the bottom of the valley. His gallop gave way to a trot, and then the trot to a walk. I looked around helplessly.

We were totally lost.

A crash or rustle would sound behind us every few minutes, but when I turned there was nothing. My heart raced.

Another crash, closer.

My throat closed up. All I could think of were Alice's feet dripping with blood. The three claws reaching through my window. The wet footprints on the porch. I squeezed my eyes shut, counting to five. Duke picked his way through the maze of trees, effortlessly. When I opened my eyes, I was shocked to find how dark the jungle had gotten. Dusk was falling quickly.

Ahead, something glinted through the trees, so brightly it burned white spots in my eyes. As we rode closer, I realized it was the reflection of the fading sun on a tin roof. My hands tightened on the reins. The roof was patchy, only a few shiny surfaces left.

Jaguar's cabin.

Duke stopped at the edge of the clearing. I studied the quiet cabin, wondering what I'd find inside. Maybe a feral jaguar, ready to slash at whatever warm, breathing thing came through the door. I climbed off Duke and tied him to a post with a quick knot. I scrambled onto the wooden porch, feeling the same fear in my throat as I'd felt the first time. The three-toed tracks had long ago disappeared, but they lingered in my memory.

I peered in the glass window, but it was dark inside. I unlatched the door before I lost my nerve. The door gave an inch but stopped, either locked or stuck. I pushed my weight against the door, then harder, and harder again, until it suddenly gave. I fell into Jaguar's cabin.

Shaken, I stumbled to my feet. It seemed as vacant and abandoned as before – even the flower was gone from the mantel. I brushed aside dead leaves with my boot and found shattered pieces of the glass vase. I ran back to the window to make sure Duke was still there, needing the reassurance.

He grazed calmly in the fading light in the front yard. I let out a deep breath and rested my forehead against the cool windowpane. I wasn't sure if I felt an urge to laugh or to cry.

Duke suddenly jerked his head up. Loose grass fell from his mouth. He seemed to stare straight at me, ears twitching, though I knew it was too dark to see into the cabin. An uneasy feeling stirred in my belly. I felt trapped. An overwhelming urge to get out of the cabin pulled at my gut. Maybe it was the pieces of deer inside me, the animal instinct, sensing a predator was near.

I flung open the door.

Montgomery stood in the doorway, his shirt torn, his hair loose.

'Juliet?' he started, but I grabbed his shirt in my fists. I touched his face, his chest, his hair, to make sure he was real.

'You're here,' I said. 'You're alive.'

'What are *you* doing here?'

I buried my face in his chest. My breath came ragged. He was alive. We were going to get off the island, all of us, in one piece. I started shaking. He wrapped an arm around my back.

'Try to calm down,' he said. 'Everything's going to be all right. Here, sit down.' He led me to the dingy bed. 'What are you doing here?' he asked again. 'It's dangerous. I told you never to return to the jungle.'

'I had to find you. Where's Jaguar? Are you all right? What happened on the beach?'

He pushed his hair back. There was a fresh cut on his arm, but it no longer bled. He started to answer, but I jumped up.

A figure filled the doorway.

'Jaguar,' I said. I slid my hand into my pocket. Found the shape of the shears.

He paused in the doorway, his slitted cat eyes shifting between us. He walked upright, but only barely. His clothes were gone. Fine golden hair covered his body like a thick mane. He'd regressed, but not as much as the others. I pulled the shears out of my pocket, but Montgomery pushed them back in.

'We can trust him.'

Trust him? Jaguar slipped in but hovered around the outer edges of the room. He moved more gracefully than ever, as though he might drop to four legs at any moment and slink closer. His long claws clicked on the wooden floorboards. He could slice our throats in a single swipe, and I was supposed to *trust* him?

His golden eyes met mine. I felt a twist inside me, fear and incredulity mixed in one.

'He's lost the ability to talk, but not his reason. He's not like the others.' Montgomery sat down in the desk chair. 'He conspired with the water beasts to flip our boat. He dragged me here.'

My head whipped to Jaguar. 'You? We nearly drowned!'

'It was me they wanted. They weren't trying to kill me. They wanted to warn me. They didn't know if you and Edward could be trusted.'

I watched Jaguar from the corner of my eye. He squatted in the corner, half hidden in shadow, so still not even his whiskers moved.

325

'Warn you of what?' I asked, breathless.

Montgomery ran a hand through his hair, his eyes shifting to Jaguar. 'The beasts are going to attack the compound. They're after the doctor, but they'll kill anyone they find.'

The hair on my arms rose, making my skin tingle. 'When?' 'Tonight.'

'Tonight? Edward's there!' I jumped up, pacing. 'We've got to leave the island. Now.' But Montgomery stayed seated. He rubbed his jaw. There was something he wasn't telling me.

'What is it?' I asked.

A low growl came from the corner. Jaguar came out of the shadow, slinking toward the fireplace. I took a step back, but Montgomery didn't seem concerned by his presence.

The heel of his boot tapped nervously against the rotten floorboards. Then he stood abruptly. 'It's nothing. You're right, we need to leave.'

He left the cabin and jumped down from the porch to untie Duke's lead. I hurried after him, but suddenly Jaguar's rough paw was on my arm, holding me back. A scream rose to my lips but died just as quickly. It took one look into his eyes to know he wasn't going to hurt me.

'What do you want?' I whispered, feeling the weight of being alone with him.

He nosed my hand palm up. I swallowed, remembering the rough feel of his tongue on my skin.

He slid out a long, black claw. He traced the tip over my forearm, lightly at first, and then slightly harder. Just enough to scratch but not draw blood. My breath caught. The pain was tolerable. What he was doing was not.

Writing.

He etched three careful scratches into my flesh. Three straight lines in a row. A crude circle around them.

'Three?' I said. Three toes? Three claw marks across the victims?

But he just growled deep in his throat and slunk back into the shadows.

FORTY-TWO

Night had fallen, and we rode home in the moonlight. Montgomery dug his heels into Duke, pushing the horse to tear at the soft ground as I wrapped my arms around Montgomery's waist and buried my face in his shoulders. Leaves whistled by, no more than an afterthought. But not fast enough. My worries hovered before us, just out of reach. I wanted to claw at the air to make us go faster. Every passing moment was a moment the beasts might attack. And Edward waited for us at the compound, unaware of the coming storm.

Moonlight glinted off mica flecks in the compound's rock walls as we arrived. Montgomery slid off Duke and helped me down from the steaming horse. We hurried to the compound and pounded on the gate.

Balthazar let us in. I stumbled through, still reeling from the breakneck ride. His face broke into a grin when he saw Montgomery. The smile faded at the hollow looks on our faces.

'Is everyone safe?' Montgomery said, breathless.

Balthazar nodded. His eyes were darting nervously. He might not be clever, but he could sense when something was wrong.

'Where's Edward?' I said.

Balthazar pointed a thick finger at the storage building. 'In his room.'

Relief showered me like moonlight. I started through the mud, but my feet stopped when I heard Montgomery speak.

'And the doctor? We should warn him at least.'

'Hasn't returned,' Balthazar said.

Montgomery threw me a questioning glance. 'He left? Why?'

I took a deep breath. We'd planned every aspect of our escape, but we'd never talked about what would happen to Father. I never intended to say good-bye, let alone bring him with us. I'd assumed Montgomery felt the same. But looking at his face now, I realized he was still caught up in their bond. Montgomery still thought of him like a father, even after everything.

'He went to the village to try to find you.'

Silence fell for a beat. I knew what he was thinking. The beasts had found my father somewhere in the jungle and sliced his heart out like those of the others. We might never see him again. For the first time, it felt real. We might leave with no good-byes, just a boat drifting out to sea, never to return.

I started to speak, but Montgomery dug his fingers into my arm and dragged me out of Balthazar's earshot. 'It doesn't matter. I'll hitch the wagon. Get Edward and collect the water and supplies. As fast as you can.'

A scream came from the jungle, sharp and piercing.

They were coming.

The gate hung open. Balthazar stumbled toward it, reaching for the wooden beam. Montgomery raced to help. They shoved their weight against the door, scrambling to seal it.

'Hurry,' Montgomery called over his shoulder.

Panic beat in time with my heart. My feet felt suspended in molasses. I couldn't move fast enough. The beasts would move like lightning, though. They'd come over the roof tiles or break down the gate.

I stumbled to my room and threw my things into the old carpetbag. A bedsheet would give us shade from the relentless sun. Mother's jewelry and the silver comb and hairbrush would fetch a price. The wooden box that held my treatment. My thoughts clutched at all the scattered things I couldn't take. Wilted lavender Alice had left on my dresser. The copy of *Longman's Anatomical Reference* I'd saved from our library on Belgrave Square. Now I never wanted to see it again.

I dragged the carpetbag outside and hurried along the portico to Edward's room. A cloud covered the moon, plunging the courtyard into shadows. My eyes played tricks on me. I thought I saw shapes climbing through the windows, over the roof. But when I shook my head, nothing was there.

Puck joined Balthazar at the front gate. They pressed their ears to the wooden boards, looking puzzled. They didn't know the beasts were just outside, planning an attack. I wondered if they'd fight back. Puck glanced at me. His scaly mouth peeled into a grim smile.

Puck might be wild enough to join in the frenzy. But not Balthazar. Balthazar would ball himself up and let the beasts tear at him. He saw me watching, and his face brightened. Again, I felt a twist of guilt at my lie. But I hadn't a choice. If he regressed like the others, turned violent in the crowded London streets . . .

A tile crashed to the ground. I jumped, scanning the roofline. I imagined the beasts there, watching, waiting, stalking, led by a black-clawed monster.

My hand found Edward's doorknob and squeezed the odd latch. 'We have to leave,' I said in a rush.

But the room was empty. The trace smell of sulfur hung in the air from a recently lit match. The lantern sat next to the pallet he used as a bed. Beside it was a pile of clothes borrowed from Montgomery, an old pair of shoes, a stack of books from the salon, and a crystal decanter.

We can sell that, I thought, and snatched it up.

The decanter left a wet ring on one of the books. The cover caught my eye. I'd seen this book on the shelves in the salon when I'd arrived, but then it had gone missing.

Edward III.

I'd read it, long ago, when it used to be in our library on Belgrave Square. It was a lesser-known play, attributed to Shakespeare by some. It was bound in dark-green cloth, standard size, nothing remarkable except for the gold foil imprint in the spine: three straight lines surrounded by a circle.

The same symbol Jaguar had carved into my skin.

My hands started shaking. I flipped through the book, nearly ripping the pages. Half the pages were dog-eared. Some had been torn out. A long gash sliced through the back cover, made by something razor-sharp. I let the book fall open to one of the marked pages. A few lines were underlined in black ink, over and over, so hard it ripped the paper.

And he is bred out of that bloody strain
That haunted us in our familiar paths.
Witness our too-much-memorable shame . . .
Of that black name, Edward, Black Prince of Wales.

Edward, the Black Prince. I tried to remember all I'd read of the Black Prince's character in plays. To the French, Edward III was a young boy raised by a cruel father – a general – who pushed him to military victory through ambition and brutality, turning the poor boy into a fiend. Not unlike the snips of story Edward had given us. The feeling went out of my feet and I knelt on the ground, frantically pawing through to the marked pages.

It was all there. The same story. The same person.

Edward had lied to us. He wasn't Edward Prince. He was *Prince Edward* – the Black Prince from Shakespeare's plays. This was his mystery. He'd stolen his identity from a little-known play.

The book fell out of my hands. This discovery meant one of two things. Edward might just be a runaway like he claimed, giving himself a new identity to flee some crime or maybe a girl he'd gotten with child. *Or it could mean . . .*

Sweat dripped down the sides of my face. I brushed it away, taking deep breaths. I fought to think with my head instead of my heart, which wanted to shout Edward's innocence. But my heart was weak. I had to cut it out of my chest and think logically.

Or it could mean Edward was one of my father's creations.

Named after a Shakespearean character, just like Balthazar and Cymbeline and all the others.

Just like me.

A faint idea seeded in the back of my head. Alice had always avoided Edward, as had Cymbeline and the other servants. Had they known? Had they avoided him because they feared him – because they knew him to be the monster?

I collapsed to my knees. No, it was impossible. The monster's murders began before we even arrived on the island. Unless . . . Edward had never been on the *Viola*. He could have left the island in the dinghy, running from something – *my father* – and fate had brought him back.

My mind raced, trying to remember where he'd been when the murders happened. Too many times he'd slipped away to his room or into the night. A hundred chances to kill. But he'd been with us in the village when Alice was murdered. *No.* That wasn't entirely true. He'd run away after shooting Antigonus. He could have raced to the compound before us, killed her, and circled back later. He'd been covered with blood and scratches, after all.

Thorns, he'd claimed. More like Alice's fingernails.

I tore through the pile of clothes, ripping at the hems, digging through the pockets, trying to find some further evidence. I yanked the sheets off his straw pallet. My heart refused to believe my head. Edward wasn't a monster. He'd protected me. He'd protected my father! I'd seen his face when he shot Antigonus. He'd gone white as a cadaver, horrified by what he'd done. He could never claw a person to death. He didn't have claws! And I'd seen the monster. I'd smelled its musky scent. I knew the weight of its presence.

I fumbled for the shears and thrust the sharp end into his mattress, ripping a gash into the burlap. I tore it open and pulled out handfuls of straw, feeling for anything that might tell me the truth.

Nothing.

I crunched handfuls of straw in my fists. Jaguar's mark flashed at me, mocking. Jaguar had known. He'd tried to warn us. Father must have known, too, but led us to believe Edward was a total stranger. Had he meant to kill him, that first day, when he pushed him into the water? Punishment for leaving, maybe. A lesson to show his creation who was in command. He'd made Edward from what – another panther? A hound? He must have done it while Montgomery was away. How proud he must have felt, to create a creature even more perfectly human than Alice, smarter even than Jaguar. Until his perfect creation had abandoned him.

Furious, I threw the half-empty mattress against the back wall. Straw rained over the damp ground that had been hidden under the mattress. My breath caught. Claw marks sliced across the stone floor. Long. Deep. Furious. And between them, dark-brown streaks of dried blood. Tracks ran through them. Three-toed.

My blood went cold. Something shiny glinted among the claw marks, and I picked it up. A silver button just like the ones on Edward's shirt when we found him in the dinghy.

My heart twisted, wanting to deny it. But the truth was evident. His scarred face was just a mask for a fiend bent on spilling blood. I didn't know how Father had done it or how Edward made those bloody footprints. Only that the truth of it chilled me to the bone.

I felt a warm breath on the back of my neck. Then a voice spoke in my ear, both familiar and terrifying.

'Don't run, Juliet,' Edward said, before his hand closed around my mouth.

FORTY-THREE

I fought him, but he was impossibly strong.

'Promise not to scream, and I'll let you go,' he said. His hand held my jaw closed, sealing in my screams. I still smelled traces of lamp oil and sulfur on his skin.

I gave a jerk of a nod. The pressure was gone, and I leapt away from him, scrambling to the back wall and filling my lungs with air. Montgomery was right outside. If I screamed, he'd come running. But would he be fast enough?

'Don't,' Edward said, reading my thoughts. 'He can't help you.'

Something primal and defensive – the animal part of me – took control of my muscles. For once my head was silent as it surrendered to that deep animal strength. With a growl I hurled the decanter at him. He blocked it with his elbow, but it shattered into shards of glass. They rained to the floor like a spring shower on stone steps, and for a moment I was back in the house on Belgrave Square, watching afternoon rain fall on the street outside. I blinked, wondering if I'd made a huge mistake. We *weren't* animals, after all – at least not entirely. This was Edward, who had saved my life. Who had come to the island to protect me.

Who loved me.

Love was a human trait. Despite whatever material Father had started with, Edward was human now. Did he deserve to die because of it?

But the primal part of me was only interested in survival, and it was stronger. I pushed past him, clawing at the door until I got it open. Outside, the courtyard pulsed with shadows. I could hear the beasts' soft footsteps and barely still breaths. They were everywhere and nowhere. I clenched my jaw and darted across the courtyard to the barn. I heard Edward scrambling just a few steps behind me. I had only one chance.

I threw open the barn door.

'Montgomery!' I yelled.

But the wagon was gone. Duke wasn't in his stall. I ran to the tack room. Empty. But it no longer mattered. Edward was already at the barn door.

I pressed myself into the tack room wall, lost among the hanging bridles and dangling saddle leathers. Edward approached slowly, his hands out, palms down, as if to steady a frightened animal.

'It's all right, Juliet. I'm not going to hurt you.'

Maybe he should have looked different – sinister, or monstrous. But he didn't. He looked just like the bruised and broken castaway clutching a tattered photograph on the *Curitiba*. His gold-flecked eyes were intelligent and deep – eyes that still haunted my dreams.

I shook my head, biting back the tender sting of betrayal. 'How could you, Edward?'

'I tried to tell you.' His dark eyes consumed me. 'Before you left, I tried . . . but what would I have said? You'd have loathed the sight of me.'

'Because you're a monster!' I hissed. 'You killed all those creatures. You killed Alice!' My foot grazed something on the ground that rang with the sound of metal. The pitchfork. I darted for it, but he was on me in a second, moving faster than humanly possible. He wrenched the pitchfork out of my hands and threw it into one of the stalls. I hurled myself at him, but he picked me up as easily as a rag doll and shoved me against the wall.

His eyes burned. 'Don't,' he whispered. Begged. 'Don't fight me. It'll only bring on the change.'

'What change?' I asked. His fingers felt like they could snap my wrist as easily as a reed. *'What change?'*

But he didn't answer. He didn't need to. I'd seen the three-toed prints, the six-inch-long claws. He was so close I could see his nostrils flare. His pupils were wide and black, slightly elongated like an animal's. My breath caught. 'It's impossible. In the woods, it was chasing us . . .'

'That was only a bobcat that had escaped the laboratory cages. You were already so scared. It wasn't hard to convince you it was the monster. I just wanted to get you back to the compound, where I could watch out for you. I never wanted to hurt you. Or any of them. I don't even remember killing them – that's how it is. I become another creature.'

His jaw twitched. 'Your father made me like this. He tried a new technique, something revolutionary that didn't involve surgery. He said he used a chemical composition taken from human blood. It changes the cellular constitution of animal flesh. He thought he had transformed me from animal to human, but he was wrong.' Edward's dark eyes could have swallowed the world. 'You can't ever destroy the animal.'

His knuckles were red and swollen, and I could feel the bones grinding unnaturally beneath his skin as he held me against the wall. I remembered what Father had said about the monkey.

A new technique. Changing the constitution on a cellular level without ever having to use a scalpel.

Edward had been his first. Now he was trying to do it again.

'I'm not a monster, Juliet. I'm everything your father intended. Intelligent. Compassionate. Loyal. But I've a darker side. I look human, but the animal flesh still lives inside me. Its bones alongside my bones. Its blood in my veins.' His eyes were glowing, hungry. 'I can barely control it.'

'From whom did it come?' I asked with a hoarse voice.

He cocked his head. 'What do you mean?'

'You said he used human blood to extract the cellular traits to make you human. Whose blood did he use?'

Edward shook his head. 'I don't know. I've never known.'

'What about the animal?' I asked. 'He must have started with some kind of creature.'

Edward cast a glance at the door, as though remembering the feel of the wild. 'It wasn't just one. He began with a jackal but added cellular traits of others. Heron. Fox. Those are just the ones I know about, but there are more – I can *feel* them.'

He flexed his hands, studying the bones as though he barely believed it himself. 'The doctor explained the process, but he kept my files secret. As far as what I was . . . I don't remember anything. I only remember waking up in the laboratory shackled to a table, and a gray-haired man taking notes. He was delighted. He thought me a great success. I knew things – words, objects. The rest I figured out through books. I read about men's clothing and the London flower markets and primate biology. I borrowed my own history from the pages of novels and plays. My name from *Edward III*. The story of Viola from *Twelfth Night*. My family's estate, Chesney Wold – that's from Dickens.'

He continued in a rush. 'The servants – Alice and the rest – they were kind, though I think I unsettled them. I stayed in the compound, never interacted with the villagers. But then after a few weeks, something happened. I was near the beach at night. A beast had cut its leg. The smell of blood . . . I don't remember the details precisely. They didn't find the body for days.'

'And Father didn't care that he'd created a monster?'

'Your father didn't know. None of them knew. I hid it. Alice saw me once rinsing blood off my hands and mouth. She suspected – but it was simple to keep her quiet. She frightened so easily. But then it happened a second time. And a third – they still haven't found all the bodies. The lack of infection here slows decomposition.' His throat constricted. 'I took the dinghy and left before any of them knew. Before I killed again.'

Suddenly he looked as vulnerable and lost as the first time I'd seen him, curled in the bottom of the boat. 'I thought I'd die in that dinghy. When your ship found me, when the doctor's own assistant brought me back to life and was headed for the very place I'd left, it seemed like escaping the island was impossible. As if my fate was tied to this place. And then there was you. His daughter. You had no idea who he was, or what he was capable of. What other monsters he might create.'

He fumbled in his pocket, pulled out a crumpled and torn piece of paper. I took it with shaking hands. The edges were so worn they were soft as fabric. The photograph.

'You asked me what it was. It's a woman holding a little girl by the hand in a garden. It used to be on the shelf in the salon with the rest of the photographs. I took it when I left because I wanted to remember why I was leaving. To remember there is good in the world, flowers and happiness and families. It wasn't a world I belonged in, no matter how much I wished I did.' He paused. 'The photograph was of you and your mother.'

I thought of him leaving the island, blood still on his

339

hands, ready to die of exposure. But he hadn't died. Above all else, we were both survivors.

He slumped against the door. 'I thought I could make up for everything. Do something right, for once. Protect you from him.'

The tiles rattled overhead. A growl, too close.

'The beasts are on the roof,' I said, my voice just a whisper. 'They'll kill us. Let me go, Edward. Please.'

'They can't get through me. They know what I am now.' A slow line of sweat ran down his face. A beast snarled again outside, but he didn't flinch.

I spied an old bucket, empty except for a hoof pick. I eased closer to it with each breath, while I tried to buy myself time. 'Father recognised you when we first arrived. That's why he tried to drown you.'

'He was furious I'd left. That first night, he told me I'd be forgiven as long as I obeyed him and kept my identity secret.'

I inched my hand toward the bucket. 'Why bother? What did it matter if Montgomery and I knew?'

He hesitated. 'He thought it would serve his purposes for you not to know. It's all one big experiment to him.'

'What do you mean?'

'He tried to match us, Juliet. He was trying to push us together, to keep you away from Montgomery. He found a use for us after all – to see what would happen if a human bred with one of his creations. We were both only experiments to him.'

My legs went weak. I grabbed a bridle to keep myself steady. *No, he wouldn't.* And yet I knew he would. Outside, glass shattered. I heard a few shouts. From Puck, maybe, but the voice was carried off by the wind. I glanced at the back wall. The big rifle was missing from the gun rack. Montgomery had it somewhere. God, where was he?

'But I'd never have gone through with it,' Edward said in a rush, oblivious to the chaos outside. 'I'd never have tricked you. It's different with you, Juliet. I can control myself better when you're near. You drown out all other noise in the room. Back in London, maybe I won't need to kill. If you help me.'

I inched my hand toward the hoof pick, but he stepped closer, his gaze dropping into the bucket. I curled my fingers into my palm, but we both knew what I'd been trying to do.

'Please. He made me this way. You can make it right.'

A gunshot rang out from the courtyard. Edward whirled, growling. I darted for the door, but he grabbed my waist and hauled me back.

'Montgomery!' I yelled. 'In here!' I struggled to get free of Edward's arms.

'He can't help you, don't you see?' Edward grunted. 'He made Alice. He's as bad as the doctor.'

I heard my name called outside – Montgomery was shouting for me. Another gunshot rang out. Something flashed by the door, leaving only dust in its wake.

Edward heard my gasp and turned.

'They're inside the walls,' I said.

FORTY-FOUR

Snarls tore the air. A shelf of tiles crashed right outside the barn. Two more gunshots.

Edward dragged me into the tack room and slammed the door, sealing us in. In the second his back was turned, I grabbed the hoof pick and hid it in the folds of my skirt.

'I can protect you, Juliet,' he said. 'We're similar, you and I. Both children of the same monster. Both capable of his same atrocities.'

I pressed the pad of my thumb into the pick's sharp end. 'That's not true. I haven't *killed*,' I said.

'Not yet. But you would. To defend Montgomery. To defend *yourself*.' He lunged at me. I gasped and struggled, but he only wrestled the pick from my hand.

He studied the sharp end, as if to prove his point. 'There's a darkness inside you. Don't deny it – you know it's true. You feel it. It's the animal in you, stirring, hungry for unnatural things. Just like me.'

He turned and hurled the pick against the back wall, where it dented the wood with a thud. I threw my hands over my ears, pressing my eyes shut. But I felt his presence in front of me, coldness and scars. His hands covered mine, drifting into my hair, his fingers running along my scalp. 'I loved you the first moment I saw you. Helplessly. Passionately. I love you more than he does.' His breath was just inches from my own.

'Stop. Please.' I squeezed my eyes harder. I should have twisted away, but my body didn't obey. 'You know it's impossible. You're a murderer . . .'

His hands tightened in my hair. 'And what do you think Montgomery's doing out there? Don't you hear the gunshots? We're all animals! We all fight to survive.'

His skin was on fire. His lips grazed my neck, and my larynx tensed, ready to scream. My eyelids shot open, my vision glassy and unfocused.

'We belong together. Not to serve your father's mad experiment. But because we're the same.' His open palm covered my heart, just grazing the exposed skin above my neckline. I gasped at his touch. Fear and thrill were divided by such a fine line that I couldn't tell which plucked at the tight strings in my chest. And was he really so wrong? I *did* know about the darkness he spoke of. As much as I loved Montgomery, he couldn't understand it like Edward.

Something thudded at the door, and the wooden latch splintered. The door burst open. Edward spun around, nearly knocking over the lantern. Montgomery stood three paces away, a gash running down his face, with the rifle aimed at Edward.

'Get away from her,' Montgomery said. Mud streaked his clothes. 'I'll blast a hole in your goddamned chest.'

'Montgomery, don't!' I yelled. I shouldn't have cared about Edward's safety. He was a monster and a murderer and the last person I should defend. But it was too late.

Montgomery paused just long enough for Edward to attack. A low growl rumbled in Edward's chest before he leapt across the room, knocking Montgomery's gun to the floor.

I screamed – it was as if Edward was suddenly a different creature, wild and violent. Gone were the gold-flecked eyes, now black as night except for an electric ring of yellow iris around slitted pupils. His clothes strained over muscles that seemed to grow larger by the second. The way he moved was calculated, threatening, like he was stalking prey.

He knocked Montgomery down with the force of three men.

I wanted to scream for him to stop, but my voice was gone. Edward was changing. *Its bones alongside my bones*, he had said. *Its blood in my veins*. The animal part of him – the jackal, the fox, along with whatever other bits and pieces of various species Father had added – really did live inside him, lurking, waiting for its chance to transform Edward into the monster Father had made him.

His knuckles were red and knobby, so swollen I thought they might split and seep blood. As I watched, his fingers seemed to grow. Tendons snapped. The metacarpal bones grated against each other. The hair on his arms darkened, until he looked nearly as beastly as the wild dogs that haunted the outskirts of farms.

I dug the heels of my palms into my eye sockets, convinced his transformation must be a trick of my eyes. But when I looked again, it was the same. The palmar ligaments in his hand twisted and popped, bending the fingers. He grabbed the door to slam it shut. The way his gnarled fingers knotted, the sweaty handprint on the door looked as though he had only three fingers. Just like the three-toed prints on the cabin porch. But what animal could he have been made from that had only three toes?

A heron. One of the animals Edward had listed. The realization nearly knocked me flat.

Montgomery struggled to his feet. Blood dripped from Edward's knuckles, though he hadn't cut them. He balled his hands in pain and growled deep in his throat. Three black claws slid out from the knuckles on each hand. They were retractable, so in his human form there had been no sign of them lingering beneath the surface. One claw was missing on his right hand, I realized – cut off by my own shears.

I stumbled and my hip connected hard with the corner of the saddle stand, but I felt nothing. Shock had rendered me blank inside. I'd wanted not to believe it. The change in Edward was hard to define. He was larger. Darker. And yet as my eyes slid over his face and body, I couldn't name one clear thing that was different. I'd have said his fingernails were black, and yet when I really looked, they were unchanged. It was like looking at stars – one could see them clearly only from the corner of one's eye.

But the claws, at least, were no trick of my eye. He raised them like deadly knives in Montgomery's direction. 'Edward, stop!' I screamed. But he didn't seem to hear me.

Edward slammed Montgomery against the wall of bridles with enough force to crack the boards. The seam of his shirt split around his shoulders. He *had* gotten larger. I rubbed my eyes, trying to make sense of it.

Montgomery managed to twist out of his grasp. Leather straps fell, tangling around them. If I could get closer, I could pull one down and try to get it around Edward's neck like a noose.

Edward curled his gnarled fist. The black claws dripped with blood. Suddenly they retracted, and he punched Montgomery so hard that the wall cracked under his weight.

'Stop!' I said.

But Montgomery got back up. Blood trickled from his mouth. Edward threw another punch that Montgomery evaded. Something silver gleamed in his hand – a broken metal bit from one of the bridles, sharp and ragged at the end, dangerous as a dagger. Or claws. He slammed it into the side of Edward's neck.

Edward howled. He wrenched the broken bit out of his flesh. For an instant he looked like himself again, and my heart twisted. I almost ran to help him.

Montgomery grabbed my arm. 'Run,' he said.

But running was useless. Edward was already blocking the door. His claws were out. His face was the dark before a storm. He lunged for Montgomery, ducking just as Montgomery brought down the broken edge of the bit. They fell to the ground, wrestling in the straw. Dirt choked my throat, blinded my eyes. Edward's claws too were like daggers. He swiped at Montgomery, grazing his arm. I pressed my back into the wall, the hanging bridles dangling over me like a curtain. I ripped one down and wrapped the leather strap around my hand, waiting for a clear shot at Edward's throat.

Just as I was ready to lunge, they rolled, bumping into the table that held the lantern. It fell to the ground. Flames leapt to life in the straw.

'The straw's on fire!' I yelled.

Montgomery thrust his fist at Edward's jaw, causing him to fall back long enough for Montgomery to stand. Edward scrambled to his feet, ducking away from Montgomery's fist. Montgomery swept out his leg, hooking it around Edward's ankle. Edward slammed to the ground, his head smacking against the corner of the table with a sickening crack.

Montgomery held his fists up, ready to strike, but Edward didn't get up. His eyes were closed. Blood pooled beneath his head. Suddenly he looked like an innocent young man again, and my heart cried out that we were making a terrible mistake. Had it all been a trick of my eyes? Or my mind? Montgomery felt for his pulse, but I grabbed his arm.

'Leave him,' I said.

'I have to finish it.' He reached for the old iron spade in

the corner. An image flashed in my head of the sharp edge coming down across Edward's neck. My stomach clenched. I stared at the blood trickling through Edward's black hair, blood that was warm and flowing. A groan so low I could barely hear it slipped out of Edward's mouth.

Still alive.

I glanced at Montgomery. The spade's rusted blade was caught on a tangle of leather straps that he tugged on angrily.

A snarl sounded outside. Heat from the fire bathed me in an uncomfortable warmth and then, with a spray of sparks, a roof beam split and fell. I shrieked and covered my head. Montgomery rushed toward me, still holding the spade's handle. I pulled it out of his grasp and threw it on the floor. 'He's no threat to us now,' I said. 'The fire will kill him. Come on, before we burn with him.'

We stumbled out of the barn into the moonlight.

'Balthazar's loading the wagon outside,' Montgomery said in a rush. 'I just need to hitch Duke.' He started for the wooden gate, but I grabbed his arm. Duchess, the little mare Father had taken to find Montgomery, stood in the courtyard. She was loosely tied to the veranda rail, her eyes white and wild in the chaos.

I froze. 'Father's back,' I said.

Montgomery paused. Shadows darted in the edges of the courtyard, stealing my attention. 'I know. He came back half an hour ago,' he said slowly. 'The beasts were after him. He closed himself in his laboratory in a panic.' He ran a hand over the back of his hair, reluctantly. 'He expects us to join him there. He said it's the only place that's safe.'

'No place is safe.'

He swallowed. 'I told him we would gather some supplies and come join him. I didn't know what else to say. I couldn't tell him . . .'

I took a deep breath, feeling the weight of the blood-red building beside us. I pictured my father on the other side of that metal door, listening to the snarls outside as his precious creations tried to find a way to kill him. Waiting for Montgomery and me, who would never come. We'd never see him again, I realized. The laboratory was a fortress. He could survive in there for days, even weeks maybe – if it weren't for the fire. Smoke was already pouring out of the barn. The laboratory walls were tin, so they wouldn't burn. He might escape. And then what? Would he start experimenting again?

Something crashed in the salon, and Montgomery grabbed my hand. 'Hurry.' We untied Duchess and rushed out of the main gate to where Balthazar was stacking jars in the back of the wagon. He'd filled the few specimen jars I hadn't destroyed with water for our voyage. They rattled against one another like the glass vials in my wooden box. The treatment was safely stashed in my old carpetbag, which Montgomery had already loaded into the wagon. I did a quick calculation – it would be enough for several weeks. I had everything I needed.

And yet an invisible hand pulled at me from the direction of the compound. It beckoned me back into the flames, to the tin building with burning red paint that bubbled like blood.

'I forgot my medicine,' I said suddenly. The lie made my mouth dry. 'I have to get it.'

Montgomery glanced at the billow of smoke rising to the heavens, then turned his attention back to hitching the last few buckles to Duke. 'Hurry,' he said from behind sweat-soaked hair.

I darted back inside the compound. The lie gnawed at my heart, but the invisible hand was too strong. The courtyard was quiet save the roar of flames – the fire had scared off the beasts. The raging blaze reflected in the salon's glass windows. Inside I could see the piano, the dining table, the photograph of Mother. The fire would burn every last scrap of memory. And all evidence of my father's terrible work.

But it was the only way. Such science wasn't meant to exist. We weren't meant to rival God. And yet a small part of me wailed to see it destroyed. That part of me – the darkness – would live in me forever, I realized. As long as Moreau blood flowed in my veins. It had driven Father mad. It wanted to do the same to me – and I didn't know if I was strong enough to stop it.

I hurried to my room and grabbed a plain wooden box so that Montgomery wouldn't be suspicious if I came back empty-handed. I didn't let my thoughts linger on the meager belongings I was leaving behind. By morning all evidence of my existence on the island would be gone, too.

I faced the red walls of the laboratory. The invisible hand tightened. The Blood House. Was Father inside right now, holed up with some Elk Hill brandy and a good book? Waiting for the rest of us to join him, never suspecting we'd flee and leave him behind?

This was what the hand had been pulling me to – Father. To say good-bye or to claw his face or just to stand outside the door and make my peace while he burned in flames. Some kind of closure.

Beyond the main gate, Montgomery and Balthazar waited for me. I only had to cross the threshold and never look back. Forget peace. Forget closure. We'd sail to London and never spare another thought for the island.

But my feet took me to the laboratory door. The heat from the nearby barn made me sweat. Paint bubbled on the tin, and I let my fingers hover a breath above it. Was he standing just on the other side, waiting for us?

He'd left me behind without a single letter, so why

shouldn't I do the same to him? The newspapers had called him a brilliant criminal, but they'd never mentioned the little girl he'd abandoned. As far as the world was concerned, Dr Henri Moreau was a collection of research papers and a grisly story. Was he more than that to me? Was he a father? He'd thought of me as nothing more than another experiment, a chance to see what happened when humans and creatures bred.

Anger curled inside me. I pressed the tips of my fingers to the burning door, letting the pain sear and stir my anger. Something caught my attention from the corner of my eye – a shadow slinking along the portico. It didn't run. Didn't attack. It came forward stealthily, its eyes glowing in the moonlight.

'Jaguar,' I muttered.

Maybe I should have been afraid, but I wasn't. It wasn't me he was after.

He stopped just paces away. This was the creature Montgomery had once called a brother. And were we really so different? We were all animals, in a sense. Even a sixteen-year-old girl needed to eat and drink and survive – and might kill to do so.

A rustling within the laboratory drew Jaguar's attention. He glided past me, his tail flicking against my feet as he slunk toward the door. His thick paw slashed at the door latch with claws as long as my fingers. He tried a few times, cutting grooves in the door but unable to grip the latch. A growl rumbled in his throat, low and angry. His golden eyes looked back at me.

I knew what he wanted.

But twisting that latch didn't just mean opening a door. It meant murder. Jaguar wouldn't hesitate to slice my father into little chunks of flesh. It was exactly what he wanted – what all of them wanted. *Revenge*. If Jaguar could speak, he'd tell me it had to be this way. Father was brilliant. He'd escape from the burning laboratory. He'd start over. There'd be another island. Another Jaguar. Another Edward. Or worse.

My fingers dropped to the latch.

Jaguar's hind legs tensed, ready to spring. But how could I open that door, knowing what lay on the other side? No good-bye. No reconciliation. Only a bitter, ragged end.

The barn roof cracked and splintered. A shower of sparks rained down. In another minute the whole structure would collapse. Edward would be killed, burned alive or crushed under falling beams. Even though logic told me Edward couldn't be allowed to live, my heart said he didn't deserve to die either. It wasn't his fault. It was that of his maker, who hid in a locked room while his children burned alive.

Edward had said I could make things right.

Maybe I could.

My fingers felt for the latch. The flames leapt to the bunkhouse. It would catch quickly, then the salon, then my room. Beside me, Jaguar's claws dug into the portico ground, ready to spring.

I squeezed the latch.

The door came open in my hand, almost too easily. Father's fail-safe had accounted for the beasts' limited dexterity, but not for deceit. He'd been too arrogant to think one of *us* would betray him.

I opened the door an inch – that was all it took, just an inch.

I fell back, my face burning from the heat. Jaguar slunk inside.

The barn roof collapsed with a roar. The heat singed my cheeks as I clutched the wooden box to my chest and stumbled back toward the main gate. Montgomery was there in the entryway, calling for me. Whether he'd seen me open the door I didn't know. His hand latched onto mine, and he pulled me from the flaming compound into the cool evening air, where Duke pawed at the ground, ready to bolt. Balthazar took up the reins as we clambered into the wagon and vanished into the jungle, leaving the smoldering wreckage behind us.

FORTY-FIVE

From the strip of sand at the ocean's edge, we could still hear the fire's roar. The beasts had started howling as the fire intensified, filling the night with wild screams. Montgomery held me close in the back of the wagon, hands pressed over my ears. But nothing could keep the sounds away. They'd haunted me since childhood. They would haunt me forever.

At the dock Balthazar stopped the wagon. Our blue-and-white boat waited, tethered to the pile, ready to take us to sea. Only when Balthazar climbed down from the driver's seat and offered me his massive hand did I remember my promise. *You can come with us,* I'd told him. But I'd never had any intention of bringing him. Someone would find out what he was and try to replicate him. Someone would take it too far, just like my father.

Balthazar cocked his head at my hesitation. I took his hand and climbed out of the wagon. Montgomery was already carrying an armful of jars down the dock. His steps were purposeful and determined, as if he was as ready to get off the island as I was, even if it meant abandoning the place he'd called home for six years.

Would he be the one to tell Balthazar or would I? We'd never spoken of it, but I knew Montgomery felt the same way. This island was my father's prison, his tomb, and all evidence of his work had to be buried with him. Even Balthazar.

Balthazar picked up two water jars, his tongue lolling out of his mouth, and followed Montgomery down the dock. My heart wrenched. Was I a monster for leaving him behind? Balthazar was the only innocent one of us. He hadn't killed. I didn't think he was capable of it.

I cradled a glass jar in the crook of my arm, watching the two of them in the moonlight. There should have been so many more of us. Alice. Edward. Their ashes tied their souls to this horrid island.

Montgomery came back to fetch a small trunk that contained an expensive china set. He glanced at me. I sensed that his resolve had hardened, as if he was steeling himself for the awful task of leaving Balthazar behind.

'We don't have a choice,' I whispered. I shifted the weight of the glass jar to my other arm. 'They were cursed as soon as they were created.'

He didn't answer but hoisted the trunk onto one shoulder and started down the dock. Balthazar took a load and followed Montgomery like a shadow. I brushed the hair out of my eyes and looked back toward the burning compound. I couldn't see the flames, but the column of smoke said enough.

I hugged the jar and hurried down the dock. Montgomery was already carrying another load. There was an urgency to his every move. I dreaded the moment when we would push off in the launch. I was afraid of what we would tell Balthazar, left on the dock, the last innocent being on the island.

'One more trip should do it,' Montgomery muttered. We took the last of the cargo, and Montgomery unhitched Duke and pushed against his shoulder.

354

'Get on, you old boy,' he chided, but his voice caught. Duke took a few steps back but didn't leave. His ears were alert, watching his master, ready to follow him to the ends of the earth. Montgomery picked up the last of the water jars and didn't look back at the horse.

Every step down that dock was one less I'd ever take on the island. One more toward England. Montgomery and I would make a life there with each other. Comfortable. Quiet. We'd never mention the past. If he'd seen my role in Father's murder, he'd never say anything, just as I'd never ask if he missed Balthazar. We'd forget about Edward – no, that was impossible.

I'd never forget Edward.

One more step. And another. And then I was at the launch.

'We don't have a choice,' I said, my vocal cords trembling. Montgomery's eyes reflected my own tangled emotions. For a moment I studied his face in the moonlight, wondering if the tie between us would be different in London. For now, it felt as though he and I would always be bound together.

I reached for the line holding the launch, but Montgomery touched my shoulder softly. He turned me back to face him again. His features were knotted and tense, but then his lips parted. 'Juliet—'

He pulled me into a deep kiss. My surprise melted and I kissed him back. My hand found the hard silhouette of his chest and pulled with trembling fingers at his shirt. I wanted to hold on to him forever. Believing in nothing except the truth of Montgomery, who for all his faults was as steady as the sea, as honest as the sun. My eyes watered with unexpected tears, and I kissed him harder, desperately. It wasn't a happy ending. He and I would return to the real world, but there was only anguish left for Balthazar and the others.

Montgomery broke off the kiss, reluctantly. Swallowed

hard. He was as afraid of the future as I was. For a moment it was only he and I and the sea and the unknown.

'All right,' he said, taking a deep breath. 'It's time.' He climbed into the boat and steadied himself. He motioned for Balthazar and me to hand him the cargo. We worked efficiently, not exchanging words. He settled the cargo carefully to prevent the boat tipping if we came across a storm. And then he climbed out and wiped his hand through his sea-blown hair.

An awful sickness roiled in my abdomen as though I'd missed an injection. But I hadn't. It was the shame of what I had to do, knotting my insides. I couldn't find the words to tell Balthazar we were leaving him behind.

At last Montgomery cleared his throat. 'Right, then. You first, Juliet.'

I looked up in surprise. Were we just going to climb in and push off, leaving Balthazar puzzled and heartbroken as we drifted away? I searched Montgomery's face, but it was like stone. He held out his hand, and I took it hesitantly and climbed down into the rocking boat. I settled between two trunks at the far end, trying to force back my tears.

'I wish it didn't have to be this way,' I said, hunching into myself. I knew he would understand what I meant. Not just leaving Balthazar, but leaving all of them – Father, Edward, the bones of all those who had died so unfairly. This island – the things that happened here – should never have existed.

'So do I,' Montgomery said, his whispered voice so low the wind might have carried it off. But he kept his gaze on me, which was odd. I kept looking at Balthazar, feeling crushed by guilt, and guiltier still that Montgomery had to be the one to tell him.

'I'm afraid this is it,' he said.

I nodded, squeezing my knees in tighter. I wouldn't look

at Balthazar's face. It might be cowardly, but I couldn't live with the image of his heartbreak in my head forever.

'I'm so sorry, Juliet.' Montgomery suddenly crouched down to the pile, unraveling the line faster than my brain could think. *Sorry?* Why wasn't he getting into the boat?

It hit me like a tidal wave. He wasn't coming with me. *He wasn't coming with me.*

The weight of it crushed me to the bottom of the launch. I stared at him, and then at Balthazar, who was trying his best not to look at me. Balthazar had known all along. This wasn't a farewell to Balthazar.

It was a farewell to me.

I jerked forward, crawling as the boat pitched. 'Montgomery, no. Wait . . .'

But he'd already pushed his weight against the bow and set me adrift. All that linked us now was a thin bit of line that he held so lightly, so loosely, poised to let go at any moment.

'Don't you dare!' I screamed, crawling to the bow. 'Don't let go of that line!' My knee connected with the sharp edge of a trunk and my eyes filled with water, not just from the pain. 'Don't you dare leave me, Montgomery James!'

But as I scrambled to reach the edge of the launch, the frayed end of the line came away from his hand. Seconds. Just seconds ago Montgomery had been holding it, and now I was totally adrift. Alone. I looked at him, stunned.

'I'm so sorry,' he said, his face broken. 'I can't leave. I've been their only family. I have a responsibility to them.'

'What about me?' I choked as the launch drifted seaward. I reached out, grappling for a hand I knew would never come. 'You have a responsibility to me!'

'You're better off without me. You can forget all of this. I would only have tied you to this place.' His voice broke. 'I don't belong there. I'm a criminal. An aberration.'

'You're Montgomery,' I called. 'We belong together.'

He shook his head. His face was wet with sweat. 'No. I belong with the island.'

The betrayal ripped me apart more than any of Father's surgeries could have done. Montgomery looked away, just as I'd planned on looking away from Balthazar's heartbroken face. A wave caught the launch and I glided farther toward open sea, gripping the edge of the boat as though clinging to life. 'No!' I screamed, one more time. Sobs choked in my throat. Hadn't I always known Montgomery was as wild as the creatures he'd created, unable to leave them? The smell of smoke lingered in the air, and it felt so wrong, like more than the compound was burning.

Maybe he said something else. I couldn't be sure. The dock drew farther away with each wave, until Montgomery and Balthazar were nothing more than a trick my eyes were playing on me. As I was swept out to sea, among the expensive baubles meant to buy me passage and the food that Edward had so carefully packed away, the island took form on the horizon. I saw the blaze that was once the compound. Two columns of smoke rose into the stars – one from the volcano, one from the compound. And then I saw nothing, as the waves spun me around in their dips and swells and the island disappeared into night, except the glowing blaze where fire destroyed the red walls of my father's laboratory.

ACKNOWLEDGMENTS

I am so fortunate to have worked with a wonderful team to turn this book into a finished product. I owe a big thanks to my incredible editor, Kristin Daly Rens, and the rest of the Balzer + Bray/HarperCollins team, including assistant editor Sara Sargent, designers Alison Klapthor and Alison Donalty for the beautiful design, Renée Cafiero for an amazing copyedit, Emilie Polster and Stephanie Hoffman in marketing, and Caroline Sun, Olivia DeLeon, and Alison Lisnow in publicity. Any author would be thrilled to have you all on her team, and I am glad I get to be one of the lucky ones.

I also owe an enormous thanks to the amazing literary/black belt ninja agent team: Josh, Tracey, and Quinlan at Adams Literary. Plain and simple, you made a writer's dream come true, and that has changed my life forever.

Thanks also to my critique group, the Secret Gardeners, as well as my beta readers: Constance, Lauren, Kim, Ameliann, and especially Melissa, who has been reading my work and giving me insightful feedback since that first awful picture book ages ago. I'd also like to acknowledge the Lucky 13s and Friday the Thirteeners for moral support, and to congratulate them on their debuts. It's been a heck of a year!

Of course, my parents, Peggy and Tim, played a big role giving me my love of literature. You and the whole Highland Books family make up my favorite home away from home and the best place for a child to grow up. Thanks also to all my friends and family who offered support through frantic phone calls, photography sessions, playlists, and book-shaped cakes. And to my husband, Jesse, who gave me the courage to believe in myself. You make each day better than the last. And lastly, I want to acknowledge my admiration for H. G. Wells, whose book *The Island of Doctor Moreau* inspired me to create this story. I'll never forget reading Wells's works when I was a teenager myself, and being exposed to such compelling and insightful ideas about the world we inhabit.

This list could take up so many pages, because I have so many more people to thank for their very generous support along the way. Holding this book in my hands is an incomparable feeling, and I will never be able to find the words to express to each and every one of you how thankful I am for your encouragement.